# COLD HEARTED RIVER

# COLD HEARTED RIVER

## Keith McCafferty

—A SEAN STRANAHAN MYSTERY—

VIKING

VIKING
An imprint of Penguin Random House LLC
375 Hudson Street
New York, New York 10014
penguin.com

ISBN 9780525429609 (hardcover)
ISBN 9780698406360 (e-book)

Printed in the United States of America
1 3 5 7 9 10 8 6 4 2

Set in Warnock

This is a work of fiction. Names, characters, places, and incidents either are the product of the author's imagination or are used fictitiously, and any resemblance to actual persons, living or dead, businesses, companies, events, or locales is entirely coincidental.

For my mother, Beverly McCafferty, with love

"This is a cockeyed wonderful country."
> —Ernest Hemingway in a 1928 letter to Waldo Peirce about the Wyoming high country
> *Letters of Ernest Hemingway,* vol. 3, 1926–1929

"Papa liked to say that all true stories end in death. I think the idea of fishing in a graveyard would have appealed to him."
> —Jack Hemingway to the author, the Graveyard Run, Thompson River, British Columbia, circa 1983

# Preface

I first heard about Ernest Hemingway's steamer trunk of fishing tackle, the lost treasure chest at the heart of this novel, from his oldest son, Jack. Jack and I were contributing editors for *Field & Stream* some thirty-odd years ago, and though not close friends, we shared a river from time to time. It was a blustery November day, easy to recall because all November days on British Columbia's Thompson River are blustery, and we were the only fishermen along a stretch of the river known as the Graveyard, just down the hill from the old white crosses where all the graves face north. On toward dark, Jack hooked a steelhead of fifteen or sixteen pounds, which I landed for him in the tailout after a long fight. We admired this great seafaring trout for a few seconds before releasing it, and celebrated with a thermos cup of hot chocolate into which I laced peppermint schnapps, in honor of my father.

After toasting the fish, I asked Jack if he thought his own father would have liked this kind of fishing—that is, wading on slippery boulders in a river haunted by the dead, casting hour after hour in miserable weather, and considering yourself lucky to hook up once every few days and manage not to drown. He said that Ernest would have enjoyed the challenge, but that he'd lost the heart to fly fish after a steamer trunk containing all his valuable gear was stolen or lost from Railway Express in 1940, en route to Ketchum, Idaho, where he was a guest at the Sun Valley Lodge. In fact, Jack could only remember his father fly fishing once after the loss, in the Big Wood River.

This was an interesting insight into the famous author's psyche, but at the time I was more interested in casting my own fly rod than the fate of another man's tackle or the sentiments it evoked.

Years passed, and I had no reason to recall the story until my wife, Gail, persuaded me to set a novel in northwestern Wyoming, where Hemingway stayed at the L Bar T Guest Ranch during five summers and falls in the 1930s, hunting, fishing, and writing. By then Jack had died and I sought to verify the details of his story with Patrick Hemingway, Ernest's sole surviving son, who lives in my hometown. I spoke with him at a local screening of the PBS *American Masters* series film *Ernest Hemingway: Rivers to the Sea*. Patrick was kind enough to indulge my questions and said he recalled the lost trunk, adding that it probably contained best-quality bamboo fly rods and reels ordered from the House of Hardy catalog. Hardy was the premier London maker, and Patrick remembered helping his father convert the prices from pounds sterling to American dollars.

Today, only one piece of Ernest Hemingway's fly fishing tackle survives in good condition, a Hardy rod in a model called the Fairy that he had with him when he first went to Idaho. It is displayed at the American Museum of Fly Fishing in Manchester, Vermont, along with a letter to *Field & Stream* that Jack wrote about the missing tackle.

As concerns the possibility that the trunk contained Hemingway treasures unrelated to piscatorial pursuits, and perhaps of far greater value, there is one way to find out.

Pour a drink, light a fire, and turn the page. I have a story to tell.

# COLD HEARTED RIVER

# CHAPTER ONE

# The Aphrodisiac Graveyard

It had started the night before, when the snow sifted down onto the carcass of his horse and there was no sound beyond the intermittent release of its gases and no stars to wish upon. That's when he began to "What if" it to death, going back to the morning, kissing her face and feeling the flutter of her eyelashes that, as he'd helped her from the saddle two hours later, were already icicling with frost.

What if he'd stopped before three kisses became four, before four became more? But he hadn't, and too long in bed gave them a slow start, their breakfast hurried, the Sunday edition of the *Bridger Mountain Star* outside the mudroom where the paperboy had tossed it. If he'd picked it up he would have checked the back page for the weather. What kind of Montanan were you if you didn't keep an eye on the sky? But he had a pannier in each hand and they were in too much of a rush to get to the property where they pastured the horses, and then to the trailhead with dawn breaking, a sifting of snowflakes she caught on her tongue, but dead calm, just cold enough that the horses blew steam from their nostrils.

It was called the Aphrodisiac Graveyard, a series of wind-scoured openings on a south-facing slope some few miles west of the wilderness boundary. Here the bulls shed their great antlers in February and March, and Freida Toliver, who had a business making antler chandeliers, wanted to get them off the ground while the beams were still that rich dark mahogany and the tines ivory tipped, before porcupines gnawed them and the weather blanched them of their value.

That was before the fairytale snowfall turned into stinging shards of ice and the temperature dropped thirty degrees in an hour, and any thought of collecting elk antlers was long forgotten.

He couldn't really say where they made the first wrong turn. Like most people who became lost, he thought that he knew where they were for some time after he didn't. It wasn't just the visibility, which had dropped from twenty miles to as many yards, but the wind blew the snow into a sea of scallops, dulling colors and swallowing landmarks to the point where it might have been a different country, or, rather, no country at all. A trail that he remembered as crossing a low saddle seemed to have vanished, along with the saddle, and so they took another trail—"This is it, right, Freida?"—and she shook her head yes, feeding into his confidence, willing it to be so. An hour of lying to themselves later, it became obvious that it wasn't.

"I thought you were an Indian," he said, trying for a smile, and failing. *Where the hell are we?*

It was a gamble, giving the horses their heads, trusting that they would find their way back to the pack trail. And their hearts lifted when they thought they had found it, only to discover that it was an elk trail that branched like a strong man's forearm veins, some bleeding back into each other, others not. The horses followed one of those veins down into a creek bottom, and it was there, in the dark heart of the mountain, and no longer sure even which mountain, that he'd made the first attempt to build a fire. But the pack of bar matches he found in a pants pocket were damp, the heads only smearing against the chemical strip.

*What if I hadn't given up smoking and had my lighter,* he'd think. *What if?*

"I might have some in my fishing vest," she'd said. It seemed absurd now, the notion that they might do a little fishing in one of the high-altitude tarns. "It's in the saddlebag," she told him. But her hands shook so badly she couldn't undo the buckle.

"Here, let me." He rummaged through the vest.

"Try the inside zipper pocket, the one with my license."

"I did."

He lifted his shoulders and let them fall. She looked at him, and did exactly the same. Like she was his echo. That's what they were to each other. He even called her that, Little Echo. She was Northern Cheyenne and had taken to it. Told people it was her tribal name.

He bent down and hugged her. He felt the frost of her eyebrows melt against his cheek and thought of the morning, holding her close, feeling her heart beat.

"I don't want to die," she said.

He looked at her, a small woman made smaller by the immensity of the country that was felt rather than seen and the fourteen hands of her horse that stood nearby, its empty saddle already frosting with snow.

"Nobody's going to die, Freida. Don't even think it."

It was the way they had together, one strong, then the other.

*I could start a fire with the gun,* he thought. It was something he'd read about, possibly in the same issue of an outdoor magazine where he'd read about a hunter who'd survived a night of thirty below zero by crawling inside the carcass of a moose.

He pulled the handgun from the holster, the single-action Ruger Blackhawk that was her birthday present to him when he'd turned fifty. Five cylinders loaded, the chamber under the hammer empty. He tried to recall the procedure. You formed a tinder nest with cloth, dried grasses, anything that was flammable. Then you pulled the bullet from a cartridge case, dumped half of the powder and stuffed a piece of cotton cloth over the remaining charge, and fired it into the tinder nest. The idea was that the smoldering cloth would catch the tinder aglow, and you could lift up the nest and coax it into flame with your breath. In the illustration, it had looked like the man was praying, lifting his hands to heaven, exhaling fire.

He had a multi-tool in one of his saddlebags, fifty feet of parachute cord and a roll of duct tape in the other. A Montanan's holy trinity. You could do anything with a kit like that—mend fence, haul a deer out to the road, splint a broken arm. Maybe even start a fire.

He broke a handful of the tiny branches that quilled the lower trunk of a pine tree and collected some larger wood to feed in later. Tinder took more thought, and she was the one who suggested that he unravel wool threads from the tops of his socks. He wadded up the threads as she searched her pockets and came up empty.

"Did I see you put on the panties with the hearts?"

She nodded, too cold to frown at the question.

"Oh, right," she said, the shoe dropping. Nothing burned like cotton.

"I'd use mine, but they're poly."

She said okay, but her hands were so numb she couldn't trust them. "I might stab myself," she said. She had bitten through her tongue from the shuddering of her jaws and her voice was thick with the blood in her mouth.

"I'll do it," he told her.

He worked her zipper and carefully cut a patch of cloth from the top of the panties. Under his fingertips, he could feel her abdominal muscles crawl from the ice of his touch.

"We're going to laugh about this someday," he told her.

She nodded, but didn't speak. The cold had started with her hands and feet. Then it had crawled up her arms and legs. Now it had settled like a pick in her chest. Even the drawing of breath was an effort. She turned away and spit blood onto the snow.

"This is going to do the trick," he said.

He tore thin strips from the cloth and wove them into the tinder nest. Pulling a bullet wasn't easy—the hard-cast .41 Magnum loads were crimped into the case necks so they wouldn't shift during recoil—but by rapping on the neck to expand the brass and twisting the bullet with the pliers on his multi-tool, he managed. He placed the nest at the base of a big pine so it wouldn't be blown over by the gas escaping from the barrel.

The first shot from the heavy revolver resulted in a brief glow in the center of the nest, but it went black before he could pick it up.

A little more powder? The second try was better, producing an orange-limned marble of smoldering tinder that died slowly enough to give them heart, but died all the same.

"What about the flies?"

"What are you talking about?"

"You can shave off the hair and the feathers. It will burn."

"Trout flies, you mean?"

She nodded. "I packed my vest in the pannier. Those big dries, the golden stones and the salmon flies, they have lots of wing material."

"You know, that's a really good idea," he said. "I knew I married you for some reason."

It looked like modern art, a softball-sized bird's nest of dried grasses, rusted pine needles, bits of cloth with pink and purple hearts, all of it woven together with ginger neck hackles, bucktail and marabou stork fibers dyed in a half dozen hues.

"That ought to catch fire just looking at it," he said.

Then the .41 spoke and for a time there was a new color on the mountain, a molten candle of hope. The matchstick-sized sticks caught fire and the flames licked up as they used their hands for wind blocks. But the ground was cold and it sapped the fire even as they fed it.

*Come on. Come on.* They blew on the struggling licks of flame.

"Not so hard. You're blowing it out. This needs a woman's touch."

*That's my girl,* he thought.

But it was like the CPR he'd once performed on a victim of lightning strike. You kept pressing the breastbone and sharing your breaths, even after the heart under your hands grew cold.

She had been waving her hat to coax the flames and pushed the frozen clumps of her hair out of her face.

"Éoseetonéto," she said. "It's really cold." And in English, "I'm freezing."

He knew soon as she went to the people's language that he'd lost her. She never did that unless she was at wit's end.

"Maybe he was right," she said.

"Who was right?"

"The man, the one I told you about. With the cat. He said that April was the best month to die."

"He's just a crazy old loon. You said so yourself."

"Yeah, I guess."

But that's when it had really sunk in, and looking down at her—she was in the dark, the fire was out—he had a thought. *This is how it ends. You wake up with the woman you'd searched all your life to find, who changed her name for you and who you couldn't think of going on without, and that night you lie down with her and die. There are no premonitions. You're just another victim of nature's impersonal calculus.*

He told himself to stop it. After all, there were still two bullets in the Ruger. He tipped out the cylinder to double-check. And thought of the horses. They were Rocky Mountain horses, not the biggest of their breed, but just as big as a moose.

He shook the cartridges into the palm of his left glove to show them to her, sensed, rather than saw, the recognition take shape in her face.

The brass gleamed in the light of his headlamp.

"Time to decide," he said. He meant they could try again to start fire or—the unthinkable. The unthinkable that had started as a half-hearted joke only an hour before, but was far from it now.

"I don't think I can do it."

"What? Shoot old Henry? You always said he was nothing but a mule with short ears."

"Either of them. They're our family."

He looked at her, her eyes squinted up against the cold, the frozen creeks of tears that ended in beads of ice.

"I'm sorry it's come to this," he said. "It's sure enough my fault."

"I'm the one with the damned business. I'm the reason we're here."

True, but little solace.

"I know what you're thinking and you can just stop it right now, Mister J. C. Toliver."

The paisley scarf she'd pulled up over her mouth was frosted from the exhalations of her breath and her voice shuddered, but the words held out a note of hope. "I thought maybe if we could just get them to lie down, we could snuggle up between them."

"You know they won't lie down in this kind of weather. Hell, old Henry barely lies down ever. And when's the last time you saw Annabel off her feet? It's the only way. If we can ride out this storm, we can walk off this mountain tomorrow morning."

"I know." For a moment the wind that swirled in the treetops died and they listened to the horses blow.

"All right," she said. A harder edge to the voice, another woman speaking now, the one he was counting on.

"If we're going to do this, let's do it while it's still light enough to see. But I'm not shooting my own horse. We're shooting each other's. Down in that little witch's heart." She gestured toward a patch of tangled timber. "If you can pull the trigger, I guess I can, too."

"All right then." And again: "It's the only way."

"I just need a minute, that's all. Just a minute with her. Go down there and wait for me."

"We don't have long."

"I won't be long. I just have to say goodbye."

He'd never seen her after that. He'd called out for her. He'd gone looking. He still had the gun and the two bullets. After a while, he used one of them.

# CHAPTER TWO

# The Witch's Heart

It was fourteen degrees with the second cup of coffee growing cold on the counter when Martha Ettinger got the call. No number she knew, a snowbird, she found out, just opening up the summer house in the Madison Valley. He'd been shoveling out his driveway when a truck pulled up, an empty two-stall horse trailer clattering in tow. The driver apologized for his appearance and assured the man it wasn't his blood, then asked if he could use the landline to call the sheriff. His name was J. C. Toliver and Martha knew him as well as you know anyone you see twice a year who only has one subject. Chuck, that's what he went by, shoed Martha's horses; you could go right down the ranch directory for three counties and he could tell you half the horses' names and bore you with the bloodlines.

His voice was hoarse, the message terse. He told her to get a hasty team up the Johnny Gulch Road to the Specimen Ridge trail access where he'd meet them, that his wife was dying up there and for Chrise sakes hurry, and the line had gone dead.

She'd hit the redial and the snowbird picked up, told her that Toliver had lurched out the door. "Like a zombie," the man said. "Like on that FX." Martha asked him to describe Toliver's condition. Did it smell like he'd been drinking? Was he coherent? Was he driving straight when he drove away?

No, he smelled like a slaughterhouse. To the other questions, yes, and yes.

Martha had taken the man's name and thanked him. She'd waited a beat as the snowbird cleared his throat. "Ah . . ." A note of hesitancy was in his voice. "You think you could thank me to the tune of a couple thousand bucks? He left gore all over a double diamond Navajo rug."

"Are you joking?"

"Not funny, is it? I'm one of those people doesn't know what to say sometimes and it comes out inappropriate. I mean no disrespect. Please call me when you get his wife out. I'd sure like to see a happy ending to this. It's the kind of thing that can ruin a man's summer."

Like most Montanans, Martha owned two Carhartt jackets, an older one for hunting and farmwork, another for town and to wear with the badge. She remembered what the snowbird had said as he ruminated a ruined summer. She zipped into the old jacket. She'd meet Toliver with open arms, and she knew that whatever she was wearing, she might be able to get the smell out of it, but the blood would be another matter.

―――

At the trailhead there was no time for introductions, just the sounds of the horses being unloaded, high whinnies, a "Come on, Trudy, settle down, now, the blanket doesn't bite." Matter-of-fact voices that didn't register circumstance, weather, or even fellow man. The masculine undertone that was the soundtrack of Martha's life.

Well, except for Katie Sparrow, who spoke mostly to Lothar, her Class III search dog, in what was a separate language altogether.

Martha called them over and they gathered around the warm hood of her truck, where she'd pinned down the corners of a topographic quad map. Walter Hess, her undersheriff, raised his eyebrows at one of the paperweights, a loaded clip from Martha's backup 10-millimeter. Hess was all angles and had a Chicago pallor that nine years in Montana hadn't changed much. He also had a sense of humor that Martha wouldn't get if she lived to be a hundred.

"Is that a Glock in your pocket or are you happy to see me?" he said, looking at the clip.

"Walt, that doesn't even make any sense."

"It's a metaphorical reference, Marth. That means—"

"I know what a metaphor is. Here's the deal." Her eyes went from Katie Sparrow to Harold Little Feather, her former deputy with whom she had shared more than the job on occasion, and who had recently climbed the rung to Criminal Investigations agent for the state office out of Helena. "Remember those hunters who got lost in a snowstorm and shot their horses so they could crawl inside them? Up in the Bear Paws? Well, that's what we got here, except one walked out this morning after a night in the carcass, and one couldn't pull the trigger when the time came and ran off with the other horse."

She gestured toward Toliver, who was standing by his pickup, changing into a spare set of clothes that Harold had had the foresight to bring when he got the call.

"Some of you know Chuck Toliver," she said. "It's his wife, Freida, that we're looking for."

"She have a gun?" Walt asked.

"Chuck says no."

No one looked at anyone else, to affirm in another's eyes what they were thinking. With no bullet waiting for a change of heart, Freida Toliver's chances of having survived the night were almost nothing.

Katie Sparrow had a face a blind person could read, and Martha watched a cloud come over it. No change of expression from Harold, not that she expected it. Words were just white noise to him. Part of him was already up the mountain, his mind working out the trail.

"Any chance she could start a fire?" Katie said.

Martha shook her head. "Not without divine intervention."

———

They were single file up the trail—Harold on his big paint, then Martha riding Petal, her Appaloosa, followed by Hess on a quarter horse Martha pastured named Big Mike, with Katie Sparrow bringing up the rear on her Rocky Mountain mare. Everyone in a line except for Lothar, who strayed here and there to hike a leg and proclaim his canine supremacy, which ended abruptly where a wolf track crossed the trail. After that, the shepherd kept his nose on the tail of his handler's horse.

It was a skeleton crew to be generous, which brought two of Martha's fingertips to the artery in her throat, a tip-off of her worry. But there was nothing to be done about it. The spring storm had dropped a blanket of trouble over the entire county, leaving more than three dozen motorists stranded, this in a place where people didn't swap out their snow tires until Memorial Day. The priority were two lost bear hunters—in any case that's what they'd told their wives they were hunting. As that call came in first, the search-and-rescue hasty team had responded, leaving the county closet more or less bare.

Martha called ahead to Harold to let the horses have a blow and crooked a gloved finger for Toliver to pull his mount up alongside.

"Can't be too much farther, huh, Chuck?"

He didn't look so bad now, in the change of clothes. He'd washed his face with snow and his blood-caked hair was covered by a hat, so except for his eyes, which had a glazed-over appearance and looked at nothing, and his gloved hands, which ran a tremor and shook the reins, Martha might have been talking to a normal person.

"I dunno," Toliver said. His red nose held a drop of moisture in suspense.

"I know you told me once, but tell me again just what happened this morning. You followed the trail she laid down when she left you, am I right about that?"

"I tried to, but it had snowed so much they were just pocks. I couldn't be sure it was the trail we made coming in, or the one she made going out. So I just started walking in circles, hoping I'd cut a fresh track if she was still moving, but I was all wet and cramping up and figured I better get back inside the horse. But by then the danged carcass was up a pretty steep slope and I didn't have the energy to climb up to it. I just couldn't get her done. So I told myself I better get on out while I could still walk a little bit."

He turned in the saddle, looking away. Martha could see his back heave, saw him roughly scrub at his face with the back of his glove. "That woman a' mine . . ." He shook his head. "She was so softhearted she couldn't even hunt anymore. Just stalked elk and counted coup. I'm the one had to fill the freezer. I should of known she'd never shoot her horse."

"We're going to get her, Chuck," Martha said. But she was looking at the depressions in the snow that were much shallower now that they'd climbed, the backtrail Toliver had made hiking out already indistinct where the wind had its way.

"Look," she said, lowering her voice. "You take as much time as you need. We'll leave when you're ready."

"I'm fine."

She watched Toliver turn his horse without touching the reins. A horse that the man hadn't set eyes on until two hours past. He was that kind of horseman. Something was off about him, though, and it took her a moment to realize what it was. With the day warming, Toliver had unzipped his jacket to expose the snap-up denim work shirt that Harold had lent him. It was a shirt that Martha had seen Harold wear a hundred times. Her favorite shirt of his, one she'd had occasion to unsnap before things went the way they did.

She chased the thought from her mind.

"Chuck, I want to ride up ahead with Harold. You hang back now with Walt and Katie."

Toliver touched the brim of his hat in acknowledgment, one in his catalog of country manners that were automatic. Martha rode to catch up with Harold, who was keeping to one side of the nearly blown trail, hanging his head to see past the withers of the horse. He called it reading the white book, deciphering the tracks in the snow.

"Can you still see that? I can hardly see it anymore."

"Plain as the sun," Harold said.

Martha could have said, "What sun?" But didn't.

———

He lost the trail a mile farther along. Or rather it was obliterated. Sometime after Toliver had walked away from the carcass of his horse, a herd of elk had wandered across the face of the ridge, churning the snow with their hooves. If the herd had walked single file, as elk typically do in deep snow, it would have been easy enough to see where Toliver's track strayed from it. But the elk had spread out to nip clumps of fescue peeking through the snow cover, the bulls that had yet to shed their antlers minding their headgear, circling from the main group to walk around trees with low-hanging branches.

"Are we fucked?" Martha said.

"No, I can work it out, but it's going to take awhile."

It cost them nearly an hour, the herd easy to follow but the going slow on the steep face of the ridge. Finally Harold found where Toliver's backtrack emerged from the maze of hoofprints to cross a saddle and head east. From this point the trail zigged down the face of the ridge, Harold twice pointing out places where Toliver had fallen, something he hadn't mentioned to Martha.

"I'm getting the heebie-jeebies about this," she said.

When the rest caught up to them, Martha pointed out the depressions in the snow. "You fell here, Chuck? Do you remember that?"

He nodded. Ice beads clung to the hairs in his nostrils. "I think it's just over the next rise, there's an elk wallow with a little creek running out of it. It's in a patch of timber there. Freida called it a witch's heart."

Suddenly he called out. "Freida! Can you hear me, Freida!" His voice echoed away.

"That'll do, Chuck. We don't want her struggling or doing anything that could get her hurt because she hears us. We'll backtrack to the carcass and go on from there. Any trace of her trail is left, Harold can follow it or the dog will smell it." She made her voice casual. "I see you're still carrying your piece. I thought the bullet you shot your horse with was the last one you had."

"It was. It's just, I don't know, rightly. I just feel naked without that weight on my hip."

"I'm on the same page with you," Martha said, patting the grips of her Ruger. And let out a breath, feeling relieved. She knew if they came up that rise and found a dead woman, her husband might well draw his revolver and put a bullet in his brain.

"Why don't you let me carry it anyway?" she said.

"Sure, if that's what you want."

"Yeah, I got plenty of room in the panniers."

Toliver pulled the handgun and nudged his mount over so he could lift the flap on Martha's pannier. "That satisfy you, Sheriff? Now if you don't mind, I want to find my wife."

They didn't. At least she hadn't made her way back to the little hollow. Toliver's horse was there, his skyward eye opaque and drawing back into the socket, his purpled intestines spilled out, the dark loaf of his liver and pink lungs pulled out. The flanks sagged hollow over the empty abdominal cavity. Bloody snow all around. Martha couldn't help but think he'd done a neat job of it, cutting through the diaphragm so it all came out in a piece, as he would an elk he'd shot.

"Field dressed to a tee," Walt commented.

"Old Henry," Toliver said. "He weren't the best horse, but he was a trusting animal and I killed him, and he saved me. How do you get your head around something like that?"

"You didn't have a choice," Martha said.

They moved upwind and out of sight of the carnage, where they dismounted. Martha edged away with Katie and Harold for a brief council.

"This is your show," she said. "Katie, does Lothar have enough to go on?"

Katie nodded. "They had extra clothes in the truck. He can isolate her scent, but eyes before nose. If Harold can see tracks, I'll hold Lothar back."

Harold nodded. "No sense having paw prints muck up the trail if there's one to follow. Give me twenty minutes. I can't find her, Katie and the dog take over. She's hypothermic. She isn't going to have made it far."

Martha looked past them. "Won't be an easy thing, telling him that we wait behind."

"You'll find a way. Like I said, she won't have gone far."

She hadn't, or at least her horse hadn't. Fifteen minutes later Martha saw Harold riding back through the timber, Freida Toliver's saddleless quarter horse shadowing his paint.

"You find her? You find . . . my Freida? You . . . tell me you found her."

Toliver rushed past Harold to the following horse. "Where is she, Annabel? Where's our Freida?" Then to Martha: "You tell me she's all right. You got to tell me she's all right." He dropped to his knees, all the cowboy gone out of him, just a man hanging his head, shaking, wavering back and forth in a personal wind. The tears came now, even before the news.

"You couldn't hear it?" Harold said. "She found her way into a bear den, no more than a quarter mile. I got upwind, that bear, it put up a hell of a ruckus. I'm guessing a sow with her newborns. All of us, we might be able to shoo her out long enough to see if Freida's alive in there. Human tracks going in. I didn't see any coming out."

"Take the horses or leave them?" Martha said.

Harold shook his head. "Ground tie them here. And Katie stays behind with the dog. He gets his hackles up, starts barking, he'll bring mama griz down on us like a bad wind."

Only Walter Hess had brought a rifle, his elk gun, a .300 Winchester Magnum. He took the lead as a quarter mile was halved, and halved again.

"That dark spot, that's the den entrance?" Martha asked.

Harold nodded. "Her tracks went right up to the entrance."

"A body would have to be desperate . . ." Hess's voice trailed away.

"You there, bear?" Harold called out.

No sound beyond the muffled plopping of snow as it melted from the laden pine boughs.

"Hey there, bear!"

Suddenly a chopping sound from outside the den in the trees up the slope, the sound of a bear clashing its teeth. Grunting roars reverberated in the confined space of the thicket.

"Cover me," Harold said.

As Harold and Walt moved forward, Toliver rose to follow them. Martha grabbed his coat. "Let them do their job."

The bear's roaring had become continuous. Up the slope from the den, Martha could see a tree whipping as if in a storm, its branches dropping heavy burdens of snow as the bear bristled up against the trunk.

Then there was the crash of Walt's big Magnum, the muzzle pointed up into the air.

"She's coming, Harold," Martha called out.

She could see her now, the bear rushing side to side, glimpses of her grizzled coat, could hear the menace of her popping teeth.

Harold was halfway back out of the den, dragging something heavy, then scooping it up into his arms and running with Walt trailing, all of them in retreat as the bear came bursting out of the pines and charged down the hill.

Another shot from Walt's rifle, the bullet kicking up the snow ahead of the bear. The bear stopped. She shook her huge head back and forth, then stood, leaning forward, snuffing at the air. She turned to peer at them, her poor eyesight unsure, then at the den behind her.

She dropped to all fours and moved toward the den. A last look around. The threat gone, she ducked her head and was gone from sight.

They didn't stop moving for another hundred yards.

"This is far enough," Martha said. "Bear's not coming."

Harold sat in the snow with Freida Toliver's body curled in his lap.

"Is she alive?" Toliver reached tentatively.

Martha felt for the pulse. She was alive.

"Let me." Toliver clutched the body against his chest.

*Let him,* Martha told herself. *It's his wife.*

Staggering under the weight, Toliver carried her back to the witch's heart. Martha hurriedly unsaddled her horse and spread the horse blanket on the snow to help insulate the motionless body. She could feel Freida's heart beating, making a thread of pulse as Harold went about building a fire, beating when Walt pulled the cord on the chainsaw they'd packed to clear a landing space for the helicopter that he'd called on the satellite phone.

Her heart was beating until it didn't and they all knew it, and nobody would admit it but the man who'd felt her eyelashes flutter against his lips the morning before. He lunged for the revolver in Martha's pannier, having one last cartridge in his revolver after all.

# CHAPTER THREE

# Dying with the Living,
# Sleeping with the Dead

For the rest of that afternoon, Martha Ettinger relived the nightmare of those few moments over and over as blood from her sodden handkerchief dropped a trail of tears in the snow.

She'd reacted instantly as she saw Toliver go for her horse, had known in that split second that it was happening and saw it in slow motion, Toliver's legs buckling as he dropped to his knees and brought the black muzzle of the revolver to the side of his head, Martha lunging with both hands, the struggle and then the crashing shot, the revolver jolting hard against her hands and Martha wresting it away as Toliver's body jerked sideways, the blood spraying her hair and face as he fell onto the snow. Then the world had spun off into the distance to leave her alone, the gun in her hand, the voices of the others distant, disconnected, heard as if from underwater. That had lasted indefinitely until she felt the rough hands of Harold hauling her to her feet and hugging her against his chest, feeling the hard snaps of his shirt against her cheek.

It wasn't until later that they realized that not all the blood was from Toliver. The bullet had also shattered the third finger on Martha's left hand on its way to Toliver's brain. Her finger, from the big knuckle to the tip, hung by a thread of tissue and Martha had looked at it as if it was a science project. She'd given it a sharp jerk and showed it to Harold.

"My finger," she said, her voice sounding distant. Harold had put it in a sandwich bag and packed snow around it.

Of all the horses, Big Mike was the most bombproof. They folded Toliver's body over the saddle and tied him to it. They tied Freida to Petal and called off the copter, no point now, and used the sat phone for the coroner instead. They went out as a pack string—Annabel, Freida's saddleless mare, bringing up the rear, Martha sitting Harold's paint, Harold and Walt walking. No one saying a word. Once, Freida Toliver's hat had fallen off and her hair drooped down to shroud her face, the stiff locks swinging against an empty stirrup. That had not seemed dignified to Martha. She called for a halt and then was unable to get the hat back on because she only had the one working hand.

"I'll do it, Marth," Walt said. His voice was gentle, concerned. "You go on up with Harold and Katie. Go on now."

Then a ringing started in her ears and she felt they were all treating her as a precious child. Twice before, Martha had taken bodies out tied to saddles, but it wasn't something you got used to. The horses' eyes went to disks like they did when you diamond-hitched elk quarters onto a packsaddle. It reminded Martha that in the end a human being was just another kind of meat, the rigor setting in so that when they got down to the trucks, the bodies came off the saddles folded and went into the coroner's Suburban the same way, though at least by then they were covered. No, there was no getting used to it, nor was there any forgetting it.

Harold told Martha he would drive her to the hospital in her truck. Everyone knew she was blaming herself for what had happened, and no one wanted to see her drive off alone. She protested, but the truth was the hand was pulsing with pain and she had become woozy and disconnected from her circumstances. So she had relented, had done what she was told.

In the emergency room, Harold handed over the finger packed in the plastic bag of snow. The doctor explained that if it had been severed cleanly, then maybe, but with the shattering of bone and mangling of the connective tissues and nerves there was no hope of a successful reattachment. If he did sew it back on, the best she could hope for was a floppy fin.

"All the Viagra in the world wouldn't get that puppy to stand back up," he said.

"That's all right," Martha told him. "It wasn't like anybody was going to put a ring on it."

———

Back at home that evening, she put the finger in a Mason jar filled with tequila and set it back on a shelf with the pickled asparagus. Then she went into her bathroom and took a long look at her face in the mirror.

"You killed him," she said out loud. It wasn't true and she knew that, but it didn't help.

Harold had made tea for her and they ate leftover elk meatloaf. The pain was there, dulled by the prescription Vicodin. She told Harold to go home, but he insisted on staying. As they were no longer a couple, Harold slept on the sofa. On toward dawn she shuffled into the living room and huddled against his chest.

"It wasn't your fault," he said. "It could have happened with any of us."

But it was her fault, that was the thing. You couldn't just wake up and say that it wasn't. Walt, who as undersheriff ran the office, had told her to take a day off, more if she needed to, and after Harold left she took a long walk with Goldie, her golden retriever. Four times over the next two days she passed by the tipi that Sean Stranahan lived in, not when his Land Cruiser was in the drive, though, and then on the third evening, coming back up the road—it was one of those cold, lavender sky evenings that you get in April in the wake of a storm—it was.

The man who had been her friend before being her lover, and who was no longer her lover but remained her heartache and her regret, as well as her friend, heard her hello and told her to come in. She undid the bits of stick that fastened the front flap as he struck a match to light a burner of a Coleman stove. He held her awhile, standing up, but thankfully didn't utter the same lame condolences she'd been getting from everyone else. When she pulled back, he indicated the folded blanket to his right. Had she been a man, he would have seated her to his left. Blackfeet custom, courtesy of Harold Little Feather, who had lent him the tipi while he was building his house. An irony if you thought about it, which Martha did often, Harold being her regret in a different way.

"When are you going to get around to raising the walls?" Martha said.

"June twenty-fourth. I'm throwing a solstice party. Pig in the ground, bean-hole beans, Sam's got some moonshine he'll uncork if you'll look the other way."

"Am I invited?"

"Of course."

"Keep your friends close, keep your enemies closer?"

"You're not my enemy, Martha."

"Going to be strange, huh, sleeping in an actual bed."

"Oh, I don't know. I seem to recall doing that a few times."

They let that one hang as he poured her a cup of tea from a blue enamel coffeepot. Sean Stranahan was a watercolor artist, a trout fishing guide, and a now-and-then private detective. It was the latter vocation that gave his body character, including a knife scar on his shoulder that Martha had liked to trace with her fingertips in the dark. He drove a forty-year-old Toyota Land Cruiser he couldn't afford to feed gasoline, had a Sheltie dog he couldn't afford to take to the vet but did, and had a history of women who fell at his feet and then, wondering how they had got there, stood up and walked away. Including Martha, Martha thought.

She found herself looking at him. She shook it off.

"I knew her, you know," he said.

"Freida Toliver?"

"She shared gallery space at the cultural center with two other artists, down the hall from my studio. She didn't work there, just displayed a few of her chandeliers. Called me Barn Owl. 'What's that good-looking Barn Owl up to today?' she'd say. 'If I had a thing for white faces I'd be looking to fly away with you.' It was a passing-in-the-halls thing, a bit of flirtation to brighten up the morning. I can't say I knew her. I wish now I had. She was a very nice woman."

"I was going to ask you the same thing she did. What do you have on the docket today?"

"Let me consult my calendar." He stood up and peered out the tipi flap. "Nice morning. Looks like fishing to me."

"I was thinking about riding back up Specimen Ridge. I could use a hand, seeing how I'm short one for the time being." She held up her bandaged hand.

"I thought there was nothing up there but a dead horse. Or is there something I don't know about?"

Stranahan had been part of the search-and-rescue hasty team that had responded to the lost hunters the morning of the snowstorm. That misadventure had had a happier outcome. The hunters were found sitting in their stuck truck, doing the Sunday crossword puzzle in the *Bridger Mountain Star,* having kept themselves warm by cranking the heater every hour. What Stranahan knew of the events up Specimen Ridge had also come from the *Star.* The headline read "Double Death in the Gravellys," with the subhead "Woman Freezes in Bear Den, Husband Commits Suicide," and the follow-up two days later: "Dying with the Living, Sleeping with the Dead."

"No, there's nothing secret about what happened up there," Martha said. "But there's two good saddles on that mountain and I'd like to bring them back before the porcupines start chewing on them. They're asking me to take some time and I really can't justify pulling someone else off a shift to do it."

"Isn't there a bear up there that might take offense?"

"It's possible," Martha said.

"I'll just get my stuff," Sean said.

———

On the drive up the valley, she told him that Freida Toliver's autopsy, performed the previous afternoon, revealed that she had died of cardiac arrest, possibly triggered by her husband hugging her to his chest. Doc Hanson, the county medical examiner, said the rapid warming could have caused the blood vessels in her arms and legs to open too quickly, resulting in a dramatic fall of blood pressure to her internal organs and triggering the attack.

"So he hugged her to death?" Sean said.

"In a manner of speaking. Doc said we should have just kept performing CPR until the chopper arrived to take her to Billings, where they have a cardiac care unit. They could have done a heart-lung bypass, removing her blood and warming it up before putting it back into the circulatory system. But by the time we got to her, her core temperature had probably fallen so far that she would have died anyway."

"If he hadn't killed himself on the mountain, he would have done it sooner or later," Sean said. "If not with that gun, with another. You know that."

Martha nodded, her eyes on the road unfurling through the valley. "So I keep telling myself."

They drove in silence, the country opening above Ennis, the white cardboard snows in the high country, the now-you-see-it, now-you-don't winding of the cobalt river, glimpsed in the valley.

"Something else about the autopsy," Martha said. "I talked to Craig Jenkins—he's the bear biologist for Region Three. He said that bears don't really hibernate, they just go into a state of torpor, which isn't as deep of a sleep. So when you get close to a denned-up bear, he smells you and he gets wide awake in a hurry. You can't just climb inside a den and snuggle up for warmth. Not if you want to keep breathing. But Freida, there wasn't a scratch on her."

"Maybe she sensed that Freida Toliver wasn't a threat. Bears are smart."

"Now you're anthropomorphizing."

"Maybe. The fact is she was in a den with a bear. Why didn't she warm up?"

"I asked Craig about that. He said that bears are so well insulated they really don't radiate a lot of heat, that it was maybe only a few degrees warmer in the den than outside."

"The things you do when you're desperate. I can't imagine what must have been going through her mind."

There was no answer to that. Martha punched the button to lock in the hubs as they turned onto the access road and began to climb. A glance at the ruts told her that someone had driven up the road in the last couple days. That by itself wasn't noteworthy. The Aphrodisiac Graveyard may not have been common knowledge among antler collectors, but nor was it a total secret. Anyone with a powerful pair of binoculars could see the openings on the ridge from the highway and might spot an elk there, or see the lines of the game trails contouring the slope.

A blue pearl Toyota Highlander came into view. It was parked at the turnaround, the windows frosted up. Idaho plates. Sean walked over to check out any prints made by the driver as he stepped out of the rig.

"Muck Boot tread, three or four hours old," he said. "He's packing snowshoes."

"How do you know?"

"They were sitting in the snow and now they aren't. Must be climbing high. You think he's a horn hunter? There's bone vultures all up the valley this time of year."

"Who else would be here?" Martha said.

"You don't approve?"

"No, there's lots of regular folks collect antlers. Long as they respect the regulations, I don't begrudge them. But for every Freida Toliver, there's a piece of Rocky Mountain trailer trash packing a medical marijuana card in one pocket and a hard-on for the law in the other."

"How many pieces of trailer trash drive hybrid SUVs?"

"I'll grant you the point." She brought her fingers to her chin. "Whoever it is, I'm not liking it."

They unloaded the horses and Martha told Sean to saddle up Big Mike. He was no horseman, so it was a way to keep an upper hand on him. Martha wasn't proud of herself for it, but all's fair. She finished saddling Petal with a bareback pad. The plan was that she would come back out sitting Freida's saddle, and they would lash the saddle that was on Toliver's dead horse to the saddle on Big Mike, and Sean would lead him out on foot.

She turned to inspect Sean's work.

"You got to get the cinch tighter," she said. "He barrels out his chest, that's because you're trying to tighten too much at once. Do it in stages. Then find something to stand on when you mount, so you don't put all the weight on one stirrup. That's just asking for it to slip, especially with a quarter horse who's got that rounded chest."

They took turns standing on an overturned bucket that Martha had brought for the purpose, and they were heading up the trail. Martha turned to check the spacing and saw that Sean was easily sitting the saddle, the rein laid over an open hand. She watched as Big Mike tested him by dipping his head, but Sean showed who was boss without making an issue of it.

She spoke over her shoulder. "I see you're sitting a little straighter on the horse. Who've you been riding with, you don't mind I ask?" Feeling the slight tightness in her chest, only the words casual.

"Etta Huntington," Sean said.

"That one-armed truck salesman? She manage to get the claws on that prosthetic limb into you?"

"I wouldn't call them claws. Actually, she doesn't wear her arm around her friends."

"Humpff."

Etta Huntington was a celebrity in the valley, a rodeo champion who had parlayed her carnivorous brand of beauty into a second career as a minor television personality. She'd been the woman who "kicked out the stars" in three Chevy Absaroka commercials that had run a half dozen years ago. Martha doubted there was a man in Montana who hadn't seen her beckon her cowboy into the pickup bed and didn't wish it was his lips she was kissing before they disappeared from sight, his belt she was unbuckling before kicking off her cowgirl boots to imprint against a screen of stars. The kind of woman that a wife introduces to her husband while digging her nails into his palm.

"Do I detect a note of jealousy, Martha?"

"No. Just a little surprised to hear the name. Chuck Toliver told me it was Huntington's ranch where they pastured their horses."

"I did not know that," Sean said.

"Now you do."

It looked like another world with the lower-elevation snow melted, and Sean said so.

"What's that?"

"I said it's finally looking like spring."

"Uh-huh."

Which set the tone for the ride, Sean offering an occasional comment, Martha the back side of her jacket. Not much else but the undertone of Specimen Creek and then, climbing, the creek falling behind and the snow—for it was still winter on the mountain—melting from the pine boughs and plopping wetly onto the withers of the horses. Sean saw Martha pull down the brim of her hat and did the same.

The trail they had been following was the one the rescue party made packing out its gruesome cargo, and had to this point been overlaid by the fresher boot prints belonging to the driver of the SUV.

As they neared the first of the clearings in the Aphrodisiac Graveyard, the boot prints diverged from the trail and Martha brought Petal to a halt. She waited for Stranahan to pull up alongside her. The snow was knee deep and it was plain to see where the hiker had dusted off a log to have a seat. Here he had buckled on his snowshoes and tapped out a pipe, though it took Stranahan a moment or two to see the pile of ash for what it was.

"Why do you think he's up here?" Martha said. "Morbid curiosity? We released the name of the drainage. Anybody who read the paper would know what trailhead we used and be able to backtrack us to the scene."

Stranahan nodded. "Maybe."

"You're no help."

"Just not jumping to conclusions. Somebody taught me that, remember? And he isn't far ahead of us now. We'll catch up to him."

A short, stiff climb brought them to the ridgeline. On the far side was the witch's heart where Chuck Toliver had shot his horse and, a few hours later, himself.

"There's likely been some critters here," Martha said. "Best dismount and tie 'em up. I don't want the horses punching our ticket to a rodeo if that bear decided on breakfast after a long winter's nap."

She unbuckled the holster strap on her revolver. Stranahan clicked off the safety tab of his pepper spray and placed his thumb on the trigger as they sidestepped down the ridge. A moment's caught breath as a pair of whisky jacks fluttered up from the patch of timber and they were there, the horse dead and then some, its smell staining the air as they came within sight of it. Stranahan looked past the horse to see a man sitting with his back to a tree, the snowshoes he had removed tipped against the trunk. The man was loading a pipe and tamped the bowl with a short stick. He said, "Don't shoot," then produced a wooden match, flicked it against his thumbnail, and set fire to the pipe.

# CHAPTER FOUR

# The Tyrolean Man

"I haven't been this high without climbing into a ski lift in twenty-five years," he said. "You must be the local authority." A nod in the direction of Martha, his eyes on her revolver. He smiled, drawing creases into clean-shaven, peach-half cheeks. "Either that or you're here to relieve me of my sovereigns."

Martha placed her hands on her iliac crests, a posture she subconsciously adopted to project authority. She rested the heel of her hand on the grips of the Ruger as the man approached. He was an inch or so shorter than her five-eight, though solidly built, with a barrel chest and an ample belly that ballooned against wool plus-four trousers that ran a burgundy stripe down the sides. Pipe between teeth, he removed a jaunty Tyrolean hat in forest green with a broad tuft of what looked like boar hair clasped in a silver fitting on the braided hatband.

"My name is Wilhelm Winkler," he said, extending his hand, his thick pink fingers clasping Martha's right hand, then Stranahan's. Sean drank in the sweet, acrid odor of rough-cut tobacco. It was pleasant enough and welcome under the circumstances. Anything to cut the stench of the horse.

"What are you doing here, Mr. Winkler?" Martha said.

"Oh, I'm sorry. Winkler, that's Winifred's maiden name. Freida, she's . . . she was . . . my sister." He cocked his head as if at some inward reflection. His eyes squinted and he pulled back the corners of his finely drawn mouth. "I hope I haven't broken any laws, but I had to see for myself. It's a tragedy. She seemed to be in such a good place in her life. It hasn't always been that way."

"What do you mean?"

"Everyone has bad times, meets people they would have preferred not to in hindsight. Freida's first husband, he made her life a living hell, left her without lint for her pockets. Then when she worked for the phone company and took that awful fall, there was a time we didn't know if she'd walk again. But she dusted herself off, got to her feet, and got her antler business in gear, met Mister J.C. That man was just what she needed, solid as granite. Though if he rose from the grave right now I wouldn't know whether to hug him or to hit him. He gave Freida a life, but I can't but think he took it away from her, bringing her this high under those conditions. No way to start a fire except a bullet? That's what the paper said. I grew up in Vorarlberg, in the Austrian Alps. You wouldn't think of going into the forest without the tools to survive and the skills to use them."

"I thought I detected a German accent," Martha said. "But I met Freida and she was Northern Cheyenne."

"She was my sister, but not my blood. My parents adopted her after her grandmother died. They were counselors at the high school in Lame Deer."

"What's the fan on your hat?" Sean asked.

"It's called a Gamsbart. Traditionally it was made from the neck hair of a chamois goat. Now it could be any old thing, but this one is chamois, from the first I ever shot." He nodded. "You're wondering why I'm here. I came to burn sweetgrass and pray for her soul. That's what I was doing before you arrived."

"I'm very sorry for your loss, Mr. Winkler," Martha said. "She seemed like very nice people."

"She was, she was. We called her Little Echo. May I ask why you are here?"

He pulled at the pipe, an ornately carved, drooping thing with what looked like bone or ivory inlays.

Martha found herself hesitating. She decided to say as little as possible.

"Sean's a tracker for the department. We need to reconstruct what happened before filing the report. The last time we were here, there were more pressing matters than reading tracks."

"Is there any reason to suspect foul play?"

"It's not that at all. We're just following the protocol."

The Tyrolean man, as Martha had come to think of him, took the pipe stem from between his teeth. He rubbed his fingers against the burl bowl as if to warm them.

"A man who is determined to top himself will find a way, one way or another."

Martha kept her face a mask.

"You rode in on horses," the man said. A statement. "I saw you at a bend in the trail, just before I topped over the ridge."

Martha nodded. "We left them a ways back. We'd offer you a ride out, but once we pack up this saddle we'll be short as it is. Sean will be hiking."

"That's okay. Walking is a good clean exercise and these snowshoes are a godsend. I have never worn them before and didn't know what to expect."

"Cut yourself a couple branches for walking sticks," Sean said. "They'll help on the downhill. Otherwise you'll be eating snow."

"Thank you for the advice. Would you like any help before I leave? Perhaps a hand with the saddle? I noticed that he dropped his mount onto the side where the latigo is buckled. You'd think he'd have removed the strap and the saddle first, but he was probably fighting frozen fingers and not thinking straight. I know I wouldn't be in those circumstances."

"A hand with the saddle would be appreciated," Martha said.

If not tall, the stout man was bullish strong. With his help, Stranahan was able to roll the front quarter of the carcass far enough over for Martha to reach under and undo the cinch one-handed. They dragged the saddle free and draped it over a log.

Wilhelm Winkler buckled his snowshoes to leave. He volunteered that he was going to hike through the openings for a couple hours and see if he could find a dropped elk antler for his mantel. That way, every time he lifted his eyes from the fireplace, he would remember Freida.

"Did you see your sister often?" Martha asked.

Winkler seemed to think about it. "No, not often. But we stayed in touch. She helped people, you know, people who had nowhere else to turn."

"How so?"

Again, he had to think about it. "It was just the way she was."

And with that he shuffled away along the contour of the ridge, a man in plus-fours and a Tyrolean hat, at home in the country if not from the continent, the spray of chamois hair sifting in the wind.

"Can you guess what he meant by 'She helped people'?"

Sean shook his head.

Martha was holding the business card that Winkler had proffered and it fell from her fingers. "Damn useless hand," she said.

Sean dusted the snow from the card. *Wilhelm Winkler and Associates. Sawtooth Appraisals and Real Estate: Ranch, Residential, Commercial.* Contact information. A street address in Hailey, Idaho.

"He didn't seem particularly upset about his sister's death," Sean said. "More . . . philosophical."

"I noticed that, too."

Following the now indistinct tracks that the rescue party had made, Sean and Martha found the saddle that Freida Toliver had pulled off her horse. It was snow-covered and they would not have seen it had they not been looking. Sean scraped the snow and ice off and hung it over a log. The twin saddlebags were attached by saddle strings to the saddle and he opened them.

"Find anything?"

"It's what I'm not. Toliver told you that he tried to start a fire with the hair shaved off fishing flies that were in his wife's fly vest, that the vest was in her saddlebag."

"That's right."

"It's not here."

"I'm guessing they just left it where they tried to build a fire. Putting it back into the bag wouldn't be a priority."

"Then let's find where that is."

They hiked back to the hollow. All dog hair thicket, trees no bigger around than a man's wrist, except for a solitary yellow pine some distance above them. That had to be the tree that Toliver had placed the tinder nest against.

The well around the trunk had been protected from the storm and held only a dusting of snow. The vest was in plain sight there, as were three fly boxes. Sean found several hooks on the ground where Toliver had shaved hair off the flies to make tinder, and what was left of the nest itself, a few charred strands of tinsel and a forlorn strip of cloth. Two of the fly boxes were of a cheaper plastic variety, the third a zippered leather wallet with sheepskin lining. The wallet had the initials "EH" burned into the leather. That meant nothing to Stranahan. He zipped the three fly boxes into pockets in the vest and shrugged it over his shoulders.

Martha bent down to pick up the cloth. The purple and pink hearts were small, like candy hearts.

"What's that?" Sean asked her.

"A desperate person's attempt at salvation. I'll tell you later." Carefully, almost reverently, she wound the cloth around a small branch. Maybe a bird would find it and weave it into its nest, so that it helped bring life rather than just the hope of it.

Sean said, "I suppose we should check out the den."

"I suppose."

"What if there's a bear in it?"

"Then we don't. What planet do you live on?"

They stopped at a hundred yards, circled around to get the wind at their backs, and talked loudly. No response. Moved closer to the den. No response.

Sean raised his binoculars. He could see pockmarks in the old snow near the den mouth, which showed as a black oval under a ledge of rock.

"I think mama bear is gone," he said. "This is the month most bears leave their dens."

"Are you asking or hoping?"

"Stalling," Sean said. He snapped the safety tab off his pepper spray. "Tell Sam the fly rods are his. You get Choti and any paintings that catch your eye. Anything in the tipi is yours, too." He shook his head.

"What?"

"Nothing. I just realized everything I own can be divided up in five seconds. Not a lot to show for a man my age."

"You're rich in experience."

"Let's hope this isn't one of them."

It wasn't. The sow grizzly and her cubs, whose tracks were the size of teacups, had left the den in single file. Compared to the tracks Harold had made carrying Freida Toliver, they didn't look quite as old. But what stopped Sean short of the den were the quite fresh imprints of snowshoes.

"What do you know," Martha said. "Our Tyrolean man was holding out on us."

Sean nodded. "I suppose it's natural, though, wanting to see where his sister was. Maybe this is where he started praying for her soul."

"The fact is he didn't tell us. He was hoping we weren't going to check out the den for ourselves. I wonder why."

Martha asked the question again, more to herself this time, pulling at her lower lip as Sean lay down and wormed into the den. He knew that most bear dens consist of little more than a short tunnel and a bedding area scarcely larger than the bear, so much the better for retaining body heat. This den was larger, a natural cavity under the rock at least ten feet wide and almost as deep. It helped explain why Freida Toliver could find refuge without having to shoulder past the bear, and perhaps even why the bear had allowed her to survive. Yet Sean could find no trace of her occupation beyond some deep pocks in the snowy walls near the cave entrance, where it looked like she'd poked something ahead of her. A stick? If so, it was a perfectly round one, for the holes were round and all alike, two inches or so in diameter. Harold had not mentioned the holes, but then Harold had a bear growling outside the den and probably registered nothing beyond Freida's body.

A bed of old leaves, tufts of pine boughs, and piles of forest floor duff covered in a layer of grizzled bear hair showed where the sow had lain with her cubs. The beam of Sean's headlamp probed the opposite side of the lair where Harold said he'd seen Freida's body curled into itself, seeming in peaceful slumber. A few red fibers, the color of the coat she'd been wearing, clung to the rock ceiling, confirming that Sean had found the right spot. The only other item that caught his eye was a small chunk of silver that looked out of place against the scattered debris on the den floor. Sean picked it up and bent his head so that the light shone on it. The bit of silver was attached to a sliver of stone and Sean realized, though it did not come to him for several seconds, that the stone was part of a tooth, the silver being a piece of filling attached to the enamel.

No, this was not a sleeping place. This was a dying place, where Freida Toliver's teeth had chattered so hard from the cold that she'd cracked off a piece of one. In that moment it became real to him. He pictured the woman whose cheerful smile had brightened up his morning, and tried to imagine what she must have gone through. It was impossible. He muttered, "Rest in peace, Freida," and then pocketed the tooth chip and crawled back out of the cave.

Martha, standing outside holding her .30-06, told him he looked like he'd seen a ghost. He showed her the piece of the tooth.

"Let's get out of here," she said.

Sean collected the saddle and carried it back to the witch's heart, where they'd left the other one. Both were trail saddles with thin horns and high forks, Chuck Toliver's a battle-scarred Billy Cook with the leather worn through at the mantle. Freida's saddle was newer, richly burnished with oak leaf tooling. "CWS" in interlocking letters was scrolled into the leather on the left fender.

"Fine-looking saddle," Martha offered.

"I think it's one of Etta Huntington's." Sean showed her the initials. "It stands for Crazy Woman Saddlery."

"I wouldn't think she'd advertise it. It just confirms everybody's suspicion."

"It's her way of saying 'Fuck you' to the world. Come to think of it, the initials on the fly wallet are 'EH.' That could be Etta Huntington, too."

"Mmm-hmm." Martha fingered her chin. "She does this kind of work with only one hand?"

"It's a point of pride with her."

Martha pressed her lips together. She was impressed.

"It's not that much of a coincidence," Sean said. "The Tolivers pastured their horses on Etta's ranch. They would know she had a saddlery business. Freida could have bought this directly from her."

Martha nodded. "I understand that, but aren't her saddles expensive? The notoriety factor and all. I imagine one like this has to run at least a couple thousand."

"More than that. But worth it. Once you've sat on hers, it's hard to go back."

"I guess you'd be the one to know," Martha said.

She abruptly shook her head. "I'm sorry, Sean. That was crude. It's no business of mine who you . . . see. It's just—" She let her shoulders fall.

"Just what?"

"When Harold and I quit, I thought, you know, the two of us . . . You *do* know I'm not seeing him now, not in that way."

"I heard. But what did you expect me to do, be a monk? It's Montana. Winter's cold."

"That's what you have a dog for."

"Some nights I need more than a dog."

"Then you get two." She shook her head. "It's just, I thought the one you were riding horses with was Katie. And I know Katie, and I know you two aren't going anywhere. There's no happily ever after with her."

"There probably isn't with Etta, either. I just bumped into her at an auction and . . ." He shrugged.

"I know. The cheekbones, the endearing dearth of an extremity. How could you resist?"

"Now you're being sarcastic, Martha. And you lost a finger yourself. Lose four more and I won't be able to tell the two of you apart."

"Yeah you will. I'm the one who doesn't sharpen her teeth when she's dressing for a date."

"That's what I love about you," Sean said.

"What?"

"Just you being Martha."

They looked at each other, the silence of the thicket gradually reasserting itself and the mountain swallowed by a dark solemnity. Suddenly it seemed absurd, talking about their relationships in a circle of blood and guts, watched by eyes that had skinned over and shrunk back into an equine skull.

"I'll ride out sitting Etta's saddle, see what all the fuss is about," Martha said.

# CHAPTER FIVE

# Sweetening the Pot

As Sean hefted the saddle from the bed of his Land Cruiser and put it on his shoulder, he recalled the first time he'd driven to the Bar-4 to call on Loretta Huntington. The occasion had not been a social visit. She had only just heard that her missing daughter was found dead in the chimney of a Forest Service cabin, and was coming to grips with that knowledge with the aid of Scotch whisky. Taking off her prosthetic right arm, she had bent all the mechanical knuckles but the middle one, then set the arm on the sill of a window casement with the one finger outstretched against the sky.

"This is all I have to say to God," she'd told him, her voice thick, then changed the subject to tell him that he had kissable lips. A few nights later, the house dark, her eyes bright, she dropped her arm on the hardwood floor and led him to her bedroom to find out if her prediction was right.

No kiss this evening. Nor did he expect one, not a casual one, anyway. "I'm not a hunt and pecker," she'd told him once, when he'd bent to kiss her cheek. "When I kiss somebody, I don't stop until it's time to light a cigarette."

She led him into her workshop and indicated the sawhorse to drape the saddle over. Sean had called her as he drove over the Bridger Pass and she knew the bones of the story leading to the recovery of the saddle.

She looked at it critically. She had green eyes with gold lights in them that reminded Sean of cat's eyes. Everything about them was wild and penetrating, except they didn't go to slits when you turned up the lights.

"I made this for a woman who owned a dude ranch in the Snowcrests," she said. "She put half down, and when I called her to take delivery, she'd split from her husband and moved to California. All my saddles are made to order, so I had to sell it for a song. Freida had mentioned how much she admired my work, so I asked if she'd be interested."

"A song being how much, exactly?" Sean asked.

"Thirty-five hundred, plus that elk antler chandelier in the dining room. Freida threw that into the pot."

She laughed, then shook her head.

"What's funny?"

"I told her that she'd bought everything but the stirrups. If she wanted those, too, then she'd have to find something to sweeten the deal. So she gave me a baggie of these thin shavings from elk anthers. Looked like coins. She said it was from the tips of the antlers, processed velvet, the primo stuff, and if I wanted the best sex of my life, what I needed to do was brew it into a tea and drink it with my lover."

"So you two were friends."

"No, not really. She just stabled her horses here. We always did a little trading to bring down the out-of-pocket for pasture fees. It was just her way. I did know J.C. He'd shoed for us for years."

"Did you see them on Easter morning?"

"No. I'd driven into church in Wilsall. I know, what's a pagan like me doing sitting on a church pew? But I understand the power of Christianity better now. It takes away the need to ask why. 'Why did God do this to me?'"

Sean saw the slight tremor in her lower jaw and moved to put his arm around her, but she pulled back. "I'm fine," she said. "What else do you want to know about Freida Toliver? Why do you want to know? It's just a tragedy. But I guess I'm the expert, so maybe that's why." She picked up a black Stetson hanging from a wall peg and centered it. "Even when I was a little girl, I always wore a black hat. My mom told me that way she could find me in the arena. Most of the other girls wore silver belly. Can you imagine me in a white hat? I don't think so."

"Do many people take their horses from pasture without telling you first?"

"Of course not. They're supposed to check in with me or the manager, so we can dock times of arrival and departure. But I was gone and Freida and J.C. were in a hurry. That's what was on the note."

"What note?"

"They left one on the front door."

"Do you still have it?"

She nodded and got it. "I decided not to throw it out after hearing what happened."

> *Hi Etta. We took the horses to go horn hunting. I'm sorry for not checking in but we're in a rush. We'll bring them back this evening and brush them down. Don't be too mad. Thanks, Freida*

Sean pocketed the note and drew out the fly wallet from his shirt pocket. "Freida had this in her fishing vest."

She examined it and zipped it open to glance at the flies. Then rezipped it. "These flies are really old," she said.

Sean pointed to the initials: "EH."

She shook her head. "It isn't mine. I did make leather goods before restricting the business to saddles, but I never did anything like this. If I had, I would have carved the initials of the person I made it for, not mine."

She gave it back to him. "Is this all you came for, to show me a saddle and this fly wallet? Or is it an excuse to see me and spend the night?

I mean, why not, now that you're here? We can even drink elk antler tea if you'd like." Bitterness had crept into her voice.

"I thought this is what you wanted," Sean said. "No plans, no regrets. Your words."

"Yes, and you agreed so quickly."

"What's that mean?"

"It means just what it sounds like. I have some quiche in the refrigerator. Or would you rather have sex before dinner?"

"Etta."

"Etta what? Don't shake your head at me."

———

Later, lying in the dark—sex had been after dinner, after all, and after drinking antler tea that she'd brewed just for the hell of it, and that left a salty taste on their lips—she said, "I'm sorry about earlier. I don't like it when I get like that. I'm the one who wanted it casual. Did I ever tell you about that guy I was seeing from Kalispell? The one who wanted me to teach at his equestrian school? No? I thought I had. Anyway, this man, he was nice-looking, had a nice smile, just lopsided enough that he wasn't too pretty. This was a few months after Cindy died, and I'd been hoping you would call and you didn't. No, you didn't, let me finish. So this guy, he was obviously interested, and I thought, 'Why not?' So we had a thing for a few weeks. But, I don't know, the pieces didn't fit. Maybe it was the arm. Some guys, it turns them on; other guys, they can't seem to get past it. Anyway, we saw each other less and less, fade to black. I thought, 'I'll never hear from him again.' Then about six months after I'd last seen him he calls me, says it didn't work out romantically but he wants us to be friends. He wants to *Skype* with me. Can you believe that? Me, looking at a face on a computer screen, telling somebody about my *day*? I don't think so. I'm not casual friends, not with men, not with women. Most women hate me, anyway."

"Why are you telling me this? I never asked you to Skype."

She laughed softly, reached over and squeezed his hand. "I'm telling you because I can't help who I am. I want you to want more from me than I want from you. That way I'm the one in control. But if I admit that I want more than I let on, I'm afraid of driving you away. This is me," she said, turning toward him and pressing her breasts up against his chest, her breath in his ear, her tears wet against his cheek. "This is me, driving you away."

# CHAPTER SIX

# The McGinty, the Coch-y-Bondhu,
# and the Woodcock and Green

The cabin belonging to the Madison River Liars and Fly Tiers Club, with its mossy roof, red-painted door, and blackened timbers, reminded Sean of a hobbit's dwelling. It showed a curl of smoke spiraling from the stone chimney. This was surprising, as Sean did not expect any of the members to have arrived so early in the spring. After leaving Etta's place he had driven up the valley to fish and to think, in that order, not to socialize. But there was the smoke, a rental Subaru in the drive, and the front door was opening even as his Land Cruiser ground to a halt.

Patrick Willoughby, the club president, stepped out onto the porch. Kenneth Winston, a hairdresser from Biloxi, Mississippi, was two steps behind. The former was a portly, moon-faced man who wore a tweed porkpie hat and the expression of a wise old owl; the latter, rail thin, had tightly curled hair sculpted by a razor and fingers that flitted like blackbirds when he talked. He was blowing the steam from the coffee in his cup.

"You didn't write, you didn't call," Stranahan began.

"And yet here you are, trespassing," Winston finished.

"I'm an honorary member."

"My point exactly. You don't pay dues. You're a simple piece of river riffraff and I'd call the sheriff if she wasn't in league with you. Or should I say in bed?"

"In league, maybe. In bed, no."

"And a fool to boot. I'd be tapping that silver star, I was you."

"Gentlemen, gentlemen," Willoughby said.

Sean stepped onto the porch and hugged two of his best friends in the world.

"What are you doing here?" he asked Willoughby.

"I wanted to fish the Madison before runoff, for once. But the real reason is Marlene finally passed."

"I'm so sorry, Patrick. I knew she was sick—"

"No, it's me who is sorry. I should have told you, but I just couldn't get the words out. It's hard to think of me overcome by inertia, but I was. It was difficult simply to speak. And you would have flown to the memorial and you need that money to build your house."

"We're all getting sick of trying to figure out where you knock on a tipi," Winston said.

"Ken has been kind enough to join me for a couple weeks," Willoughby continued. "I've always been an optimist, despite a career that served to confirm the opposing viewpoint. But I've spent the past months in a very dark place. Each morning I would awaken, hoping that the other side of the bed was cold, that Marlene had found freedom from pain in a better world. That kind of anticipation saps your soul, no matter how strong you believe you are. Now that she is finally departed, I find that I can neither stay in the house where we lived for forty years, nor can I stand to be alone. What I needed was trout therapy, that and to be with good friends. We tried calling you yesterday to come to dinner, but you must have been out of cell range. In any event, now that you're here, you're not going anywhere. I won't allow it."

"How long have *you* been here?"

"Just a little over a week," Willoughby said.

Winston nodded. "And already we've been visited with something of a mystery. I blame you. It's the curse of Sean Stranahan. Just knowing you casts a pall."

"But interesting," Willoughby said. "It's one of the reasons we were trying to contact you. And I must say it has been liberating, to focus my mind on something other than Marlene."

Sean asked them to elaborate, but Willoughby said in good time, there was just enough of the afternoon left to pull on waders and see if there were enough *Squalla* stoneflies about to bring a trout or two to the surface. There weren't, but an olive marabou streamer fly worked through the softer water coaxed the trout from their torpor. Sean landed two—a smallish brown, and then a rainbow with spawned-out colors that was active enough to make the rod throb. The anglers had split up, and by the time Sean hiked up the bank to the cabin, a bourbon and branch water was sweating at his place setting on the dining room table.

Kenneth Winston was sitting before his vise—the table doubled as a fly-tying bench—and didn't look up as Sean sat down. His ebony fingers were palmering grizzly and ginger hackles ahead of the quill body of an Adams dry fly, tied in the traditional split wing style. Like all of Ken's flies, every wrap of thread was perfectly executed. The fly, which he removed from the vise and pushed across the table toward Sean, stood at attention on its hackle tips, a slight drifting of wind coming through the screen door breathing it to dancing, quivering life.

"Fish that one when the drakes come out next month," he said.

Sean would do nothing of the sort. Ken was a renowned fly tier, arguably the finest Catskill-school fly tier in the world, and this fly, like others he had given Sean, would find its way into a shadow-box display on the wall of his art studio.

Dinner was an appetizer of sautéed morels that Willoughby had collected up the West Fork, followed by a second-day bourguignon featuring venison sliced from the haunch of an impala, courtesy of a club member who lived in Zimbabwe. Willoughby opened a second bottle of a French Margaux, and by the time it was finished Sean had helped his dinner companions into their saddles, ridden them up the mountain, shown them the bear's den and the carcass of the horse, mimicked the accent of the Tyrolean man, and introduced them to the bird's nest of tinder, complete with its tiny hearts. The dishes cleared, he retrieved the two fly boxes and the monogrammed fly wallet from the tackle bag.

Sean opened the larger of the plastic boxes. "See where the wings have been cut off the salmon flies and the elk hair caddis?" he said. "My guess is that they shaved them off right here in the box and then tipped the feathers and hair into the nest of tinder."

Willoughby shook his head. "What a nightmare that had to have been. Failing at fire and knowing the only way you could survive was killing your horse. I thought that only happened in movies."

"You knew the man?" Ken said.

"No, it was her I knew," Sean said. "Freida."

"Very well?"

"In passing."

"You see, this is why I never come here in winter." Winston tapped his forehead. "My mother didn't raise her boy to crawl inside a horse. 'Course, in Mississippi, you'd have to use a gator."

"Alligators are cold-blooded, Ken," Willoughby said.

"Then a pig. One of those Hogzillas they're always putting up on the Internet. You could sleep inside and have your side of bacon in the morning. 'Course you'd have to eat it commando style, like the eastern Europeans."

"Did you look inside the wallet?" Willoughby asked.

"It's just some old flies."

"May I have the honor?"

Willoughby unzipped the wallet, which was the size of a grocery store paperback Western. One side contained three small wet flies already knotted onto a coiled fly leader, the hooks secured in the sheepskin lining. The other half contained a half dozen or more wet flies in patterns similar to those on the leader. A curious expression worked across Willoughby's face. He handed the wallet to Winston.

Winston nodded. "I'll tell you right now that a wallet like this, in this condition, would be worth . . . what do you think, Patrick? Seventy-five dollars, a hundred? I'd say a hundred, tops. Most collectors want pewter Wheatleys and the like. Not much demand for fly wallets. But this one is quite well preserved."

He put on the magnifying glasses he used for fly tying and raised his eyebrows. "What do we have here? Catgut?"

"I do believe," Willoughby said. He took the wallet and handed it back to Sean.

"See how stiff the leader material is? You're still a young man, so you would never have fished with catgut, nor you, Ken. But I did, and let me tell you it was a problem. You had to soak it to make it limp enough to cast without kinking. Knot strength was poor, and it wasn't strong for its diameter in the first place. But it isn't the catgut that piques my curiosity. It's the fly patterns, the ones tied to the leader. Are you familiar with them?"

Sean fingered the stubble on his chin. "They're traditional wet flies. The one that looks like a bumblebee is called McKenzie, something like that, right? My father had a box of old wet flies."

"Close," Willoughby said. "It's a McGinty. Quite a popular pattern back in the day—the day being the first half of the last century. The others are more obscure. This one, with what looks like a turn of badger hackle, is called Coch-y-Bondu. The other is a Woodcock and Green. Wet flies like this were often sold prerigged in Britain and a three-fly cast was typical."

"Down-and-across presentation," Winston interjected. "A. H. E. Wood called it greased line fishing."

"Quite," Willoughby said. "The slow lift of the flies as they swing around imitates the rising of insect pupae to the surface."

Sean sipped at his bourbon. "You harbor a mischievous look, Patrick."

"Do I? I suppose I am drawing this out, but it isn't often one comes face-to-face with a page of history, and this *is* a page of history. 'Okay, Patrick,' you must be thinking, 'what is so unusual about these particular patterns?' What makes them more interesting than any three other wet flies of the period? Do you want to tell him, Ken, or shall I?"

"I'm embarrassed to say I don't know," Winston said. "I'm familiar with the patterns but not their significance. They are all old standards, if less well known than, say, the Leadwing Coachman or Gold-Ribbed Hare's Ear."

Willoughby pulled his glasses down to peer over the lenses, first at Winston, then Sean. "Have either of you heard of the L Bar T Ranch? It is, or rather was, a dude ranch about ten miles east of Cooke City, near the northeast entrance of Yellowstone Park. Just across the state line into Wyoming, actually."

Neither had.

"Back in the 1930s," he continued, "this ranch hosted an American sportsman who came to hunt big game and fish for trout in the Clarks Fork River, which flowed through the property. It's a matter of historical record that he favored a cast with these three fly patterns, tied to the leader in precisely the order that these are—a Woodcock and Green on the uppermost dropper, then a Coch-y-Bondhu, with the McGinty on the point—and that he bought his leaders prerigged from Hardy Brothers in England. Essentially, what we are looking at is a custom order. The odds of another angler requesting these three fly patterns in this order are, in my opinion, slim. As Ken pointed out, with the exception of the McGinty, the patterns are obscure."

The club president raised a pair of woolly bear eyebrows. "In addition to being a sportsman, our angler was a man of letters, a prominent American writer. Now can you hazard a guess?"

Sean swallowed the information. Then, deliberately, he folded the wallet, zipped it, and turned it over so that the initials engraved into the leather became visible.

For a time no one spoke. They just looked at the discreet "EH" in the upper right-hand corner of the wallet. Sean saw Willoughby and Winston exchange a curious glance.

"I amend my appraisal," Winston said. "The value just went up."

———

In the pregnant pause that followed, Willoughby stood and splashed whiskey into their three glasses. He walked to the small kitchen, where he cracked an ice cube tray and came back and added two cubes to each glass. "Gentlemen, if you would excuse me for a moment," he said, and they could hear him opening a drawer in one of the bedrooms.

"Recall when I mentioned that we had been visited by a mystery?" Winston said to Sean.

"Yes, you somehow blamed me."

"And I stand by the statement. But in the light of what is before us"—he indicated the fly wallet—"our little mystery just got a little bigger."

Before Sean could ask him to clarify, Willoughby was back. He showed Sean a manila envelope with a canceled stamp in the corner and a Billings, Montana, postmark, which restricted its origin to half of Montana. No return address, the mailing address in blue-black ink, in a rather ornate cursive script.

> *Patrick Willoughby, USN Ret'd*
> *President, Madison River Liars and Fly Tiers Club*
> *#7 Madison Bend Trail*
> *Cameron, MT 59720*

The envelope contained two sheets of plain white paper. One, Sean could see, had a hand-drawn map. The other was a letter. Like the address, it was handwritten in ink. Willoughby pushed up his glasses and read.

*Dear Mr. Willoughby,*

*Your stature as a collector of vintage fly fishing gear and classic fly patterns tied by the world's masters, including yourself and your fellow club members (prominently Kenneth Winston and the late Polly Sorenson), is well documented, as is your honesty and the content of your character.*

*A private collection of classic fly fishing gear once owned by a famous person has recently come into my possession, or will be transferred into my possession soon. Some of the pieces are signed with the owner's signature or initials. The collection, I am told, may include samples of the owner's writing. The individual pieces I have examined can be described as desirable collectables from notable makers in very good to excellent plus condition. But, as I'm sure you are aware, the worth of a collection such as this cannot be established by comparative values. If provenance can be determined, the collection is in my opinion priceless, with the pool of prospective buyers not restricted to the angling fraternity.*

*I am testing the waters of my options at this point— please forgive my pun—with my first priority to establish authenticity. If they are what I think they are, I wish to sell the collection as a whole. It is my hope that the buyer display the collection for posterity, so I am, at least at this juncture, limiting my enquiry to foundations, museums, and private parties who are in accordance with my wishes. As I wish to keep my name out of the transaction—there well may be others who seek this collection or lay claim to ownership—I am initially approaching private individuals such as yourself.*

*Would you be interested in examining a selected item from the collection, with the aim to establish provenance and estimated value? If so, would you entertain making an offer, or seek to secure backing funds from other sources to do so?*

*I will be at the location marked on the accompanying map from noon to 3 p.m. on Friday, April 22—rain, shine, or, as this is spring in Montana, snow. I have copied this letter to your Connecticut residence, overnight delivery, to allow for travel time, should this epistle find you there instead of the clubhouse. Please come alone, dressed as you normally would to fish. So that I may identify you, I ask that you carry a bamboo fly rod with a Hardy reel of your choice. I am sure you have several such outfits within reach.*

*Thank you for indulging my enquiry and please forgive the cloak and dagger.*

*I am respectfully,*

*Your fellow angler*

Willoughby pulled his glasses onto his nose. "In case you've lost track of your calendar, the rendezvous he suggests is tomorrow."

He opened the folded sheet of paper with the hand-drawn map.

"The river he has directed me to is our very own Madison, in the Bear Trap Canyon Primitive Area. Sean, you know this water better than I do."

Sean peered at the map. It was drawn in the same ink and showed the river in its toothy half smile that suggested the jaws of a bear trap. The map included three sets of rapids known as the Kitchen Sink, the rapids marked with a series of X's, as well as several tributaries. In one of the bends of the river was a line drawing of a fish, with a small dun-colored dry fly hooked into the paper near the fish's lip.

"The parachute *Baetis* is a nice touch, wouldn't you say?" Willoughby said.

Sean tapped the map with his finger. "It's a good run, that bend. I've caught some nice trout there."

Willoughby pressed his lips and slowly nodded. "I was intrigued, of course, when the letter arrived. But my initial inclination was to decline the invitation. Many famous people fly fish and I was thinking it was probably from a movie star's collection, someone like Gary Cooper, or a politician such as Herbert Hoover. Which would make it valuable, undoubtedly, but frankly I am not interested in celebrities who happen to have fly fished with expensive tackle, even ex-presidents. But if the collection was owned by our 'EH,' who, dare we say, is Ernest Hemingway . . ."

He flexed his eyebrows and looked from one to the other.

"Mind now," he continued, "I don't think I'm jumping to conclusions. Your fly wallet making its appearance in the same time frame leads one to think that they are connected. It changes the game. We are talking about the most famous American novelist of the twentieth century. And this collection, so we've been informed, may include samples of his writing. You are aware"—he took in Stranahan with his glance—"that a valise containing most of Hemingway's early short stories and a draft of his first novel was stolen?"

Sean shook his head.

"From the Gare de Lyon train station in Paris, in 1922. Hemingway's first wife, Hadley Richardson, was going to join him in Switzerland where he was covering the Lausanne Peace Conference. She decided to surprise him by bringing the stories so he could work on them. After she placed the valise on her seat, she got off to buy a newspaper at the kiosk on the platform. When she returned, the valise was gone."

"Are you suggesting—?"

Kenneth Winston cocked his head and waited for Willoughby to complete the thought.

Willoughby shook his head. "No, I'm not suggesting the collection our mystery man speaks of includes any contents from the long-lost valise. If it did, it would be a literary treasure on the order of Tutankha-men's tomb. But any words it may contain, even snatches of phrases or scribblings, would undoubtedly be much more valuable than the tackle itself. Kenneth, what's your opinion on this? Should I go?"

Ken Winston frowned. "My *opinion*," he said at length, "is no mat-ter what I say, you're going to go. My *concern* is for your welfare. That's why I insist that you take Sean with you. I'd go if I didn't stick out like a black widow on angel food cake."

Willoughby nodded. "He stipulates that I go alone, but it's public water and another angler on the same stretch shouldn't raise suspi-cion. Especially if he drives a separate rig. Sean, would you be up for it? Keep your distance and see what unfolds?"

"Of course."

"I'd pay your day rate, naturally."

"That isn't necessary."

"What's necessary and what I'm going to do are not the same. You will unearth that contract you keep in your fly-tying kit and I will sign my name. Then"—he smiled up at Sean—"let's see if our fellow angler has the fortune he speaks of."

# CHAPTER SEVEN

# Secrets

Sean probed at the streambed with his wading staff. Although this reach of the Madison, a couple hundred yards above the clubhouse, was his favorite in the entire length of the river, it was not a pleasant stretch to wade. The boulders were slippery, the current turbulent, with slots of heavy water to negotiate if you wanted to fish in the slicks near midriver. It was heart-in-your-throat wading, and that was in daytime, when you could see where you were planting your boots.

He took a step, then another, reaching a shallow bar where he could relax. No longer needing the support of the staff, he reached into a pocket in his fly vest and removed the Meerschaum pipe that, along with two bamboo fly rods and a folding knife, were the most treasured possessions he'd inherited from his father. He had not smoked a bowl for at least two years, and wouldn't have thought of it, if not for meeting the curious gnome on the mountainside whom Martha had christened the Tyrolean man.

Sean brought the pipe stem to his lips. He glanced at the luminescent hands of his watch. Midnight. When the hearth fire in the clubhouse had burned down and they had, at least for the evening, exhausted the subject of Ernest Hemingway, Sean had found that he could not fall asleep in the club's bunkhouse. Typically he slept quite well there, soothed by the lullaby of the river outside the window. But he could not sleep, and so he had risen and found himself at the water's edge, above him a sickle moon reflected on the surface, with, just beyond its arc, a single shimmering star. The pipe lit, its cherry bowl glowing,

Sean regarded that star. He had a feeling—it had been building since he'd come back down the mountain with Martha—that he was about to embark upon a journey. It had happened before when a seemingly insignificant detail took on a life of its own. This time it was a three-fly cast on a leader made from catgut, and a fly wallet's curious, if tenuous, connection to the most famous of American writers.

Before this evening, Sean's knowledge of Ernest Hemingway had been sketchy, if specific. In a high school literature class, he'd been given the choice of reading *The Great Gatsby*, by F. Scott Fitzgerald, *Light in August*, by William Faulkner, or *A Farewell to Arms*, by Ernest Hemingway. He had asked the teacher if he could substitute Hemingway's *In Our Time* because several of the stories were set in Michigan, where he had once gone on a camping trip with his father. Sean had chosen the volume because it was thin, and his teacher's face, as she pondered the request, told him that she suspected as much. Nonetheless, she agreed. Most of the stories in the volume Sean skimmed and promptly forgot. But two had made indelible impressions.

The first was "Big Two-Hearted River," which Sean liked immensely as a fishing story, unaware until he read the Cliffs Notes that it was the subtext that gave it gravity—a young man, shell-shocked by war, trying to find solace in the constancy of a river, and who, by attending to ritualistic chores such as chopping wood and pitching a tent, could reclaim a sense of who he had once been. The story left Sean with a series of images—trout holding in the current among mists of sand and gravel that spurted from the streambed; the slow bubbling of pancake batter in a frying pan; the coffee "according to Hopkins," which Sean tried to make and found horribly bitter; the sudden flame of a match incinerating a mosquito on the ceiling of a tent. Sean had tried that trick the next time he had gone camping with his father, who was not pleased by the hole the match burned in the canvas of his tent.

The second story was "Now I Lay Me," which followed the long night of a soldier who was afraid to fall asleep, feeling that if he did so the soul would fly out of his body. He passed the hours of darkness by fishing trout rivers in his mind, starting at a point upstream and fishing them all the way downriver, then turning around and fishing them back to the place where he had started. Sean did not fear for his soul, but he did identify with the soldier, for he, too, found sleep elusive and had often lain in a half-waking state, fly fishing his way through currents both recalled and invented. Usually, those streams were real waters he had fished, like the Deerfield and Battenkill rivers in Vermont, and the Au Sable and Manistee rivers in Michigan. But sometimes he made them up, and if you were to ask him when he had first seen the Madison River, his favorite trout stream in the world, he would have said not until his early thirties after he moved West, but that was not entirely true. He was only a boy when he'd seen a photograph of the Madison in an old *Field & Stream* magazine. He had torn the page out and taped it to his wall, and at night he would fish that river from a point far upstream where the water was small and the mountains tall, and, reaching the stretch where the photograph was taken, he would fish it all the way downriver, from peaks to plains, until its currents joined those of the Gallatin and Jefferson rivers to become the Mighty Mo, the Missouri River.

This was very curious, even surreal, for there were stretches of the river that, when he actually saw them for the first time, he would swear he had fished them as a boy. In fact, he had never been within fifteen hundred miles of Montana. Thus the river of his mind joined currents with the river of geography to become a river both real and unreal, and that as a consequence was his and his alone.

He knocked out the ashes of the pipe and touched the bottom of the bowl to the water's surface to cool it. He placed it back in his vest and began to fish, swimming a mouse fly with a strip of muskrat for a tail through the apron of smooth water that pooled below a logjam. He did not expect to be rewarded with a fish—as a rule, strikes are few when night fishing, fewer still when the water is cold—but big trout don't get that way by following rules. This one took violently and crashed the surface, shattering the reflection of the moon and scattering the stars. By the time the trout had quit jumping and was pulling away, Sean stumbling after it, it had taken almost his entire fly line. When he had finally got enough control to keep it from wrapping line around exposed rocks and breaking the leader, he was so far downstream that he could make out the silhouette of the clubhouse.

For a long moment he thought about calling out, for even without seeing the fish, he knew from the way it fought that it was an old hook-jawed brown trout, and that it was probably the largest he had ever hooked in the Madison River. Willoughby and Winston would surely like to see it, and he would like to see the expressions on their faces when they did.

But he did not call out, although when he finally slipped his hand under its belly and switched on his headlamp, he saw that the trout was not only the biggest he'd caught in the Madison, but the biggest he had caught in any river. As a form of crude measurement he held his hand against the cool underwater feel of it. He walked the hand down the length of the trout from its lip to its tail. Three and a half turns—about twenty-eight inches. Perhaps eight pounds, perhaps nine. Its spots were the size of Canada dimes.

He removed the hook and supported the fish with a hand under its belly, its head into the current so that the water worked across the gills that shone regularly in pulsing red ellipses. He opened his hand and the trout settled to the bottom, where it wavered indistinctly in the smoky current, regaining its strength. He thought of Nick Adams watching the trout on the streambed in "Big Two-Hearted River," the fish as much shadow as reality. Then the trout was gone.

Sean clipped off the deer hair mouse, which had been mangled by the trout's teeth, and found a compartment for it in one of his fly boxes. He would never fish it again, but keep it to serve as a reminder that the trout had actually existed. Though, having been caught in a river that was both real and unreal, the fish itself was suspect and Sean wondered if he might someday wonder even about that. He knew that he could sleep now and slowly walked the bank back to the log house, the star that danced outside the sickle of the moon showing the way.

——

In the morning, when Willoughby handed him coffee and asked him how his fishing had gone, Sean only smiled. Rivers, dreamed and un-dreamed, had always acted as mirrors in his life, showing him his reflection while keeping their secrets, at least those that had spots the size of dimes. He knew that he had been afforded a rare glimpse be-neath the surface, and being as superstitious as the next angler, he wondered what he had done to deserve it, and whether talking about it would prevent it from ever happening again.

He decided to keep the secret of the trout. No one would have be-lieved him anyway.

# CHAPTER EIGHT

# Straight Through the Heart

When Sean pulled into the turnaround at the lower end of the Bear Trap Canyon, he saw that the club's Subaru was already parked at the access. He took in the other vehicles in the lot—a baker's dozen or so, the expected smattering of dusty trucks and paint-peeled SUVs—Willoughby's rental a spit-and-polish exception. No clues there. He pulled on his waders and opened the sign-in box at the trailhead. No clues there, either. It was empty save for a stub of pencil and the resident arachnid, in this case a wolf spider as big as a poker chip.

He started to hike up the riverbank, something nagging at him. He snapped his fingers, turned on a heel, and walked back. He used his camera to take photos of the parked vehicles and their license plates, all Treasure State except for a black F-150 with West Virginia plates.

The map showed his destination to be a little more than two miles upriver, below the narrow canyon where Bear Trap Creek bled into the river. Sean knew every rock; it was one of those pieces of water he had fished as often in his dreams as he had with a fly rod. He walked the two miles slowly, and as he rounded a bend where a copse of willows, half of them gnawed into sharp stubs by beaver teeth, obscured his view of the river, he stopped. A few more steps would bring him into an open area from which he would be able to look down on the long run marked on the map. This was where he expected to find Willoughby, and with a few more steps he did. Willoughby had waded out a short distance from shore and was fishing, although Sean was too far away to see the sliver of his bamboo rod.

Leaving the trail, he worked his way down through the maze of willows to the tailout of the run and began to work out line. A midge hatch was in progress, with trout poking their noses out of the water to sip them in. He knotted on a pattern that his friend Sam Meslik called a Missouri River Boner, a stub of red ultra chenille tied at the bend of a #18 hook with two turns of grizzly hackle. An hour passed quickly enough, and then another, good fishing if not good catching. He looked at his watch. The window for the rendezvous was closing. More to the point, the trout had stopped feeding, and he glanced upriver to see Willoughby walking the bank in his direction.

"I really thought he was coming," Willoughby said.

"So did I. He still might. It's only half past."

Willoughby shook his head. "When I was in naval intelligence, it was my experience that when we set a meet, the meet was made in the specified hour or not at all."

"This isn't the Cold War."

"I suppose you're right. Give it another what, twenty minutes?"

"How about until someone catches the next fish?"

"I'll take that as a challenge," Willoughby said.

Sean changed reel spools to a sinking tip line to swim a streamer fly, but Willoughby had already made a dozen casts and was into a fish, a small rainbow trout that took his pheasant tail nymph.

"For once I best you," he said. "Shall we call it a day?"

They did and hiked down the path toward the trailhead, hearing notes of a faint voice in that direction, followed by pitched shouting.

"Jupiter, come on, boy, get over here!"

A woman was standing in the path, a hand on her hip, her fingers tapping a holstered GPS on her belt. The dog she was calling to showed in blurs of color among the bushes that choked the riverbank down the hill. She looked at Sean and rolled her eyes theatrically. She was what Sam would call a Montana Hardbody. Crow's-feet under the brim of a sweat-stained red ball cap. Lank hair. Chapped lips. No bra, and a glance at her flannel shirt, half unbuttoned with the sleeves rolled up and the shirttails knotted over her brown belly, showed little that required support. Her body was sinew and skeleton and alive with nervous tics, the muscles in her forearms rippling like snakes. A friendship bracelet made from colored strings encircled her left wrist. She brought her left forefinger to the side of her head and twirled the hair around her ear, exposing an elk-tooth earring in a silver setting.

"If that hound gets into a skunk, he's going to trot home leashed to the bumper. I'm not aimin' to let a skunked dog into my car, not this year." She put fingers at the corners of her lips, revealing a pair of very long cuspids, and whistled sharply. "Come on now, Jupiter, come on, boy." And to Sean, blowing at a strand of hair that had fallen across her face, "There must be something dead in there. He hear'd the whistle, he's usually a-comin'.

"There's a good boy." The dog, a big, gangly-looking creature with a wasp waist, was bounding up the bank toward them, carrying something in its mouth.

"What you got, a hat?"

The woman reached down as the dog called Jupiter beat at her legs with a wet tail, jangling the keys that hung by a carabiner to a belt loop of her jeans. "Give." A command. The dog opened its jaws.

On the ground at Sean's feet was a green felt hat with a braided hatband. The Gamsbart sticking from the hatband was mangled, and long strands of chamois goat hair were caught in the dog's mouth, so that it looked as if he'd grown a goatee.

"He likes dead things, does he?" Willoughby asked the woman.

"Yeah, that hound's plumb dumb. He'd sooner hump a roadkill possum than a bitch in heat."

———

The body was face up, lying partly submerged, the head and torso in the shallows, the short, thick legs on shore. Waders, fly vest, mirrored sunglasses that reflected the high passing of cumulus clouds. A crawfish, mottled brown and blue, had crawled onto the face. One of its claws pinched the left nostril.

"Jesus," Martha Ettinger said.

She stood with her hands on her hips, an hour of light in the sky, the canyon caught in that profound silence as colors die, before the sound of the river is amplified by nightfall. She looked at a wispy cloud of blood issuing from the back of the man's head before washing away downriver. What had done the damage—it was a guess, for without rolling the body she couldn't see the head wound—was a triangular-shaped rock partly sticking out of the water. The rock was a few feet out from the shore and about six feet upriver of the victim's head, and it held a smear of blood.

A second wound, in the chest, was easier to read. It looked to have been caused by the sharp stub of a willow sapling growing on the bank. The sapling had been gnawed about eighteen inches from ground level by a beaver's teeth, and looked to be as sharp as a spear. The stub was no different from a hundred others, except that the entire length was slicked with blood and shone bright crimson.

"So we figure what?" she said. "He trips, spits himself like a rotisserie chicken, picks himself up, reels into the water, falls and hits his head on the rock?"

"Or was pushed," Sean Stranahan said. "You can see where the blood dripped. The tails indicate direction of travel." He pointed to a trail of blood, red splashes shaped like tears, leading from the bright stub in the willow jungle to the river's edge a few yards away.

"Why can't people die normally anymore?" Martha said. "A woman in a bear's den, now this."

"Do you think they're related?"

"The deaths? Winkler said they were brother and sister, even if they didn't share DNA. So at least in that sense, yeah." Martha shook her head. "Just tell me it wasn't you who found him."

"Actually, it was a Plott hound."

"I didn't say 'what.' I said 'who.'"

Sean didn't say anything.

"Uh-huh. Did I ever tell you, you manage to step into—"

"Yeah, Martha, once or twice."

"Okay." She burbled out a breath. "Here's how it's going down. When Walt's done taking Little Red Riding Hood's statement"—she pointed to the woman wearing the red hat, whose shirt also was red—"he's going to take yours. Meanwhile, I'll talk to Mr. Willoughby. We aren't going to bring the body onto shore until Doc gets here and the CSI shows with her bag of tricks."

"Do we pick off the crawfish?"

"No. He has dibs."

"Did you see the Highlander in the lot?" Sean asked.

"Winkler's? The one up the Specimen road? Yeah, it's there."

"It wasn't when I drove in. He must have come in after, within the last couple hours."

Martha stared off across the river. "So you figure our Tyrolean man is the letter writer, the guy with the Hemingway stuff?"

After discovering the body, Sean had asked a passing fisherman to call the sheriff's office when he got into cell range, and then had waited with Willoughby and Jolene Bailie, for that was the name of the woman with the dog, for someone with a badge to arrive. When Martha showed up, Sean had handed her the letter.

"More of a coincidence if he wasn't," Sean said.

She nodded.

"Something came to me while we were waiting for you. Or it came to Willoughby when I told him about the guy we'd met on the mountain. I don't know whether to bring it up now or later."

"Bring it up now."

"Vorarlberg, where Winkler said he was from, that's where Ernest Hemingway went on ski vacations in the 1920s. A town called Schruns, Willoughby said. And the ID Winkler showed us says he's from Hailey, Idaho. That's near Sun Valley, the ski resort where Hemingway stayed in the 1940s. According to Willoughby, Hemingway bought a house in Ketchum, which is only a few miles from Sun Valley."

"What are you saying? There's a connection between crawfish bait here and Hemingway?"

"He could have met Hemingway way back when, stole some of his gear. Or maybe Hemingway gave him some stuff. That's how a piece of it got into Freida's effects. Now he's trying to unload it. *Was* trying."

"He'd have to have been a little kid to have known Ernest Hemingway."

"People take care of themselves now. Older people look younger. Say Winkler's seventy. *Was* seventy. Hemingway died in—"

Martha held up a hand. "Let's not get ahead of ourselves. Anyway, it's too late in the day for me to be wrapping my head around numbers." She blew out an audible breath. "Well, shit," she said. "This puts a damper on the evening. I had a date and he's going to think I stood him up."

"You had a date?"

"No, but is it so hard to believe that I could have?"

"Not from where I stand."

"Where's that?"

"From about five feet away."

"Do you want to be my date? I mean, unless you're seeing that one-armed Chevy salesman. The techs will be here any minute and they'll just tell us to steer clear. We can be out of here in another hour."

"You want to go out tonight?"

She shrugged. Then her face changed, and the river behind her bled away, and the body gone with it, and he was looking at Martha, way out on a limb.

"Tonight's good," he said.

———

At four in the morning, heading to her bathroom, he tripped over the duty belt lying on the bedroom floor.

"Are you okay?"

"Yeah, I just stumbled on your Ruger." It had been their ritual once, Martha removing her belt and letting it drop before taking him to bed. Or the other way around, Sean reaching to unbuckle it.

"I should have remembered," he said.

"Take the bullets out and bring it back to the bed."

He dropped the cartridges onto the floor.

"Put the muzzle on my chest."

"No, Martha, that's—"

"Just do it."

He hesitated, then pressed it against her sternum.

"More to the right."

He moved it onto the swell of her left breast.

"Cock the hammer."

He thumbed the hammer back.

"Shoot me," she said.

"Won't dry firing damage the gun?"

"Not a centerfire revolver."

"I thought—"

"Don't kill the moment. Just shoot me."

He pulled the trigger and the hammer dropped with a loud click.

"Straight through the heart," she said. "That's where you always get me, straight through the heart."

# CHAPTER NINE

# Flip of a Coin

In the morning, they lay together easily, drowsy and warm, and to Sean it felt as right and as natural as he had ever felt with any woman. But then she lifted the arm that was around her and padded into the kitchen, and Sean could hear the water boil.

When he joined her she was looking down at her cup, as if seeking her fortune in the stray leaves that had escaped from the ball tea strainer. Her face was as pink as the sky. "Coffee's in the pot," she said, not looking at him.

"Martha."

"That wasn't me last night. I violated the cardinal rule of firearms safety—'Never point the muzzle at anything you aren't prepared to destroy.' Even if it's only my own heart."

Sean poured coffee. "Technically, I did the pointing."

"Nonetheless." She shook her head. "If you had a gun you'd have another notch for it, but then you don't have a gun. What kind of Montanan are you?"

"A lucky one."

"Yeah, a rodeo queen with one arm and a sheriff with a shot-off finger. We must fulfill a fetish."

Sean didn't say anything and she didn't lift her head.

"It felt special to me," he said.

Martha looked off toward a corner of the kitchen. She spoke under her breath. "Why do I do this to myself? It's like something good happens, so I deliberately sabotage myself." There was a pause, and just as Sean thought she was working around to answering her own question, she looked again into the teacup.

"I have a hard time getting it out of my head," she said, "the way that the blood looked when it mixed into the water. I've seen some horrible things, but there's something about it. It's like you're watching the soul seep out of the body."

"When's Doc doing the cut?"

"He's got it at three tomorrow."

So they would talk about business, he thought, return to a safe topic.

"Something's missing," Sean said. "It's been bothering me."

Martha shook her head. "Yeah, my marbles are missing. Sometimes I just do things without any thought process at all."

"Are you talking about last night?"

"I'm back to that vicinity. I don't regret it. It's just I don't know where this goes. Does it mean you come back here tonight? Or next week? Or never? I don't want to be one of those women who are anxious all the time. 'He's thinking this about that. I'm thinking that about this.' 'I'm here. He's where?' 'If he isn't with me, who's he with?' *That* kind of woman. It puts me at a disadvantage because most men, they don't think it to death. They just get on with their lives."

"I'm not most men."

"No, you aren't. But still, I'm the one brought it up."

"You're the one who left me, Martha. You turned the light out."

"I know. It's not rational. But still, I'm going to ask you. If you're going to see someone else, like Katie Sparrow or Etta Huntington, particularly Etta, I don't want to know about it. I'm not that evolved."

"The same goes for you. If you're seeing someone else."

"Yeah, like that's going to happen."

The silence came back. Her eyes went anywhere but his. Then, abruptly, she sighed.

"Did I ever tell you my dad called me Maudlin Martha? Even when I was little, I was always dwelling on what I couldn't change, always worried about stuff I had no control over. It seemed like I lived half my life regretting the mistakes of the past. Dad, he'd say, 'Regret is the past crippling your chances for the present.'"

"He's right," Sean said.

"It doesn't make it any easier to be me."

"I love you for who you are." The word was out before he knew it.

She paused with her cup halfway to her lips. "You mean, as a person?"

"I wasn't qualifying it."

"You can't say something like that if you don't mean it."

It was silent in the kitchen, and then a bird started up.

"Robins are as common as dirt. But they sing like angels. That's something else my dad said."

"Martha, look at me."

She looked at him. "I'm just scared," she said. "You wouldn't know the feeling. I don't mean that the way it came out. I just mean your confidence in things."

"I'm not confident. I just act like I am. 'Always certain. Often right.' That was the motto *my* dad lived by. In that way I'm his son."

"I love you, too, Sean. I always have."

"Well, hell, should we go back to bed and talk about it some more?"

"I'd like to, but I have to get to the office." A briskness was back in her voice, but it was just the business side of Martha, without any note of frost.

"You said something was missing," she said. "What did you mean?"

"Here's a man wearing waders, wearing a fly fishing vest, who presumably is carrying a valuable piece of fishing gear, good guess a fly rod. Where's the fly rod?"

"We've been over this. He could have dropped it into the river when he fell."

"Maybe. But in my experience, rods don't go very far before snagging up on the bottom. Especially with a reel attached. I've gone into the drink a dozen times to retrieve rods that my clients dropped overboard, and they're never far downriver."

"You're saying somebody took it. That someone helped him fall, that someone killed him and took it?"

"It fits what we know."

Martha nodded thoughtfully. "We'll think about it. And on that thought . . ." She stood from the kitchen table. "I got work to do. Believe it or not, this isn't the only thing going on in the valley."

"What else is going on?"

"A deputy sheriff in Wyoming hired a couple prostitutes for an early graduation present for his son. This is up at MSU. One of the pros at the party complained that she was raped."

"Can you rape a prostitute?"

"Yes, if she doesn't consent. But it's hard to work up sympathy for her, so prosecutors drag their heels. Anyway, the deputy is an asshole, a disgrace to the profession. Forget I mentioned him. What are you up to?"

"Sam's coming into town to price a couple boat trailers. Molly's given him a day off baby duty and he wants to go fishing."

"How's the dad thing working out? Has it made him a grown-up?"

"To tell you the truth, I don't see that much of him."

"Then you just answered my question. They have a daughter, right?"

"Sarah Jane."

"Well, you tell him congratulations from me."

"I'll do that."

"So, where are you two going? And don't tell me Bear Trap Canyon."

"What's the difference? The story will be in the paper today. There's no secret to keep."

"Maybe not. But if he goes there with you, he'll tromp around like an elephant. One of the techs might go back looking for evidence to corroborate something she's found on the body, and those big boots will have destroyed it. Right now there's no police tape, and that's on purpose. All we've released is that a body was found in the canyon."

"We usually flip a coin. Heads the Madison, tails the Yellowstone."

Martha fished a quarter out of her pocket, flipped it, caught it, slapped it on the back of her hand. "Call it."

"Heads."

It was heads.

"Keep him on a leash," she said.

———

The bikini barista at Lookers and Lattes pressed up against the sill of the kiosk. A lilac streak in a bleached blonde pageboy. Black lashes. Lipstick with a dark outline. Cleavage as deep as a family secret.

"The usual," Sam said. "What's yours, Kemosabe?"

Sean ordered a twelve-ounce drip.

"You want that with a Happy Ending?" The barista looked down at him, her implants stretching a sequined halter. Everything about her was fake but her smile.

He said yes and she poured the cream.

"Cute dogs," she said.

They'd decided to leave Sean's rig in town and take Sam's Nissan pickup, Sean riding shotgun, Killer, Sam's big Airedale, and Choti, Sean's little Sheltie, sitting on the bench seat behind them.

"Yeah," Sam said. "It's a regular Montana double date. So what's the story, Marsha? This is Trudy's shift."

"She was here, but she was wearing a T-shirt with an arrow that read 'My eyes are this way.' She thought it was cute, but Bill, he's the manager, he told her the arrow was pointing the wrong direction and to go home and change if she wanted to keep her job. Asshole."

"You aren't going to tell me where to look, are you?"

"You're a married man, Sam. You should be ashamed of yourself, especially when your wife's got a rack like Molly's."

"I know. I'm incorrigible. But my friend here doesn't have a conflict."

She looked at Stranahan. "You look like a young George Maharis."

"Who's he?"

A TV star my grandmother had a crush on. *Route 66,* you hear of that?"

"It's a road, isn't it?"

"He's funny," she said to Sam.

Her eyes flicked back to Sean. "Do you have a steady girl, honey?"

"Would George Maharis have a steady girl?"

"Maybe. But he had boys, too. Broke my grandmother's heart."

"If you two are done flirting, can we go fishing, please?" Sam said.

"You didn't answer my question," she said to Sean.

"I'm not sure."

"Tell you what, you find the answer to that is 'no,' you come back and see Marsha."

Sean smiled back at her. He was a sucker for baristas, fully clothed and otherwise, had had an affair with one who'd worked at this same kiosk the year that it opened. Martinique Carpentras had given him all he wanted and some things he wasn't aware that he needed. But she'd gone to veterinary school in Oregon and they'd drifted apart, with her doing the drifting.

"I just might do that," he said.

They were halfway to the Bear Trap Canyon before Sean asked Sam if he'd read the paper. Sam hadn't, but he'd heard about the floater and listened, fingering his beard, as Sean filled him in about the letter that Willoughby had received.

"Mmm-hmm," Sam said.

"Mmm-hmm what?"

"Mmm-hmm like it rings a bell. I had a client who told me something about Hemingway's fly rod going missing. At least I think it was a client. Maybe it was a reel. Or maybe it was . . . fuck, I don't know. It was a long time ago, after I got back from Iraq. I was putting a lot of shit up my nose and the years sort of blurred together."

"Keep thinking," Sean said. He wasn't really surprised, but he wasn't optimistic, either. Sam's connection to the unvarnished truth was at best tenuous. All kinds of nuggets floated around in his shaggy head, some gold, most fool's gold.

At the Bear Trap Canyon, they hiked upriver and fished the same run where Sean had fished the day before. But that afternoon had been calm, today was clear and raw and the wind was a broom that swept the insects off the river. They might as well have been fishing in their dreams, because they would have done better. But they fished as men do, because they can, and because it feels virtuous to sit on the bank afterward and let the river run through you and wash you of your past and bring hope to your future. It was cheaper than an hour at the psychiatrist's, a point Sam made regularly.

"You're in better shape than I've ever seen you," Sean said. He meant it. The big man had lost weight, his eyes were clear, there was a bounce to his step where before he lumbered like a bear standing on its hind legs.

"Kids," he said. "They either make you or break you. Here's the deal about becoming a father. It's the best thing in the world, because you no longer have to look for the meaning of life, because it's throwing up on the rug in front of you. The downside is you can't walk out the door without making a plan. So what you end up doing is sacrificing the life you had for someone else's life. It's a big fucking deal. What we're doing here, it's not about the fishing anymore. It's about catching your breath. It's the same thing with hiking. I try to fit in an hour before breakfast every morning. It's the only time I'm alone and have a clue who I used to be."

"Fatherhood has made you fit *and* eloquent, Sam."

"Fuckin' A."

They looked at the river and drank coffee from a thermos and chewed venison jerky. The dogs, which had been bounding up and down the bank, settled in with them and begged scrids of meat.

"So this is the spot, huh?"

"Downriver about a hundred yards is where the Plott hound found the body. Martha told me not to take you there, it could disturb evidence if this turns out to not have been an accident."

"So fine, we'll wade down. Won't venture a foot onto dry land."

"I suppose that would be all right. But what about the dogs?"

"We'll 'stay' them."

"Killer will stay?"

"If I can work up the right tone of voice."

The dogs stayed and they waded down, but there was nothing to see but a pencil one of the techs must have dropped into the drink and the bloodstain on the protruding rock, which was now brown. Sean pointed out the position of the body, brought up his reservation about a wading angler tripping, hitting the back of his head, and falling where the body was found.

"Yeah," Sam said, "I get that. But he could have tried to crawl out and then passed out."

"If he crawled, why would he be face up?"

"People kick the bucket all which ways. I saw it in the war. Bodies in these grotesque positions. Fucking haunting. Did he have water in his lungs?"

"The autopsy's tomorrow morning."

Sam pulled a white bone toothpick from his shirt pocket. "Look around, Kemosabe. This is the most secluded stretch for a mile in either direction. If the body's here, nobody sees it. You said the hound found it, but what if it hadn't? It might have laid up here for a week before some fisherman stumbled onto it. But if somebody pushes him into the current, cat's out of the bag. He wouldn't float a quarter mile before somebody spotted him or he washed up against the bank in an open spot. If I killed somebody, I'd want to have time to hike out and drive away before somebody with a badge shows at the parking lot."

He revealed the grooves in his front teeth as he worked his toothpick around.

"What is that made from again?" Sean said.

"Raccoon penis bone." Sam worked the pick.

"You do that much longer and I'll have to tell Molly."

"She's bi. I tell you that?"

"No, I would have remembered."

"She dropped it on me before the wedding. Said not to worry, but she couldn't rule out seeing another woman at some point in her life."

"Really?"

He pocketed the toothpick and brought out a rumpled-looking cigarette.

"What can I do? I love her."

He frowned at the cigarette and brought it to his nose. He inhaled, his broad chest expanding, pushing against his wader tops.

"When Molly got pregnant and gave up drinking, I gave it up, too. A beer now and then, but always somewhere she wasn't. Out of respect. She said while I'm at it, why don't I give up smoking, too. I was going to be a father. I needed to live a long time. So I surprised myself by actually quitting. Now I just sniff at one once in a while. It's like looking at Marsha's mu-cha-chas. It's okay long as you don't touch. How about you? You still knocking on Katie Sparrow's door?"

Sean hesitated.

"Hey, I'm not criticizing. You don't let the lion loose once in a while, it affects your fishing."

Sam repocketed the smoke. "You're thinking this is all about the rod. That somebody killed this guy and took the rod. I understand the logic. But what I'm saying is, look at it from the victim's perspective. What's his name? Winkler?"

Sean nodded.

"My cousin married a Kraut. Must have been six-eight, but a cadaver. Man had an Adam's apple you could play tennis with . . . Where was I?"

"The victim."

"Yeah. Your Winkler, he asks Willoughby to meet him upriver. Now, does he know Willoughby personally? Does he even know if Willoughby will come alone? Nuh-hah. He's walking into an unknown situation, and he's got a rod with him, or some other piece of gear, that could be worth a lot of money. So what does he do to ensure somebody doesn't just take it from him? He hides it. Then he can go to the meeting place with peace of mind. If everything's kosher, then he goes and gets it. I put myself in this guy's place, I'd find a spot with a lot of brush, like right here, and I'd stash the rod until I knew it was safe to bring it out. How thoroughly did they search?"

"The techs were still here when I left. But they were concentrating on the body and it was getting dark."

"It could be five feet away and you wouldn't see it. Hell, you know how hard it is to find a lost rod. Break it down, it just looks like a couple sticks."

"Martha won't like it if we kick around here."

"When did you start doing everything she tells you to do? And what would they do anyway? Come back and grid the place. They'd muck it up a lot more than we will, and who said anything about kicking? We'll stick to the paths, be discreet. Five gets you ten we'll find that rod."

But they didn't find anything, not in a full hour of looking. Late afternoon found them fishing again, clouds of caddis flies pulsing above the willow tops and now and then a trout coming up, leaving a disappearing ring on the surface. Not enough to target individual trout, but enough to fish blindly with an elk hair caddis and do a little rod bending.

They called it a day and were hiking back when they saw it.

On the river side of the path, snared in the charred branches of a blackened clump of sagebrush, was a metal fly rod case. Even with the sun behind clouds the metal glinted, and Sean felt the flutter in his bloodstream as he approached it. A piece of paper peeked out from a red bandana knotted around the tube. He untied the bandana to read the note, which was inked in bleeding letters on a doubled-over sheet of toilet paper.

*I found this in the bushes on April 23. If you are the owner,*
*I'm sure you'll be relieved to have your rod back. If you aren't*
*the one who lost it, please do the right thing and leave it for*

*the deserving party. Tie the handkerchief on the bush. I'll
pick it up next time in.*

Sam itched at his chest. "This is the twenty-third, right?"

Sean nodded. "Somebody must have found it in the last three hours.
We didn't see it on the hike up and I don't see how we could have
missed it."

"We didn't miss it, Kemosabe. Are you going to unscrew that cap
or just look at it?"

Sean hesitated. "If this is what I think it is, then I want to wait until
we can do it in front of Willoughby. It's his dime I'm working on. He'll
know what we're looking at."

"It says Gillum right on the case. Was he famous?"

"I know he made good rods, not much more."

He scribbled a note onto a piece of paper torn from his lunch bag. "My
phone number," he said in response to Sam's lifted eyebrow. "In case the
guy who found the rod comes back. I'd like him to give me a call."

He knotted the bandana around the note and they were dragging
their shadows back to the trailhead when the hound came bounding
up, the woman, Jolene, trailing it. She registered her surprise by crin-
kling up her eyes. Same red flannel shirt and trucker cap, same sharp
cuspids showing in a grin.

"Fancy meeting the like of you a-gin," she said. She shook Sean's
hand.

"I figured this would be the last place you'd come back to walk
your dog," he said.

"Yeah, that crawdaddy give me the heebie-jeebies. But Jupiter didn't
get into no skunks here and that trumps it. I'd kiss a copperhead snake
if it meant no skunks." She looked at the three dogs. They were being
dogs, circling each other, sniffing butts, getting acquainted.

"This is my friend, Sam," Sean said.

"Pleased to meet you." She pumped Sam's hand with vigor. "Jolene,"
she said. "Like the Dolly Parton song. She's my favorite."

Sam asked where she was from and she said Centralia, West Virginia. She dismissed her birthplace with a roll of her eyes. "The dam broke and washed away our first house." She pronounced washed as *warshed*. "There still ain't no cell phone. About all we had growing up was WWVA and rabbit ears."

Sam asked what had brought her West.

She said a no-account man.

Where was the man?

"Back down Hoopie," she said.

What did she do?

She said she house-sat a place in Virginia City for a snowbird and did pet-sitting. Housecleaned for summer people "all over the durned place." She was an actress, she said, offering no specifics, and played live music, was trying to write songs. If the dog howling was a compliment, then she was the next American Idol. If they hadn't put the hiatus on the show. She used the word "hiatus."

She jangled the keys carabinered to her belt and said she was hoping to get a five-mile hike in and better get a-goin'. Sam said, "Then you better get a-goin'." It wasn't mockery. He had ingratiated himself with his rough charm as effortlessly as he did with almost everyone— and they watched her push her shadow up the same trail they'd just come down.

"You know what that was, Kemosabe? That was a Big Sky moment. Only thing spoils it is she's a chick."

Sean nodded. Open skies, ready smiles, and paths to nowhere were the best roads to friendship that he knew, especially when they converged at water. You met a fellow angler and exchanged a few words— the weather, the hatch, your dogs—and the next time you exchanged a few more, maybe swapped a couple flies, and then there was a beer to share from the back pocket of a fly vest. Twenty-five years later, you were planning your fifth trip to Alaska together. Such chance acquaintanceships might not be what brought someone to the state, but it's what made them stay.

Sean nodded absently. It did seem like a bit of a coincidence, seeing her again. She'd glanced at the rod case he was carrying without comment. But had her eyes lingered on it a second longer than one would expect?

Sam read his mind. "No law against walking your dog," he said.

# CHAPTER TEN

# Pinky Gillum's Little Finger

Patrick Willoughby used his right thumb and forefinger to unscrew the knurled brass cap on the fly rod tube. The metal surface of the case was worn to a silver patina. He bent the gooseneck lamp on the fly-tying bench to read the faded lettering on the glued-on label.

> H. S. Gillum
> *Finest Custom Built Rods*
> Ridgefield, Conn.
> Length 8 feet
> 4⅝ ounces

He drew out a cloth rod sock and offered Ken Winston a sniff. Winston brought his nose to the cloth, drinking in the rich scent of tung oil.

"What the fuck?" Sam said. "Do I need to turn my back and let you two have a moment?"

Willoughby extracted the sections of the rod from the sock. As expected, it was made from milled strips of bamboo and was lightly varnished, with copper-colored wraps tipped by a darker mahogany. The rod was built in a hexagonal design and included a spare tip, customary among better rods. Willoughby handed it to Sean, who had donned blue latex gloves. He rotated the rod sections, examining each bamboo flat. On one flat, ahead of the tapered cork grip, was the maker's full name: *Harold S. Gillum*. On the flat below—*Custom Built* framed by quotation marks. There were no other markings. Sean placed the three sections on the table and pulled off the gloves. Evening light was streaming in the picture window that overlooked the river, and the rod glowed softly.

Willoughby looked over his glasses at the assembled—Ken Winston, his fingers massaging his cheeks; Sean, brushing back a comma of hair from his forehead; Sam, itching at a hole in a T-shirt with a marabou streamer fly on the front and the logo *Sam's Skinny Minnows*.

"You do understand—Ken, I know you do—that we are looking at a very special rod." Willoughby regarded Sam's cocked eyebrow. "I'm not talking about provenance. As we can all see, there is nothing on the tube, the label, or the rod itself to suggest ownership. The mere fact that this is a Gillum is more than enough. Particularly one in this condition, and from this period of his career. Pinky Gillum stands alone among his peers, not because his rods were better than those of Payne or Dickerson—they weren't—but because of their scarcity. Gillum is thought to have produced no more than a thousand over a forty-five-year career, dating from the mid-1920s to his death in 1969. This is an early-middle-years model, if I am not mistaken. Before he began adding serial numbers."

"Why is the period important?" Sean asked. "Did he make fewer rods then?"

"No, but there was a decade or so, starting, I would say, about 1930, when he used an inferior glue. The rods from that era tended to delaminate and very few examples remain. Postwar models glued with resorcinol have a much higher survival rate."

"What does any of this have to do with Ernest Hemingway?" Sam said. "I mean, to cut to the fucking chase."

Willoughby smiled at Sam's impatience. "First, the rod's manufacture roughly coincides with the period in his life when Hemingway did most of his fly fishing for trout. As I've told Sean, it was during the 1930s that he was a regular guest of a dude ranch outside Cooke City. The Clarks Fork River ran right through the property." He peered at Sam. "To cut to the chase."

"Would he have known Pinky Gillum?" Sean asked. "I mean, of him."

"Quite possibly. We know Hemingway fished with bamboo fly rods. Many photos support that. Patrick, his middle son, once told me that they would get the Hardy Brothers catalog each year and pore over it, trying to convert pounds sterling—Hardy is a London firm—into American dollars. Hemingway ordered from Hardy regularly. His favorite rod was a model called the Fairy. I dropped out of the bidding for one at around a thousand dollars a few years ago. One of Pinky Gillum's rods from the same era, by comparison, could bring between five and ten times that amount. That's because it is a rare find, and also because the best American-made rods are more desirable than the best English rods."

"It's our colonial snobbery," Ken Winston said.

Willoughby braced his hands on the table and leaned forward out of his chair until he hovered over the rod. "Tell us your story, my darling," he said. "You lovely, lovely work of art."

"Why did they call him Pinky?" Sam said.

Willoughby sat back in his chair. "One explanation is that Gillum had red hair. He indeed had light hair, though black-and-white photos don't show the hue. The more romantic story is that he lost the little finger on his left hand in a beveler, while cutting the angles on bamboo strips. I took the liberty of refreshing my acquaintanceship with Gillum when you phoned from the road. You know my ambivalence about the Internet, but the dial-up came in handy enough today. Ken, would you be so kind to bring me our laptop?"

Winston retrieved the laptop from the coffee table by the fireplace.

Willoughby opened the lid and three heads craned over his shoulder. On the screen were two photographs displayed alongside a photostat copy of Gillum's obituary in the *Ridgefield Press*. One photograph, blurred and grainy, showed him holding an Atlantic salmon that the caption said he'd caught in the Black Rock Pool of the Margaree River. In the other photo, Gillum stood in hip boots on the riverbank, his hat brim tilted at a jaunty angle. Three fingers held his fly rod just in front of the cork grip. The little finger looked to be missing.

"He was a cantankerous cuss," Willoughby said. "He would refuse to sell a rod to someone whom he thought would abuse it, and for-swear repair if it broke. Rumor is that he saw a fisherman who owned one of his rods catch a tree limb on his backcast, and he was yanking on it with the rod. Gillum helped him unhook the fly from the tree, then took the rod and refused to give it back."

"My kind of man," Sam muttered.

"Irascible," Willoughby agreed. "But a master craftsman. Would Hemingway have purchased one of his rods?" He shrugged. "As a col-lector, I can assure you that you never have enough. I must own three dozen cane rods. Ken?"

Winston flashed the fingers on both hands.

Willoughby nodded. "A Gillum is as close to a Stradivarius as any fly caster is likely to see, let alone cast. Hemingway would have known this."

"Is there a way to establish a connection without an inscription?" Sean asked.

Willoughby frowned. "You have been careful not to erase any fin-gerprints?"

Sean nodded. "I was thinking about prints left by Winkler, or, if he was a victim of foul play, by his killer."

"A reasonable caution. Latents can persist for quite some time, especially on smooth surfaces such as aluminum or varnished wood."

"How long?" Sean saw where Willoughby was going.

"That would depend upon many factors, paramount among them handling by other parties, because they would easily wipe away. Still, it is conceivable that Hemingway's own prints would remain on the rod or on the case, especially if it has languished in storage since his handling."

"Say they were," Sean said. "What could you compare them to?"

"Hemingway's prints, of course. As a noncombatant correspondent during the Second World War, he would have been fingerprinted."

"Wouldn't you need permission from the FBI or someone to see them?"

"Reasonable to think, but no." Willoughby allowed a smile to cross his lips. He drew the laptop to the edge of the table and made a few keystrokes.

"The miracle of modern technology," he said, and leaned back so the others could peer more closely. They were looking at Ernest Hemingway's official certificate of identity, EH-C6226D, issued by the United States Army on May 20, 1944. The certificate listed Hemingway's rank as captain, for purposes of treatment should he become a prisoner of war. A photo, showing the writer in full beard and wearing a pinstriped suit coat and tie, appeared below identifying information listing age, weight, hair, and eye color. The right half of the document displayed the fingerprints of his thumb and the four fingers on his right hand.

"Perfectly suitable for determining points of similarity," Willoughby said. "If there are prints to be lifted, I have faith your Ouija Board Gigi could uncover them."

He closed the lid of the computer. Once more he peered at the rod. "I think you have told us all you can for now." He dropped the sections of rod into the cloth sock and slipped it into the rod tube.

He picked up the brass screw cap, then hesitated. Frowning, he pulled out the cloth sock and reinserted it into the tube. He canted his eyes.

"It's catching on something," he said. "Very slight, but it's catching."

He rose from the table and rummaged through the pocket of his fly fishing vest, which hung from a peg inside the front door of the clubhouse. "Ah," he said. He brought a pencil flashlight back to the table, pulled out the sock, and shone the light into the aluminum tube.

"Don't keep us in suspense," Ken said.

Willoughby slowly nodded. "There appears to be some sort of paper rolled in the tube, way down by the bottom. But let's not let our hopes get too high. Rod builders sometimes inserted shipping information into the tube, but they also slipped in instructions for rod care. The latter would tell us nothing. Ken, we're going to need a rod tip with a hook on the tip-top to pull it out. You have the steadiest hands. It's your honor."

A minute later Ken's dexterous fingers were working a rod tip into the tube. Carefully, very slowly, he drew the tip out, the hook of the streamer fly he had knotted to the tip having caught on a roll of paper. The paper was oil-stained and yellowed with age. Winston placed it on the table and pulled on the latex gloves first Sean and then Willoughby had been wearing while examining the rod.

"Don't force it if it starts to crack," Willoughby cautioned.

Winston nodded. "Bring me four tumblers from the kitchen," he said to no one in particular.

Sean returned with the heavy glass tumblers. He pinned down the corners of the paper as Ken carefully unfurled it. There was only one sheet. The typed letters were smeared but legible. They all looked at the letter, Sam moving his mouth as he read, the rest staring. Outside the open window, the sound of the river, the trill of a robin. For a long minute no one spoke.

"I'll get the whiskey," Willoughby said.

# CHAPTER ELEVEN

# Smoothing Feathers

In the morning Sean beat everyone to the coffee maker except, apparently, a solitary redwing blackbird that sung as if he were on his second cup. Sean opened the front door to hear his challenge—the song of the male redwing was one of his favorite sounds on earth—and brought his coffee to the fly-tying table. He took a sip and read again the writing on the faded stationery, which was still pinned to the table by the whiskey glasses.

*May 4, 1933*

*Mr. Ernest Hemingway*
*907 Whitehead St.*
*Key West, Fla.*

*Dear Mr. Hemingway,*
*I apologize for the condition of the rod you returned to the shop. Once delamination has begun, it is difficult to work glue between the strips without removing the winding checks and the thread wraps holding the guides. This can be done and the rod re-varnished and restored to new, but I hope you don't mind that I have chosen to replace it with the same model rather than send you the repair with which you had the unfortunate experience. You are an esteemed client and it is my pleasure to do this. I take responsibility*

*for using bad glue, a problem that has been rectified going forward. In accordance with your wishes, I am sending the rod to your Florida residence, where it should arrive in timely fashion for your annual trip to Wyoming.*

*Thank you for your business. I believe that Harold S. Gillum rods are the finest fly casting tools on the planet and that you will agree when you fish this rod on the Clarks Fork River.*

*Respectfully yours,*

*Harold S. Gillum*
*323 Stonecrest St.*
*Ridgefield, Conn.*

*PS You will note that the tip sections are lighter in color than the rod's butt. This is caused by the tempering process which is altered through a rod's length to obtain its best possible performance.*

"Has the leopard changed his spots?"

Sean had heard Patrick Willoughby pad into the kitchen on bare feet and didn't turn around. "It reads the same," he said. "Did you sleep well?"

"Yes, soundly, but solely due to practice. In wartime, a life sometimes hung in the balance when one shut his eyes, a life that may have ended before you opened them. If one was to sleep at all one learned to compartmentalize, to use the modern terminology. Now then—bacon, scrambled eggs, toast with that exquisite Indian marmalade Robin brings back from Botswana? Suit you?"

"To a tee." It was Ken Winston's voice.

"Good morning," Willoughby said. "Sleep?"

"Forty winks, minus about twenty-five. Hard to sleep when you're sitting on a treasure."

Willoughby grunted sympathetically. He busied himself and, breakfast made, they sat at the table and pointedly ignored the letter, which
by this time they could have recited blindfolded.

"Please pass the marmalade," Ken said. Spreading it on his but-
tered toast, he nodded to Sean, and after taking a mouthful and making an appreciative noise, spoke. "Pat and I had a powwow last night
after you turned in. Or rather Pat sought my opinion and I was in concurrence."

"Concurrence on what?"

"On hiring you, of course," Willoughby interjected.

"You already did."

"I paid you for one day's work, accompanying me to the Bear Trap
rendezvous. I'm talking about uncovering the secrets behind the dis-
covery of this rod, which might take some time. Mind now, I'm not
asking you to withhold evidence or keep Sheriff Ettinger out of the
loop. But the county has limited funds and manpower, and should
Winkler's death be classified as an accident, I fear that the larger issue
of the Hemingway gear—not to diminish the gravity of a man's death—
may become of secondary importance. The events of the past few days
incline me to believe that a substantial collection of fishing tackle belonging to Ernest Hemingway has been recovered, and two of the
people who possibly knew something about it are dead. The window
on solving this mystery, let alone recovering gear or any written words,
is fast closing. I am willing to front your rate for two weeks, plus, of
course, cover any and all expenses. Hemingway was a traveling man
and I would not be surprised if the scope of your investigation goes
beyond the state border, so I understand that this could get expensive.
You aren't to worry about that. What do you say?"

Sean considered. "If I do manage to recover something and it turns
out to have the Hemingway stamp, what happens then?"

"A question I have asked myself," Willoughby said. "I believe that
anything of note should be donated to the Hemingway Trust, which

manages the affairs of his estate and includes several of his surviving relatives. My sole request to the trustees would be that the gear, or any letters such as this one, should be publicly displayed, preferably at the American Museum of Fly Fishing in Manchester, Vermont. Prose—one might as well pipe dream—would be better housed at the Kennedy Presidential Library and Museum. They have the Hemingway Collection. Of course the ultimate decision lies with the trustees. But I am friendly with several board members and count on their generous natures."

"So you would receive nothing?" Sean's glance took in both Pat and Ken.

Ken held up his hands. "Don't look at me. It's Pat's money you'll be playing with."

Willoughby's smile was accompanied by a self-effacing nod. "Sean, when you look at me, what do you see? Do you see the naval hostage negotiator who once traveled under three passports and lived, as invisibly as he could, in the smoky gauze of espionage? Most who know my background, that's the person they want to see. But when I look into the mirror, the man I am looking at is a widower who has lost his best friend, and who is rapidly approaching his dotage. I have a substantial government pension and my consulting work is lucrative. For years I have been a student of fly fishing history. Now a small piece of that history has become enshrouded in mystery, and through no design of my own, I have been chosen to play a role in it. You will understand that as the recipient of the letter, I feel an obligation to see through to the light of this matter. In fact I want to, for to tell the full truth, it is a much-needed therapy. A way of living in the moment again. If I was a younger man, I would pursue the matter myself. But you're a close friend and the natural choice, and I will stand in the shadow of your investigation as a consulting detective, if you will."

"Sherlock to your Watson," Ken piped up.

"Not exactly, but I will certainly help you any way I can. Ken, too, naturally. Now, if you will retrieve one of your contracts I will rummage up a pen, and may our misadventure begin."

———

Anticipating that he'd be on the road, Sean said goodbye to Choti, who spent large parts of the summer at the clubhouse anyway. Sam dropped him at his tipi, where he made a peanut butter sandwich and grabbed an apple, and twenty minutes later he was at the Law and Justice offices in Bridger, where Martha Ettinger kept him waiting. She finally beckoned him, raised an inquisitive eye at the rod case, and heard him out, glancing at her wall clock as she distractedly rolled a dart in her fingers. She dug her nails into her curls as she examined the correspondence between the rod builder, Pinky Gillum, and Ernest Hemingway, then leaned back and laced her fingers behind her head.

"There's no proof that this rod is the same one mentioned in the letter," she said. "Or even if the letter is genuine. This could be a hoax."

"It could be, but Willoughby dates the rod to the time frame of the letter, which corresponds to a period in Hemingway's life when he did a lot of trout fishing and had the money to purchase expensive tackle. He thinks Hemingway's fingerprints could be on it."

"Good luck with that," she said. But she had pinched her chin as she said it, and Sean knew that she would approve his investigation as long as he didn't tread on the department's toes. Martha told him that Wilkerson was holding off on the blood spatter and tissue analysis of matter found on the willow stub and the rock near Winkler's body until the results of the autopsy were released. Sean said he could drop the rod off at the lab and Martha said no. Finding the rod and turning it over to authorities was one thing, but beyond that his involvement required authorization. She regarded him with disapproving eyes, not having to elaborate on the obvious breach in protocol committed when he showed the rod to Patrick Willoughby and Ken Winston.

A stretched moment of silence, which Sean broke.

"Do I recall right, that Toliver said they had intended to do a little fishing up in the high-altitude lakes?"

"He mentioned it. I think the idea was hatched before the temperature dropped fifty degrees."

"Freida had her fly vest in her pannier. If they were going to fish, they needed a rod. You didn't mention finding one."

"That's because we didn't."

"Don't you think that odd?"

"Not that odd. It could have been scraped off one of the horses and covered with snow. Could be practically anywhere since they first got lost."

"I'm thinking of those circular pockmarks I found in the bear den."

"You think it was a fly rod case? The one you and Sam found?"

"I think there's a good chance. Maybe Freida used it as a walking stick when she was stumbling around in the dark."

"And you're thinking that Winkler found it when he went into the den?"

"Why else would he be there? He said he was burning sweetgrass for her. Where was the sweetgrass? I didn't see any burned-up grass. And the den reeks of grizzly bear. Would you go in there if you didn't have to?"

Martha stroked her jaw. "Say I agree. We already know he had the rod. What's it mean?"

"I think it means that Freida was the one with access to the gear, not her brother. When she died, he drove over from Idaho to see what he could get hold of before any of us got to it."

Martha grunted her acquiescence. Then she cocked her arm and the dart flew, vibrating as it struck one of the Wanted posters pinned to a corkboard on the wall.

"Right eye," Sean said. "Is that anyone in particular?"

"He's committed six bank heists wearing a domino mask and mails postcards to local authorities calling himself the 'Scion of Zorro.' Spray-paints a 'Z' on the floor before making his getaway."

"Where?"

"New Mexico. Arizona." She shrugged. "Not my circus, not my monkeys."

She looked up at him.

"I'm heading over to the morgue. I'll drop the rod with Wilkerson on the way."

"Will you tell her it's from me and that I'll check with her later this afternoon?"

"You think that will speed things up, huh? The magic of your charm? You know she has a bun in the oven."

"I knew she was married. I didn't know she was pregnant. Good for her."

"Not good for the department when she goes on maternity leave. You think she'd be more considerate and pop the kid in the winter, when it's too cold to commit crime. But no, she's got to go and have unprotected sex with no thought at all that a baby could arrive just in time for the creeps to crawl out of their dens."

"Martha," Sean said.

"I know. I'm just kidding. Well, mostly. I'm happy for her. And I'll drop your name, I know she likes you."

"Can I come to Doc's with you this afternoon?"

Sean saw her hesitation. "No, I think I better go alone. He likes to stick to tradition."

"You mean he has a thing for you and wants some alone time."

"No, he's got a girlfriend now. But he's a crusty old coot. If I'm by myself, I can smooth his feathers. Are you going to stick around town this evening?"

Sean could read the moment of vulnerability in her face, before the mask came back on.

"Do you want to have dinner tonight, Martha?"

"Like a date?"

"Like a date. Not just go to your place and rip our clothes off, like we did a couple nights ago."

Martha blushed from neck to hairline.

"In public?" she said. "We'll get looks. You know how small this county is."

"I'm not ashamed."

"Yeah, but . . . this, the you-and-me thing, it's hard enough, I mean—"

"I understand."

"No, the hell with propriety. Where do you want to go?"

"How about Over the Tapas in Bozeman?"

"The big city. That's kind of la-di-da, isn't it?"

"You can wear your cowgirl boots with the roses. I'll make a reservation for seven."

"You'll pick me up at the house and everything?"

"I'll even take the dog blanket off the front seat of the Land Cruiser."

# CHAPTER TWELVE

# Armed and Beautiful

They kissed European style, the county medical examiner and forensic pathologist tickling Martha's cheeks with the bristles of his mustache.

"You take a month in Rome and now you're Omar Sharif," Martha said.

"I was in Tuscany," Hanson said. "And Omar Sharif, if I recall, was Egyptian."

"Potato, po-tah-to. You look tanned and healthy, Bob."

"I feel tanned and healthy."

"And Sabrina?" Sabrina was the reason he'd taken the month's leave, his first serious relationship since his divorce.

"Tanned and fingers crossed. The latest CT scan showed no enlargement of the tumor. But lymphoma teases you. You learn to live in the now." He met her eyes. "I have you to thank for that. It was a big step for me, confessing my admiration for you. Or love, to call it what it really is. And you handled my advances with grace and consideration for my feelings. Then, with Ariana, you opened my eyes to other possibilities."

"I set you up with a sexual adventuress and you cheated on your wife of thirty years. I could have arrested myself for pandering."

"I call it an act of mercy, and no money changed hands."

"Have you seen her?"

"Ariana? We don't stay in touch, but as far as I know, she still works at the Bozeman Library." He glanced at the wall clock. "I have a deposition at three. We should get to this, if you don't mind. But thank you for your concern and for just being Martha. I mean that."

The heartfelt nature of his compliment caused Martha unease.

"Let's see him," she said brusquely.

She always insisted on seeing the body, even if it was in an advanced stage of putrefaction. It made the connection between a name and the person behind it. It made the death personal.

Or it sometimes did. She looked at the cadaver of Wilhelm Winkler and felt nothing. This wasn't the pipe smoker she had met in the wilderness, with his jaunty hat cocked at an angle and his smell of rough-cut tobacco. This was not a man at all, just a carcass that the innards had been spilled from and samples taken, before the organs were sutured back into the body cavity.

"Cause?"

"Head trauma, cardiac arrest, drowning, blood loss. A perfect storm. Should I pull the sheet back up?"

"Show me the head wound."

Hanson arranged the position of the body. With the blood cleaned away and the head shaved, she could see the denting of the skull and the purpled bruising around the slitlike wound.

"Looks like one of those little fish tacos they serve at the Bacchus," Martha said.

"That's not the analogy I'd use."

"You know how I talk. It's a coping mechanism."

"Morgue humor takes many forms."

"So what came first, the chicken or the egg?"

"You're asking what the autopsy revealed?"

"I'm asking your opinion."

"Those are different things. From a purely medical standpoint, it's hard to say. The coronary could have occurred before his fall, or been triggered by the impact. It also could result from pulmonary edema.

The latter is my educated guess, pending lab results. You're shaking your head."

"I'm just trying to keep up."

"Okay, let's look at the sequence. You say there was blood spatter leading from the stick to the river's edge. That suggests that the first wound is the pulmonary laceration, the puncture in his chest. He would be experiencing hemopneumothorax, with both blood and air invading his chest cavity. A life-threatening injury, but it would not be immediately fatal."

"So he staggers around and falls in the drink," Martha said.

"That's a reasonable assumption. He would already be in shock. His heart rate would be skyrocketing and he would be losing blood pressure. Losing his footing? In his disoriented state, I would be surprised if he didn't."

"So he hits his head on the rock," Martha prompted.

"Yes, and that's where it gets interesting. With primary drowning, you inhale a large amount of water and drown in a couple of minutes. But his lungs weren't full of water. They had some water in them, but they contained bodily fluids as well. What that indicates is that he aspirated a small amount of river water when his face submerged. The body, feeling the effects of dilution of the alveoli, rushed to send more fluids from the bloodstream into the lungs. The accumulation of fluids, including blood from the initial chest injury, prevented oxygen from entering his bloodstream. It's referred to as secondary drowning, but it's actually cardiac arrest."

"Are you saying he would be conscious when he fell?"

"Possibly. There might have been a window when he could even have spoken."

"But he could have just as easily been pushed and hit his head, leading to the same result. Correct?"

"Or pushed so he fell onto the sharp stick, and everything followed from there. In any case, your killer, if there is a killer, could have watched this man die for some time."

"Do you see any evidence that would lead you to think that?"

"No. But if he was given a push, there probably wouldn't be any transference of fiber. Especially if the other person was also wearing waders. Was it raining that afternoon?"

"No. What are you getting at?"

"If the other person was wearing waders *and* a rain jacket, he would effectively be wearing a body condom, in terms of fiber transference."

"What about blood? Is there any blood that isn't the vic's?"

"None. Wilkerson already performed a DNA comparison. The blood on both the stick and rock is a match. I found dog saliva on the face, but you say the dog found him, so it would be normal to find transfer saliva from its muzzle or tongue. Dogs lick things."

"You aren't helping me, Bob. It's hard to justify contributing the county's resources to this case without any determination of crime."

"It's what it is."

"It is. Thanks for fitting it in so promptly. I'll look for the lab report." She nodded to herself. "We'll just have to hope for help from other avenues of investigation." She was thinking of Stranahan.

"There was something, though I doubt it will be of help." Hanson removed his glasses and used two fingers to hook back his unruly eyebrows. "Intriguing, though."

Martha raised her own eyebrows. "I like intrigue."

"I examined Mr. Winkler's stomach contents—that's routine to place time of death. He had consumed a thin broth on the morning that he died, perhaps within the hour. It contained a mixture of herbs in suspension with minute solids composed of protein and ash, with small amounts of calcium and phosphate. I had never seen such a composition, so I consulted with an old colleague at the University of Michigan, who specializes in gastropathology. He is Korean, and said he'd found the same combination of substances in several autopsies he conducted when he worked at a hospital in Seoul. The first time he'd encountered the substances, he'd brought in the hospital's resident

pathologist, who'd shrugged and said, "Antler soup. He was just trying to keep his wife happy."

"You're saying that Winkler was drinking an aphrodisiac soup?"

"He was drinking what some call the elixir of life. Antler velvet is
a traditional Chinese medicine that dates to before Christ. It's used
to treat all kinds of maladies and is increasingly popular in the U.S.
with professional athletes, both for performance enhancement and to
hasten recovery from injury. Several double-blind studies suggest—
mind now, I use the word 'suggest'—that it can actually work. I'm not
speaking of erectile dysfunction, but for other legitimate medical uses.
I had my assistant send some links to your e-mail address. They ought
to be there."

Martha fingered her lip. "Next thing you know, they'll find a medical use for rattlesnake poison. With all the dens in this county, it will
be like striking oil."

"Martha." Hanson shook his head.

"What?"

"They already have. The compounds in venom are used to thin blood.
It can help stave off a heart attack."

"Humpff. Didn't help Winkler, though, did it?"

———

The corrugated steel Quonset hut off South 19th Avenue in Bozeman
looked more like a helicopter hangar than what it actually was, the
crime lab that served much of south-central and southwestern
Montana. Recently renovated under the supervision of Georgeanne
Wilkerson, the region's chief crime scene investigator as well as one
of the state's senior forensic scientists, the unit had proved a godsend for
several Montana counties, including Hyalite. Prior to its opening, the
department had had to collect, label, and transport evidence for criminal analysis to the state lab in Missoula. With the new facility, a simple
fingerprint analysis that could have taken weeks unless red-flagged
could now be completed in days, or sometimes even hours.

Sean entered the building and had the receptionist ring down for Wilkerson, who greeted him wearing her scrubs and pink plastic Crocs.

She said, "The last time you came by you wanted to talk about semen. You promised we'd talk dirty and here you are with nothing more salacious on your mind than fingerprints."

"Gigi, you look . . ." He searched for the delicate word.

"Huge," she said. "Wanna touch?" She took his hand and pressed it against her abdomen.

"I can feel a knob here."

"That's a foot."

"When are you due?"

"Yesterday."

"No, really."

"Yesterday."

"Then I better get in my questions."

He followed her to her desk, which was pressed up against the arching inside wall. Sean saw the same photo of her and her husband, then boyfriend, kayaking in Alaska. She opened a drawer and fanned several rectangles of paper on her desk, all about the size of playing cards. Each displayed a fingerprint in a contrasting color.

"Before we start," she said, "I'll get the bad news over with. I found no usable prints from the letter. I didn't really expect any. Prints on paper, especially rough paper, are much harder to lift than prints on metal. I tried disulfur dinitride, which is the tried and true, but all I came up with were areas of smudge with a few partial ridge patterns. So the letter this Gillum guy sent to Ernest Hemingway, it's a dead end. Who is he, by the way? I didn't have time to look him up."

"Gillum's a bamboo rod maker."

"No. Hemingway. I know the name, but I feel like I ought to know more. Was he a movie star?"

Sean felt suddenly old. He'd assumed that everyone knew Ernest Hemingway, but obviously, with the millennial generation, you couldn't take that for granted. Wilkerson, he guessed, was in her early thirties. Hemingway had been dead for twenty-five years before she'd been born. He told her, saw the big eyes swim with excitement.

"Cool," she said.

"Where are these from?" Sean indicated the cards with the finger-prints.

"I used white powder to isolate the prints from the darker surfaces, including the rod and the reel seat, which is mahogany." She pointed to the dark cards, which had white prints on them. "I used black powder for the ones on the aluminum rod case." She indicated a lighter card with darker prints.

"Are they a match with the victim?"

"The ones on the rod have up to eleven points of similarity with prints lifted from the victim. This one, on the case, had fourteen. The state legal standard is twelve. So, pretty much bombproof."

"All Winkler's?

"Almost. It's safe to say that he handled the rod."

"You said almost. Not all?"

"No. There were a few smaller prints, but they were obscured by the victim's larger prints."

"That could have been his sister's prints."

"Siblings will share points of similarity. I found none."

"I should have said stepsister. She was Cheyenne."

"Then that explains it."

"What about the prints on the reel seat?"

She shook her head. "I can tell you that those were from somebody else, too, but without latents to match them to, about all I can say is that this fella had big fingers."

"Can you determine how old they are?"

"No, you can't age fingerprints. You can guess, sometimes, by their orientation and location, and by the pattern of overlap. But Martha didn't give me the circumstances when she gave me the rod. She didn't even say it had anything to do with Hemingway."

"I assumed she had."

"We're talking about Martha. Three words and a grunt and she's out the door."

Sean laughed. "Our Martha? Do you have time for a story, Gigi?"

"I can make time. Everybody's saying I shouldn't be here at all, even though I keep telling them not to worry. If my water breaks, I'll get the mop."

Sean told her the story of the rod, gauging her curiosity by the quicker movements of her eyes.

"You said there's a Web site with Hemingway's prints on it?" she said when he had finished. Sean recited it from memory as she typed at her computer.

She sat back a few inches. "Now I call that a beard," she said. She glanced from the computer fingerprints to those on her display card. "The ones I lifted from the reel seat are overlapping, which is a bummer, but I can see similarities. Yes, I can see at least four points of similarity with the Hemingway prints."

"Let me look," Sean said.

"You can look, but all you'll get is a headache. Overlapping prints create an optical illusion. You have to have a trained eye to separate them."

"Four points, that's not enough, is it?"

"Well, officially, we don't engage in probabilities, so, officially, I would have to say that the match is inconclusive."

"And unofficially?"

"What I see suggests the possibility of a match, but I can't speculate beyond that. This guy's been dead awhile, though. Right?"

"Hemingway committed suicide in 1961. The rod was shipped to him in 1933. The prints would have to have been transferred between those dates."

Wilkerson nodded. "It's possible. Back in North Dakota I matched prints from an ax handle to a man who had buried the ax in a graveyard in 1946. I know, that's not much help in this case. I wish I could tell you that Ernest Hemingway held this rod in his hands. I still might, if you can wait a couple days."

"Oh?"

"The match is inconclusive, *as it stands*. But we have a machine that isolates overlapping prints. We can match a skeleton image of each print on the reel sent with the actual Hemingway prints."

"Why a couple days?"

"Because the software's being reconfigured to include the latest algorithms. It's still new technology. I could call you with the results."

Sean handed her his card, the one that read *Blue Ribbon Watercolors*, and underneath, in discreet script, *Private Investigations*. He had another card advertising his work as a fishing guide under Sam's outfitter's license. That one featured a Royal Wulff fly.

"You owe me a pencil sketch," she said.

"What do you want?"

"A buffalo in the Lamar Valley. That's where Chris proposed to me."

"You got it. What are you going to name the baby?"

"Jessie Rose or Thomas Hart, depending."

"I thought everybody knew the sex these days."

"Call me old-fashioned, but I like mysteries. You go now, I have real work to do."

Sean left her, a woman with real work to do, never mind a baby to be born. He climbed into the Land Cruiser, but stopped his hand from turning the key. If Hemingway's prints were to have survived the decades, it made sense that they would be found on the reel seat. The first thing a fisherman did after jointing the pieces of a rod was screw the reel onto the reel seat. With the reel foot covering it, prints on the bottom of the mahogany reel seat would be protected from smearing. Maybe the rod had been in storage with the reel already attached. Or hanging on a wall as a decoration.

Which got him where, exactly? He already believed that the rod had belonged to Hemingway. A positive fingerprint match would only confirm it. He thought of Freida Toliver, who quite likely had left her smaller prints on the rod as well. Was she the pilot fish who had unearthed the source of the treasure, and had then led her brother to it? Sean recalled that she had paid for part of the saddle that Etta Huntington sold to her with an elk antler chandelier. Martha had told him that it was a successful business, that Toliver personally installed chandeliers in many of the second homes and log mansions in the valley. Maybe she'd come across the Hemingway tackle in one of those places. If she kept good records, it shouldn't be hard to compile a client list. He could burn a couple tanks of gas and see where that led. At the least, he'd be driving through country showing the promise of spring, cause enough for celebration.

The buzzing of the phone in his pocket broke his train of thought. He glanced at the number and flipped it open.

"Kemosabe," Sam said.

"Are you still in town?"

"No, I just got back to the shack. Anyway, this guy I bought the trailer from, we got to talking about outhouses."

*Here we go,* Sean thought.

"So he has this book, *Grand Thrones of the West*. Catchy title. One of the outhouses in the book was his own shitter, had your standard quarter-moon cutout and inside there was a built-in bookcase with stacks of *Fly Fisherman, Fly Rod & Reel,* all your standard trout porn. And one of those old railroad lanterns was hanging from a cord so you could read if the call of the wild came in the night. I mean, you could unpack your bags and set up house in there, never have to go hunting for a bathroom again."

Sean waited. This was what you got when you asked Sam a simple question.

"I know, I digress. Anywho, where was I? Oh yeah. The reason I called is, when I saw the magazines, it was like something snapped and I knew who it was."

"Knew who *who* was?"

"You know, the client who told me about Hemingway's missing rod. The name I was trying to remember."

Sean kept the excitement out of his voice. "Go on," he said.

"Well, first thing is, it was a chick. She was a journalist for *Esquire*, I think. I remembered because she had come out here to write an article about Al McClane, the fishing editor of *Field & Stream*. Told me he was supposed to have been a Cold War spy, that all the fishing trips were just a cover. Talked as if she'd met him before. 'Al this, Al that.' He used to rent out a cabin on the Madison. I guided him a couple times. He was so good, it was like he caught trout as an afterthought. Like, he'd be talking to you about wine or some shit—he was a gourmet cook—and then he'd make a cast and catch a fish, and then go back to whatever he was talking about. A fucking trout wizard."

"How could you forget a story like that?"

"I didn't forget *that* story. What I forgot was, this woman had told me this other story about meeting Ernest Hemingway's son. The oldest one, Jack. She said he was the real fisherman in the family, and it was him who told her the story of his dad's tackle getting lost."

"What can you remember?"

"Not a goddamn thing. I was more interested in the Al McClane connection. Ernest Hemingway, that didn't mean much to me. But she was a looker, so I was probably looking at her boobs while she talked."

"What was her name?"

"I can't remember. I drove all the way home, Bridger to Ennis, I just can't bring it back. I have a vague recollection it was initials, not like a whole name."

"Do you have guide records going that far back?"

"I was afraid you were going to say that. Yeah, I got my journals. But I'd have to do some digging, 'cause they're sort of unorganized. Shit, you know me."

"I do. I'll be there at eight tomorrow morning to help. Does Molly have coffee or should I stop at Lookers and Lattes?"

"Just because we don't drink doesn't mean we don't drink coffee. But hold off 'til nine. Sarah's not sleeping through the night yet and sometimes that couple hours, six to eight or nine, that's the only time we have any peace."

———

Sean dressed for his date with Martha in clean jeans and a snap-up shirt, what passed for black tie in Montana, and she walked out the door, waving as he drove up. He got out to hold the door for her.

"You're all tricked out, Martha. I hardly recognize you without your duty belt."

"I slipped my Walther PPS in my boot."

She turned her calf, showing him her boots with the roses.

"Armed *and* beautiful, that's my girl."

# CHAPTER THIRTEEN

# One Eye Open

Sam Meslik's Fly Shack slouched in a rain haze as Sean turned up the drive. He idled down and let out a long breath. It had been tight-grip driving over the Norris Hill, what with the poor visibility and the sudden ghosts of deer caught in the fog lights, and though the ground he stepped out on was hard enough, he experienced a floating sensation as he walked to the high bank overlooking the river. The long snake of the Madison shone in smoky coils, the riffles pewter and the quiet water gunmetal, the same noncolor as the sky. With the Gravellys swallowed by the clouds it could have been a river anywhere and the taste of the rain on his lips carried him back, his mind unreeling to the night before, the quiet booth in the restaurant, the rain streaking the window, and the ruby trails of taillights out on the asphalt.

He and Martha had surprised themselves by having a quiet, easy time, drinking sangria, dining on lamb kebabs and patatas bravas and grilled asparagus with aioli sauce, leaning close to talk and only drawing the line at touching hands.

"We're like an old married couple," she'd said as they walked out into the rain, though Sean had to amend her opinion when she leaned across the car seat to kiss him.

"I think old married couples wait until they're home," he'd said.

A half hour later, he heard Martha's voice from her bedroom.

"You can come in now."

A candle, a glass of whiskey on the bedstand, and Martha, slipping off her silk robe with Chinese pheasants on it, naked except for the boots.

"Are you still packing the Walther?"

"You never know when you're going to run into a bad guy," she'd said.

His reverie was broken by Sam's voice calling out to him from the porch, telling him to get the hell out of the rain. He did and followed Sam up the stairs to the apartment above the fly shop. Molly was sitting cross-legged wearing a sweatshirt, little Sarah on the floor next to her, naked except for a diaper, arching her head, her mouth moving like a guppy's. Sam's Airedale, Killer, was sacked out in his dog bed in a corner. Molly stood and Sean hugged her, her rich earth smell tempered by the sour odor of regurgitated milk.

"Some mermaid, huh?" she said. "To think I used to be an object of man's desire."

"You still are, Molly."

"That's the response I was angling for. You hear that, Sam, that's another use of the word 'angle.'" She turned back to Sean. "He didn't think it could be a verb. Hey, it's been too damned long. Where have you been hiding yourself?"

She scooped up the baby and passed her to Sam, who enveloped her in his Popeye arms while Molly set about making Sean what she called a European cappuccino. Sean told them where he'd been hiding himself and an hour passed, little Sarah going from Sam's arms to Molly's left breast, to the floor, back to Sam's arms, to Molly's right breast, Killer's eyes opening occasionally to make sure no one needed protecting. It was a very domestic affair all around and something Sean longed for in his own life, though he would not admit it, not until the small hours, anyway.

"Can she crawl yet?" he asked.

"No," Molly said, "not for another few months. We've got about half a year and we're going to have to be living on a ground floor."

She pulled a jumpsuit over Sarah's diaper to ready her for a walk. Out on the porch, Sam opened a collapsible baby carriage and pulled up the plastic hood after Sarah was buckled in, although the rain had let up.

"You better get that barn shipshape, and I mean eight inches of insulation, up-to-code plumbing, real electricity, not a crank-up generator. You got that." Molly kissed the big man on the nose and started pushing the cart up the lane, led by Killer.

"Can the owls stay?"

"As long as they're not in the finished part of the barn." She tossed the words over her shoulder.

"Don't say it, Kemosabe."

"I didn't say anything."

"You're thinking it."

"All I'm thinking about is your record keeping."

"Oh. Yeah, about that." He scratched his chest. "I started rummaging last night and I found her, the client."

"Why didn't you call? You could have saved me the drive."

"Fuck that. I wanted to see you, man. We're friends, you know. Friends see each other. They go fucking fishing."

"Okay. I'm here."

They'd walked back into the shop, where Sam picked up a fly rod from a rack and gave it a wiggle. "I don't know what you're supposed to be able to tell from wiggling a fly rod. I think customers just do it to annoy me." He set the rod down.

"Who is she, Sam?"

"In time, in time."

"Sam."

"I'm playing with ya. Her name is Margarethe Jane Harris. Called herself Margee with a hard 'g.' I remember 'cause I called her Margie and she corrected me in no uncertain terms. I even have a Polaroid of her." He hefted a logbook onto the case that displayed fly reels. He slapped the cover and pushed it across the glass top. It wasn't so much a logbook as a journal, with Sam's fishing notes including dates, weather and water conditions, and trout caught. Here and there a fly was hooked into a page, whatever the pattern of the day was, and the journal was thick and lumpy with photographs.

"You see I floated her July second, 1987."

Sean turned the journal so he could read. "Says she caught five rainbows and two browns," he said. "One over sixteen inches. McAtee Bridge to Burnt Tree." He knuckled the stubble on his chin as he studied the photo. She had stepped out of the drift boat, a slim woman wearing a khaki shirt and hip boots, ash blonde hair falling in a wave. Her rod was high overhead, bent to a trout, and she was looking back over her left shoulder, smiling for the photographer.

"You took this?"

"Proof of the crime."

"There was a crime?"

"We went out to dinner and she put her fly in the water, so to speak, and I swam after it all the way back to her motel room." The slabs of his shoulder muscles shifted, the tattoo of Mickey Mouse on his left biceps coming to life, fighting a trout that leapt with every flex of his muscles.

He nodded, thinking back. "I remember the drugstore was closed and the only condoms I could get were out of the bathroom vending machine at the Exxon. A three-pack—red, white, and blue. I asked her what color and she said it didn't matter, it was the Fourth of July in a couple days and we were going to be patriotic and use all of them. I assume we did, but like I told you, some of those years are blurry in the rearview."

"You remember the condoms but you can't remember what you did with them."

"Isn't that a pisser?"

"And you never saw her again."

"No. She was going to meet McClane the next day. Took a shower, shook my hand, said, 'Wish me luck.' I got the feeling she was like a birder, you know. I was another exotic to add to her list."

"Did she say where she was from?"

"I think it was somewhere back East, but I can't even swear to the time zone. Sorry, buddy."

"That's all right. Let's see if we can find her on the Internet."

Sean keyed up her name, no dice, skipped to a people finder site that he subscribed to and found plenty of Margaret Harrises, plenty more Jane Harrises, but no Margarethe Harrises. He drummed his fingers on the top of the glass counter.

"You said she might have gone by initials, right?"

Sam nodded.

Sean got a hit on M. J. Harris, but the woman's namesake was a building contractor in Ireland.

*Add A. J. McClane to the soup, you idiot,* Sean said to himself.

That did the trick. The two names were linked in a post on an angling forum called *Under the Surface.* The poster's handle was "Hell Hound from Trout," showing a thumbnail of a demented biker holding a fly rod. The corners of Sean's mouth rose fractionally.

> I remember an article in a magazine called Rural Free Male (I think) that said Field & Stream fishing editor A.J. McClane was a Cold War spy. The article was by M.J. Harris and titled "Angler, Scribbler, Soldier, Spy—The Many Lives of A.J. McClane." He seemed to be personal friends with everyone of high military rank in the country, and managed to wet a line in 140 countries. I know you don't travel like that on a magazine writer's pay. But I can't find the article. McClane was my favorite fishing writer growing up, and I'd like to see if this is true. Can anyone shine a light?

But no one else on the forum had any light to shine, and all Sean could find out about the magazine was that it had been a bimonthly glossy with a brief run in the 1980s. The post was seven years old and Sean got nowhere trying to find Hell Hound from Trout. That didn't matter, though, because he had Margarethe's nom de plume, and with a few more keystrokes he found one article by her and then a second, both fly-fishing-related and both more than twenty years old. One, a reminiscence titled "Under the Cedar Sweepers," had been reprinted in *Fly Rod & Reel* only two months before, and was linked to their archives. The essay was about growing up in Grayling, Michigan, as the daughter of an Au Sable riverboat craftsman, and was followed by a two-sentence editorial note:

> M. J. Harris is the owner and head guide of the historic Wa-Wa-Te-Si Fishing Lodge, located on the Holy Water stretch of Michigan's Au Sable River. The lodge will reopen its doors to discerning fly fishermen for the first time in a decade this spring.

It was this spring. Sean Googled up a phone number and used Sam's landline to call it. Straight to message, the voice a woman's, not old, not young, and not much in the way of warmth or invitation.

"The Wa-Wa-Te-Si Lodge is now taking reservations for the spring fishing season. Please leave your name, number, and a brief message, and we will get back to you soon. Thank you."

Sean clicked the off button without leaving a number.

"Did that sound like her voice?" he asked Sam.

Sam shrugged and Mickey's trout jumped. "Too much water, too many bridges. Leave a message. She'll call back and you can ask her if she knows anything about Hemingway's rod."

"I don't know if I want to do that."

"Why? What's she got to hide?"

"I don't know, but she's my only lead who's still got a pulse. If there's any chance she's involved, I don't want to run her off with a lot of questions."

"Killer, what do you think?" Sam said. "One eye open, call. Two eyes open, don't." And to Sean, "This is the way I answer all life's persistent questions." He snapped his fingers. Killer opened one eye. Sean hit redial.

"This is Sean Stranahan from Montana," he said at the beep. "If the Hendrickson mayflies are hatching, I'd like to stay at the lodge and hire you as my guide. Do you have any openings later this week or next week? I'd like to fish at least a couple full days. Thank you." He gave his cell number and hung up.

"Going undercover, huh?" Sam said. He gave Sean his sly dog look. "I seem to recall that's where she's right at home."

# CHAPTER FOURTEEN

# The Woman with Lake Storm Eyes

The Wa-Wa-Te-Si Lodge at the end of Wa-Wa-Te-Si Road could have been a trout lodge on the banks of the Madison River, some fourteen hundred miles to the west, or on the Neversink River in the Catskill Mountains, another seven hundred and fifty miles to the east. It could be any lodge where after-dinner anglers sit in a screened-in porch and sip their bourbons while the fish they catch grow longer in the telling. Sean had fished the Au Sable once, on a camping trip with his father. At the time, it was the farthest west he'd ever traveled. They had rented a canoe with a garish red Indian painted on the side from a livery in Grayling, then floated and fished their way to Mio, a five-day trip that Sean recalled with the smile that you smile when someone can no longer smile with you. How old had he been? Thirteen? Fourteen? Around there, that age when the rough edges sharpen and a distance grows between boys and their fathers, when voices are raised and silences follow.

Fishing had become the solitary grace note in their relationship. Sean's father visibly relaxed when they were on the water. His voice toned down and you could almost see him take deeper breaths. The trip down the Au Sable had been the best and the last of those times. His father had died in an auto accident only a few months later.

Sean climbed out of the rental into a light rain. He stepped up onto the porch, passing an upside-down wooden crate and stopping under the weathered skull and antlers of a moose. He rapped on the door with a heavy iron knocker in the shape of a leaping trout. Receiving no answer and expecting none, for he had seen no cars in the drive, he unlatched the door and pushed it open.

"Anyone home?"

In the hollowing silence, his voice rang with a slight echo. The grand room of the lodge was furnished in vintage Adirondack style—leather-covered armchairs that looked like they'd take the weight of a black bear, slat-back couches with leaf pattern cushions, a solemn river stone fireplace, whitetail deer mounts and old oils with gold-washed frames hanging on the walls. Sean noted several watercolors in the school of Ogden Pleissner, angling art with a Canadian flavor—canoes, men in red plaid shirts digging with paddles, brook trout jumping against bent rods, and against their nature, because brook trout don't jump. Heavy shuttered windows let in dust-mote shafts of light, striping the gloom abstractly.

Something was missing, and it took Sean a minute to figure out that there were no stuffed trout on the walls. His eyes were drawn to an old tintype portrait. It was an Indian chief. A nameplate identified him as David Shoppenagon, a guide and woodsman who had built the property's first lodge in 1880, and had christened the place with its Ojibwa name.

"Wa-Wa-Te-Si means 'Plain View.'"

Sean had heard neither a car pulling into the drive nor the steps that brought her into the room. The only noise was the soft tocking sound of a grandfather clock.

"I was just reading about that," he said.

"You could see from here to eternity back then, or at least to the bluffs in the Mason Tract, after they cut all the white pines." In person the voice was not as businesslike as it had sounded on the phone, but was warm and ran toward reflection. "Now that land's all grown back in porcupine quills. Remember when Ronald Reagan said, 'You've seen one tree, you've seen them all.' He must have been talking about Michigan jack pines."

Sean hadn't yet turned to face her.

"We have lodgepoles where I live," he said. "It's a sister species, and the same story how we got them. At least you still have your cedars."

He heard her rapping steps on the hardwood floor and turned to meet the outstretched hand with his own. A firm hand, but cold to the touch.

"I have Reynaud's syndrome," she said. "It's a fancy term for poor circulation. If you'd come here an hour earlier, you'd have walked in on me sitting in my underwear with my hands in a bucket of hot water."

He smiled, not knowing how else to react. It was a strange introduction.

"It's biofeedback," she continued. "You stand outside until your teeth start to chatter, then come inside and put your hands in hot water for ten minutes. Then you walk back outside and put your hands in a bucket of hot water on the porch for ten minutes. You're tricking your body into sending blood into the hands at cold temperatures. The technique was developed by the Army. You don't want soldiers with icy trigger fingers."

"Does it work?"

"You felt my hand, so there's your short answer. But you do the biofeedback over the course of a few weeks. I tried it last year and it worked for a couple of months. At least nobody said that my touch was as cold as ivory, which a man did once. How insensitive, but then I've never had particular luck with that particular kind of man. I'm Margarethe Harris. You must be Sean Stranahan."

Sean nodded. "Margarethe." Repeating the long 'e.' "That's a beautiful name."

"Lake Margrethe's west of Grayling. My father, Everett, said my eyes were the color of the lake before a storm, when the phosphorus and calcium carbonates were stirred up by waves. It created a luminescence. He added the 'a' in the middle to make it three syllables, so it would sound more lyrical. But you know kids, that's too long a name, so I grew up as Margee. Now I prefer my father's choice, God rest his soul."

Sean looked at her, the woman whose eyes were a lake before a storm. She was dressed little differently than she'd been in the photo Sam had taken of her nearly thirty years earlier. Khaki shirt tucked into khaki pants, leather belt, a tangerine-tinted bandana knotted at her throat the only splash of color. She wore jodhpur riding boots pulled over the cuffs of her pants, like a horsewoman, or a lion tamer, which was the image that came to Sean's mind. Her shoulder-length ash blonde hair was going gray, or colored just enough to maintain the illusion. She had a strong nose, a straight mouth framed by commas worn into her cheeks, and luminous eyes that were set just a little too close to be a model's. Sean remembered what Sam had said about her being a looker. The woman standing before him had seen some weather but was still strikingly beautiful, or, better said, beautifully striking. Sam had guessed her age at twenty-five. That would put her in her middle fifties now. It was an age where insecure women look into their mirrors and pull back the skin at their temples to see how they'd look with a lift. Margarethe Harris didn't strike Sean as someone who fell prey to her vanity, but then the face that looked back at her every morning didn't ask for much attention.

"I'd help you get your bags," she was saying, "but it stopped raining just as I walked up and I'd like to show you the river. You said this trip was nostalgia, so I take it this isn't your first visit?"

"I floated by this place in a canoe once, but it was a very long time ago." He told her about the trip he and his father had made as he followed her outside to a plank dock, where a slim, elegant craft with a pointed bow, a squared-off stern, and folded cane seats was moored. The river swirled with foam lines and looked lazy and made a sigh. Downriver, on the near bank, a weeping willow with low branches trailed lime-colored fingers in the current.

The Au Sable seemed much more at peace with itself than the brawling Western rivers Sean had grown accustomed to, and he told her so. She was standing with her hands on her hips, and as he watched her watching the river, a trout made a quick circle on the surface.

"He rose to a mahogany dun," Margarethe said. "All the mayflies are three weeks early this year. I wouldn't have told you to come last April. Too much rain. You'd be fishing in a cup of first flush Darjeeling and a few hours later it was as dark as Pu-erh tea. But the Au Sable always runs with color. It's the seepage springs draining the tannins from the cedar roots. That's part of what I love about it. Fishing can be such a sensuous experience. The colors and the sounds and the smells and the way a trout feels underwater. Some fishermen I've guided, all they care about is the strike. 'The tug is the drug,' that's their mantra. That's like making love and only caring about your orgasm. So limiting, don't you agree?"

Sean agreed.

"I'm a very sensuous person, Sean. Some people don't know what I mean by that."

He didn't say anything. He wasn't sure of the definition.

She seemed to read his confusion. "Sensual suggests sexuality. But only some people take time to experience nature with their senses, to be *sensuous*."

She held her palms out, as if to receive whatever sensuous gifts the heavens were offering, which, starting a minute or two before, was a bit more rain.

"Aren't you cold?" Sean said.

"I'm always cold, but you have to get really cold before the biofeedback works. I'll do another session after I show you to your room. You can rest up from the flight. Cocktails are at six down in the Great Room, as my father called it."

"Are there other guests?"

"You're my first of the season, the first in several years, for the matter of that. I kept this place open through thick and thin, mostly thin. I had to shut down for a time. So it's just the two of us for dinner. I live in that little green cottage you passed driving in."

They walked to Sean's rental, where he grabbed the duffel with his waders and gear and handed her his rod cases.

"This one's the length for a three-piece," she said.

"It's a bamboo rod my father milled. I have two of them, a four-weight and a six."

"I'm not surprised. As soon as I saw you I said to myself, 'Here's a man who loves a classic cane rod.' You have that old-fashioned look, and I mean that in the very best way. I always say, if you're going to fish the Holy Water on the Au Sable—that's what we call the stretch from Burtons Landing to Wakely Bridge—you need a rod made from a living material. I fish a Paul Young 'Martha Marie.' Young was a rod maker out of Detroit. He stayed here many times, fishing mostly on the North Branch. You're a man after my heart."

She led him up a steep staircase to a second-floor room that offered a river view and left him there, the man after her heart, thinking about her interest in bamboo rods. Could it be a coincidence that she'd introduced the very subject that had brought him to her door? When she'd returned his call earlier in the week, she'd asked why, if Sean lived in Montana, he wanted to fish a Michigan river, especially during an iffy month like April. The tone had been more "why on earth" than "why." So he'd told her it was nostalgia, and now, having established that as his purpose, it would be awkward to raise the subject of Hemingway's missing gear without raising her suspicion that memories had nothing to do with his trip at all.

A shower in the shared bathroom down the hall refreshed him, though it brought him no closer to a strategy, and he walked to the bedroom window with a towel wrapped around his waist. The bit of rain had turned into a bit of snow, big wet occasional flakes and the lovely river no longer so inviting. The view included a corner of the covered porch. Margarethe Harris was there, sitting on the upside-down wood crate with her bare forearms disappearing into a five-gallon bucket that rose a steam. She turned her head and they were looking at each other through the liquid gauze that sheeted the windowpanes. He must have been an impressionistic painting to her, as she was to him, her tangerine bandana a reckless stroke of the paintbrush in an otherwise monochromatic scene. Yet even so he felt the voyeur and stepped back from the window. He realized he'd been wrong, comparing her to a lion tamer. In fact she was the lion, a woman painted all one color.

He was in the Great Room at the appointed hour. A few minutes later she came from some farther recess of the lodge carrying papers, which turned out to be a fishing license form. "I'd like to be on the river early tomorrow, so let's get this out of the way." They got it out of the way and she asked what his was. Sean was about to say Scotch when she suggested a martini.

"I make the best this side of Manhattan," she said. "I mean a real martini with Plymouth gin and vermouth, straight up with a twist, like they serve at the Bemelmans Bar at the Carlyle. Or did. It's been a long time since I was in New York."

They drank the martinis standing, exchanging background talk—his painting, and her upbringing, a small-town girl fishing the river out the front door, for, as it turned out, she had grown up in the lodge back in the 1960s. At that time the Wa-Wa-Te-Si belonged to a Detroit auto magnate and her parents managed it, her father pulling double duty as the head guide. He'd built his riverboats in a workshop just up the road. She described an outbuilding that Sean remembered passing on the drive in, a long, low shed covered with Tyvek sheeting.

The idyll of her childhood, she said, hadn't lasted. Her mother had died when she was twelve, her father six years later. A small-town romance had resulted in a too-young marriage and inevitable divorce, college a lost opportunity but no children, "thank God."

"I wanted to be a painter like you, but I had no talent so I turned to writing, because it's a skill you can develop."

Literary flair carried her from the *Crawford County Avalanche* to the *Saginaw News*, where she'd penned an outdoor column, kick-starting a mildly promising career as a magazine writer that she had never seriously pursued. Saginaw was also where she met the man who'd become her second husband, a story, she assured Sean, that wasn't worth getting into, and then did in some detail. The husband was an art dealer from Toronto who had his fingers in other ventures besides art, including art forgery, and another part of his anatomy in as many women as would have him. A ten-year slice cut from her life—"and with a very dull knife," as she put it—but when the blood congealed from the divorce and other legal proceedings, she found herself with enough money to combine with an inheritance from her mother's mother to buy the Wa-Wa-Te-Si from its Motor City owners, who were more than happy to unload it.

"I knew the place needed work," she said. "The attic was nothing but bats. It was like Dracula's castle."

But it was her castle, finally, and despite setbacks she'd managed to keep its doors open until the last recession, both as a promise to herself and to her father, who had gone to his grave in the river.

"My father," she said, "after Mama's funeral he was never the same man. He had a dream of renovating the property, but I was in school and you can't rebuild with good intentions and a bottle of Chivas Regal. We were losing the place one rotten board at a time. He drowned in the swamp that you can see from your room, where the river bends around that big cedar sweeper. He was testing out a new boat and the water was deep, and it's faster than it looks down there, and he got knocked off the boat by the sweeper. He got wedged under the limbs. I found his body later that day."

"Is that the boat moored at the dock, Margarethe?"

"No. I burned the boat he was in. Burned it with him in it. Scraped his remains into the river. Dad had loved the Au Sable so. God, where else could his bones find any rest?"

All this, and she still had half of her martini. She drained it, raised her eyes in a question that Sean answered with a fractional nod, and took his glass and came back with two more. He was her confidant now. They clicked glasses.

"To the Holy Water," she said. "And to Dad, the best man I ever knew." And let her shoulders sag a little, as if that was wishful thinking.

It was the second time, Sean thought, that she'd felt the need to qualify her measure of him, even if only by gesture.

"To Dad," Sean said.

# CHAPTER FIFTEEN

# Song of the Solitary Angler

"That's when I started collecting fishermen," she said.

They had moved on to dinner, a baked venison lasagna, and had moved past it to brandies in the chairs before the fireplace. She was the kind of talker who repeated herself and took her time getting back around to the point, and now she was sipping her brandy and nodding.

"Down by the river, when I said you had an old-fashioned look, what I meant was you reminded me of my father. After his death, the world moved on—that's the way of life—but my concept of what a man should be never changed. I never stopped looking for the best of him in every attractive man I met. Do you know the kind of man I mean?"

She answered her question before Sean could venture an opinion.

"I mean the gentleman angler, someone who has that quiet center and is kind and sure of himself and has no need to plump up his feathers. You sense the decency in a man like that and warm up to him like you warm up to a fire."

She smiled to herself.

"You see," she said, "I've known a few of those men. They were the fishermen who came here, summer after summer, usually in June and July for the big nighttime mayfly hatches. They were part of Dad's informal club. He called it the Au Sable Club. It was modeled on the Fario Club, the fly fishing club started after World War II by Charles Ritz, the hotelier in Paris, and Al McClane, the *Field & Stream* fishing editor, and the third was Ernest Hemingway. They all used to fish the Risle River together in Normandy. They fished the Au Sable, too, at least McClane and Hemingway did. Of course, Dad's club wasn't quite so grand. Instead of an annual banquet at the Ritz, courtesy of Escoffier, Mom cooked. But after dinner, they'd sit right here if it was cold, or out on the porch. You're actually sitting in Daddy's chair. All I can say is you better be able to cast a fly line as well as he could."

"Looks like I have a lot to live up to," Sean said. And to himself: *Hemingway was here?*

"Follow me," she said. "I want to show you something."

Sean rose, carefully—two martinis, two glasses of cabernet, and a brandy was the sum of alcohol he drank in a week, not a night—and followed her into a dark-paneled study with a heavy desk and a swivel chair. On the desk was an old-fashioned manual typewriter under a gooseneck lamp. She switched on the lamp.

"This used to be our office before I moved it into the cottage," she said. She pointed to a photograph in a standing frame on the desk. "Dad," she said simply.

Sean was looking at a spare, angular man with broad shoulders and a heavy wing of black hair. The man was sitting in the stern of a green-painted Au Sable riverboat, holding a long wood pole.

"I have a lot of his features, but I inherited my mother's eyes and hair," she said. "You asked about the boat tied to the dock. This is that boat."

"Are these members of the Au Sable Club?" A half dozen photos, mostly posed shots of Everett Harris standing beside other fishermen, competed for eye-level space on the wall.

"That man with the wavy hair and craggy grin, that's Al McClane. My mother said he was the handsomest man she'd ever seen. He could take a ninety-foot fly line and cast the whole thing, just with his hands, no rod at all. There's a photograph my dad took of him doing it, it might be stacked in the frame behind this one, at least it used to be. I grew up with a crush on him. Later I visited him in Montana and wrote a story for a magazine. I wrote a couple pieces about other famous fishermen, one on Roderick Haig-Brown and one on Bud Lilly, two other fine fishermen."

"Who's this?" Sean was looking at a flash photo of a man holding a large dead trout by the gills. The man was smiling and his teeth showed in the flash of the camera.

"Guess."

"Is it Hemingway?"

She nodded. "The two Papas, my mother called them. They were thick as thieves. He spent three nights here in 1947. He caught this trout on the South Branch, up around a stretch known as the Castle. Signed his name in the register and left a very nice note to my parents. Drank them out of Scotch, but he was a great talker. Made you feel like you'd known him all your life."

"I'd like to see that register," Sean said.

"It's gone, I'm afraid. Somebody broke into the place when it was vacant and tore out the page. Maybe they thought it was worth money."

"That's too bad," Sean said. "Do you remember him?"

"Hemingway? No, I wasn't even born for another fourteen years. The closest I ever came to meeting him was meeting his son Jack. A magazine called *Rural Free Male* paid me to fly up to Kamloops in British Columbia, where Jack fished for steelhead in the Thompson River. I wrote the profile, but the editor wanted me to rewrite so it included more about his father. Jack told me that he'd spent his life in the shadow of his father, and then later in the shadow of his daughters, the actresses, and the only place he was fully his own man was on the river. I'd promised him that he would be the focus of the piece, so I sat on the story, and then the magazine folded its tent. So it was never published. Jack would have made a fine member of the Au Sable Club."

"Did he talk about his father to you?"

"Some." Her eyes flashed past him to the wall, then seemed to swim away to some indeterminate point of focus.

Sean felt a flush of excitement. Here, much sooner than he had anticipated, was the chance to bring up the missing fishing tackle, or rather to keep her on the subject of Hemingway, so that she might be the one who broached it. But she was speaking again before he could form a question.

"I'm not as old as you thought I was, but I'm not so young, either. I'm going to get some sleep. Please feel free to sit up as long as you like. I realize you're still on a Montana clock. With the water this cold, there won't be a hatch until later in the morning, if at all. I'll have breakfast ready by seven-thirty, and you can help me shuttle the pickup to the take-out. We'll put in right here at the dock. Can I get you anything else?"

*Don't act like you're too eager,* Sean told himself. He said, in a voice that said it would be nice but no big deal, "I'd like to read that piece you did on McClane." Then, as if it were an afterthought, "And the one about Jack Hemingway." He shrugged. "If it isn't too much trouble."

"All my clips are back at the cottage. Do you mind waiting until tomorrow?"

"Not at all."

"The Hemingway piece . . ." Again her eyes slid past him. "I haven't seen that in years. I probably put it away somewhere it would be safe, which means it's probably safe from me ever seeing it again."

She laughed, a low sweet music with a hint of sadness that made Sean acutely aware that he was alone in a lodge, in a forest, in the night, with an exceedingly attractive woman whose greater years on earth were only a number. That knowledge pulsed between them like a heartbeat, and he was relieved when she pooh-poohed his offer to walk her back to her cottage.

"I've been walking this road after dark since before you were born."

Sean stood at one of the big panes of window that looked out toward the river. He watched as the beam of her flashlight swept the surface of the water, painting a milky stripe that illuminated the pines on the far bank. He realized that, like him, she was unable to resist one last glance at the river that was as much her lifeblood as the plasma in her veins. The light bobbed as she walked back up the road, the beam diffused by the misting rain. It was as though she was being led by the cold breath of a ghost. Sean waited for the light to fade away at a bend in the road. Moonless dark, all the land gripped in the moonless dark. He stood at the window until a haze of lemon grew beyond the bend. She had turned lights on in the cottage.

Now that he was alone, he walked back to her study and looked toward the wall where twice her eyes had strayed. There were at least a dozen photos, but his attention focused on a color photograph of a man with apple cheeks and a wide smile. The man was kneeling in a river, holding the tail wrist of a big steelhead with a ruby blush on its side. Behind him was a broad expanse of current, box cliffs beyond, a train winding up the far bank, maple leaves stenciled on the boxcars. A Kodachrome image somewhat faded, the colors still a little too painterly to be true. Sean guessed he was looking at Jack Hemingway. Why would Margarethe Harris raise Jack Hemingway's name, but not point out his photograph?

He pondered that as he lifted the framed photograph of Al McClane from the wall and set it on the desk. He thumbed back the swivel tabs that kept the cardboard backing in place and found three other photographs behind the facing photograph. One was the photo she'd mentioned—McClane casting the fly line without a rod.

Sean left the frame disassembled on the desk and lifted down the one of Jack Hemingway. Sean liked Hemingway's smile and he liked the way he cradled the steelhead with its gills underwater so it could breathe, and he wished he was fishing that river. On the back of the frame, in ink:

> *Jack Hemingway*
> *14 pound hen steelhead*
> *Green Butt Skunk*
> *Thompson River B.C.*
> *11/04/1986*

He studied the photograph. The steelhead had a kype on its lower jaw. That marked it as a male, not a hen. The fly showing in the corner of its jaw was orange. A Green Butt Skunk had a black body and a white wing and no orange, not even as an accent. It wasn't the steelhead the words described. *Hmm.* Margarethe had stacked several photographs of McClane in the same frame; perhaps she had of Hemingway as well?

She had. Behind the cardboard backing was a second photo—the same man, Jack Hemingway, the same river, the Thompson, but a different steelhead. And this fish did have a fly with a white wing in the corner of its jaw. If the second photograph had been all that was revealed when he took apart the frame, Sean would have merely been envious. But he scarcely glanced at the fish, because the photo was sandwiched among several sheets of onionskin paper that were folded once and showed the ridges raised by the keys of a typewriter on the off side. His fingers felt cold as he unfolded the typewritten sheets and he quelled their shaking. *Now who has the Reynaud's?* he thought.

A glance at the title—"Hemingway's Ghosts"—confirmed his suspicion that this was the unpublished profile that Margarethe Harris had written about Jack Hemingway.

Sean took the stairs two at a time to the second floor. He rummaged through his duffel for the waterproof point-and-shoot he carried on fishing trips and then bounded back down to the lobby. He stepped to the big picture window and looked up the road toward the yellowish tinge in the pines. Just checking, making sure she was still there. Reassured, he was startled to hear a muffled clacking noise from the porch. He shrank back from the window as a shape moved by, felt his heart pounding and then let out a breath. The deer was a silhouette within the greater darkness beyond. It was a doe. She had her head outstretched and was no more than half a dozen feet from the pane of glass. She was stealing from a bird feeder Sean had noticed on the porch earlier.

He walked back to the study. Placing the typewritten pages on the desk—seven, double-spaced, including the title page—he crooked the lamp over them and then photographed them one at a time. He enlarged the playback images to make certain the typewriting was legible. Done. He folded the papers and was putting the frame back together when again he heard a tapping noise. He heard the abrupt snort of the startled deer. Silence. Then the heavy iron latch on the door ratcheted, metal scraping metal, and the door opened and he felt the cool kiss of the night.

Thumbing two of the tabs into place and hoping it would be sufficient to keep the picture together, Sean hung the framed photograph back on the wall. Two long steps back to the desk chair, and with glass of brandy in hand he was studying the photographs of Al McClane when she reached the door of the study.

"What are you doing?"

Sean turned to her. "You startled me."

"You didn't hear the deer snort?"

"No." Sean sipped the brandy. He waved a hand over the spread photos. "You were right about McClane, but I wanted to see for myself. He really could cast the entire fly line without a rod."

"I didn't give you permission to take apart my photographs." Her voice was cold.

"I'm sorry. You told me about them, so I thought it would be okay."

"You should have asked."

She was wearing a black-and-red plaid wool jacket over her khaki shirt and pants, which made her look like an L.L. Bean model. The bandana knotted at her throat had changed. It was a red to match the plaids. So, Sean thought, vanity after all.

"I'm sorry," he said.

He began to stack the photographs into the frame and caught sight of the Hemingway picture out of the corner of his eye. He'd hung it so that the top right side was a half inch too low, but what sent a shiver up through his body was that the other photo was facing out, the one of the female steelhead. In his hurry, he'd put the wrong photograph against the glass. They were almost identical poses taken from the same run of the river, but there was no train in this photo and the steelhead had a Green Butt Skunk in its jaw. Not looking at Margarethe, he slipped the tabs into place on the McClane photograph and rehung it on the wall. He felt her eyes on his back.

"Bring the right side up," she said. "Here, let me."

She squared the photograph and brought the finger of her left hand to her chin, pinching it. If she shifted her eyes a foot to the right, she'd be looking at the photo of Jack Hemingway and couldn't fail to see that it was the wrong one. But she stepped back and nodded once. Then, frowning, she stepped forward to the Hemingway photograph and took it between her hands.

"Looks like a drunk hung this picture," she said. Her hands straightened it. She looked at it critically. "Did I tell you this is Jack Hemingway?"

Sean said she hadn't. He couldn't feel his feet on the floor.

"He got two fish that day. Not an ounce of bravado in him, or none I saw. Oh, I know he drank and I heard his daughter talk about him on TV, that he maybe molested her sisters, but I choose to believe otherwise. I think it comes down to Jack being about the only person in that cursed family who didn't seek attention."

Sean found his voice. "How many days did you fish with him?"

"Two, but you can get to know someone in that time if they really open up. I had a gift then of getting people to do that. I wasn't always so skeptical of people's motives. I wasn't always someone who was cold as ivory. I don't just mean that literally."

Sean was only half listening. He couldn't believe that she hadn't noticed that the frame on the wall showed a different photograph. But then, when the same picture stares back at you for years, perhaps you don't see it at all. As an artist, Sean knew that better than most.

"Why did you come back tonight?" he heard himself saying.

"I left a bag of groceries on the back step. I'd already taken a couple bags in and then I got a call and blanked it out, and I was in my pajamas when I remembered. Nothing was going to go bad in this weather, but we have a family of raccoons that think they own the place. They'd have taken the bacon and we'd have gone fishing tomorrow without a proper breakfast."

She smiled. In the turn of her heel that brought them face-to-face he had become her friend again, improbably as that had seemed only a minute ago. And when she said good night a few minutes later, Sean for the second time watched the ghost made by her flashlight lead her past the bend in the road. Now he didn't know whether to switch the Hemingway photographs back to their original order, or leave them as is. Apparently she hadn't noticed the change, but if he switched them a second time?

His gut told him to leave well enough alone. He thumbed all the tabs so the frame wouldn't fall apart and squared it on the wall.

"It's our secret, Jack," he said.

This time he took the stairs thoughtfully, and one at a time.

# CHAPTER SIXTEEN

# Hemingway's Ghosts

Sean undressed for bed and brushed his teeth, his prolonging of the ritual deliberate. He wished he had brought his laptop to transfer the images to. As it was, he'd have to enlarge the images on the camera card and view them through the playback feature, scrolling side to side and up and down to read the story a few lines at a time. He had taken the photos without the flash and they were dark. But then, as he began to read, so was the story.

> "HEMINGWAY'S GHOSTS"
> BY
> M.J. HARRIS

Jack Hemingway whistles through the tombstones in the somnolent pre-dawn canyon. The tune, which cuts through the undertone of British Columbia's Thompson River and returns from the bluffs in stringing echoes, is the theme from the movie "The Great Escape," and Hemingway whistles as if he is marching off to war. Forty odd years ago, he whistled himself off to a real one, World War II, where he parachuted behind enemy lines and endured the atrocities of a German prison camp before the Allied liberation. This time around he is marching to do battle with one of the giant steelhead that have ascended throbbing rapids and all he really has to be concerned about is staying on his feet while negotiating the slick boulders that stud the riverbed. But for Jack Hemingway, the demons that haunt his existence—the suicides that run in his famous family, six over four generations, the schizophrenia, manic depression, and the alcoholism—are never too far away, and the irony of fishing in a run of the river that is called the Graveyard is neither lost on him nor denied.

"I don't know why I love this place," he says as we reach the bank, the river before us a shimmering of coins that spill away into lambent smoothness in the pool below, "but I think it has something to do with rebirth and the possibility of miracles."

Turning his back to the current, he switches on his headlamp to clip off the fly he'd fished yesterday and ties on a new one with Halloween colors—orange and black with a white wing that he ties with roadkill skunk. "That's the key ingredient," he says.

I ask what he calls it.

"Hemingway's Ghost," he says. "Or Hemingway's Curse, it depends."

Depends on what, I ask him.

"On whether it catches a fish." He winks, a scrunching up of one eye that creates craters of shadow on his face. He is a whistling, winking kind of man, gregarious among friends, of whom he has a great many, but by choice a solitary angler.

"All the most memorable fish I've ever hooked," he will tell me, "I've been alone."

Sean read on, the fishing good, the catching poor. Her prose was a little precious for his taste and she inserted herself into the story too often, but he began to like Jack Hemingway, or the portrait of him that she painted. He read, interested, but learning nothing about what had brought him to Michigan.

And then, on the next-to-last page, he read something that made him become aware of his breathing.

I take a chance and ask Jack if his father would have liked this kind of fishing. It is a chance because I told him that I wouldn't ask about his family, but he is interested in the question and looks far away. He tucks the butt of his spey rod in his arms crossed in front of his chest, and with each breath he takes, the rod, which sticks far above his head, quivers like an antenna. He begins circumspectly.

"When I was a little boy, fishing was the forbidden fruit. My father would permit me to accompany him when he fished on the Clarks Fork River, back when we took our summers at the L Bar T, but I wasn't allowed to carry a rod and I had to stay upstream of him, so I wouldn't scare away the trout he was fishing for. I literally became his shadow. Sometimes he'd let me feel the rod when a trout was on the line or net it, but not very often. People who consider this cruel and proof of his selfishness haven't thought it through. What better way of ensuring interest is there than to give someone a taste of something delicious, but refuse him the second bite?

"It was Papa who made me the fanatical fisherman I've become, and you have to be a fanatic to fish for steelhead in this river, because you might go a week between fish. We shared the temperament that makes a masochistic endeavor such as this attractive. But it really would have depended upon what stage in his life he was. In his later life, Papa got much more into big game fishing, trolling for marlin and tuna, than river fishing for trout. And he lost all his fishing tackle, and it had sentimental value so I think that had plenty to do with it, too."

He explains that almost all his father's fly fishing gear, rods from the Hardy Brothers in London, from the best makers in the States, all his reels and lines and flies, were packed in a steamer trunk and sent in 1940 by Railway Express from Key West to Ketchum, Idaho, where he was living with Martha Gellhorn as a guest at the Sun Valley Lodge. The trunk never arrived. It could have been lost, or more likely stolen, especially if it had the Hemingway name on it, for with the publication of "For Whom the Bell Tolls" that same year, Ernest Hemingway had become one of the most famous people in America.

Jack is speaking again. "I think what my father regretted more than anything, what I certainly did, was he had written a story about the two of us, sort of as a sequel piece to 'Fathers and Sons,' which was about his own father. He said it had some uncomplimentary references to Pauline in it, they were going through a divorce at that time, so he'd slipped the story into the trunk with his fishing gear to keep it private. He thought he'd taken it with him when he drove out to Idaho in the spring, but he couldn't find it and decided it must still be with the fishing tackle. It was his only copy."

We are sitting on the riverbank eating our lunch as he confides this to me, and I see the wink in his eye.

"Are you pulling my leg?" I ask him.

"No, he really did lose the trunk. But he only told me about the missing story once, when he was melancholy with drink, and we were shooting buzzards from the second-floor window at the Finca. I'd confessed some regrets to him and had to hit him up for money, and he'd written me a check and said 'We all have our regrets,' and then he told me about the lost steamer trunk. Papa was an honest exaggerator. He'd stretch the size of fish, but not lie about catching it. So maybe there really was a story. I'll never know."

Sean read through the passage again and then to the story's conclusion, with the evening dying and Jack hooking a great steelhead. It had run to midriver and jumped, falling away, and jumped again, falling away—"like dominoes falling," she had written, "if dominoes came in chrome and weighed twenty pounds." Hemingway had finally pulled the great trout close, "a yard long if it was an inch," but the hook pulled out before he could land it.

> Jack doesn't seem chagrined, but only reels up and shows me where the hook of the fly had been straightened by the leverage the steelhead worked against it. He smiles.
>
> "That one will keep the ghosts away," he says.
>
> I ask what he means and he says that when he fishes here he builds an imaginary campfire to keep the ghosts from crowding too close. That the longer he fishes without catching a steelhead, the closer the ghosts advance and the more they haunt him, and that the best remedy against them is to feel the line tighten. He says that with the fish on the line, the ghosts recede beyond the fire, up onto the hill where they belong, and hours can pass, even days, before they come back to dance at the edges of the light.
>
> Softly, he laughs. "Papa liked to say that all true stories end in death. I think the idea of fishing in a graveyard would have appealed to him."
>
> "Do they come back?" I ask him. "The ghosts?" We are walking back up the hill now, past the tombstones that are an eerie, thin milk color under the waxing moon.
>
> He stops and turns to face me, his round face bathed in this ethereal light. He brings a hand up to scratch at the hairs escaping under the brim of his Scottish cap.
>
> "We'll see what happens tomorrow," he says.

She had typed the old journalism symbol, "- 30 -," to indicate the end.

Sean thought the story was stronger by not mentioning the two fish that Jack had landed, presumably when she accompanied him to the river the following day. He zipped the camera into his fishing vest and slept fitfully, his mind returning to her story again and again. It confirmed Sam's account of what Margarethe had told him so many years before. There really had been missing gear. Had the trunk been the source of the fly wallet engraved with Ernest Hemingway's initials? Had it housed the Pinky Gillum fly rod that Wilhelm Winkler, the Tyrolean man, wanted Patrick Willoughby to authenticate? Sean thought that likely. But was it too far-fetched to believe that Hemingway's own writings were part of the fortune the steamer trunk contained? That was the question.

Sometime in the night, Sean woke and stood for a time at the window. The sky had cleared, revealing a moon with a haze ring that shone a vaporous light on the river downstream, where the Au Sable bent into the swamp. It made him think of the swamp in Hemingway's short story "Big Two-Hearted River," where the fishing would be "tragic." He remembered his teacher telling him that the deep, swirling waters brought back Nick's memories of war and represented the reservoir of his fears. She told him that the swamp was a *lodestone,* a word Sean had to look up in a dictionary, and that its magnetic pull would prove irresistible, that in time he would have to face the swamp and overcome the darkness that had come to live inside him. At the time, Sean had been more interested in the mechanics of landing a trout if he hooked one in such an unforgiving place.

Looking at the water now, he felt both the attraction and repulsion of the poles. There were real ghosts here, at least one, for this was the bend that had claimed Margarethe's father's life. She had said that the current was deceptive. It was not a place where you stepped in too deeply. And yet Sean suspected that he was on the verge of doing just that, and that the waters were darker and far deeper than he had imagined.

# CHAPTER SEVENTEEN

# First Kiss

The morning passed without a fish. Then the early afternoon, though it scarcely mattered to Sean. It was what fishing was in cold, penny-dark water, not very good, and with the river still rising from yesterday's rains, unlikely to get better.

But the country the riverboat passed through could not be spoiled by weather. For an artist it was a palette that ached for the brush—forests of black spruce and white pines, straight as sentinels, soft maples that would turn to fire in the autumn, even the swamps extending a dark invitation.

"How are your hands?" he asked Margarethe when she poled the boat to a stop below the tail of a long island.

"Better than I thought they'd be. Maybe there's something to this biofeedback after all. I hope so." She tied the boat off to a cedar root and pulled a rod from its tube.

"This is the Paul Young 'Martha Marie,'" she said, handing it to Sean.

"I'm honored," Sean said.

"You should be. It was my father's. I've never let anyone fish it, ever."

"Why me?"

"Because I've seen how you cast. You don't try to push bamboo farther than it's meant to be pushed. And because I have a bet with myself that you'll be able to get a rise from the trout that's working in that soft slot of water on the far side of the island. Did you notice that it was man-made?"

Sean shook his head as they waded up to the island, which was at least sixty feet long, with tag alders and a solitary tamarack growing out of it.

"It looks pretty natural to me," he said.

"That's because the boy who made it was artistic. He worked for one of the state river crews that built trout habitat. He came up here his summers off from college and lived in a tent on the river. I met him when his crew was putting in a riprap just downstream of the lodge. I brought everybody iced tea when they stopped for lunch."

She cocked her head as she spoke of him.

"He isn't the one you married, is he?" Sean said.

"No. He was the one I should have, though. He named this island for me, Margarethe's Island. Right where we're standing, this is where we had our first kiss. Here, I want you to try a parachute quill."

As Sean tied the mayfly imitation to the leader, one of its real counterparts landed on Margarethe's hat, the ephemeral sails of its wings opening and closing. It flew away and a few moments later its twin floating down the river disappeared in a tight swirl made by a trout. Sean made the cast, throwing slack into the line so that the fly would drift naturally. The trout rose and the slender shaft of bamboo bent deeply.

"I'll take a picture," she said.

"No, that's all right."

But she had already moved up to him and was reaching into his fly vest. Sean had taken several photos during the float, so she knew which pocket he kept his camera in, and she clicked the shutter as he fought and then released the trout, a beautifully spotted brown that Sean looked at without seeing, because in the corner of his eyes he was watching Margarethe tapping at the back of his camera.

"I'm sure you got a couple good ones," he said.

"Let me just check."

She was using the playback to scroll through the images. Sean felt the air go out of his lungs when her face changed, went dead gray as the blood left her cheeks. Her eyes skimmed over so that she was looking somewhere behind them. He saw her mouth moving, but there was no sound but the murmur of the river.

She opened her eyes. Still not looking at him, she said, "I have to sit down. Here, here's your camera." She held it out. Her voiced quavered. "Take your damn camera."

"Margarethe, I can explain."

She brought her hand back as if to throw the camera, then her shoulders sagged. Opening her hand, she let the camera drop into the water at her feet.

"I'm going to sit down," she said. She sat down on the island and dropped her head onto her hands.

"I want you gone," she said. Where before there was a mechanical resignation in her voice, a dispirited sadness, now something close to real hatred broke through, her tone turning as cold as her touch. "After we shuttle the boat back, I just want you gone."

"Don't you wonder why I took the pictures?" Sean sat down a few feet away from her. "I can explain."

They sat in silence.

After a time she spoke. "When I told you I wasn't always so skeptical of people's motives, this is what changed me, men like you. You invaded my privacy and took something from me. What do you want with an old story? It wasn't even published, for God's sake."

"I'm sorry, Margarethe."

"No, I'm the one who's sorry. Did you even fish here with your father, or was that just playing to my emotions, knowing I'd lost my own on the river?"

"No, that was true. Margarethe, do you remember a man named Sam Meslik? He calls himself Rainbow Sam. He's a fishing guide on the Madison River."

Her "yes" was so soft Sean barely heard it. "I remember him. He had a face like a wolf." She shook her head at the memory. "He was just my type back then. I'd flown out to Montana to interview Al McClane."

"Do you remember telling him about Ernest Hemingway's missing fishing tackle?"

"Is that what this is about?" she said. "A few fly rods?"

"Well, two people who might have known something about it are dead within the past two weeks."

She looked at him for the first time in minutes. A mayfly flew into the space between them. Another. One landed on the sleeve of Sean's shirt, its delicate twin tails pulsing up and down. On the far side of the island, Sean heard trout rising, the regular cadence of smaller trout punctuated by the deep, hollow burbles that the good ones made.

"You *would* have to ruin the first good hatch of the season." She didn't smile. It was an accurate statement. "Go on," she said. "I'm listening."

———

She would not kick him out of the lodge after all. They would share the martinis before dinner that night, the brandies before the fire. There would even be a second day on the river, a downstream reach called the Trophy Waters, though no big fish came their way.

But though she accepted Sean's apologies, she had been either unable or unwilling to expand upon his knowledge. When pressed upon the subject of the trunk, she recalled little beyond what was in her unpublished story. She did remember that Jack told her that he had seen the trunk once on a visit to Key West, and that he had opened it, just being inquisitive, and had been drawn to staring at the trout flies in the little compartments in the fly boxes, his eyes mesmerized by the gemstone colors. Had Jack offered an opinion on what had happened to the trunk, beyond the possibility that it was stolen? No. Nor had he recalled seeing any of his father's writing in the chest, but he was enthralled with trout, not words. A page of prose might not have registered deeply enough to be recalled.

Sean considered himself a good judge of character, but there was a distinction between judging character and gauging truth, and several times he suspected that Margarethe had not met his probing with complete honesty.

"Where do you go from here?" she'd asked. It was his third night at the lodge, his last, for he had to drive to Traverse City to catch a flight the following morning.

"I'll follow the trails of the dead. The rod we found on the Madison had to have come from somewhere."

"You said it came from that Wilhelm Winkler."

"I'm working on that assumption, but he was just a link in the chain. I need to go further back, all the way to when the trunk first went missing. If I can solve that mystery, maybe the rest will fall into place."

She was at the bar, stirring the ice in the martini pitcher. The noise stopped.

"Everybody needs something to live for," she said. "Whether it's a martini at six o'clock or a good man at ten."

"Is that something Hemingway said?" Sean was aware of the clock in the room, the tock with each swing of the pendulum.

"No," she said. "It's something I said."

She handed him his drink, and he watched the sadness come into her eyes as her shoulders fell of their weight.

"Are you just going to let me stand here?" she said.

# CHAPTER EIGHTEEN

# Running with Wolves

**W**hen he reached for her in the morning, the place on that side of the bed was cold. He walked to the window and braced his hands on the sill. A watercolor morning. The vague shapes of whitetail deer with dropped heads in the yard.

Sean got dressed and found her in the kitchen, standing over a skillet, still in her nightgown. He reached around her and cupped her breasts, and she leaned back against him.

"I fly all the way from Michigan, and the weather here is the same weather I had there."

"You weren't complaining about the weather last night. You know what I think? I think you thought about it long and hard. That's why you bought me the necklace."

Sean released her. "She's twenty years older than me."

"All cats are gray in the dark."

"Martha . . ."

"Do you know who said that? It was Benjamin Franklin. He was counseling young men on their choice of mistresses. He said older women were discreet and they didn't get pregnant and they knew more tricks in bed."

"She wasn't my mistress. All I did was hold her awhile. Can't you just say you like the necklace?"

"I do like it. It will go with my hair when I get gray." She turned and kissed him good morning. "I'm just giving you a hard time. I think."

The necklace's pendant was a Petoskey stone, a fossil coral found in Lake Michigan, with a hexagonal design brought out by lapidary polishing. Sean had stopped at a roadside stand on the outskirts of Traverse City on the day he'd flown in and bought it on a whim, *before* he'd met Margarethe Harris.

"Sit down," she said. "We'll have breakfast and then I have something to show you."

"Show me now."

"No. In this house we follow the rules."

"What rules?"

"We don't talk about work at breakfast, we don't talk about work at dinner, and we don't talk about work in bed."

"When do we talk about work?"

"During work times."

"But we don't work at the same place. You haven't thought this through."

"Don't tell me what I have or haven't thought through. Anyway, you know what I mean. Now eat your eggs."

The three sheets of paper Sean was studying ten minutes later were in Harold Little Feather's handwriting, which meant they were in cursive and took concentration to decipher.

"This is a ledger of some kind?"

Martha nodded. "It's a client list. These are people Freida Toliver sold elk antler chandeliers and whatnot to. The figures on the right-hand column are installation fees. Freida worked as an electrician for the phone company before her accident."

"Four thousand dollars for a chandelier?" Sean whistled.

"It's a lot. But I don't think it's out of line with other outfits that sell them. Freida didn't keep very good books. Harold put this together from a couple half-assed ledgers, envelope scribblings, this and that."

"Why give them to me, if Harold's on it?"

"Harold isn't on it. There is no 'it' to be on. She died of hypothermia, remember? But he found the body and I instructed him to look into her background, which led to what you're looking at. I thought this was an avenue you were anxious to pursue."

"I am—will. Thanks for this. So Harold's done, right? I don't want to step on his toes."

"Harold's work was preliminary to cause of death. We were just covering bases. He's not even in the county as of yesterday. The state investigative office has him doing something with an Indian connection in Lewis and Clark County. He was up in the rotation. Nothing you need to concern yourself with."

"You make him sound like a number. Is that for my benefit?"

"No. I've always managed to separate work from play. That's not the right word."

"Hardly."

"Harold's the past, you know that."

"I'm just teasing you."

"Is that a way of saying you don't care about my relationships?"

"No. How the hell did we get started on this?"

"You being attracted to what's-her-name in Michigan. Her with the lake storm eyes. What is it with you and every woman having a name starting with 'M'? Martinique, Margarethe, Etta—"

"Etta?"

"Loretta. 'L' is only one letter over from 'M.'"

"You're crazy."

"Oh, and don't forget Martha," Martha said. "That's what I am, a familiar letter of the alphabet. You probably picked me because I had a name that would be easy to remember."

"I can see I'm not going to win this one. But I don't want to leave here today on this note."

"What do you propose, that we go back to bed? Will that patch things up?"

"Now that you mention it."

"Give me five minutes to freshen up."

"How will I recognize you? I mean among all my 'M' women."

"I'll be the one wearing a Petoskey stone."

Forty minutes later, she watched him walk down the lane toward his tipi, a man with his hands in his pockets, whistling. She loved watching him walk. She fingered the stone resting against her breast-bone. Goldie had come up from behind and Martha reached down to pat her head.

"I do love you, you know." Working her fingers into the dog's coat, feeling his touch all over again.

———

"So how did you like the famous Au Sable?" Patrick Willoughby asked. He gave Sean his owl eyes. "I always meant to fish the Hex hatch there. Drifting a dry fly at night, a pipe to keep away the mosquitoes. It has a romantic allure. I've heard it can get quite crowded, though."

They were sitting on the porch of the clubhouse, talking softly as Ken Winston read the story about Jack Hemingway. Sean had transferred the photos of the manuscript to his computer and printed out a copy before driving up the river.

Winston placed the papers on the table and set a rock on them so they wouldn't blow away.

"You've both read it now, what do you think?"

"I think I'd like to catch a steelhead in the Thompson River," Winston said. "But I'm not sure they let black people into British Columbia."

They shared the laugh, except for Willoughby, who folded his arms across his chest and lifted his moonlike face, regarding a vista in some indeterminate distance.

"He gets the same look before he howls to the pack," Winston said.

That was true enough. A wolf pack had moved into the Gravelly Range and they had heard the wolves howl from the clubhouse and joined the chorus.

The president of the club found that his pipe had gone out and relit it.

"The cult of celebrity is an odd phenomenon," he said presently. "Here we are, more than half a century since the man was buried, and we are still enamored of objects solely because he has touched them. I am reminded of the elk antlers stolen from Hemingway's Ketchum residence by the journalist Hunter Thompson. Even he fell under the spell of the man."

"Speak for yourself," Winston said. "I'll add a Gillum to my quiver even if the only one who's fished the rod was Lucifer himself."

Willoughby conceded the point. "I'm not helping, am I? That's because I see no solid thread to follow, unless Margarethe Harris knows more than she's told you. I consider that probable, but as she isn't here, we must follow any thread available to us, however fragile and likely to break. Sean, you are in possession of a list of Freida's clients. What leads you to think that one of them would have given her the fly wallet with Hemingway's initials? Or the Gillum rod that ended up in her brother's hands?"

"She tried to throw the wallet into the pot when she was haggling over the price of a saddle with Etta Huntington. Etta told me that Freida liked to barter and they'd horse-traded before. I can see her getting it in a deal with someone else."

"A fine Native American tradition," Willoughby said. "Let me play devil's advocate for a moment. Why would someone deal it away to her, if they knew its provenance and thus the value?"

"Perhaps the owner didn't, but Freida did."

"Gentlemen," Kenneth Winston said. "We can go round and round on this, or we can start knocking on doors."

They agreed to reconvene for burgers and beers later that afternoon. Willoughby, who was the voice of authority in any room, or on any porch for that matter, took command of distribution. The original list included fifty-two names, of which Harold had found addresses for forty-one. Of those, twenty-three were not in the Madison Valley at all, but spread across neighboring counties. Those could be saved for a later day. The remaining addresses were rather evenly distributed from Ennis to West Yellowstone, a span Willoughby divided into three geographic sections. He would take the dozen or so clients whose addresses were in the lower valley north of Varney Bridge, Winston would take their second rental car to visit a similar number residing from Varney upriver to Lyons Bridge, while Sean concentrated on the upper valley. Quite a bit of driving for each, and an ambitious day's work—that is, until you took the month into consideration. Most of the Madison Valley's residents were snowbirds who were sipping chardonnay in the Sunbelt, their summer homes silent except for the periodic snapping of mousetraps set by property caretakers.

"Shall we say the mermaid bar at six?" Willoughby said.

They were agreed.

———

Vic Barrows, the bartender at the Trout Tails Bar & Grill, scratched the new tattoo on his left forearm as he took their orders. The tattoo was a date in February, underneath the words *Free at Last*. He was wearing a starched white shirt with the sleeves rolled up, and his gold front tooth shone under prisms of light cast by a multifaceted chandelier. The battered upright piano on the south wall, the warm wall, just collected dust, and the mermaid tank behind the bar showed a six-foot-long crack in the inner layer of its triple-glazed glass. It hadn't held a drop of water since Labor Day. Vic said they were hoping for a Memorial Day opening, but the owner, who lived out of state, was balking at the cost of fixing the tank. Barrows shrugged. He'd done two months in the Hyalite County Jail for breaking the head of an innocent bystander as collateral damage while breaking up a fight between two fishermen smitten by a woman flaunting a vulcanized tail. Hence the date of his release on his arm. Hence the gold tooth. Hence his indifference about the future of this particular mermaid tank.

"Tits, tails, and drunken fly fishermen," he said. "What could possible go wrong?"

"This place is starting to become depressing," Patrick Willoughby said after the bartender had turned his back.

"It's April in Montana," Kenneth Winston said. "Everything about it is depressing."

The beers came and Willoughby placed a legal pad on the table. "Shall we begin? Kenneth, do you want the honor?"

Winston sipped the foam from his Cold Smoke Scotch Ale. He said he'd knocked on nine doors, three of which had opened, three sets of eyes registering surprise at seeing a black man in southwestern Montana, then trying to be blasé about it. Two couples ushered him in the door, shook their heads when he brought up the subject of the fly wallet—yes, Freida Toliver had sold them an elk antler chandelier; no, they had paid in full with personal check; hmm, what are you trying to get at?—and ushered him back out the door. The third door was opened by a woman who insisted Ken drink a cup of tea with her. She was a college professor on sabbatical and she was writing a book, and he was a lot more interesting than the subject, which was personality projections based on spatial models in urban living situations. Ken had sipped the tea sitting under an antler chandelier. The woman was a friend of the home owner, who wintered in Santa Fe, and she didn't know anything about the chandelier. Could he stay for dinner? She'd made barley soup and had baked gluten-free bread. Her body language said she was available, and she was attractive enough in a faded hippie kind of a way, and he was, alas . . . married.

You know what they say, she'd told him. What happens in Montana . . .

"Stays in Montana?" Willoughby finished the thought.

"What she actually said was, 'Dot, dot, dot.'"

"I'm afraid I have nothing so exciting to relate," Willoughby said. "I talked to more people than Ken, six out of the twelve names allotted, but none of them knew anything about a fly wallet or a bamboo rod, and I took them at their word. Sean, you look far away. Did you have any better luck than we did?"

# CHAPTER NINETEEN

# The Elixir of Life

Sean had been gaining mileage but losing heart by the time he found the turnoff to the last residence on his list. The property, called Typey Acres, belonged to a character actor who raised polo ponies and had made a career impersonating blueblood politicians on the screen. His name was Carson Bostic and he was the kind of person, in person, who you knew had to be somebody, even if you didn't know who that was. Sean had met him once, at a Fourth of July party, and remembered a man with silver hair who looked taller than his six feet one, who had a sly sense of humor and a toothy smile and whose voice was as deep as a midnight river.

The single-story cabin, situated on a height of land overlooking the silver winding of the Madison, wasn't as ostentatious as many of the log mansions in the valley, and the truck in the drive was older than most, and the man who opened the door was dressed in pajamas at 4 p.m. The face was craggy and haggard, the gone-white hair was unkempt, but the eyes were a cold steel blue and they looked into Sean's, unblinking, then past him.

"Seventy-five FJ40," he said. "When a Land Cruiser lived up to the name."

"Close. It's a seventy-six."

"Are you one of those pricks from AMC who was sent here to get me to sign on as the vice president in the *Beltway* pilot? I'll tell you what I told them last time. You can't pay me enough money to play one more goddamn glad-hander, but I'll sniper one from a rooftop for scale."

"Would someone from AMC drive an FJ40?" Sean said. He matched Bostic's height, but knew if he stood down even an inch that he'd have the door shut in his face.

"Yeah. That's exactly what one of those pricks would drive."

"Would it have the blood of last year's elk in the back?" The elk part was a lie, but it might lift him out of the prick category.

The laugh was a low rumble.

"Come on in. I don't give a shit what your business is, but you sound like good company. What do you want to drink? I just opened the place so I don't have any wine. I left half a case of an '82 Pomerol in the cellar the first year I was here and all the bottles froze. An '82!"

"Did you drink it?"

His face looked stricken. Then broke into a grin.

"Of course I drank it. I had the son of the maharaja of Sonepur here with two women from his harem, they were as beautiful as sunset from my back porch. He said it was the best Bordeaux he'd ever had, and he'd had a 2010 Château Lafleur the night before."

"Hindus have harems?"

"All rich men have harems, they just call them personal assistants. He told me he had seven women, but times being what they were, he'd pared the traveling retinue to two, one for himself and one for his largesse. I guess even the sons of maharajas feel the pinch. Next thing you know, he'll have to fly without anyone to screw. Good fisherman, though. Brought me a piece of the rock Jim Corbett hid behind when he shot the Thak Man-Eater in 1937, up on the Mahakali River. Are you familiar with a book called *Man-Eaters of Kumaon*?"

Sean wasn't.

"Corbett hunted down man-eating tigers and leopards, the locals put him right up there on a plane with the gods. Schoolkids sing songs in his honor in that part of India. I lobbied anyone who would listen to fund a biopic, but I kept hearing you can't have a white guy be a hero in a movie set in India. I tried to explain that only his skin was white, that Corbett's family was four generations in India and the British Raj sniffed at him like he had an odor. But the guy from the one studio that expressed interest dug in his heels. Could Corbett maybe be played by an Indian? Could the tiger be rehabilitated and live happily ever after? I told him to suck on my dick. I have a bottle of Selección de Maestros ten-year-old rum in the cabinet. *Gostoso,* as they say in Portuguese. Quite tasty. We'll drink it in my fly-tying room."

Sean had heard that the actor was a fly fisherman and soon saw that for himself, for the room that Bostic led him to was stacked three shelves high with multidrawered storage boxes housing a various ilk of fur and feathers, each drawer neatly labeled. A brass-fitted HMH vise squatted on the table, a minuscule dry fly clamped in its jaws.

"I didn't know *Baetis* mayflies ran that small."

"The farther you go up the river, the smaller. This is a size twenty-four." Bostic handed Sean a snifter of a deep copper-colored rum. "Are you a fly tier, Mr.—?"

"Stranahan. Sean Stranahan. Yes, I am." He sipped the rum.

"Why, I've heard of you. Damn it, man, I have one of your paintings in the guest bedroom. Love it. I'll show you."

They climbed stairs and Bostic showed him. It was a murky oil with dead snags jutting from the surface of Quake Lake, where a 6.5 on the Richter scale had bitten off half a mountainside and slid it into the Madison River. A haunting piece, for the slide had buried twenty-eight people. Seeing old paintings was like seeing long-lost children, and Sean thought the oil had stood the test of their separation. It wasn't one that he would have chosen to look at just before turning out the lights, though.

"I sold that piece to Charlie Strean," Sean remembered. "From San Francisco. He has a house up in the Sundance development."

"Yes, you did. And he can't shoot pool for crap."

"You won it in a game of pool?"

"I played a hustler in a movie about Willie Mosconi that went straight to video. I know my way around a table. I also know how to look like I don't know my way around a table."

"What was your side of the bet?"

"I put up a Browning Sweet Sixteen over and under. A Belgium Browning, the best."

"I'm glad to see that my painting was worth something."

"Alcohol may have inflated its value. But I liked it. I wanted it. I sunk the eight and I took it. That's pithy enough for a gravestone."

Carson Bostic smiled. They really were white teeth.

"So you've seen my lair. You've drunk my liquor. You don't seem to give a shit that I'm a household name. Why are you here? I don't mean to pry, but I have things to do today, like take another nap."

"I'm here because of Freida Toliver."

"Freida Toliver?" He repeated the name. An expression of genuine perplexity crossed his face, but then, he was an actor.

"The woman who died in the grizzly bear den," Sean prompted.

"Oh, sure. I heard about that. A tragedy."

"She made elk antler chandeliers. You have one in your dining room. You didn't win that shooting pool, did you?"

"No." They were standing and Bostic brought his face within a foot of Sean's, close enough that it blurred. "You have to understand, someone in my position gets hit up for this and that all the fucking time. I don't volunteer my friends, my connections, to just anybody. So, sure, I knew Freida. Happy?"

*Connections?*

Sean told him why he'd come, the real reason. It had been the agreed-upon strategy, working on the assumption that the person who gave Freida Toliver the fly wallet didn't know its provenance, and therefore would have no reason to deny having owned it. Bostic had poured two more rums and they were back in the tying room in chairs to sip them.

Bostic dropped his chin onto steepled fingertips.

"I don't know anything about this Hemingway stuff. Freida's a talker, was a talker, but that name never came up in any context. But it's intriguing. You ever find that trunk and there's any of his scribbling in it, even if it's written in shit on toilet paper, you come to me. There's a movie in this and it can't be any worse than the others made from his books."

Bostic clamped a new hook in the vise and threaded a bobbin. His voice was even.

"Do you know who might be taking over her trade?"

"You mean the antler business?" Sean said.

The actor looked curiously at him, then pursed his lips. "What to tie? What to tie?" he said under his breath. He pulled on magnifying glasses and wound thread onto the hook. "I'm going to ask you a serious question, man to man. Would you begrudge a person stepping outside the law to perform an act of kindness for his fellow man?"

"I suppose that would depend if anyone else was hurt by it."

"No one would be hurt."

"Then I wouldn't have a problem."

Bostic dubbed a body on the hook, then added tiny upright wings. Sean thought that anything he might say would be wrong, so he waited. Bostic used a needle to apply a drop of lacquer to the head, then he sat back.

"We'll just let this dry," he said. Again, he looked at Sean with curiosity. It was a small room, and the silence grew in it.

"You really don't know, do you?"

"I guess not."

"That chandelier in the dining room, how much do you think I paid for it?"

"Three thousand dollars."

"You must have a copy of her ledger."

Sean nodded.

"How much do you figure it would go for in one of the artsy-fartsy stores in Big Sky? Same size, same quality of craftsmanship."

"I have no idea," Sean said.

"Try nineteen ninety-nine. So ask yourself, why would I pay an extra thousand for Freida's chandelier? Do I look like a soft touch to you, a patron of the local arts?"

"No."

"How many names are on that list of yours?"

"Around fifty."

"That's more than I thought, but I'm not surprised. You can't go to a dinner party in this valley without poking your eye out on an antler tine, and at least half are hers."

*He's enjoying making me wait,* Sean thought. *Say as little as you can and let him enjoy himself.*

"You're wondering why I'm telling you this. I'm telling you because you look like a smart fellow and there's money to be made in a vacuum. Because I'd like to see somebody pick up where she left off, and the sooner the better. I didn't open up this place in April because the fishing was good."

"Why did you?"

Bostic laughed, a short bark. "I like a man who can sit on a small pair and not give himself away. You want to know so bad you're wetting your pants. I could spit in your face and I'd still have to use a pry bar to get your ass off my chair."

"Thanks for the rum," Sean said. "It was gostoso." He stood, taking a gamble.

"Don't be so fucking touchy."

Bostic made a show of exhaling his breath. He gave Sean the crooked smile he gave to the camera. "Okay, okay. I'm an asshole. Everybody seems to agree on that point. Drink some more rum with me. You look ridiculous standing there."

Sean sat in the chair. "What was the extra thousand dollars you were paying her for?"

"Finally, an intelligent question." Bostic leaned forward over his tying desk and pulled out one of the dozens of tiny drawers in the plastic work cabinets. He placed a small reclosable plastic bag on the fly-tying table. Inside were tan wafers about the size of a nickel. "You're a hunter, what are we looking at?"

"Elk antler shavings." Sean was remembering the baggie Etta Huntington had shown him before brewing tea from the shavings and the taste of her when they'd kissed after drinking it. Had it worked? It hadn't not worked.

Bostic was nodding. "Viagra on the hoof. For most people that's the end of the story, Chinese octogenarians sipping tea through the hairs of their Fu Manchus, trying to scare a little blood into their dicks. But antler has been used in traditional medicines since the Han dynasty."

Bostic held up one finger after another as he spoke. "Arthritis, cartilage restoration, muscle growth, mood enhancement, medicine for your ticker, stimulation of the immune system, reduced tumor growth, you name it, there's a double-blind test backs it up. Or at least some of it. Fuck, man, the stuff's been banned by the NFL and Major League Baseball. Why? Because it contains human growth hormone. Self-medication with antler juice isn't just grasping at straws."

"Freida was your supplier?" Sean said. "The extra thousand was for this stuff?"

"No, not this stuff. This *stuff*"—he emptied the baggie of wafers onto the table—"isn't much better than sawdust. It wouldn't lift your dick to a forty-five-degree angle, let alone reduce your PSA count. That's because it's cut from hardened antler, what you see on an elk in the fall, and contains the least amount of nutrients. What you're looking for, for maximum benefit, is the velvet antler, which is the fastest-growing animal substance on earth. A bull elk you see in July, those fuzzy-looking antlers, that's white gold."

He opened a different drawer and removed a vial of gel capsules the size of kidney beans.

"These are from a commercial red deer farm in New Zealand. They saw the antlers off, dry them, and grind them into a powder. Controlled conditions, supervision by a veterinarian. I had a friend from down under fly over for a visit to make sure it wasn't being cut with baby powder or rat droppings."

"So this is better than the hard antler?"

"Yes. But it's overprocessed and can't begin to compare to antler that is consumed raw, right after harvest, or flash frozen after being cut. Raw, of course, that's almost impossible to come by unless you know an elk rancher. But that would be domesticated elk, fenced elk, and I want wild elk. What I'm looking for, what Freida had for her select clients, was vacuum-packed velvet taken from the tips of antler tines from wild Rocky Mountain elk."

He stood, walked out of the room. Sean heard the refrigerator door open. The plastic package Bostic brought back looked like it contained a finger sausage and was ice cold to the touch.

"That's more valuable to me than gold, frankincense, and myrrh," Bostic said, placing it on the table. "Freida told me she was going to bring some by this weekend. That's why I drove up from Napa, nine hundred miles sitting on my hemorrhoids. She said it was the dregs from last summer's supply. She wouldn't have any new product available until July. I told her I'd take whatever she had left and place an advance order for the new."

He flicked a finger on one of the small drawers of the fly-tying chest. "I have five one-hundred-dollar bills in here waiting to change pockets. That's why I invited you into my house. I was hoping you'd taken over the pipeline."

"How much is this piece worth?"

Bostic weighed the package in his hand. "Three ounces? Two hundred fifty an ounce. Do the arithmetic."

He made a face. "The cost isn't here nor there to me. Money isn't that much of a factor when you have stage three prostate cancer. I can use penile suppositories or intracavernous injection if I want to get it up, but I'm really not concerned about my sex life. I just want to get some quality back in everyday living, stick around long enough to catch a few more trout on dry flies and see my grandchildren grow up. The doctors have tried radiation and hormone therapy, that's the standard one-two punch, and the tumors aren't spreading"—he rapped his knuckles on the tabletop—"but cancer's like a whore in Havana. You pay her off and she keeps coming back." He stopped, shrugged. "You think this is all voodoo. I probably would, too, if I could piss a five-foot rainbow off the stern of a boat. But when you've gone down the road far enough to see the end, and it isn't a pretty way to go, you start grasping." He made his right hand into a fist and squeezed it so that his forearm veins stood out. "You grasp hold of whatever hope you can."

"How did you get hooked up with Freida?"

"Same way I met you. She knocked on the door. Asked me if I wanted to buy a chandelier. Mind now, she wasn't out to make a killing selling antler velvet. She used it herself because she had arthritis so bad it was getting so she couldn't work or ride a horse. It made a difference in her life, so she wanted to pass the word and maybe make a buck doing it, and the third or fourth time she came she found a way to work it into conversation. If you bit, fine, if you didn't, that was okay, too. But if you bit, then the price of the chandelier went up thirty percent. The chandelier went down on the books as a sale. The velvet didn't."

"That's money laundering."

"I call it not drawing attention to yourself. Anyway, a thousand dollars took you a few weeks in, until you could judge whether it was doing you any good. After that, if you wanted more, it was a cash transaction off the books. Or a swap. She traded three ounces of velvet for a painting she saw hanging in the dining room once. She came across as a little mousey, some of that self-effacing deference Indians wear like a mask, but there was more to her than you thought. You got to know her, she was a shrewd woman."

He leaned back in the chair. "Why am I telling you this?" Talking to himself, removing the second fly from the vise and clamping another hook.

"How did she get the antler?"

"Don't know. Not a question you ask."

"There's no legal hunting of elk in July. It would have to be shot out of season."

"Like I said, I never asked. Here," Bostic said. He held out his cupped hand. In the center of his palm were the two tiny mayfly imitations. "What you do is wade the river at the second island above the Slide Inn. You'll have to put your big boy pants on and you'll need a staff. You manage to cross without drowning, there's a slick about a hundred feet up from the tip of the island. That's where the flies come off. An overcast morning's best, but I don't have to tell you that."

He turned back to the vise, started wrapping thread.

"I'll let you see yourself out. You can thank me later."

———

When Sean finished his recitation, Ken caught the attention of Vic Barrows for a second round. Sean saw Willoughby studying the flies hooked to a sheepskin patch that was safety-pinned above the buckle set on his hat.

"I appear to have lost an olive crystal bugger," Willoughby said. "No matter, my own fault for putting it there."

He put the hat down as the drinks arrived. "I now know what Martha Ettinger meant when she said you were a man who would step in shit even if there was only one horse in the pasture."

"So what does 'Typey Acres' mean?" Winston scrolled quotation marks with his fingers.

"And this would be apropos of what, Ken?" Willoughby said.

"Nothing. I'm curious."

Sean nodded. "He said it meant a good polo horse. If a horse was typey, it possessed the right proportions."

Willoughby frowned thoughtfully at his beer. "This narrows the field."

"You're a step ahead of me," Sean said.

"Start with human nature. Freida Toliver likes to barter. She did so with Etta Huntington, also Carson Bostic. But not with just anyone. You had to have established a friendship, or at minimum a friendly acquaintanceship. So I think we can eliminate the names of people who paid a fair price and simply bought her chandeliers outright, and narrow it to those who overpaid or who she visited more times than necessary for installation. Thanks to the ledgers you have provided, they are now easy to identify. If you will hand over your lists, I can do the weeding while we finish these excellent drafts."

———

Etta Huntington was standing on her porch. She froze as the Land Cruiser's headlights illuminated one tree and then the next as they searched up the drive.

"You caught me looking at the stars," she said.

"What do they mean tonight?"

"Nothing," she said. "Not a single thing. Do you know what negative capability is?"

Sean stepped onto the porch beside her. He said he didn't.

"It's the ability to wonder at the world without wondering why. Like touch without thought, like when you make love. It's one of the best therapies I know."

"Making love or not thinking about it?"

"Both."

"About that, Etta."

She began to shake her head even as he reached out to her. "Don't touch me," she said. "If you're going to say what I think you are, then I don't want you to touch me."

"Etta."

"'Etta' what? 'Etta, I won't be seeing you again'? 'Etta, I've found someone else'?"

"It's just that—"

"It's her, isn't it?" She let out a breath. "Of course it's her."

"She invited me to move in until I get the walls up on my house."

"How convenient for you."

"It just happened. We were involved before."

"And she left you. And now she's changed her mind. And I'm out of the picture. Just like that."

She was right, and anything he said would be wrong.

"Tell me one thing. What were we these past few weeks? Going out to look for my Cindy in the Milky Way. Going back to bed and making love. That was real, at least I thought it was real. It felt real. Silly me."

The favor he'd come for was not going to get any easier to ask if he waited. When he told her what he wanted, she shook her head.

"For her? How dare you ask that?"

"No, for bait." He told her why, the bones of it.

"Sure. What use for it will I have without you to share it with? Just come in and make yourself at home. You should know your way around by now. We've only had sex in almost every room in the house."

So he followed her inside and she found the baggie in the freezer and handed it to him, avoiding his eyes.

"Thank you. This doesn't mean we can't be friends, Etta. We can still Skype."

She met his crinkled-up eyes, and he listened to her laugh softly in spite of herself.

"You don't forget anything, do you?"

This time when he reached for her, she allowed him to pull her to his side. She rested her head against his chest as he ran his hand over her hair. They stood like that for a while.

"Go now," she'd said. "You think I'll see you off with a kiss, and I won't. You made your choice. It has consequences."

A tear fell from her right eye. She'd once told him that she sat on the right side of people so they wouldn't be looking at the stump of her right arm, and that she had learned to cry out of her right eye so that no one could see.

"I'll miss you, Etta."

"You bet you will."

# CHAPTER TWENTY

# The Top of the World

There are places in the Rocky Mountains where the rivers flow north, serpentining through lush valleys with the mountains enameled in distant snows, where the spring creeks are as smooth as glass and dimpled with rising trout. They are places where the eye follows the flight of the bluebird and the ear the song of the meadowlark, and it is so serene that you would want to die here, although death in such country seems very far away.

Then, too, there are places in the Rockies where the rivers flow east, foaming and pummeling through hard rock walls, where the dipper bird dives into the whitewater for insect larvae and crows caw and the trees are like spears, and the peaks above them are like the points of spears, and loom close and forbidding. They are places where you wouldn't want to die but can't help thinking about it, for death in such country seems quite close at hand.

It was along a river in one of these hard, uncaring places where Sean thought his dark thoughts. He idled the Land Cruiser across a bridge constructed of oiled timbers and pulled up to the locked gate marked by the X on his map. He switched off the engine and stepped into the sound of the river. He zipped his jacket against the chill.

It had seemed like a good idea last night, after he'd left Etta's house and was driving home, to save gas and time and simply call the names on the condensed list that Patrick Willoughby had compiled of Freida Toliver's clients. Martha Ettinger had once told Sean that he could charm a snake over the phone, and in any case several of the residences on the list were more than a hundred miles from Bridger, so there was a logistical aspect to consider.

A man's voice answered the first number on the list.

"Howling Wolf Guest Ranch. Bill Shaunnessey speaking."

Sean had offered his name and said he'd been a friend and associate of the late Freida Toliver, and that he was trying to reach out to her clients and assure them that her business would continue, should they have any problems with chandelier repair or installation, or be in need of any other services Freida offered.

And had waited.

Sean imagined he could hear the breathing on the end of the line. Then: "I'm very sorry to hear about your friend's passing. But I don't own one of her chandeliers. I think you're trying to reach Peter Jackson. He rented a cabin from me for a couple of summers. I do recall an antler chandelier. He made me an offer on the cabin and I sold it to him."

"Do you have a number for him?"

Sean heard a short laugh, almost a bark.

"To my knowledge he's never had phone service. There's no cell reception up or down the Clarks Fork for miles. He used to make calls from the landline at the ranch house. That's why you have this number."

"The Clarks Fork? In Montana?" Sean was sure the number he'd dialed had a Wyoming area code.

"Not that Clarks Fork. We're on the Clarks Fork of the Yellowstone, in Wyoming. We're a few miles outside Cooke City, just across the state border from Montana."

"You say he used to live on your place. Does he no longer live in the cabin, then?"

"I sold the cabin, not the land under it. He trailered the logs to a piece of property he bought from an adjoining ranch. Nailed it back together himself. Bought the table and chairs that went with the place, oil lanterns, even a tatty old mount of a wolverine. I sold him the Crawford stove, too, quite the relic; he took everything but the fire."

"He must have really wanted to keep the cabin as it was."

"I suppose. It isn't far from here, just a couple acres up on Froze-to-Death Creek and not the main creek, just a side shoot you could jump across. There's nothing up there—no electricity, plumbing, nothing. Just an old man who thinks he's writing the great American novel, of which I doubt he's written a word. Oh, and a cat. Can't forget the cat. He calls his place 'the Top of the World.' It isn't the top of anything."

"So you still talk to him?"

"You ask a lot of questions for a chandelier maker."

"I'm sorry. I know this is an intrusion. But he and Freida had become friends and I'm in the area today. I thought I'd reach out to him."

"Now I really don't know who you're talking about. The Peter Jackson I know doesn't have friends. He could get on a jag and talk your ear off, used to hold forth on all sorts of subjects in the bars in Cooke. Told me he'd been a college professor back in the Midwest somewhere. American and Spanish literature. Said he was Cuban on his father's side, but you wouldn't know it to look at him. Walked around quoting Kipling, Keats, Shakespeare, Gabriel García Márquez, you name it, he could recite it. English, Spanish, French, whatever. But he was one of those people, the first time you meet him, you sit at his feet because he's seen some of the world and he's interesting. You bump into him a second time, you make an excuse for leaving the bar. Good to have around the ranch, though. He could mend fence, fix the sump pump, your basic jack of all trades. I can put up with a lot of hot air if it means you don't have to call the plumber."

Sean had asked for directions to Peter Jackson's cabin and got them.

That had been three hours ago, a long hundred and thirty miles ago. Sean opened the rear door of the Land Cruiser to change out of his tennis shoes and lace up his boots. In this part of the world, spring was a source of water or something that you wound like a watch. You had winter, and then you had mud. There was no in between.

Sean walked out onto the bridge. Under the piled timbers the river galloped like a horse with his tail caught on white fire. To the west, straight up the corridor of the river, the perfect spire of Pilot Peak rose like a gun sight. Sean pointed an imaginary rifle and pulled the trigger. Then he skirted the gate and started up the two-track to find the cabin at the Top of the World.

# CHAPTER TWENTY-ONE

# The Anthill Tiger

The road climbed through forest and meadow, Sean's breath forming dissipating puffs along the walls of the evergreens. Too early for many wildflowers, although the odd clumps of sage were greening. But the peace was only a veneer, broken by the shrill bickering of male bluebirds staking out territory, and Sean hiked with the heightened alertness he always summoned in grizzly country, a little anxious, but for half a mile or so without a moment's unease. Now he stopped, feeling a tightening in his chest, and became aware of his breathing. The tightness went away but not the feeling of unease. He looked around and felt the isolation of the place. He looked up at the bands of buff-colored cliffs that towered to the south, then down at his boots. It had rained earlier in the morning, softening the mud so that it registered tracks, and for some time he'd been following the trail of a house cat that was perambulating the road. Cats are perfect trackers, placing their rear feet directly into the prints made by their front paws, as this one had done. But something was odd about the track, and it was only after following it for another dozen yards that he realized the cat's stride indicated a very small animal, whereas the size of the paw prints belonged to a larger one. All wildcats have outsized paws compared to their domestic cousins, and Sean wondered if he was following a bobcat or a lynx kitten. Perhaps the mother was nearby, her green eyes fixed on him, and though there was no danger to be apprehended by a bobcat or a lynx, this was what had heightened his sensitivity to his surroundings.

Whatever the cause, the feeling ebbed away and he followed the road into a strip of the wood that still held patchy snow, and then, the trees thinning, he came in sight of the cabin. It was set in the middle of several cleared acres, with blackened logs that had been rechinked, giving it a striped appearance. A stone chimney on the side of the cabin exhaled like a dying dragon, the smoke hanging low over the road. Old-fashioned wooden snowshoes in a teardrop design hung from ten-penny nails driven into the log walls. Sitting on the stoop in a folding lawn chair was a man with snow-white hair and a beard, which registered before Sean could make out the features of his face. The man was running a patch through one of the bores of a double-barreled shotgun. He looked incuriously at Sean approaching, then down as he ran the patch through the other bore. He dropped two shells into the chambers and brought the barrels up to engage the action. The shotgun closed with a solid thunk.

"You just ruined Tatie's hunt," he said. "She was stalking a blue grouse that flushed when it heard you coming."

Sean put the man's age as late sixties, but he seemed older the closer Sean approached. His hair was lank and pasted to his head, with unhealthy-looking streaks of grayish yellow. The skin of his sagging cheeks was sallow and blotchy, and the hands that rested on the shotgun were heavily spotted and curled like claws around the oiled stock. He had been a big man once, a Saint Nicholas of a man, Sean imagined, with heavy broad shoulders and an ample belly, and was still the shell of one. The black-and-white-checked flannel shirt he wore had once served a much larger body. Now it wrapped around him like a flag and was held in position by a length of thick rope square-knotted at the waist. He was wearing moccasins as broad as kit beaver tails, and as he rose, the bores of the gun briefly traced a diagonal line across Sean's torso. Intelligent hound dog eyes looked Sean up and down. They were sad like hounds' eyes, too, world-weary and cloudy. Haunted eyes that saw winter coming.

"Have you been hunting?" Sean asked. He heard his voice as if from some distance away.

"Not for years," the man said. It was a midwesterner's voice, serious, and without much music in it. "I do pay my neighbors a visit to shoot gophers. You can't coax the DNA out of a black-footed cat. I tried feeding her cat food, but she likes to crack bones and drink the blood." His eyes drifted past Sean as he called out, "Here, Tatie. Kitty-kitty-kitty." Sean turned round as a small, spotted cat with a very short tail darted past him. The man sat back down and the cat leapt onto his lap. The man stroked its back, the cat disappearing under his hand.

"In Botswana they call it *miershoop tier*," he said. "That translates as anthill tiger. They are nocturnal and sleep in abandoned termite mounds. According to San legend, they can kill a giraffe by piercing its jugular vein. That, I believe, is folklore, but it is a testament to their ferocity. Tatie only weighs three pounds, but I have seen her drive away a black bear that climbed onto this porch."

The anthill tiger poked its head out from under the hand and fixed Sean with slitted eyes. It opened its mouth in a silent hiss. The canine teeth, like the paws, were very large.

"How did you get her?"

"My last safari to Africa. We were in Tanzania, up on Selous Game Reserve. That was the middle of nowhere then and I suppose it still is. And we were on the road and this tout, a Mohammedan from the Sudan, stepped in front of the lorry so that we had to stop. He was a snake oil salesman—this tincture for your spleen, this for your liver— and he had animals for sale. Had a monkey, had a rock python draped around his shoulders, a few macaws in bamboo stick cages, and then he had this tiny cat, just a kitten really, that had been on the road with him all the way from Namibia. All the animals except the snake were cooped up in cages scarcely bigger than they were, bugs swarming around their eyes, terrible conditions. I bought the kitten against my guide's wishes, but she was skin and bones and I've always had a soft spot for cats. I intended to release her, better to have her die in the teeth of a wild dog than to waste away in that cage. But she had spunk and I couldn't just abandon her. I had a friend in the U.S. embassy in Mombasa who pulled strings for me. Luckily, a black-footed cat looks enough like a house cat to pass muster. It wouldn't have worked with any other African wildcat, too obvious it was a native species. It took six months before my friend could get her out of quarantine and ship her to America, and then it was another six months before she came out of a culvert pipe in my backyard to do anything except eat a few bites before disappearing again. I consider gaining her trust to be one of the great accomplishments of my life."

The object of this accomplishment had climbed up the front of the man's shirt to perch on his shoulder. Four eyes, two with rounded pupils, regarded Sean with unveiled suspicion.

Sean asked the man if he was Peter Jackson and told him why he was there, rushing to get it out, the proximity of the shotgun hurrying the words. At the mention of Freida Toliver's death, Sean watched the blood drain from the man's face. Clearly he had not heard, and now, knowing, he appeared unable to absorb any detail of the news beyond the circumstance of the tragedy.

"Freida," he said, repeating her name several times. "In the den of a bear." He shook his head. "Those the gods can't break . . ." His voice trailed away.

He held out the shotgun. "Please set it on the table." Then without a further word he walked into the dim interior of the cabin. The cat, still perched on his shoulder but facing backward, with his eyes fixed on Sean, flexed his whiskers and hissed.

Sean bared his own teeth in response and glanced at the weapon, which was rose-and-scroll engraved with *W & C Scott* etched in a banner on the action. The London address of the maker was etched into the barrels and the stock had been carved from gorgeously fig-ured walnut. Sean suspected it was worth a great deal of money, per-haps more than the cabin. The "table" the man had indicated was nothing more than two-by-tens supported by opposing sawhorses. Nearby was a chopping block with an ax sticking into it and a pair of leather gloves folded neatly on top. Sean noted that the sawdust on the floorboards held swirling comb marks from being broomed. He set the gun down on the table and went through the open door into what turned out to be a kitchen. It was a gloomy space, with small six-paned windows, the furniture consisting of slat-back wood chairs and a rough-hewn pine table studded with candles that had dripped pools of wax. A vintage blue enamel woodstove commanded the room. On a kitchen counter were mismatched utensils and a plastic five-gallon container half full of water.

Jackson poured two coffees from a metal flake coffeepot and set it back down on a warming burner. Sean brought the cup to his lips; the coffee was piping hot.

"It's the way Hopkins made it," Jackson said. "Bitter as a turnip, but we must honor the Hophead."

Sean remembered the reference from the short story of Hemingway's he'd read in high school.

"Like the coffee in 'Big Two-Hearted River,'" he said.

"Yes, you know it? It wasn't the Two-Hearted that Nick Adams fished. It was the Fox. But that didn't have the ring. It's like the Clarks Fork. I call it the Cold Hearted River because it carries the feel of the country better. And over the years many people's hearts have grown cold here, died in the mountains or drowned in the currents."

"Did Hemingway call it the Cold Hearted River?"

"He's said to have been the one who christened it. It was dear to his heart, everything you can see in any direction. 'A cockeyed wonderful country,' he called it. Most people don't realize how important it was to him, both personally and as a writer. He spent five summers and autumns at the dude place up the valley. It was the L Bar T then, this was in the 1930s. Fished, rode horses, hunted bighorn sheep on Pilot Peak, even hunted grizzly bear. He finished *A Farewell to Arms* here and wrote some of *For Whom the Bell Tolls,* parts of *Death in the*

*Afternoon* and *To Have and Have Not*. Many of his best short stories as well. The original manuscript for 'The Light of the World,' which he wrote here, brought $127,000 at Christie's in 2000. I ought to know. I bid on it.

"Mind now"—Jackson lifted a finger—"when I say here, I mean this cabin. I numbered the logs and rebuilt it exactly as it was. The artifacts are, or were, Hemingway's. A few—the elk mount in the study, for example—I've duplicated to the extent of my means, back in the years when I had means. The cabin originally had an antler chandelier, which the property owner sold. That's why I bought the one from Freida. When I moved the cabin here, I had to sell it. No electricity. I was sad to see it go."

"Who did you sell it to?"

"Why, back to Freida, of course. Traded for some of her sweet elixir. Would you like to see the rest of the house?"

Sean absorbed this information as he walked into the "study," which, in contrast to the dreary kitchen, was light and airy, with its north- and south-facing walls supervised by, respectively, the shoulder mount of the bull elk Jackson had mentioned, and a full-curl ram. One bay of windows revealed the bands of cliffs that rose in back of the cabin, while the largest picture window on the west-facing wall was pierced by the towering spire of Pilot Peak and the neighboring fist of volcanic rock called the Index. Jackson put the cat down on the floor. It darted through the open doorway back into the kitchen and was out the cracked front door. Sean drew up beside Jackson to admire the view.

"I prefer the original name for Index," Jackson said. "The prospecting company that founded Cooke City called it Dog Turd Peak. I'm told it looks like one from a certain angle."

Under the window stood a rolltop desk with chips in the cherry-wood veneer. On the pullout leather writing surface, which was gray and worn thin with stiff gray hairs sticking out of it, stood a vintage manual typewriter, similar to the one Sean had seen in Margarethe

Harris's study in Michigan. Lines of typewriting were visible on the sheet of onionskin paper that was rolled onto the platen. Beside the typewriter, several other typed pages were weighted down by a fist-sized chunk of copper ore.

"Is this Hemingway's typewriter?" Sean asked.

"There's no proof it is, though it came into my possession with the cabin. Papa worked on many typewriters—an Underwood Standard, various Coronas, and, certainly, the Royal Quiet Deluxe model identical to this one. The scrap of lesser kudu neck hide it's resting on is similar to one in Hemingway's home in Cuba."

Sean wanted to see what had been written, but resisted the temptation. He didn't want to be seen as prying.

Instead, he studied the mantel on the other side of the room. It was imposing, built of smooth river rocks that would have taken a very strong back to carry, and held the embers of the morning's fire. Over it, perched on a ledge built from a slab of black rock, was the full-body mount of a snarling wolverine, with pebble eyes and cobwebs stretching across its open maw.

Sean lowered his eyes from the petrified beast to a coffee table that stood on ornately carved cat's paws. The table's surface was polished to gleaming and carefully arranged with small tools and bric-a-brac. Many objects were of African origin or theme—a set of curved warthog tusks, rifle cartridges as long as Panatela cigars, miniature wood carvings of cheetah, lion, and rhino. In addition, there was a brass-handled magnifying glass such as Sherlock Holmes would use to solve a riddle, an eyeglass case opened to show wire-rimmed spectacles, a skeleton key, a carved bowl filled with stones, and, underneath a cover of heavy glass, a scattering of photos, some in sepia tone, some black and white.

The photos looked to have been taken on two African safaris separated by a decade or more, for in the black-and-whites Jackson appeared as a darkly complected, strikingly handsome man who could have sold Marlboro cigarettes on highway billboards. In the later ones, his face was bloated and he was going gray with a stubble beard. A haunted look had begun to gather at the corners of his eyes. Sean studied the photos—Jackson standing with his arm around a woman who was nearly as tall as he was, with fair hair in loose curls and the sharp features of a young Lauren Bacall, tents with acacia trees and Kilimanjaro for a backdrop, the obligatory trophies expired on the savanna, dark stains on their muzzles from coughing up lung blood.

Jackson pointed a thick finger, drawing Sean's attention to a photo of a young man with dark curls. "That's Harry Selby beside the lorry. He was my professional hunter, the best in Africa. Selby was Philip Percival's protégé. Percival guided Theodore Roosevelt's 1910 expedition and later Ernest Hemingway's two safaris to Tanganyika. Hemingway called him Pops."

"Has anyone told you that you look like him—Hemingway?"

"Is that a compliment?" Sean detected a note of challenge in the voice.

"It's an observation."

Since entering the room, Sean had the feeling he should be walking with his hands clasped behind his back, that he was not in someone's house but in a carefully constructed memory, where the wheel that is time had ground to a stop many years before.

"I was persuaded against my better judgment to enter the Hemingway look-alike contest in Key West once. I missed out on the 'In Papa We Trust' medallion by a few votes."

"Why was it against your better judgment?"

"Because Hemingway Days is about the caricature. Hemingway the person is among the most misunderstood, vilified, and yet the most celebrated Americans of his generation, and I would venture among the most iconic figures of the twentieth century. He defined the American male, was labeled a misogynist, yet his relationships were with strong women and he championed their accomplishments. He could be shy behind his glasses, or generous and instructive. A bully and a bore, but by and large his friends forgave him his transgressions, because most of the time he was simply the best company you would ever find. His intelligence and enthusiasm were piercing lights to which people couldn't help but gravitate."

Jackson frowned, warming to his subject.

"Today, psychologists might argue that his mood swings were governed by bipolar disorder, and it's been postulated that his bouts of paranoia and occasional grandiose delusions indicate schizophrenia. I would argue that the brain damage he suffered in an airplane crash in Africa was just as crippling to his work. Would he have written more, or written well longer, if he hadn't drunk to excess, or if he'd remained with his first wife, Hadley, had her steadying influence and not been seduced by the fiesta lifestyle foisted upon him by the rich? We'll never know. But I believe his accomplishments are remarkable given his physical and mental challenges. We must always judge the whole man, not one plucked from a moment in history."

At some point it had become a speech, and for Sean a domino had fallen. Jackson's remarks had shown more than a passing knowledge of Hemingway, but that familiarity could be written off as study; the man was, after all, a literature professor. But here was someone absorbed by the personality of the writer, and whose defense of Hemingway sounded a lot like self-defense. Sean felt certain now that the key to the mystery of the artifacts that had cropped up in the Madison Valley was here, at the Top of the World.

"Bill Shaunnessey said that you were a writer also, that you were writing a novel."

"I was a literature professor."

"You weren't a writer?"

"Young man, there is no such thing as a humanities professor who arrives at his station without discovering that his talent does not measure up to his ambition. The desire to create, and the failure to do so, is a prerequisite for the job. You've heard the saying 'Those who can't *do,* teach'? It applies equally across the board of artistic endeavors."

Despite the self-effacement, a measure of pompousness had come into the voice, an attitude of condescension that gave Sean a glimpse inside the carapace. He asked, "Do you live alone up here? I noticed the woman in your photographs. Is she your wife?"

"Virginia *was* my wife. I have outlived two wives, although they come back to visit me frequently. I have a unique ability to summon the dead."

Sean let the odd remark pass. He noticed that Jackson's face held a sheen of sweat, although the room was more cool than warm. For some reason, Jackson had become unsure even as he was asserting the vigor of his personality. Sean decided to play his card.

"Mr. Jackson," he began, and saw the eyes gather focus, as if the man could divine that Sean's next words would be of importance to him. "As you might know, Freida sold more than chandeliers. She sold . . . hope."

Jackson's smile was unsteady. "And . . . did you happen to bring some of that hope with you?"

"I only have this for now." Sean reached into his pocket and drew out the shrink-wrapped package that Etta Huntington had given him.

"I may be able to get more, I'm not certain."

At the sight of the package, Jackson began to pace the room, rubbing his thumbs against his forefingers, a gesture Sean took as a manifestation of avarice.

"Same arrangement as before?" he asked. He had stopped at the coffee table and was picking up one object after another, distractedly examining them before setting them back down.

"I don't know about that. I only have Freida's price, three hundred dollars."

*Make him say it,* Sean thought. *See if he makes an offer.*

"My financial situation is tenuous," Jackson said. "Transporting the timbers and rebuilding this cabin drained what little capital I had, though I don't regret it for an instant. I can only offer what I offered Freida."

"What's that?"

"A piece of Americana. It's worth far more than three hundred dollars."

"You'll have to be specific," Sean said. The second domino teetered.

"Wait here."

Sean caught a glimpse of a cot covered by a green wool blanket as Jackson opened the door to what he presumed was his bedroom. As the door shut behind him, Sean took the two strides to the desk and read the words on the sheet of paper. It was a half page of pica type-writing and he read the passage twice more, trying to memorize the lines by giving them cadence, and was reciting them silently to him-self, looking pointedly out the window at Pilot Peak, when Jackson came back into the room a minute later. In his right hand he clutched an old-fashioned wicker fishing creel with a leather front pocket and an intricate linked-diamonds motif built into the weave. It was beau-tiful and Sean said so.

"It's Salish."

"I didn't know Indians built creels."

"Not many people do. They are among the best ever crafted, mostly early twentieth century, but it isn't for sale." He lifted the lid of the creel and drew out a circular fly reel case. Jackson unzipped the case and removed a fly reel nested in the sheepskin lining. Sean recognized it as a model called the Perfect, made by England's Hardy Brothers. It had a rippled brass reel foot and an agate line guide and was definitely worth more than three hundred dollars, perhaps twice that.

"This is an English-made reel," Sean said. "You called it a piece of Americana."

"Did you not read the etching on the spool?"

Sean read the inscription aloud, and the domino fell.

House of Hardy

By Appointment to HRH the Prince of Wales

Made for Mister Ernest Hemingway

Sean whistled, hoping he wasn't overdoing his reaction. "Do you have the provenance?" he asked. "A traceable serial number, or a letter of transaction?"

"No." Jackson shook his head. "But I'm sure an antiques dealer could determine that the engraving was true to the period."

"That's no proof it belonged to Ernest Hemingway."

Sean saw a sag in the shoulders, the big frame slumping. He realized that Peter Jackson really didn't have much money, and that he was desperate, for the seriousness of his predicament registered plainly on his face.

"How did you meet Freida?" Sean said.

"I met her several years ago, at the antler auction in Jackson Hole. I heard that Korean brokers would be buying velvet, and I thought maybe I could find someone who would part with a little. My health had been in decline—high cholesterol, autoimmune complications, joint wear and tear—the general malaise of age. The problem was that the drugs I was taking had side effects that made it difficult to work. I told you earlier that I was a failed writer. For years I've been trying to rectify that. So I tried a more naturalistic approach. I drank herbal drinks. I ate turtle eggs. I even had testosterone injections. For stamina and vitality, understand. I have a mission in life to complete, and I need the energy to see it through. I had read about the anti-aging properties of antler and wanted to try it."

He said that Freida had a booth where she was selling her chandeliers. He bought one for the rental cabin—he'd had money then—and she'd accepted his offer of a drink. They'd had another drink in her truck camper, an antler tea brewed on her propane burner.

Jackson looked at Sean and shrugged.

"I hadn't made love to a woman in a long time, Mr. Stranahan. As I've told you, I wasn't in the best of health. I didn't know if I could. But I don't delude myself into believing that her tea had anything but a placebo effect. It can take months before one realizes the benefits, so I suppose it was the romance of the situation. In any case, that was the start of it, and the medication has given me a new lease on life. I have macular degeneration and have been able to see better. It's hard to write when you begin to see double, so it's of vital importance to take advantage of the window I've been given, and to do everything in my power to keep it open. This would be of no consequence if it was only for myself, but my work is important to others."

"Who is it important to?"

"Why, many people. Those who have eyes for a sunrise, for example, or for last light on water. Everyone who is moved by art, but especially those who understand the fleeting nature of life, the sad finite song of it. Too few realize that the full living of the time we are given is not a response to be measured or doled out, but instead an opening of one's self, a willingness of the heart. It is for these people I write."

"Did you always pay Freida with antiques or pieces of Hemingway memorabilia?"

"No, I paid cash. As I said, it's not until the last couple years that I fell on hard times."

"What have you bought velvet with, other than money?"

"The paintings that were on these walls. They were the first to go, mostly to Freida. The last time she came here I gave her a fly wallet that had Hemingway's initials on it. She took it, but didn't take much stock in it. I think she thought I was a dreamer on that subject."

"Were you still romantically attached to her?"

"No, that was over long ago. She married a farrier and I wished her the best. We remained friends. It's still hard to believe she's gone."

"Do you have a large collection of antiques?"

"Besides the paintings? I did, but the cupboard is close to bare. I still hold on to a few of the better pieces, like my shotgun. They were to be my nest egg in retirement. Now I know I will never retire and also that I will never again have money. It is a sobering self-assessment. But it is my sacrifice and my calling to finish what I have set out to do. Not to do so would be a sin."

"Mr. Jackson, I will trade you the velvet for this reel, but I would like to see your collection. Perhaps we can do more business in the future."

"I would oblige you, but my more valuable pieces aren't here. Valuable is perhaps not the right word. Distinguished. Historic."

Sean realized that the missing steamer trunk might be separated from him only by the thickness of a bedroom door.

"Perhaps if you let me have a look," he said.

"That is impossible. Even if I was willing to sell, it would take some time to retrieve them. They aren't just lying around. Now I really must get back to work. When may I expect you to call again? Freida said she would have more velvet available in the summer. This is scarcely a month's supply. I really do need it, you understand. It is vital to the mission."

Sean said maybe sooner than later, and asked if there was any other way to get in touch besides a three-hour drive from Bridger. Jackson said no, but he was almost always at the cabin. He hitched into Cooke City every couple weeks for groceries, often with one of the wranglers at the Howling Wolf, but he was always home before dark.

"I used to close down the bars," he said. "But I had to sell my truck and there is too much at stake. Also no money for whiskey."

He turned his back to Sean, indicating that the conversation was over.

Sean said he'd see himself out, and passed through the doorway back into the kitchen. He could hear Jackson padding on his moccasins a few feet behind. On the porch he turned and offered his hand, and the man took it in a powerful grip.

"Goodbye, Mr. Stranahan. Please come again when you have medicine."

Crossing the clearing, Sean looked back to see Jackson standing on the porch, the shotgun cradled in the crook of his left arm. When he turned back to the trail, he saw the cat. It had locked onto a grouse with its teeth on the back of the bird's neck. The grouse was thrashing, thumping its wings, actually lifting the tiny beast off the ground. Dun-colored feathers rose in a cloud over the battle, but the anthill tiger's grip was fast, and as Sean passed the struggling animals, he could hear the thumping of the wings less often.

*"I used to think that November was the best month to die,"* Sean said under his breath. *"It is a gray month. The salmon are dying and the leaves are blown in the river, scattered like petals cast by mourners onto a grave."*

They were the first lines that Sean had read on the sheet of onion-skin, and as he left the victor to his spoils, he recited the passage from memory, picking up where he had left off.

*"But now I think I was wrong. Now, I think, it must be April."*

Then what? What was next? Something about walking on a path with a boy. *Talk, don't think,* Sean said to himself. And in a few strides the rest of it came, the words spilled out in a rush.

*"Don't say such things," the boy said. He was fair-haired and small for his age, though sturdily built.*

*He looks like her, he thought.*

*"I only tell the truth," the man said. "Last year I was leading you to our secret water. Now you are ahead. Soon you will be holding my hand when we wade the deep part. Then I will know it is March, and April coming."*

*"You are being macabre," the boy said.*

*"That is a very big word."*

*"We read an Edgar Allan Poe story. The teacher said he was a master of the macabre."*

*"I wouldn't want to be macabre," the man said. "I only mean to be honest. It is a virtue, you know."*

*"No, you are macabre. And it is spring. Nothing bad can happen in the spring."*

*And the man smiled and forgot to knock wood, and on the path through the cedar swamp, wood was all around, too.*

Sean had always had a memory others remarked upon—good for

detail, precise for rivers and other places of the heart. He knew he might have missed a word or reversed a couple sentences, and there were several subsequent lines he hadn't had time to memorize, but the beginning he was sure of. Back at the gate, he found a pencil in the Land Cruiser and wrote it all down, another domino falling as he drove back over the bridge, looking west, toward Pilot Peak.

# CHAPTER TWENTY-TWO

# Running with Hounds

"**S**o what *is* the best month to die?"

Martha Ettinger sat back in her office chair. She linked her hands behind her head. "I'd go with February," she said, answering her own question. "You're sick of the snow and you're always catching a cold from someone in the office, and it's more winter as far as you can see down the road. Yeah, February gets my vote."

"I don't know," Sean said. "The highest suicide rate is in April."

"That's because in February people are too depressed to act on the urge."

"Fishing can be good in February, Martha. And the crime rate's down, you have to give February that."

"I don't have to give February fiddle-de-dee." Martha shook her head. "This antler thing sounds like a bunch of voodoo to me."

"It isn't voodoo to him, that's what matters."

"I suppose." She leaned forward. "Gigi got back to me about the fingerprints this morning. The partials under the reel seat that you thought could be Hemingway's actually were Hemingway's. She said to tell you she was sorry for the delay. I thought you'd want to know, though I don't know where that gets us."

"It tells us we're not just howling at the moon."

"I suppose." Martha nodded to herself, as if coming to a decision. "Time for me to knock off. You want to take a ride up the valley? I have the key to Freida Toliver's place. Now that her brother's dead, the next of kin is a half-Cheyenne sister from Kentucky, or maybe West Virginia. One of those states where cousins kiss their cousins. She's coming out to lay claim when the estate clears probate at the end of the month. Harold did a once-over, but we never had a forensic team on the premises or made a detailed search. In light of what you're telling me, maybe we should have. The gas and my good company are on the county."

———

So they drove up the valley, and as they topped the Norris Hill and began the descent toward Ennis, Sean told Martha he had a confession to make.

"You saw Etta Huntington."

"You know?"

"Walt was up in Wilsall. A rancher shot his neighbor's pointer because it got into his cattle. He mentioned that he'd seen your rig turning up the Shields River Road. Wilsall. Shields River Road. Crazy Mountains. I can add to three."

"I just went to borrow the antler velvet."

"I told you not to tell me if you saw her."

"I'm telling you because I was saying goodbye to her. I thought you'd want to know."

They drove on in silence, slowing down for the three blocks that comprised Ennis's business district and crossing the span of the Madison River.

"Was it a long goodbye, or did you just stop by for a quickie?" Martha pulled off the pavement onto the shoulder. "This is where the fox had the den last summer, in that field with the llamas. You know, the fox and the kits the *National Geographic* photographer shot for the cover?"

"I saw them," Sean said. "Everybody did."

"Yeah, they did. That pointer the neighbor shot? Its owner put the rancher in the hospital. He told Walt he wouldn't have hit him so hard if he'd only been screwing his wife. But the dog had better bloodlines. This state, you gotta love it."

She closed her eyes. "I'm sorry. I shouldn't have said that about you and Etta. I realize you were involved, that you can't just walk away without being honest with her. And maybe it scares me, the thought of nobody standing between us. It's up to us now if we keep this thing going. And what's going to happen after you get your walls up? I can't move out of my farmhouse. It's my home. And I have animals to consider."

"We're only a few hundred yards apart. We'll work something out."

"Will we?"

That was the question they were still mulling over when they reached the Wolf Creek turnoff.

"It's up about a mile and a half," Martha said. "Harold said there's a sign says 'Elk Creek Creations.'"

"There's no Elk Creek here."

"No, but there's a place where Wolf Creek splits for a hundred yards, so Freida renamed the channel that runs by her house. Makes business sense."

It was a typical home before money came into the valley, a white one-story rancher, a kitchen out of the '50s, a nice big living room furnished with farm auction pieces, with a wing added onto the north end that turned out to be the workshop. Homey, and oddly without a single elk antler chandelier. Not one hanging, anyway.

"And you say she lived here alone?"

"It was one of those marriages where both parties keep their houses and live together off and on. J.C.'s place is up Jack Creek."

Sean's eyes roamed the walls, lingering on the artwork—country pastorals, fox and hounds, and fish and game still lifes.

Martha scratched her throat. "They look like pictures you'd see in a manor house in Yorkshire."

"Have you ever been to a manor house in Yorkshire, Martha?"

"No, but I've seen *Masterpiece Theatre*."

Sean nodded. "Sporting art is a relatively new genre. I have a general appreciation for the period, but this isn't in my wheelhouse. About all I know is that it was denigrated as an inferior art form and didn't become collectible until the 1800s, and then more for its historical insight into the life of the times rather than the quality of the brushwork."

"Humor me. Put a value on, say, that piece." She pointed to a fox-and-hounds oil with a rolling landscape and hunters strung out in the chase. There was some age laddering, but the painting retained vivid colors, the red of the hunters' jackets splashing against the background.

"I wouldn't guess."

"Guess."

Sean stepped closer to see if it was signed. "H. Calvert," he said aloud. "Three thousand to maybe eight. Higher-end if Calvert is a name I should know, but don't."

"But the low end is three thousand dollars?"

"If it's original, and I think it is."

"I count fourteen pieces in this room alone. Would they all be worth three thousand or more?"

"The miniatures might be less, it would depend on the name."

"Still, any way you cut it, Freida Toliver took fifty thousand dollars' worth of art in trade for a few pounds of elk antler velvet."

"That's a small price if you believe it's the fountain of youth. Jackson thinks it will give him a window to complete his life's mission."

"Which is? Remind me."

"The rancher who told me where he lived said Jackson was writing the great American novel. I'm not sure if he was being facetious, or it was something Jackson had told him. I do know he was trying to write. Or at least it looked that way. There was the start of a story in his typewriter."

"Yeah, so you said. The best-month-to-die thing."

"I'd like to run it by Patrick Willoughby. I thought we could drop in at the Liars and Fly Tiers Club later. We're already up the valley."

"Sure. So what are we doing here again, beside art appreciation?"

"You're the one who suggested we come."

"So I did. Let's see what else Freida was up to, besides selling the fountain of youth."

They found little of note, save a baggie of marijuana in a jam jar in Freida's medicine cabinet and six shrink-wrapped packages in her freezer that were the size and shape of Vienna sausages. They each had a date, going back to the previous July, in blue permanent marker.

"Is this what I think it is?" Martha asked.

Sean nodded. "Carson Bostic said she was down to the end of last year's supply. Maybe we should try some."

"Is that what you did with Etta, drink antler tea?"

"I'll take the Fifth. I'm just saying it might make you howl at the moon."

"Officers of the law don't howl at the moon."

"I seem to recall—"

"Hush." She felt her face color with heat.

"Or we could smoke the weed. I'm told it has the same effect."

"You do that. I'll save a cot in the jail."

"You wouldn't."

"Try me. Come on, let's have a look at the workshop."

It was a larger-scale business than Sean would have thought, the workshop occupying an add-on room that was the size of a double garage. Half of the floor space was stacked to the ceiling with shed antlers graded for size, symmetry, color, and species. The rest was occupied by two workbenches, vises with heavily padded jaws, precision drills, and racks of drill bits. There were saws, spools of electric wire— everything needed to turn the raw material into chandeliers, lamp bases, coffee tables, drawer pulls, dog chews, and antler chic whatnot. It told them little about Freida Toliver beyond that she was organized and professional, the mild chaos of her ledgers notwithstanding.

And she was armed.

A gun cabinet in her bedroom held an L.C. Smith double 12-gauge, as well as a Remington .22 semiautomatic and a synthetic-stocked, stainless steel Tikka T3 Lite in .300 Winchester Short Magnum, with a bipod for steady aim and a Leupold eight-power scope. On a velvet-lined shelf in the case stood three marksmanship trophies, one from a state championship turkey shoot in Billings, plus a sterling silver belt buckle with an embossed cartridge on it and Freida's initials.

"Any elk steps within five hundred yards better have written his will," Martha said. She drew back the bolt of the rifle to make sure it was unloaded, and dry fired it. "Nice crisp trigger pull." She nodded and passed the rifle to Sean.

He squinted his eyes, lining up a distant imaginary target.

"Either that, Martha, or . . ." The gun made a click as he pressed the trigger.

"Or what?"

"I was going to say an insurance policy on his antlers."

Martha raised her eyes to question the comment, then she understood. "I always said you were an idiot savant," she said.

"I'll take the savant part," Sean said. "Think about it. The antlers that go into her chandeliers are sheds. We know she buys some and collects them in the spring; that's what she was doing when she died. But how does she get the antlers when they're in velvet a month or two later? I figure she either shoots a bull and saws his antlers off, or she just shoots the antlers off and the elk runs away with a bad headache. She wouldn't need many. A couple big six-points would put her clients in velvet for a year. You're nodding."

"I'm remembering something her husband said. He said Freida was so softhearted she didn't hunt anymore; she just stalked close and counted coup. Chuck was the one who had to stock the freezer with venison."

"Maybe we should check with an elk biologist. See if hunters have reported shooting elk that only had one antler."

"Why one?"

"Chances are the elk would run before she could get another steady shot. She'd have to collect an antler from each elk she lined up in the scope."

Martha nodded. "I see what you're saying. I don't see where it gets us, though."

"I don't know, either. I'm just the idea man."

She nodded absently, chewing for an answer on her lower lip. Then shook her head.

"Let's get out of here," she said. She collected the packages of velvet from the freezer.

"Are you going to take that bag of pot in the bathroom or am I?" Sean said.

"Take it. It could be evidence."

"Of what? Having fun?"

"I'll think of something," Martha said.

# CHAPTER TWENTY-THREE

# The Theory of Icebergs

Kenneth Winston set a squat glass on the fly-tying table, inched it toward Patrick Willoughby, brought it back, and inched it forward again. He circled his fingers above the rim, as if coaxing a genie from the amber liquid.

"You tempt me," Willoughby said, "but I will not be persuaded." He glanced across the table at Sean and Martha. "When you are within shouting distance of fourscore, you become judicious with your bad habits. Alas, cognac and caffeine are among the first fatalities."

"Be that way," Ken said, and took the glass and pushed it to Sean. "You're the whippersnapper at our soiree, drink up and say thanks."

Sean drank and said thanks. It was fabulous brandy. The red that came before it had been fabulous as well, as were the eland steaks served with the wine.

Willoughby bent his eyes to the table, where he studied the scrap of paper with Sean's handwriting.

"You're wondering if this is imitation Hemingway or, dare I say, a page from the master himself? Wouldn't that be pretty?"

"Not to mention," Ken interjected, "that it makes it more likely there actually is a cache of tackle."

Willoughby's nod took in Sean and Martha. "Ken is more interested in the possibility of another Pinky Gillum rod than he is in a lost story from the hand of our country's most famous author."

"Damn straight," Ken said.

"The rancher who sold Peter Jackson the cabin said he was working on the great American novel," Sean said.

Willoughby's brow knotted above his spectacles. "Peter Jackson is this man's name?"

"Yes," Sean said. "I thought I mentioned that at dinner."

"You did, you did. And I thought I'd heard the name before. I have just now drawn the connection. When Hemingway was a newspaperman, he wrote under several pseudonyms. One was John Hadley, which stuck in my mind because he had used his first wife's Christian name. Another was Peter Jackson. It meant nothing when I was doing the research. I'm not altogether sure what it means now."

"It means he was so obsessed with Ernest Hemingway that he took on his name," Ken said.

"Indeed, it does." Willoughby pulled his glasses down and turned his attention back to the paper. "To me, the passage reads as a first page of a short story, rather than a novel. But let's set form aside for the time being. Does the writing itself follow in the style of Hemingway? Sean, while you were in Michigan I reread several of Hemingway's short stories, as well as *The Sun Also Rises,* which I believe is the longer work that best exemplifies his technique. And I would have to say that, yes, this sample does follow Hemingway's example. The writing is unadorned, direct, and musical—short words, deliberate repetition, vivid imagery, an emphasis on nouns with few adjectives, and not a single adverb. And the story, simple on the surface, a man and a boy, presumably his son, walking through the woods, an easy camaraderie between them, an obvious shared love. Yet there is an undercurrent of tension, a foreboding. The Iceberg Theory is at work. There is much under the surface that is unstated. The woman that the boy looks like, who is she? A wife? An old lover? Omission makes the reference stronger.

"Then there is the theme of death so prevalent in Hemingway's canon. What is the best month to die? What month is it now? The

boy, in his innocence, thinking that you live forever. The man knowing you don't. And knowing something else as well that the reader
doesn't. It really is . . . not bad, I think."

"But is it Hemingway?" Sean said.

"That's impossible to say. If we had the actual page, then perhaps
we'd know. But I don't have to tell anyone at this table that the odds
of fingerprints lingering so many decades on onionskin paper are poor.
Martha, I don't believe you've said a word since dinner. What's your
take on this?"

"My take?" She slid her lips back and forth as she considered. "My
take," she said, "is that two people are dead, and both possessed the
kind of memorabilia you're interested in. That aspect seems to have
been lost in all this talk of an undiscovered story. But northwest Wyoming is out of my jurisdiction. The deputy there owns a bar in Cooke
City and indulges in his inventory, which just makes him mean, plus
he's got a hard-on for me. Sean, this is the guy I mentioned."

"You called him an asshole."

"I understated. Anyway, I arrested him for soliciting at his nephew's graduation at MSU. He hired Ginny Gin Jenny and a couple of
her girls to entertain. She blew the whistle when he tried to stiff her,
and claimed that one of the girls had been raped."

"Who's Ginny Gin Jenny?" Willoughby asked.

"She's the Elk Camp Madam," Sean said, "because servicing hunters at their camps is her specialty."

"Ken, we lead a sheltered life here," Willoughby said.

"I take it you're persona non grata," Winston said.

"He threatened to chain me inside a culvert trap and bait it with a
T-bone steak if I ever crossed the state line."

"You mean like they catch bears with?" Winston raised his sculpted
eyebrows.

Martha nodded.

"Did the charges stick?" Willoughby asked.

"For soliciting?" She snorted. "When your star witness includes the county attorney as her client, your case tends to go up in smoke. And the woman who claimed rape wanted to keep her name out of the paper and didn't press charges."

"So what's our next step?" Willoughby said. "What would you do if you didn't have to worry about someone throwing you into a bear trap?"

"I'm not scared of Leland Stokes, but that's not answering your question. Everything you've been talking about points to this Jackson character as being the source of your fancy fishing tackle. And he's vulnerable because he's bought into the antler velvet hoopla. It's crack cocaine to him. I'd go down there and pry the lid off and see what kind of worms crawl out of his skull. But you have to remember that even if he has this stuff, trading a fly rod or a painting for elk antler velvet isn't against the law. You can't confiscate his possessions, no matter who you think they once belonged to."

"Our aim is to save these pieces for posterity," Willoughby said. "Not to steal them for profit."

"Then you'll have to get him to give them to you or you'll have to pay for them."

"We're prepared to do that."

"Something to bear in mind as well," she said. "If you coerce this man, or you perform an illegal search and seizure, then any evidence that points to his involvement in a crime will be inadmissible in court."

"Are you suggesting Peter Jackson had something to do with Wilhelm Winkler's death?" Willoughby said.

"I'm not suggesting anything. I'm just eyeing your brandy and rethinking your invitation to spend the night. What do you think, Sean? It's a long drive back to Bridger."

"It's late," Sean agreed.

"Then it's decided," Willoughby said. "Martha, you may have the guest bunk room. Sean, I'm afraid it's the couch."

"We can stay in the same room," Martha said.

She looked at Sean, who tried not to register his surprise.

"Promise I won't bite."

"Certainly," Willoughby said. He sounded uncertain. Sean glanced at Ken, who mouthed the words "You dog."

———

At six the next morning, Sean walked her out to her truck.

"Do you have any last-minute advice?" he asked.

"Yes. Be careful."

"Do you know something I don't?"

"No, it's a feeling. But last night, after you had fallen asleep—"

"—You mean, after you were done 'not biting' me."

He saw Martha's cheeks color in the dawn light.

"You didn't seem to mind. But yes, later. I came out into the kitchen to get a glass of milk, you know how I am about that."

Sean nodded. She was a wee-hours-glass-of-milk-before-the-fireplace reader, and he had often felt the emptiness when she was gone and would walk out and take her by the hand and bring her back to bed.

"Well, I went into the living room and Patrick had moved one of the stuffed chairs over by the window and he was staring out into space. You know that look of his."

Sean nodded. "We called it his 'Iron Curtain' face."

"That's the one. So of course he got up and bowed, and pulled up a chair so I could sit beside him and asked me how my finger was healing, and we sat there passing time and being comfortable, and then he started in that way he has of talking that isn't to you so much as for your benefit. He said that Peter Jackson possesses grandiose illusions, and that they could be caused by lesions of the brain's frontal lobe, that Jackson might well be obsessed with Ernest Hemingway to the point of adopting his pen name, but there's a chance it's gone beyond that."

"What do you mean?"

"Patrick thinks it's possible that he thinks he really is Ernest Hemingway."

"He never claimed that in my presence," Sean said.

"Patrick said the delusions can come and go. There's a word for them. Melagomania. No, megalomania. Anyway, like that. He might actually hear voices. It's a symptom of schizophrenia."

"Hemingway himself might be speaking to him?"

"Jackson might convince himself of it, yes. Patrick's point was that we're dealing with someone who can't be trusted to act rationally, and that sufferers can react hostilely to people who attempt to shatter their illusions. He said he'd run into someone in Berlin who thought she was Marlene Dietrich, and that she was so seductive men opened up to her despite their better judgment, and that she could have never pulled off the act if she didn't really believe it herself."

"She was one of Willoughby's agents?"

"He called her an asset." She looked up at Sean. "By the way, Patrick was impressed with your memory. He said he could have used you on his team back then."

"I'll take that as a compliment."

"I thought you'd be pleased. Anyway, to get back to the story, I asked him how it ended with her, because he had this haunted look. He said he'd fallen in love with her, and she'd talked him into letting her stay behind the wall when he should have pulled her in, because he had a premonition she was blown. He said she was the fourth person he'd sent across who didn't make it back. He said his wife's name was Marlene, and though that was a coincidence, it's kept the memory of the other Marlene alive to him, and he prays for her and for the others who didn't make it back every night before going to bed."

"I've never got that close to Patrick," Sean said.

"I think it's maybe because I'm a woman, and with his wife gone there's no one who knows what he's gone through. He's lonely."

"If Patrick thinks Jackson could be dangerous, why didn't he tell me?"

"He is telling you. I'm just the one saying the words. He made me promise I'd warn you."

"Then thanks for the warning."

"I have something else you can thank me for. Are you driving the blue Suby?"

Sean nodded. "Patrick said I could borrow it."

"I'm putting a package on the rear bench. Promise that you'll open it before you leave the car."

"Why not now?"

"Just promise."

"Sure, Martha."

"I'm going to give you a proper kiss, before God and everybody."

She did, even if "everybody" only extended to a robin pulling a worm where the feeder creek crooked to the river.

# CHAPTER TWENTY-FOUR

# A Scent in the Forest

Sean reached into the back for the package as the engine ticked down. It was heavy, a shoe box with an oily scent that he'd been smelling ever since leaving the clubhouse, and he had a pretty good idea what it was.

The drive had taken him up and over Targhee Pass into West Yellowstone, where he'd bought a season pass before entering Yellowstone Park. At Madison Junction he turned north to Norris and then drove on up to Mammoth, the road just plowed in that stretch, then Mammoth to Roosevelt Lodge, and east up Slough Creek, with the most sophisticated cutthroat trout Sean had ever cast a fly to. The Lamar Valley with its panoramic vistas, its vast elk and bison herds, its wolves, its grizzly bears, was as close to an American Serengeti as there is.

He left the park at the northeast entrance at Silver Gate and idled up through Cooke City. He stopped in at the general store where the locals used to buy ammunition by the cartridge, or so the man behind the counter claimed, saying, "That's how the West was won, one bullet, one Indian at a time." He tipped his Polaris snowmobile cap and offered Sean a glimpse of stubby teeth stained by chewing tobacco.

Sean walked across the street to one of the two bars where Peter Jackson was said to have warmed a stool. The Pilot was closed, but a woman swamping the place out opened the heavy door and asked him what he'd forgotten, bars in the West having the biggest lost-and-found closets of any business. When he asked about Jackson, she said sure, she knew him, yeah, he was a talker, no, he didn't get into any trouble, she hadn't seen him in months. How was the old badger? This was the bar owned by the deputy who'd threatened to throw Martha into a bear trap. Sean knew because the walls were plastered with photographs of the man, several in his officer garb, many more in Wild West period clothing—Stetson, bolo tie, paisley patterned shirts. In one photo, blown up to poster size, he was in a crouch, a pencil of fire coming out the barrel of his Colt revolver.

"Who's this?" Sean asked the woman, though he recalled the name Martha had mentioned.

"That's Leland in a quick-draw contest in Reno."

"Leland?"

"Leland Stokes. He's the deputy sheriff on the Wyoming side. He owns this bar."

Sean pointed to a glass wall case displaying shelves of trophies under a tooled leather double-holster gun belt, complete with matching ivory-handled, single-action revolvers.

"Says these were won by the Ringo Kid."

"Everybody in the Cowboy Fast Draw Association goes by a handle. He also did cowboy action events as Red Bart, because of his hair."

"Sounds like you know him pretty well."

"Leland's not one to miss an opportunity to tell you about his exploits. If I got a dollar every time I heard him talk about Tombstone, the day he busted a balloon in point one six seconds—that's drawn, cocked, aimed, and fired, which he won't let you forget—I could move someplace warmer."

"Tough to be his wife," Sean offered.

"I was his wife."

"Then sorry for bringing it up."

"No reason you ought to be. The problem with Leland, he was as fast in the sack as he was with a gun. Over before it started, and shooting blanks at that."

It was one of those I'm-an-open-book conversations that flow like water between strangers in the West, but Sean's mind was already a few miles down the road, and he left her polishing glass with one more stop before climbing to the Top of the World.

———

The turnoff was well marked. The road crossed a sturdy one-lane bridge, left forest for open land, and wound through a cluster of guest cabins before reaching the main lodge, where a life-sized iron sculpture of a wolf howling at a quarter moon reminded you of the name of the place, the Howling Wolf Guest Ranch. Sean had phoned ahead and Bill Shaunnessey was standing outside the door as he pulled up. He was a big man in the way that ranchers who have traded the saddle for the desk can be big—heavy jowls on a clean-shaven face, a tan line where the hat rests, a rodeo belt buckle glinting from under an overhanging gut. Shaunnessey offered Sean a meaty, crooked-fingered hand that would betray his cowboying days as long as he lived, gave him his welcoming eyes, his professional, at-your-service smile.

Sean asked to see the foundation where the cabin had been before Jackson moved it down the road and Shaunnessey said sure, we'll take the four-wheeler. They did. The stone foundation was a couple hundred yards down the hill toward the river, weeds growing through the cracks of the gray granite rock.

"Like I said when you called, not much to see." Shaunnessey tipped his hat back.

Sean nodded. "Did Jackson tell you why he wanted to buy it?"

"Why don't you just tell me why you're here and get that out of the way first." The smile stayed. The welcoming look in the eyes didn't. "And don't give me, 'He was a friend of a friend,' like you did on the phone. He didn't have friends. Now, he might have had people who wanted something from him, but that isn't the same thing, is it?" Now the smile was gone, too.

Sean said, "Freida Toliver actually was his friend. She was trying to get him to move in with her in the weeks before she died. He was good with his hands and her business was suffering because of her arthritis. But Peter is delusional, and he has relatives who stand to benefit if he can be declared incompetent to manage his own affairs."

"So you're the vulture in the tree, waiting for the lion to leave so you can pick over the bones."

"No. I share Freida's wish that Peter leads a decent life. When she died, I started looking around for some other living situation. I have friends who own a place on the Madison River. They do philanthropy work for Warriors and Quiet Waters, introducing servicemen with PTSD to fly fishing. It's not only fishing. There's immersion in nature, history, literature, and so on. They've agreed to offer Peter a job this summer, and he can start by building the guest cabin he will be staying in. One of my friends used to be a naval psychologist. He believes that bringing Peter into a social situation could help keep him on keel."

Sean had run the gambit past Martha and Willoughby the night before, and the story would hold up. At least Willoughby would back up the therapy aspect and the job offer. The unnamed relatives were spun from whole cloth.

"Okay, I give up," Shaunnessey said. "You're looking out for his welfare. What business is it of mine anyway? And hey, I know he's getting pretty far out there, especially with the Hemingway stuff. That's why he wanted the cabin in the first place. He thought Hemingway stayed in it when he was a guest of the ranch way back when."

"Is it the cabin?" Sean asked. It was the real reason for his visit, to get an opinion from someone in the know.

Shaunnessey shook his head. "Hemingway's cabin? Nah. Well, maybe. The first summer he came to the ranch—understand, now, the original owners aren't here to say one way or the other—Hemingway did stay in one of the cabins. This would be 1930, 1931, thereabouts. Moose Johnson worked out of the place going way back, he was a mountaineer, horse wrangler, guided Hemingway when he went bear hunting. They took to each other, both being world-class blowhards looking to bend an ear. Moose was said to have said that this was the cabin, that he'd swing by in the saddle and Hemingway would be writing on the shady side of the porch. Moose said Ernest told him that he'd renamed the Clarks Fork, from now on it would be called the Cold Hearted River. Said all trout streams were coldhearted bitches. You could fish them with the best rod, the best-tied fly, even drizzle a nip of whiskey from your flask into the water, and there were still days that the trout weren't going to put out."

Shaunnessey's shrug said maybe Moose's recollection was true, maybe it wasn't.

"This Hemingway history is all third- or fourth-hand by now," he said. "What I do know is that the second summer Hemingway came here, the owner built him a brand-new cabin that was closer to the river. It's the first one you saw after crossing the bridge. That's where Hemingway always stayed after that, and that cabin isn't for sale. So whether Peter bought the original cabin or he didn't, I don't know. But if he thinks it is, who am I to tell him otherwise? And he might be right. I do know he paid an honest dollar for it. I didn't inflate its value."

For some time Sean had been watching a garter snake that had emerged from the stone foundation, the snake flattening its body to receive the maximum warmth from the rock.

"See how his tongue comes in and out. He's tasting the spring," Shaunnessey said. He hitched his blue jeans and bent to pick up the snake, then paid it out from hand to hand, like a rope. He allowed it to slip free and the striped snake poured itself into a crack in the rocks. The big hands were gentler than Sean would have thought. He'd built up a label for Shaunnessey upon meeting him. It wasn't true. But then that was life.

The big rancher straightened. "You want a cup of hundred percent Kona coffee? The missus won't be up until Memorial weekend and I'm right on the cusp of crazy. Like that character Jack Nicholson played in *The Shining*. Scariest goddamned movie I ever saw."

"He was a writer," Sean said. "The character."

"Don't think I haven't made the connection. Old Moose used to say that he could feel Hemingway's ghost in the big house. But then he would have seen that snake and read all kinds of meaning into that, too. You winter up here, every canyon's got a bad wind, every creek sings a tragedy. You like that? I made it up. Just the names alone are enough to spook you—Froze-to-Death Peak, Dead Man Mountain, Crazy Cascades, Hoodoo Creek. Hell, there's even a Hemingway Creek."

"Where's that?"

Shaunnessey pointed north across the river. "Up on the state border, feeds a lake called Widewater."

"Froze-to-Death Creek is where Jackson rebuilt the cabin," Sean said.

Shaunnessey nodded. "'Bout six, seven mile up from there is a lake by the same name—Froze-to-Death. Said to be almost two hundred feet deep. Moose said it's where Hemingway threw the Civil War pistol his father used to commit suicide. There's a horse trail in there, but you want to know why I never rode it, it's because I carry the image of that pistol in my head. My father had the cancer, it ate him up. He wanted a gun and I wouldn't give it to him. Now, did I do the right thing or the wrong thing? You tell me."

They had the bitter nectar of the coffee, and Sean pried himself away, liking Bill Shaunnessey and feeling bad about the deception. He said he'd take him up on his offer to fish the Clarks Fork when the snowmelt cleared, see if it really was a coldhearted bitch, and drove up to the bridge where the trail took off for Jackson's cabin.

He lifted the lid off the shoe box in the backseat. The barrel of the revolver had a dull polish and looked as deadly as a mamba. It was a Smith & Wesson .357 with a shark's fin front blade inlaid with a red fiber optic sight. Sean checked the loads and put it back into the box. The last thing he wanted was to give Jackson a reason to feel threatened. Even if he could conceal it under the back of his jacket, the fact of it would add a static charge to their conversation. One thing Sean had learned about guns, their barrels spoke even when no sound came out.

He was sure of his decision as he hiked up the trail, still sure when he saw the fresh paw prints of the black-footed cat, more than sure when he passed the place where he'd felt the tightness in his chest two days before and felt none now. Then, coming through the trees, the cabin in view, no smoke from the chimney, he wasn't sure at all.

He helloed from a distance, the walls of the canyon tossing it back to him. Nothing to see. No one to his knock. He pressed the iron door lever down. Locked. The kitchen window over the table didn't have a lock. He opened it and hoisted himself to the sill. He crawled through the small opening, cutting his left hand on a shard of glass, and dropped to the floor.

He sucked at his hand as he walked into the living room. It was as before, with a notable exception. The sheet of onionskin that he'd seen in the typewriter was missing. As was the typewriter.

He opened the door to the room in which he'd caught a glimpse of a cot on his first visit. Calling it a bedroom was a stretch. Military wool blankets neatly stacked on one end of the cot, single pillow on the other, kerosene lamp on a nightstand. A novel in Spanish—*Love in the Time of Cholera*. A story about obsession.

Sean's eyes were drawn to the foot of the cot, where more stacked blankets covered something that was large and rectangular. If he was a finger trembler, his fingers would have trembled as he lifted up the blankets. It was a steamer trunk, and for a few moments he allowed himself to be convinced it was what he was searching for. Wishful thinking. The trunk, wood-paneled with iron fittings, had been made to look antique, but it wasn't. And the only items in it were more blankets. He unfolded an Indian print blanket and brought the soft wool to his face. A long-disused, musty smell. He checked to see if the trunk had a false bottom hiding a secret chamber. That was wishful thinking, too.

Sean's unease had returned. He felt like he was not alone, but when he went back into the living room, the only eyes that looked at him were the lifeless ones of the wolverine.

He looked briefly for the shotgun, which he had not seen in the bedroom and didn't find here, either. He went back outside.

Hearing the quick scampering of feet, he turned round and looked up. A flitter of red as a pine squirrel materialized on the roof. It jumped into the upper branches of a touching aspen tree, darted around the trunk, then stopped in a fork, giving its alarm bark.

*Kuk! Kuk! Kuk!* The squirrel's tail jerked.

Sean saw the cat. It was on the ridgeline of the roof, not paying attention to the squirrel at all, but looking off toward the woods beyond the clearing. And its back was up.

Sean could see movement there, a flickering between the tree trunks. Something big enough to scare the cat was there, something dark. Black bears in the Rockies come in shades from dirty blonde to soot, grizzlies cover almost as wide a color spectrum. The shape was gone, leaving only the wall of trees, and Sean found that he was resting his thumb on the trigger of his pepper spray.

He began to walk toward the trees, pausing every few yards to stop and listen. Behind him, the chatter of the squirrel faded. He was entering Darwin Award country. You don't walk toward movement in a forest, not in this part of the Rockies, not until you're positive that whatever it is doesn't have long teeth.

*You don't have to do this,* he told himself. He felt his heart beating, but took another step toward the trees. One more. That's when he saw it. A dark shape, coming fast, snapping like a band of elastic toward him. He thumbed back the safety tab, stumbled, and fell. He scrabbled for the spray as the shadow of an animal fell across him and a rank, sour odor invaded his nostrils. He struggled to his knees and turned, the pepper spray in his fist.

It was a dog. Sean sat back on the ground. The flush of adrenaline had made him light-headed and for a minute he just breathed. He reached out a hand and the dog nosed it. It began to circle him, its head down.

When he reached to pet it, it bounded off into the trees, then slunk back and dug its wet muzzle into his hand.

He stood up. The dog moved off again and he began to follow it. It led him into and then out of a stand of aspen, their new leaves curling in a breeze. Then into pines, the forest of trunks closing behind him. He continued to follow as the dog led him up a rise of land. From the top he could see the silver glinting of Froze-to-Death Creek below and to the south. Patches of old snow clung to the slope, and on the trail that the dog had taken, Sean saw boot tracks. The tracks were large and only a little distorted by snowmelt, and the trail they made partly obscured a second set of smaller tracks. Ahead in a little hollow was the dog. The dog was trailing its nose in a figure eight, snuffing the ground, which had been freshly turned over a fairly large area. Presently it lay down, resting its head on crossed paws and making a small, intermittent keening sound. A flag of red cloth protruded from the ground where Sean assumed the dog had tugged at it.

He recognized the color. It was the color of her shirt on both occasions he'd seen her, and after he dug with his hands, exposing the side of her head, he recognized the elk-tooth earring. He recognized the dog, too, but he'd known the dog the second he'd seen it. He even remembered its name, although it took a moment to bring back hers.

"I'm sorry, Jupiter," he said. He squatted down and dug his fingers into the thick hair on the back of the hound's neck. "Jolene isn't coming back."

Sean began to work the connections—Jolene Bailie had found the body of Wilhelm Winkler, who was brother to Freida Toliver, who had bartered antler velvet to Peter Jackson. Sean wasn't sure what that meant, but he knew he'd have to report the body, and that as soon as he did, his access to the area, let alone the body, would be prohibited. There was a line he could cross or not cross, and he pulled out his camera and crossed it. He took pictures of the scene from different angles, then started to scrape the dirt away from the body with a piece of wood splintered off a deadfall pine tree. She'd been killed, all right.

There was a hole in her back as big as a softball, although surprisingly little blood, most of it having seeped into the turned earth.

Scissoring his fingers into the back pocket of her dirty jeans, he extracted a cell phone, and reaching underneath the body—the woman had fallen facedown—he pulled a GPS from the holster on her belt. The GPS was probably the same one he'd seen her consulting in the Bear Trap Canyon, and he frowned at it as he contemplated crossing a second line, deciding against removing evidence from the scene. Instead, he photographed the liquid crystal display with the most recently added waypoints on the GPS, then did the same with the most recently called numbers on her phone. He looked for the carabiner of keys she'd worn on her belt, but didn't find them. That was no surprise, as there had been no truck where he'd parked the Subaru. Whoever killed her had taken her truck, that much seemed clear. He wiped away any prints he might have left on the smooth surfaces, touched the phone and GPS to the clawlike fingers of her right hand to transfer her prints to them, and, wrapping his own fingers in a handkerchief, replaced the items into her pockets. He used the scrap of wood to reposition the soil as he'd found it and then threw the splinter as far as he could into the forest.

He nodded to the dog, which obediently trailed him back toward the bridge over the Cold Hearted River.

# CHAPTER TWENTY-FIVE

# The Ringo Kid

Sean looked out the window of the phone booth. It was a dinosaur of its kind, with a folding door and a light that turned on when you opened it. The wood paneling was old and inked with phone numbers.

"What did you touch?" Martha said.

"Everything. And nothing. I stopped back at the cabin and wiped away any prints I might have left in the bedroom."

"But this Bill Shaunnessey, he knew you were going up there today?"

"He did."

"Where's the dog?"

"It's in the Subaru."

Another silence.

"And she was murdered? You're certain."

"I don't think she fell on the shotgun."

"And you think Jackson did it?"

"Well, he has a shotgun. I saw him wearing moccasins, and moccasins don't leave a tread pattern. The tracks I saw at the scene were smooth."

"Where are you exactly?"

"I'm in the lobby of the Soda Butte Lodge."

"You know the deputy's office is across the street, at the back of the Pilot Bar."

"I know that, Martha. I suppose it's my next stop."

"Am I hearing a question?"

"Maybe."

"Don't even think about it. You went into his bar asking about Jackson when, three hours ago? Then you told Shaunnessey you were going to go visit the cabin. Even if you hadn't done either of those things, I'd advise you to come clean. You skip out, you're digging yourself down into the same hole she's in."

"I've been first to the scene of two violent deaths inside a week. It won't look good. And something I forgot to tell you, I cut my hand. There may be some of my blood in the cabin. That's not good, is it?"

Silence.

Sean's voice found a note of optimism. "I suppose I could use you as a character witness."

A pause. "I'm glad you can find some humor in this. I can't."

"Well, thanks for the advice."

"About that package I gave you . . ."

"Already taken care of."

"Meaning?"

"Meaning don't worry about it. It's under a rock a few miles back."

"I'm not the one has to worry."

Sean was thinking up a reply when the phone went dead. His quarters had run out.

———

The deputy's office was a low room in back of the bar, with a window overlooking a steep mountainside of charred pines. Some of the blackened spires stood within fifty yards of the window.

"First thing I did that day, this would be nineteen and eight-eight, summer of the Yellowstone fires, September four to the best of my recollection," Leland Stokes was saying, "I got my Colt revolvers and gun belts. Next thing I took were the photos of the folks. Third was a bottle of Woodford Reserve. Opened the safe to make sure there wasn't anything but change money, and I was out the door. Guns, family, whiskey—in that order. There's some might read into that and pass judgment, but if they'd have looked closer, they'd see I had my priorities. My wife and I are divorced, no kids. My dad was a son of a bitch, my mother ran off when I was ten, and I have a sister in Albuquerque I haven't seen in five years. Closest kin, you're talking geography, is a no-account nephew who's at MSU. None of the bunch would shed a tear at my demise. Plus the Colts are worth at least half the insurance value of the establishment. As for the whiskey, well, when your place of business is about to go up in flames, you need something to wet your whistle while she burns."

He smiled, showing overlapping teeth in his pinched mouth.

"I see you thinking," he said, "and you're saying to yourself, 'This here Leland Stokes, he's got a sense of humor and that's fine and dandy, but shouldn't we be getting up there?' But I say, 'What's the hurry, Mr. Stranahan, what's the hurry?' She's got a hole in her back. I'm going to go out on a limb and say she's not going to go zombie on us and start eating her own flesh. Sure, a bear could put his nose to the wind, maybe take a nip out of her, but I doubt that's going to happen in the next hour or two. So what we're going to do is put your statement on the recorder. I always like to get a fellow's first impression, that's so I can see the look on his face when it bites him on the ass later, not that I'm implying you're being anything but a Samaritan. Then I'll ring up Joe Hoss, who's deputy on the Montana side—he lives up out of Gardiner— and leave word with the Montana Highway Patrol, because we're all one happy family here, what with the county seat in Wyoming being to hell and gone in Cody. Confusing, I know. Two adjoining counties with the same name, in two different states. But with the distances involved, what works best is whoever happens to be closest responds to the call and we sort out the jurisdiction later.

"Then, once we got everyone informed and the gears crunching to get the coroner and a forensic team on the road, you and me"—he patted his belly—"we'll take that drive."

The clichés, the aw-shucks manner, the way the man swung himself around the room, invading Sean's personal space to show his authority—everything about Leland Stokes grated. He was a short man, and what excess weight he carried, he carried in a potbelly. His face was possumlike, his features scrunched around a pointed nose. Boiled lobster forearms, the right as big as a ham hock, popped from rolled-up sleeves. Carroty hair. Freckles. But for all the bluster, Stokes could put on a poker face when called for, and he had that face in place as Sean talked. Sean saw no way out of telling him about his previous acquaintance with the victim, which raised the question of why he was in the Bear Trap Canyon on the day when Jolene Bailie's Plott hound had found the body of Wilhelm Winkler. That meant Sean had to broach his off-and-on profession, he had to mention Freida Toliver.

Stokes leaned back in his chair for the recitation, snorting in amusement at the mention of antler velvet but not interrupting, nor commenting when Sean had finished. He was one of those people, Sean decided, who could give you his attention while keeping his thoughts to himself. He tapped at the computer squatting on his desk and watched the screen for a long minute, occasionally pushing the mouse around with his fingers. He patted his belly, left hand, right hand, left hand, right hand, like it was a tom-tom. Then he craned his head to look out the window.

"I'm thinking I shouldn't have got out of bed this morning," he said at length. "I'm thinking you shouldn't have, either." He hefted himself out of his chair. "You got the winder cracked for that hound? Seeing's how he's the key witness for two might-be, could-be, probably-are murders, I want him healthy."

He buckled on a double-holster gun belt different from the one in the glass case, with black-handled revolvers, mimicked a double-handed fast draw, blew imaginary smoke from imaginary barrels, wrinkled a pair of expressive nostrils, and made the calls he'd been talking about.

"Time to giddy up," he said to Sean, cocking a finger.

Stokes's Dodge Ram—he said the county vehicle was in the shop— sounded like a submerged chain saw as it worked through the gears. It was loud enough to make silence seem comfortable, and they drove the nine or ten miles to the rickety bridge without a word spoken that wasn't a direction. Stokes had pale blue irises the color of a glacial melt river that Sean had once fished with Joseph Brings the Sun, a young Blackfeet man he'd met on a case and with whom he'd lost touch and wished he hadn't. When they parked just before the bridge, the deputy made no move to step out of the truck.

"Here's the deal," he said, "and I want you to tell me the truth. What I was looking at on the computer screen back in the office was a Web camera set outside the Soda Butte Lodge. It's an advertising gimmick got nothing to do with law enforcement, but it's got east- and west-facing lenses, so pretty much anything happens on the street, you see what it was. I saw you walk right past the bar to go into the hotel at 2:27 p.m., and you left to cross the street and come into the bar at 2:46 p.m. So I asked myself, 'What did he do in those nineteen minutes? Doesn't take that long to take a whiz. So did he have a drink in the hotel bar to work up his nerve to pay me a visit? Upchuck into the toilet? Or did he use the pay phone in the hall to talk with a lawyer about the pickle he's got hisself into? Far as I know he's deciding whether to run, and decided against it. But he was doing something in there and I wonder what it was.'"

Sean knew that the number at the phone booth was traceable and decided to come clean.

"I called Sheriff Martha Ettinger in Hyalite County. I told her about finding the body, because the victim has a connection to a case she's working. I told you about the man we found in the Bear Trap Canyon. I wasn't asking her advice on whether to run."

Stokes's face remained passive.

"Martha Ettinger," he said. "Now there's a name doesn't come easy to the lips. No sir, it surely doesn't." He looked at Sean. "So am I to assume you're her emissary, or are you down here on a private dime? Not that it matters much. On the county coffer or off it, you aren't licensed to investigate a lost dog here unless you make a courtesy call and clear it with me. See, the problem with the West is, it's full of cowboys. Act first, ask later. Gets my dander up."

Sean took in his dander, his carroty hair longer on top in a baby Mohawk. Something glistening in it, not sweat.

"I'm sorry. I should have dropped in earlier. I did, actually, I talked to your ex-wife, who said you wouldn't be in until noon."

"Caroline didn't mention that. She tells you we were married, then she doesn't mention you stopping by. Women, it gets that time of month, they can get sort of funny."

Slowly, he nodded. "All right." He lifted his hands from the steering wheel, facing his palms. "You and me, no need to get our stirrups crossed. No sir-ee." He climbed down from the truck and buckled on the holster from the gun rack, where it had been hanging during the drive. Sean could read the history of Stokes's spreading waistline from the wear on the notches. Another ten pounds, he thought, and he'd have to get a longer belt.

They walked out onto the bridge.

"Reason I didn't drive across," Stokes said, "is we'll get a tread analyst up here who can decode all the tire tracks in the mud. So we'll skirt that area and walk to the side of the ruts you followed up to the cabin."

"The only human tracks I saw were up higher, near the burial site. It snowed up there, just enough so that they registered. They could be melted by now. I'd guess a day old, maybe not even."

"You know something about tracking?" Stokes said.

"I was taught by Harold Little Feather. He's a state investigator now, learned from his grandfather."

"Hell, I remember Harold. He taught a seminar in Cody, first year of my hire. Fifteen, sixteen years ago. Man was a fucking *Indian*. He could track a spider up the side of a porcelain toilet bowl and right on down to the waterline. Yes, I believe he could do that."

By the time they reached the thinning trees with their first glimpse of the cabin, Stokes was wheezing and blaming it on getting over a cold.

"Damned bar is like a Petri dish," he said. He put his hands on his knees and breathed. "Imagine the work," he said. "Tearing it down and putting it back together in this godforsaken place."

He was still stalling.

"Son," he said, straightening to his height, "I do believe I'm looking at a feral animal."

Ahead, on the path, the black-footed cat flattened itself, then streaked off into the trees. Stokes pulled the Colt from the right-hand holster and said, "Bang."

He holstered the gun. "Only good cat is a dead one, huh? Now a dog, they say he's man's best friend, and I haven't found any reason to argue."

Sean had met many men who talked in clichés, and had always thought it was the hallmark of an unexamined life. Why think of something to say when you can fall back on what someone else has?

"Yes sir," he said.

Stokes looked hard at him. "You making fun of me?"

"I don't like cats, either," Sean said.

A moment's pause. "Then we're of a feather."

Fifteen minutes later they were in the hollow, standing on the windward side of the body, though it was fresh enough that the only discernible odor was the heavy, cloyingly sweet scent of blood. The two sets of tracks that Sean had followed to the site had been all but obliterated by the day's snowmelt, though it was still possible to differentiate them by size.

"You didn't have a smartphone on you, take any pictures here?" Stokes said.

Sean thought of his camera, which he'd left in the center console compartment of the rental Subaru. "No," he half lied, and felt the constriction come and go in his chest.

Stokes grunted. "I can't even see any goddamned dog prints," he said.

"It was the dog who led me here."

Sean buttoned up his jean jacket. It had started to rain, and now that he was just standing around, pointedly not looking at the body, he was cold.

"Well, 'shee-it,' as my grandmother used to say. You're just being no help at all. Just none at all. But then it's only the third body you've seen lately, so maybe you're getting too jaded to care. Or maybe drinking that antler tea's making you squirrelly." He had started to walk around the site, taking photos of what tracks were left, plus what they could see of the body.

"I'm going to have to scrape some of the dirt away so you can see the face and positively ID it as the woman you saw up on the Madison River. Your Jolene Bailie. I wrote that down with a 'ie,' not an 'ey.' I'm right about that, aren't I?" He tapped his belly.

Sean nodded.

Stokes squatted in a catcher's stance and whisked his fingers, exposing the left half of the face.

"It's her," Sean said.

Stokes worked his fingers on the point of his jaw.

"When will your people get here?" Sean asked.

"Depends. They'll be coming from Cody or Livingston—two hours one way, three the other. We'll go check out the cabin, you can give me the tour. Then we'll drive back to the office and you can be on your way. Can't detain a man for being an unlucky dumb ass, least not until you got reason to believe that ain't the case. But we'll be in touch, of that you can rest assured. And you tell Martha Ettinger hi for me. No hard feelings about what happened in Bozeman at the U. Man has to stand up for his kin, even if he's no-'count."

He nodded to himself. "We're done here," he said.

They were halfway back to the truck when they saw the cat. This time it was twenty or so yards off the track, and the gun was out of the right-hand holster so fast Sean didn't even register a blur. At the shot, the cat jumped four feet into the air and somersaulted when it hit the ground. A second shot. The cat humped up, then sprung like a catapult and was off and gone into the bushes.

"Gol-dang-it, now. Did I get 'im? I could a swore I got him." Stokes was running in a crouch toward the place where the cat had disappeared, the revolver in his hand. "I got hair!" he shouted. He seemed to have turned into an animal himself, jerking his head with feral intensity, the cold blue eyes searching.

"Well, I clipped the bastard, anyway," he said as Sean came up. "What? I thought you hated cats. Now you're disgusted with me. I see it in your face. You think you're superior and I'm just some knee-jerk yahoo, don't you? You hope I missed. I hope he's dragging his guts. Fuck you. Fuck Martha Ettinger, too."

Sean didn't say anything.

Stokes holstered the revolver. Then he pulled the left one from the gun belt, cocked it, and pointed it at Sean's chest. Sean felt his insides crawl up as he watched the finger take up the slack in the trigger. "I can't think of the last time the Ringo Kid missed three shots in a row," Stokes said. And as Sean's muscles instinctively tightened, he fired.

———

Sean was lying on the hard ground. He felt the hatred build up in him and come to a point, then ebb away. Again the black rage came to the front, again it ebbed away. Each time it receded, he was left with the pain in his chest and the cold of the ground. The pain was a searing poker on the point of his breastbone that intensified with each intake of his breath. There had been an hour, deep in the night's stillness, when, listening to the creek and focusing on the pain, he would gladly have killed Leland Stokes by beating his head with a rock. He would have, and in all his life Sean had never felt that level of hatred for another human being.

The cold was constant, too, though he could shift it by hugging the dog to his chest or by facing away from it and pushing his back against it. The thing was, he didn't know where he was. He remembered being shot, he remembered Stokes looming over him, saying, "We call that 'beat and release' where I come from. It'll teach you to mind your manners."

Sean could recall writhing on the ground as Stokes smiled down at him.

"I'm going to give you a choice, boy-o," he'd said. "We get back to the truck, you sit in the passenger seat like a quiet little mouse, I'll drop you at your car and you can drive home and give your sheriff a kiss from me. You can tell her I dream of her regular, you can do that, and I won't raise a finger to stop you. Or"—he'd rubbed his chin—"you can be a smart-ass and try something. In that case, I guarantee you the next bullet will be from the right-hand gun. I shot you with the wax bullet we use in competition, just the primer and a few grains of powder. But the loads in the other gun, why, a gerbil will be able to wriggle in one side of you and see daylight out the 'tother. And your fingerprints, they'll be all over the gun, 'cause it was you who wrassled me for it and shot first. So what's it going to be, the gun or the mouse? I think the choice is clear, myself."

Sean must have been out for a while, because when he opened his eyes, a figure was looming over him. The pointy hat the man wore made an elongated shadow in the slant of morning sunlight.

"Slough Creek is hard-sided vehicle only," he heard the man saying. "It's against regulation to sleep in a tent."

"I'm not in a tent."

"You're in the open. That's also an infraction. And you have an at-large canine. That's in violation of park regulations. And you didn't register for the site."

"I guess I won the trifecta. Call Katie Sparrow. She's a ranger in the Lamar Valley. Tell her it's Sean Stranahan, he needs to talk to her."

The shadow of the hat moved back and forth. "I'll do that, sir, but your acquaintance with another ranger won't change the citations or the amount of remittance."

*Jesus,* Sean thought. *Speak like a human being.*

He heard footsteps as the man walked a few yards away to use the radio in his patrol car. There was a crackle as he spoke.

By the time the ranger returned, Sean had coaxed the Plott hound into the Subaru and, with great effort, had climbed behind the wheel. The pain in his chest, which had receded to a dull, aching throb, was again tearing at his nerve endings.

"Sir, Ranger Sparrow is on backcountry patrol."

*Good,* Sean thought. He shouldn't have made the request in the first place. He wouldn't have if he had been thinking straight. Unless he planned on bringing charges against Leland Stokes, the less attention he drew to himself in this area, the better.

"Are you okay?" the ranger asked. "You look peak-ed."

"I'm fine."

The ranger wrote him up. "You have a good day now."

Sean looked at the citations, seeing that his good day had already cost him two hundred dollars. He'd bill it out to Willoughby as operating expenses if the county didn't pick it up.

"Sure," he said. "I'll just stop eating for a while."

He left the ranger puzzling over this, his furrowed brow working under the Smokey the Bear hat.

# CHAPTER TWENTY-SIX

# An Appreciative Date

**M**artha Ettinger tut-tutted over him in her bathroom.

"You were lucky," she said. "You can see where the bullet caught the edge of the button; there's a smear of wax. It went through your jacket and stopped. If your jacket had been unbuttoned, it could have slipped between your ribs. You could be dead now."

"Martha, it didn't even break the skin."

"I'm going to tape some gauze over it, but I'm not sure what good it will do. There could be inflammation under there. You could have a hematoma pressing against your heart. A Band-Aid's not going to fix it. I think you should see a doctor."

"I don't have health insurance and I don't have any heart pain. I'll be okay." He shook his head.

"What?"

"Nothing. Last night, I was lying on the ground and I thought about how you asked me to put the muzzle of your gun on your chest and shoot you through the heart. But I'm the one got the bullet."

Martha blushed.

"Just funny what you think of, that's all. Mostly what I thought about was murdering Leland Stokes."

"I want you to reconsider about pressing charges."

"His word against mine." Sean shook his head.

"The man was suspended for six weeks last year for using too much force. He knocked down a drunk and the guy fell on a broken bottle. Gouged out his eye. If he wasn't such an asshole to start with—I'm talking about the guy who lost his eye—the infraction wouldn't have gone away. Leland's a rogue. The only reason animals like him exist is because they're off the grid where not a lot happens. The fact that he was suspended once tells me he got away with using unnecessary force more than once, probably a lot more. I doubt you're the only one going around with a bruise from a wax bullet. I'm sure if we look into it, there's a pattern of behavior that will work to your advantage before a judge."

"He called it 'beat and release.' You've got to hand it to him, it's a good line."

Martha frowned at him. "Be that way. Make light of it. It's only your heart."

"Is it mine?"

"I'm serious?"

"So am I."

"What are we talking about?"

"My heart. I think."

Martha sighed. "Here's the situation. This isn't TV, where everybody's fighting over jurisdiction. It's more like the opposite. 'It's on your side of the line.' 'No, it's on yours.' Everybody looks to pass the buck, and so everybody ends up with a piece of it. This investigation will be a three-way street—Leland in Wyoming, Joe Hoss on the Montana side of the line, and us because of the Jolene Bailie connection. What that means is you may end up seeing him again. Leland's like a Georgia peach. Polite to your face. About as friendly as an eastern diamondback under the smile. But as long as you aren't alone with him, he probably won't misbehave. So your job is to not be alone with him."

"I'll do my best. What do they have so far?"

"After you called from the park, I got a call from Joe Hoss. He was at the scene with the evidence crew. They found the dead woman's wallet. Same driver's license she gave us in the Bear Trap. Jolene Bailie. And they found gloves that were too big to be the victim's. That's something you didn't mention."

"That's because I never saw them. At least not at the scene." Sean told her about the leather gloves he'd seen on Jackson's chopping block.

"Joe said they were near the body."

"I don't think I would have overlooked them."

"Are you suggesting they were planted?"

"No, just that I didn't see them. She was stiff when I found her. Did they determine time of death?"

Martha nodded. "She was in rigor when Joe got there, but the body temperature was still up. So that means three to eight hours. It's a big window."

"She died this morning?"

"Early. Before you arrived at the cabin."

Martha took out the notepad in her shirt pocket. "The shotgun charge was through and through, back to front. Pellets recovered at the scene were number six shot. Pheasant loads."

She repocketed the notebook. "Looks like she was killed where she was buried, from maybe ten feet away. Far enough that there aren't any powder burns, but close enough so that birdshot still en-ters as a fist. Joe said there was no evidence of struggle, but of course they'll do a transfer analysis, check for debris under the fingernails, fibers on her clothing, that sort of thing. And process the gloves. There might be skin cell DNA to match against Peter Jackson's. State crime lab's in Cheyenne and there's a pecking order, so I suggested they use ours and Wyoming agreed. Shouldn't take more than a few days."

"She was shot in the back?"

"That's what the evidence says. The impact site was higher than the exit wound, so the shot was at a downward angle. The charge entered high on the back on the medial line, with the exit above the right hip." She crooked a hand around her back and tapped the right side of her abdomen with her other hand to illustrate.

"The victim was in the hollow and the shooter was above her?" Sean said.

"Maybe. But I've seen this trajectory before when a victim was pleading for his life."

"You mean like an execution."

Martha nodded. "A lot of killers have a hard time facing someone when they pull the trigger."

"Did they put an APB out for Jackson?"

"Of course."

"What's his motive?"

"You tell me. But the place to start looking is only about forty miles away, up in Virginia City."

Sean nodded. "Jolene told me she was house-sitting. Shouldn't be hard to find. It's a ghost town, after all."

———

Some of the two-lanes that capillary through the Madison Valley weren't marked on Martha's dash-mounted GPS, but the Plott hound, which shared the passenger seat of the Cherokee with Sean, didn't need technology to know which way to go when the road forked. His head would turn one way or the other and Martha turned the wheel accordingly.

Canine directions led to a right turn off Wallace Street, the main road of Virginia City, just past the blacksmith's shop where a red stagecoach sat idle behind a team of bored-looking horses. The road wound to a sagebrush bench above Alder Gulch, which was suggested by a line of greening trees punctuated by glints of water. Alder Gulch was where William Fairweather, after being run off Crow hunting grounds at the point of an arrow, stumbled onto a treasure of gold, which turned out to be the richest placer deposit ever discovered. That had been 1863 and the town swelled to five thousand residents inside a year. For two decades it served as the capital of the Montana Territory. Now there were probably more chickens than people. But it still served as the Hyalite County seat, with a grand courthouse completed in 1876. Martha admired the brickwork and the stately columns, but she had sat in the witness box too many times, wishing she was anywhere else.

"What are you thinking about?" Sean said.

"Retirement."

He let the remark pass, as the hound had stood and was nosing the windshield, making a whimpering sound. They pulled up to a house that matched the address Jolene Bailie had provided when she'd been questioned. It was in keeping with the town's architectural façades—a weathered gray-board front with plain windows and a wicker trout creel that served as a flower box, nailed up beside the door. The mailbox in the drive had the flag up. Martha lifted the lid—junk mail going back a week. No truck with West Virginia plates, but none was expected, the working assumption being that Bailie had driven her truck to Peter Jackson's place and that, after she'd been killed, Jackson had driven away in it.

The front door looked like it would splinter under a hard knuckle and was in fact unlocked. The kitchen was modern and unremarkable. The living room doubled as a dining room, with a walnut leaf table and matching chairs. Twin love seats were covered with mismatched throws matted with dog hair. Fireplace, coffee table, fan of magazines. A marijuana roach in an ashtray shaped like a paw print made Martha raise her brow. The walls added color, being papered with playbills from the Virginia City Players, advertising the past season's performances—*The Lodger, Sleeping Beauty,* and *The Legend of Sleepy Hollow.*

The first bedroom was just a place to sleep, with an opened roller suitcase on a bench and a few clothes in a closet. A chest of drawers revealed underwear, T-shirts, jeans, casual clothes in three drawers and fetish clothing in three others—frilly lace corsets, lingerie, push-up bras, like you'd see in an old-fashioned burlesque. There were clothes on the floor and discolored rings on a nightstand. The bed was unmade.

By contrast, the second bedroom was spotless and designed for, well, not exactly sleeping. A four-poster bed had a gauzy curtain drawn around it. Twin lamps with ruby-beaded shades topped the nightstand tables, the lamps in the form of carved wood nymphs with bare breasts, the nipples tipped by red glass inlays to catch the light. An antique maple vanity with a three-panel mirror was angled to reflect a woman giving her hair a hundred strokes, or, at a further remove, any shenanigans the bed might inspire. Erotic, tasteful art hung on the walls among more amusing and ribald offerings.

"You need to hire a new decorator, Martha," Sean said.

Martha didn't respond. She was looking at a framed photograph showing a young woman sitting on a bed that was being pushed down a street by two men and two women, the men sporting mustaches and sleeve garters, the women dressed, or rather undressed, in frilly working-girl attire. Everyone looked like they were having a roaring good time.

"What's this?"

"Brothel Days," Martha said. "The 'Running of the Beds.' The team with the first mattress across the finish line wins beers at the Bale of Hay Saloon."

"You've seen it?"

"I was in it once, as a pusher. It was the department's idea. Put a human face on your sheriff."

"Did you wear a corset?"

"I wore a miniature pearl-handled revolver tucked into each garter."

"Did it soften your image?"

"It might have, but a jealous wife started a catfight with one of the brothel reenactors. I threw her into a stock tank right there on Wallace Street, went into the drink, and hauled her out. A lot of tourists reaching for their iPhones. Guess who was on the front page of the *Star* the next morning? Talk about a bad hair day. Anyway, take a close look at the picture. Recognize anyone?"

"Is that our Jolene?" Sean was looking at one of the bed pushers, who was wearing a red satin dress with a deep scoop front.

"Check this out," Martha said, leading him back to the living room. She pointed to a framed photograph of the prior season's Virginia City

Players, tapped a woman garbed in buckskin fringe who was holding a shotgun.

"I wasn't sure before. Now I am."

"So she's in the Virginia City Players? She told us she was an actress. No law against that."

"No," Martha said. "But I'm reminded of something Oscar Wilde said. 'A man's face is his autobiography. A woman's face is her work of fiction.'" She crossed her arms over her chest.

"Meaning?"

"What did I call her before? Little Red Riding Hood? Well, my guess is she isn't the hillbilly she had us thinking she was. I'm betting the closest to a yokel she's been is playing Ma Kettle onstage. Now why she would pass herself off as someone she isn't, unless she has something to lose by talking like an educated person?"

"Maybe because she's supplementing her housecleaning income by turning tricks. It's against the law."

"That doesn't answer the question." Martha nodded to herself. "I'll have Huntsinger do a search, see who she really was. But what all of that"—she cocked a finger toward the bedroom door—"has to do with her winding up in a shallow grave, that's the sixty-four-thousand-dollar question. What are you thinking?"

"I'm thinking we should go back to town and rustle up someone connected to the Virginia City Players. Then we should grab a bite at the Virginia City Cafe. Sam says they have the best BLTs in the county."

"Well, he's one who should know."

They were in luck. The Opera House where the Players staged their shows was a month away from its opening night, but an amply endowed woman with hair dyed the color of an Irish setter answered Martha's knock. She said she was the company manager and offered a smile that faded by degree as she took in the news of Jolene Bailie's demise. She sat them down in her office and wound a strand of hair around a finger as she tapped keys to find her employee's application form.

While the computer worked, she said this would have been Jolene's third season with the company, that she'd been the lead in *Annie Get Your Gun* two summers ago, but was otherwise a middle-bill performer with a commanding contralto, who got along with everyone, as far as she could see. Yes, she'd known that Jolene was house-sitting, she knew the Santa Fe couple she was house-sitting for, had had dinner up at the place on several occasions. And she knew that Jolene did house-cleaning. She knew, in fact, exactly what Sean and Martha knew, except about the second bedroom.

The manager had found the form and summarized it aloud.

"Jolene May Bailie, place of birth, Centralia, West Virginia. Thirty-eight. Unmarried. Listing for a mother in Staunton, Virginia. Bachelor's at WVU, School of Theatre and Dance. Summer theater gigs in Harbor Springs, Michigan; the Finger Lakes; Bangor, Maine; and so on. Shakespeare in the Parks in Montana. Dinner theater in Taos, New Mexico. Summer camp artistic director at Nesowadnehunk Lake, Maine."

"She talked like a hillbilly," Martha said. "Is that the way she spoke in person?"

The woman shrugged. "She could do a half dozen Southern voices, from coal miner's daughter to coastal Carolina. She could do 'Well, howdy, partner' as well as anyone. River City, Iowa, for *The Music Man*. Slip in and out of character, which gets a bit tedious, to tell the truth. You never knew which voice you were going to hear until the words came out. Usually she spoke in the accent of a part she was studying for."

"What would that be this summer?" Martha asked.

"We're reprising *Annie Get Your Gun* come August."

"Then that explains the accent," Martha said. She nodded a grudging inch.

"How about boyfriends?"

"She had some." Something about the tone of voice suggested disapproval.

"Were they older men?"

The woman hesitated.

"This is a murder investigation," Martha said.

"There was talk, you know."

"I don't know."

"Like she went out with guys who might slip her something once in a while. I wouldn't call her a prostitute."

"What would you call her?"

"I don't know. An appreciative date? I don't like putting labels on people."

"You mean she was a sugar baby," Sean said.

"They're your words, not mine."

And they proved to be among the last words of the interview. The manager either could not or would not provide any names of men Jolene had "dated." She had never heard of Peter Jackson, and knew Wilhelm Winkler's name only because his death had made the front page of the *Bridger Mountain Star.* She didn't like where the conversation was heading.

"Just because we dress up like hookers doesn't mean we aren't good Christian women." She said she had to get back to work, although what work that might be she didn't volunteer.

Martha thanked her for her time, took down contact information, and said she might have more questions later.

They walked down the street to the café, where Martha had vegetable soup and Sean ate the best BLT he'd had in Montana.

"I know that might not have seemed productive," Martha said, asking for the bill, "but I think we learned something."

"You mean now we know what the connection could be, the way Jackson might have known Jolene. She cleaned his house."

Martha rolled her eyes. "More like she wet his whistle."

"I just said that to see your expression."

"I figured. Say she was offering sex. How did she meet him? For that matter, how did he pay her? Man alone in a cabin, no visible means of support, he tells you he has no money."

"He pays her the same way he paid Freida," Sean said. "He parcels off his Hemingway memorabilia."

"That's what I'm thinking, too. Makes you wonder about what really happened in the Bear Trap. We've been operating under the assumption that Winkler was acting alone, that he got the rod from his sister and was trying to barter it to Patrick Willoughby when he met with his accident. Now I'm thinking Winkler and Jolene were working together, or else she followed him. And maybe it wasn't an accident. Maybe she didn't like the idea of someone else cutting into a piece of the pie."

"How does she come to know Winkler?"

"Through association."

"You mean she knew Freida?" Sean said.

"She did or she didn't, once Freida and Winkler were out of the way, she had free rein to milk Peter Jackson for anything he still owned."

"Then what? He finds out she doesn't really love him and kills her?"

"Maybe she was stealing from the trunk. He caught her at it. Or maybe Papa in the sky told him to off her. You said he could be schizophrenic. Maybe he heard voices."

Martha thumbed her credit card and placed it on the bill, shaking off Sean's offer of cash. "On me," she said. "Got to keep you solvent until the walls of your house go up."

Sean swallowed, feeling the pain in his chest, which had leveled off but was still hard to ignore. "So where do we go from here?" he said.

"Back to the house. See if we can find anything that looks like it belonged to Ernest Hemingway. Use sharper eyes this time."

A grim smile played on her lips.

"What?"

"I thought of another quote."

"You seem to be full of them this morning."

"That's because I read. You could try it sometime. Besides *Field & Stream*, I mean."

"All right, what is it?"

"'I ain't afraid of loving a man. I ain't afraid of shooting him, either.'"

"Who said that?"

"Annie Oakley."

# CHAPTER TWENTY-SEVEN

# What Goes On in Martha's House . . .

"**P**ass," Martha said.

She was standing before Jolene Bailie's four-poster bed, hands on her hips. Sean, who'd been impertinent enough to ask if she wanted to try out the mattress, leaned in the doorframe.

She chewed on her lip. A long minute ticked off. Then she cocked a forefinger at her temple. "It's not in the house," she said.

"What do you mean?"

"I mean it's in plain sight, only not in the house."

She waited. Sean thought.

"The flower box," he said.

They took the creel to the hood of the Cherokee and emptied out the petunias. The bottom of the creel had a copper lining to keep the wicker from rotting and had turned green over time. Sean exchanged a glance with Martha. He pried out the lining. There was nothing underneath but feathers, bits of stick, and white deposits that made Martha turn up her nose.

"Looks like a robin tried to build a nest before somebody lined it," Sean said. "But I'll tell you right now this isn't the same creel I saw at Peter Jackson's house. That one was much fancier. It was built by Salish Indians."

Martha wasn't giving up. "Do you know anything about the value of these things? This one's pretty well preserved. Usually, you see an old wicker creel, the leather's dry rotted and the clasp is missing."

"It has an ink stamp on the lid with the number five."

"Be nice if it had 'EH' carved into the leather trim."

"That would be too easy, Martha."

"Nothing wrong with easy." She put the creel in the Cherokee and called the number that the Virginia City Players' manager had given her, asked if she had ever noticed the creel when she visited the owners of the place. She listened and punched off.

Stranahan didn't question her and they were down the road and out of the ghost town, leaving two clicks of a century behind before Martha spoke again.

"She said she visited half a dozen times over the past few years and can't recall there being a creel, either used as a flower box or anything else. That doesn't mean Jolene put it up, but I'd say good chance."

Sean nodded.

"Not out of the question that Jackson had two creels," Martha said.

Sean nodded again. He was finding that just talking hurt. It felt like a constricting snake had taken up residence in his chest and tightened a coil around his heart.

"I guess," he said.

"You guess what?"

"I don't know."

"Why do I feel like I'm talking to myself?" Martha said under her breath. Then, "Hey, are you okay? You've been sort of monosyllabic since we left town. Pain's not getting worse, is it?"

"What makes you think that?"

"Is it?"

"Just sort of an ache."

"Good. I was afraid if you were agreeing with me too easily, it meant you were in too much pain to argue."

Stranahan laughed, then grimaced. "Don't make me laugh," he said.

He didn't make the mistake again, and Martha didn't say anything that encouraged it. Forty minutes later she pulled up to his tipi, but he just sat there.

"You're sure you're okay?"

"Yeah," he said. "I'm just not thinking very well. I forgot to tell you something and now I'm afraid if I do, you'll be pissed and I won't have the energy to defend myself."

"I've been pissed at you before. It's the bedrock of our relationship."

"About Jolene Bailie . . ." He told her then, the part about finding the body he hadn't told her before, using his camera at the scene to take photos of the footprints, the body, and the data from the woman's GPS and cell phone. "You have to understand, Martha, I was afraid I'd be cut out of the loop. I'm still working this case, at least the Hemingway angle."

"Oh, I understand. I understand tampering with evidence. It's in Law Enforcement 101."

"I put everything back where I found it."

"That doesn't make it acceptable." She raised a hand before he could object. "I'm going to need your camera. And that notebook." She lifted a hand from the steering wheel and snapped her fingers.

"Why? The actual phone and GPS will be in evidence with the Park County sheriff's office. I didn't erase any data."

"Nonetheless."

"Don't you want to know what I found on them?"

"I do or I don't, it doesn't justify copying evidence. I took an oath to uphold all the laws, not just those I have a mind to."

"Okay, I'll hand my camera over, but you're going to look at the pictures with me before you give them to anyone else."

"Why? Do you have any reason to think Stokes isn't investigating this murder on the level?"

"Yeah. A bullet to the chest. Stokes was the first officer to see the body. After he dropped me back in Cooke City, if he drove straight back up there, he'd have had an hour at the scene before anyone else showed with a badge or a fingerprint kit. Probably more than an hour."

"Why would he tamper with evidence?"

"I don't think he went to the same law academy that you did. I don't think they teach 'beat and release' where you went to school. Maybe he shot me for the fun of it, or maybe the wax bullet was a warning. 'Don't stick your nose into my business.'"

"You know I've aged two years for each one on the calendar since meeting you." She shook her head. "Tell you what we're going to do. You're going to rest up a couple hours while I go into town and take care of a few things. Then you're coming over for dinner, and afterward, when we're both off the clock, we're going to stick the camera card you didn't give me into the Mac. I don't trust that bastard, either."

"What goes on in Martha's house stays in Martha's house?"

"Go get some rest."

# CHAPTER TWENTY-EIGHT

# Might as Well Be the Moon

Three hours dead to the world followed by two codeine pills originally prescribed for his dog, Choti, the last time she'd got into a porcupine, dulled the pain while restoring his spirits. The half glass of wine with dinner added just enough glow to make him careless.

"I had lasagna with Margarethe Harris on the Au Sable River," he said. "Yours is better."

He hadn't meant to bring the name up, and there was an awkward pause.

"Still pining for her, huh?" Martha said.

"No. It's just that she started all this talk about a missing treasure chest with her story about Jack Hemingway. It's just the way of life. You meet someone, they trigger something that takes you in another direction, and then you never see them again."

There was a silence.

"I'll drink to that," Martha said.

With that they were back where they'd begun the evening, relaxed with each other, their minds turning toward the riddle that had started with a woman dying inside a bear's den on one mountain, and that now, a little over two weeks later, centered on another woman's demise on a different mountain. Sean cleared the dishes and they took the remaining half bottle of red into Martha's study, where a polished, hundred-and-fifty-year-old ponderosa stump served as her desk. She keystroked her Mac out of its slumber and a few minutes later they were studying the images she'd transferred from Sean's camera card. Besides the photos he'd taken at the burial scene, there were several images of footprints in the patchy snow.

"If you blow up this section of the photograph, you'll see that there's no tread pattern in the larger, overlapping print," Sean said. "It's smooth. That's what makes me believe it's Jackson's moccasin."

"So you told me before."

"You don't agree?"

"No, I'd just be more willing to take your word if it was Harold's word. No offense."

"None taken. He'd certainly have a better idea if the small tracks and the larger ones were made at the same time, or if the moccasins came in later. One would imply that Jackson killed her, the other that he found her."

"Yeah, well, Harold's up on Rocky Boy. Tell you what we'll do, though. He checks in at the tribal headquarters in Box Elder every other day or so. He can get Wi-Fi there. We'll attach these photos to an e-mail and see if he can clear the air."

Sean nodded his agreement. "Do you want to see the pictures of the GPS and phone screens?"

Martha was reversing through the images. She paused at one that showed the elk-tooth earring on Jolene Bailie's dirt-smudged ear.

"Looks like a tooth from a three-year-old cow," she said. "A bull's would be more round." She raised her eyes from the image and looked away. "I heard you about the GPS," she said. "I just want to spend a minute with her first. It makes her death real to me. It makes me want to get to the bottom of it."

She clicked through the photos again. The left side of the face. The left hand and wrist, which Sean had scraped the soil from, exposing the friendship bracelet that he'd first noticed in the Bear Trap Canyon. A close-up of the left eye, not so much staring as what?

None of the adjectives people used to describe a dead person's eyes got it right. Opaque, glassy, unseeing, lifeless—none were right. In fact Martha saw the opposite. She saw eyes that still possessed sight, and that reflected a dreamy sort of acceptance of death. It was as if the eyes were lazily observing whatever it is that people observe when their hearts cease to beat. Martha had seen wonderment in the eyes of the dead; she had seen, she thought, bewilderment. But she had not seen pain or terror or even anxiety. No, dead eyes were calm eyes, they had all the time in the world. In a few hours they would begin to skin over, in a few more to shrink back into the skull. But by then they would only be husks, and it was only then that the adjectives applied.

"The coroner said three to eight hours dead," she said. "But I can tell you right now that when you found her she hadn't been dead more than an hour or two. I can see it in her eyes."

Martha shook her head, as if to chase the images out of her mind. "God have mercy," she said. "Okay, let's have a gander at the calls."

Most of the incoming and outgoing calls were Montana numbers, but there were half a dozen or so with a 208 area code.

"That's Idaho, right?" Sean said.

Martha nodded.

"Didn't Winkler say he was from Idaho?"

Martha nodded again. "Hailey."

"If that's his number, it's probably still connected."

Martha tapped at her phone. Five rings before the recording. *Please leave your name, number, and a clear message at the tone.* No name, but the accent was sufficient to identify Winkler as the speaker.

"The next photo is the only text message I saw." Sean advanced the images. It was from Winkler's number. *It's on. Bear Trap. 11 a.m. Agreed about Jupiter.*

Martha bit her lip as she read the text. "It confirms the rendez-vous. But why the dog?"

"Because you could walk a dog from one end of Montana to the other without anyone asking you a question," Sean said. "It makes her presence at the river legit."

Martha nodded. "I'll put Hunt on the technical extraction stuff tomorrow. If something's been erased, he'll find it."

"How can he do that if all he has is a picture?"

"All I know is that you give him a raindrop of blood, he can coax a vampire out of his coffin."

Martha laced her hands behind her head. "Well, what do you know?"

It was a rhetorical question, and Sean's "Well now" was an echo of the sentiment.

"She didn't mention anything about being with Winkler in her statement," Martha said. "Makes you wonder if she wasn't the one who gave him a friendly shove onto a spiky stick."

"Or Jupiter did. Did Doc check the body for dog saliva?"

"He found some on the face. But as he said, 'Dogs lick things.' Winkler could have already been dead. It doesn't mean the hound knocked him down. And the man was wearing waders, so even if the dog did jump up on him, there wouldn't necessarily be transfer evidence."

"Where is Jupiter, by the way?"

"I dropped him at the shelter."

Martha was nodding to herself. "While you were resting up, I called Jolene's mother in Staunton. She'd already been informed as next of kin and said she'd been estranged from her daughter and hadn't seen her in three years, ever since she'd moved west. She said Jolene thought she had glitter in her veins and was too good for her old momma. I asked if she wanted the hound and she said no, but he was a pedigreed coon dog and she knew a teacher at the high school who might. She was going to have the teacher call us back, because he wanted to hear the dog bay, because he hunted coon for the music." She shook her head. "Like we're going to arrange a conference call and have the dog sing into a mike."

"Maybe Sam will take him," Sean said.

Martha murmured to herself. "I'm murmuring to myself," she said. "What do you know, it's another new bad habit. Let's move on to the GPS."

"I transcribed the waypoints into my notebook. The numbers are easier to read."

"Then give," Martha said.

It took a few minutes, transferring the GPS waypoints onto a Google

Earth topographic mapping system. While the computer cooked, Martha corked the wine and brewed tea. They sipped at it, studying the markers superimposed on the digital rendition of the country. The waypoints included the dates they were entered into the positioning unit and showed one along the Madison River, below the confluence with Bear Trap Creek. Sean pointed with the eraser of a pencil and Martha nodded. It was the rendezvous point that Winkler had mentioned in his letter to Patrick Willoughby, and was dated only the day before they had found his body.

A nest of overlapping waypoints, all dated within the past two months, cluttered the map near Cooke City. Martha spread thumb and forefinger on the touch pad, zooming in to distinguish the markers.

"That's the bridge where I parked," Sean said.

"Don't touch the screen."

"Sorry."

"I'm to assume this one is Jackson's house?" Martha said.

"Yeah. It's right alongside the creek."

"How about up here?" One of the waypoints marked a peninsula extending into a body of water that, counting the contour lines, had to be at least two thousand feet higher in elevation than the cabin itself.

"That's Froze-to-Death Lake," Sean said. "Bill Shaunnessey said it's where Hemingway threw the pistol his father used to kill himself."

"You don't say."

Sean moved the eraser farther up the swirl of contour lines to a broad area above the treeline. The marker on the east side of flat ground there, near the final approach to Froze-to-Death Peak, was the highest-elevation GPS waypoint on the map.

"Froze-to-Death Plateau," he said.

"Are you saying that because you've heard of it?"

"No. I'm just reading the name on the map. Why? Have you?"

"They call it the 'Roof of Montana,'" Martha said. "It's so barren up there the only mammals are pikas and mountain goats. Anyway, it's a godforsaken wilderness."

She shook her head, remembering. "We got called across the county line for a search and rescue, this would be back in oh-six, oh-seven. I wasn't on the force then, but I volunteered SAR. Two hikers had signed the register at the trailhead and then just disappeared. Boyfriend, girlfriend, plus a dog. We climbed up there, twenty-six switchbacks, three-thousand-feet elevation gain in two miles. July snowstorm."

"Did you find them?"

"Not for four years. Finally a climber found the remains under a ledge. Their faces were gone. We figured they got lost and died from hypothermia, and golden eagles got to them."

"What about the dog?"

"It showed up at the trailhead two weeks into the search. Made us believe they died early on."

"How long would it take to climb up there?"

"This time of year? Only about six weeks."

"Winter's a long time going, huh?"

"You can get a blizzard at that elevation any day of the year. I know what you're thinking, Sean. You're thinking that Jackson stashed his steamer trunk up there and Jolene wangled the coordinates out of him."

"It's logical. He seemed fit enough to make the climb and he wouldn't have had to haul in the trunk, just backpack the contents. If not on the plateau, how about the lake? That's waypointed as well."

She shrugged. "It's lower, but it's still got to be nine thousand feet. This time of year, might as well be the moon."

Sean thought about that as they checked the other coordinates on the map, most of which marked high-altitude lakes in Hyalite and surrounding counties and dated to the prior summer.

"She was a hiker, that Jolene," Martha said. "I don't think any of these coordinates mean anything, though. Do you?"

Sean shook his head and she put the computer to bed. She told Sean that he was sleeping over.

"No funny business, though," she said. "I don't want to put any strain on your heart."

She kept her word and lay quietly beside him while he felt sleep coming on, and it was right there, just one more breath and then the liquid slipstream into his dreams . . . but something in him fought against it. He got up and went outside under the haze of the moon, waxing ever since he'd caught the great trout on his mouse fly in the Madison River, and only a couple days off the full now.

*Might as well be the moon.*

Well, they'd reached it, hadn't they? Landed on it. One small step for a man, one giant leap for mankind. You never knew unless you tried.

# CHAPTER TWENTY-NINE

# Froze-to-Death Lake

The Ruger with the shark's fin sight was right where Sean had stowed it, six miles east of Cooke City under a slab of slide rock that wore a pattern of lichen shaped like a lightning bolt. He wiped away a spider's web that arched across the cylinder and checked the loads. Five live with the one under the hammer empty except for the web's weaver. He gently blew into the cylinder, coaxing the spider out, then zipped the gun into the side pocket of his backpack and picked his way through the boulders down to the road.

Sam Meslik was leaning against the hood of his pickup, grinning, showing the grooves in his teeth.

"Are we armed, Kemosabe, or are we just going to go up there with swinging dicks?"

"We're armed."

"Good. 'Cause if anything happens to me, Molly will cut your heart out."

"It's you who insisted on coming."

"I know, I'm just talking. It's different, though, having someone who cares. All my life I've gone where I wanted, when I wanted, and no-body home to worry if I don't come back."

Sean met the big man's carnivorous grin, but it had been against his better judgment, acquiescing to Sam's adamancy about tagging along, and he would never have agreed if he'd thought there was any chance that Peter Jackson was still in the vicinity. But his working supposition, shared by law enforcement, was that Jackson had fled in

Jolene Bailie's truck after killing her, and he was up here on a hunt for treasure, not for a fugitive. The truth, if he permitted himself to admit it, was that he wanted the companionship. Plus Leland Stokes didn't know Sam's Nissan pickup. Sean had been driving the club's rental Subaru when he met Stokes, but Stokes had asked for the make and model of his own rig and Sean had given it to him.

He felt the heft of the revolver in his pack and thought about Martha. They loved each other—they had said the words for the second time only last night—and yet here he was, betraying her trust, creating the separation he could have bridged just by being honest. But then he would have come up here anyway, even under the weight of her disapproval. No, she wouldn't approve one bit, and there you had it, the price to pay later.

"What the fuck?" Sam said. "Are we going or are we going?"

"We're going." Sean climbed into the cab.

"Fuckin' A."

Sam motored the remaining five miles down Highway 212 and crossed the rickety bridge where Froze-to-Death Creek spilled into the Cold Hearted River.

"This is the path up to Jackson's cabin," Sean said.

Sam eased off the pedal.

"No, keep going. The trailhead to the lake's another mile."

They found the turnaround at the trailhead empty, no surprise this early in the year. A signboard warned that it was grizzly country and included an illustration of the proper method for hanging food. Sean studied the topographic map fixed to the signboard under a protective sheet of Plexiglas. It showed the broken line of the trail as requiring a switchback climb of some fifteen hundred feet right off the bat, before the trail zigged down to the creek. The trail then followed the creek all the way up to the lake's outlet, on one side of the blue line on the map or the other. Sean had anticipated having to ford the creek and they had packed Croc sandals for the crossings.

"Piece of cake," Sam said.

It was wishful thinking, dry ground giving way to mud, giving way to slush and, before they'd even reached the ridge, a fresh pelt of snow that rose halfway up their shins in vanilla swirls. Topping out, they regarded the unrolling of the country to the north and east, the rock escarpments windswept and barren. What was the word Martha had used? Desolate? No. Godforsaken. It was that, all right, but nothing prepared you for the scale, the utter immensity of a landscape as yet unchanged by the hand of man, where only the hardy or the very fool-hardy dared to tread.

Sean and Sam took their packs off and sat on them. Sean tried to ignore the sharp pain each time he drew breath. It was getting easier— the ignoring part, not so much the pain. Far below them the creek shone intermittently, banging its way through a narrow canyon, the water more white than blue. Sam's "I don't know, Kemosabe" hung in the air as they began to switchback down.

Reaching the bottom, the trail hugged the bank, then crossed to the other side of the creek, the way shown by piled-up cairns of rocks. Five creek crossings, the last two iffy with the water above their knees, saw them to a few acres of level ground where the creek spread in a bog. A month from now the standing water would sing with the hum of mosquitoes, but now it was covered by a pane of ice and the quiet was the quiet of wilderness. Sean advanced a foot onto the bog. Put his weight on it. The ice fractured, crow's-feet radiating in four directions. Water burbled up through the cracks. So much for the idea of crossing on the ice.

Skirting the bog took longer than expected, the snow crusty but not hard enough to support their weight, the going a slog, what moun-taineers called postholing. At the upper end of the bog was a rock out-cropping that was dry enough to sit on. Sam said, "From this point forward, I will fight no more forever." He stepped onto the ledge and lay back and looked at the sky. Wet and exhausted, Sean followed suit. He unfolded the map in his jacket pocket.

"What's the verdict?" Sam said. "Are we fucked or are we fucked?"

"Both. The lake's two more miles and another thousand feet up. The snow will be up to our waists."

Sean watched Sam digest this news. He was so disheartened by their failure that he shut his eyes and began to snore. Sean took Sam's lead and dozed, and had been dozing for some time when the sound of a falling rock brought him to a state of alertness. Looking across to the concave slope of the ridge on the far side of the bog, he saw a puff of snow. Then there was a thunderclap, followed by an echoing roar as the slope began to avalanche, the snow rushing in a billowing wave, clouding the sky until there was nothing but white and the avalanche, still roaring, trees snapping like gunshots, slowed, spreading in a V. It settled in a hem of mogul-shaped deposits over the bog.

In the profound silence that followed, Sean found himself in a copse of stunted white-bark pines fifty yards up the slope behind him, having fled the slide instinctively, and without having the slightest notion how he'd got there. He heard Sam shouting his name and his name echoing, and then he saw him, some distance away, even farther up the slope.

Sean waved and climbed up to him.

"I'm beginning to think God's trying to tell us something," Sam said.

Sean rested his hands on his knees, breathing hard, sweating in the cold. He shook his head and straightened up. As he did, his eyes settled on a disturbance in the snow. No more than a dozen yards up the slope, a line of tracks showed as shadows. A glance at closer range revealed that the trail had been laid down by snowshoes. The imprints were distorted by age—two days old? Three? No more than that. He remembered the snowshoes he'd seen outside Peter Jackson's cabin. Had they been there on his last visit? He couldn't recall.

"We aren't alone up here," Sam said.

Sean stepped into one of the tracks, which were shaped like giant teardrops. Snow, when disturbed, sets up hard, and the firm crust supported his weight. He stepped into another track. It, too, held.

"There's your fucking miracle," Sam said. "Now you're like Jesus. You can part the fucking sea. Or maybe Moses. He walked on water, right?"

"I think you got your testaments mixed up."

"Whatever. They taught us the Bible in Sunday school, but it's hard to concentrate when you're trying to look up Gretchen Little's skirt."

Sean shook his head. This changed things. He'd packed the revolver only as a hedge against his bet that they'd have the high country to themselves. Now they were following the tracks of a man who was probably armed and likely a murderer at that.

No, not probably armed, Sean thought. Positively. He could see where the butt of a shotgun had been used as a walking stick.

"Not the safest way to carry your weapon," Sam observed. He jabbed the butt of an invisible shotgun onto the snow and said, "Boom."

"Maybe we'll get lucky," he said. "Maybe he'll shoot himself."

Sean smiled, but only with the half of his face that faced Sam.

"We're turning back," he said. "We'll report it and they can wait and take him when he comes back down."

"Like hell we will," Sam said. "We can be there in an hour."

Sean shook his head. "You have a family to consider. It isn't like before, you said so yourself. And I'm not just talking about Jackson. You saw what happened. We trigger another avalanche, they might not find our bodies for months."

"I'm my own man," Sam said. And as if to prove it, he stepped with his right foot into one of the snowshoe tracks. He lifted his left foot, and for several heartbeats he was on top of the snow. Then his right boot broke through, jarring against the ground underneath. He tried again, better, got two steps, then abruptly broke through the crust.

"Shit," Sam said. "How much do you weigh?"

"I haven't stepped on a scale in at least ten years."

"I got you by thirty-five pounds, I figure. I'm what Ali weighed at his peak."

"Now you're Ali, huh?"

"I'm in fighting trim."

"Tell that to the snow."

Sean looked at the sky, the sun already over the shoulder of the escarpment. It would be dark inside an hour.

"Let's sleep on it," he said. "Maybe you can lose the weight overnight."

Sam snorted. "I hope you brought something to eat."

"I got this and that."

"I got a flask of schnapps."

"Then we have the basic food groups covered."

They settled on a bench of timber, far enough up from the creek bottom to be out of the cold wind that would flow down the canyon in the night. Sean tied off the corners of his tarp to tree trunks to make a crude shelter, and they dragged downfall and built a fire, piling logs to act as a reflector. It was a good idea, although the wind didn't cooperate, and every twenty minutes or so they had to move around to dodge the smoke. "This and that" turned out to be antelope jerky that Sean had made on Martha's smoker and a hard-boiled egg apiece, the yolks frozen so that they had to put the eggs under their shirts to thaw.

"Tell me again why I came up here," Sam said. He knocked the flask back and said, "Ahh."

"Because you wanted to have a hand in finding fishing gear that belonged to Ernest Hemingway."

"Yeah, it's coming back. It's just that with all the fun, I forgot."

He took another swallow and passed the flask to Sean.

After awhile: "Say I can't get up there. What then?"

"You stay while I check out the waypoint on the lake. I'll climb up and come back early, before the sun gets up and increases the avalanche risk. Then we'll go on down together."

"We don't have sleeping bags. You think we'll get any sleep?"

"No," Sean said.

———

That would prove true for at least one of them. Sean had brought two thin foam pads as insulation against the ground and gave one to Sam, who curled beside the fire and began to snore almost immediately, oblivious of the smoke. Sean turned himself as one turns a steak on a grill, braising one side, then the other. He spent the night the way he had before on a cold breast of mountain, rising to pee, to stoke the fire, to add another stick, to reposition his pad as the wind changed its mind. To do everything, that is, except sleep.

Giving up when the moon told him that the night was on the wane, Sean rummaged in his pack for coffee. He dumped a small handful into the pot of water sitting next to the fire. He let it simmer up, then added the leftover eggshells to make the grounds settle. They didn't. Maybe that worked only with fresh shells. It was still coffee. He sipped at it, straining it between his teeth. He spit out the grounds.

Sam stirred. His mane of hair glowed copper in the firelight. "You really going to try it, Kemosabe?"

"If I don't come back, you get the Burkheimer five-weight."

"I want the Bruce and Walker, the fifteen-footer."

"Anything else?"

"That Ellefson belt knife you carry. And I'm sure Molly would like a painting."

"Any she wants."

"Not to get all gooey, but you're the best friend I have. At least the best one doesn't give me a hard-on you could hang a moose head from. So be safe up there."

"Gee, Sam. Thanks . . . I guess."

"You get to be a father, you can't just fish and fuck around like you used to. I hate to say anything nice about Martha, but she's thrown her chips into the pot and ain't the neither of you getting any younger. Maybe it's time to settle down."

Sean grunted.

"You even sound like her," Sam said.

Sean told him there was coffee in the pot and started off, the snow squeaking under his weight, but holding. Sam had been right. It was like walking on water.

"Did you say something?" Sean stopped

"This guy sounds like he's got a screw loose." Sam's voice was thick with his watch cap pulled over his nose.

"I'll be lucky if it's only one," Sean said.

# CHAPTER THIRTY

# A Man of the World

The lake looked to be entirely frozen. It was a long lake, nearly a mile on the map, pinched into a black widow's hourglass by a peninsula that jutted from the far shore. A vast, black pearl surface.

Stars, some dead but with their echoes still shining, glanced off the pool of open water at the outlet. The trail of snowshoes had skirted the outlet to a higher vantage, and where Sean stood, only the occasional deep note of the creek's lament reached his ears. Already, a wafer of gray painted the horizon. Sean raised his binoculars to study a firefly of yellow light that shone across the lake. He switched on his headlamp, using the red LED cluster to prevent the glow being seen at a distance. Consulting the map, he assured himself that the yellow light had to be in the immediate vicinity of the waypoint Jolene Bailie had marked on her GPS. Sean had that feeling that hunters know when the tracks are fresh, of impending action, of a need to swallow. It had been mounting inside him ever since leaving Sam at the camp. He bent and scooped up a handful of hoarfrost, its crystals glistening like shards of glass. He put the snow in his mouth, felt the nothingness of it, as if chewing on cold air, then the slippery feel as it melted. He swallowed the few drops of water. He switched the light off and felt the reassuring weight of the .357 pulling at the stitching on one side of his pack. He began to contour the lakeshore.

There was no path, only a jumble of boulders and ledge rock, and in the forty minutes it took to circle the southern rim of the lake, the yellow light grew from a shapeless smear into three distinct lights, a large dull orb topped by two blisters of bright light, the effect roughly that of a glowing snowman.

For some time Sean thought he was approaching a dome tent, but as dawn crept down the walls of the basin, he saw that it was an igloo, the larger of the lights emanating from the entrance, the middle light from a rectangular window, and the upper and smallest light coming through what he assumed to be a vent. Lifting his binoculars for a better look, he saw a figure emerge through the entrance, walking on all fours like a bear and then, standing up, still bearlike, propping its weight on a walking stick. Except it wasn't a stick, for as the figure stepped forward, the light of the igloo's window glanced off metal. Sean didn't need the eight-power glass to know what that was.

Peter Jackson's voice echoed in the rarefied air of the basin. "It's my practice never to shoot anyone until the sun is over the mountain. Come on up. Welcome to the Top of the World."

Sean climbed into the range of the shotgun, passing the place at which the pellets would burn and bury under his skin, to the place where they would punch a hole through him the size of a cannonball.

"I hope this means you've brought me some of the angel dust that Freida dispensed. Else why are you up here? And a fool to boot. I heard the avalanche last night. I hope that wasn't you who triggered it."

"That was God's doing," Sean said.

"He's letting you know that he's angry," Jackson said. "Next time he might not be so forgiving."

Sean was close enough now to make out Jackson's face, the tangled hair and beard, white against an expanse of windswept rock on the slope behind the igloo. His smile was skeptical, bemused. Not at all the expression one would expect from someone on the lam from the law, let alone the prime suspect in a murder investigation.

"Are you armed?"

"There's a revolver in my pack."

"Only an idiot packs a gun where it would take an act of Congress to draw it. But then we've already established your mental deficiency."

"I didn't climb here to pull guns. I just want to talk."

"Then have your say. But I hope you don't harbor any illusions of changing my mind. What Americana or objets d'art I may still possess are not for sale, at least not for pieces of paper issued by the U.S. Treasury Department. I may suspect your intention, but I don't know how you've arrived at this temporary domicile, and that is a concern. My privacy is important to my work. Watch your head, now."

Propping the shotgun against the outside igloo wall, Jackson ducked inside. Sean shrugged his pack off, leaving it beside the shotgun, and followed him, pushing aside the thin blanket that draped over the entrance. In the four years that Sean had been living in a tipi, he had twice built igloos to survive the coldest weeks of winter, using a YouTube video as his guide, and this one was typical of those he'd constructed, though with a larger footprint.

Made from compacted blocks stacked so that each layer formed an ascending, inward-facing spiral, like a perfectly coiled rattlesnake, the igloo was nearly tall enough to stand in. The living space near the back was elevated to trap warm air. In addition to a sleeping platform, which was carved from snow and draped with a luxuriant elkskin robe, the major piece of furniture was a work table nailed together from wrist-thick lengths of pine. A tanned animal hide had been tacked across the top of the table, the stretched skin having dried to make a drum-tight surface. On the table, a hurricane lamp with a cracked globe cast light onto the matte black manual typewriter Sean had seen in the cabin. A sheet of onionskin typing paper was rolled onto the platen.

"As you can see, I have all the creature comforts."

The livered hand swept the igloo's interior, encompassing the sleeping platform and the elkskin robe, on top of which was the same wicker creel with the diamond design that Sean had seen at the cabin. He noted a cache of groceries and a dual-fuel Coleman stove with which to cook them.

Everything but the cat, Sean thought, and in the echo of his thought, if thoughts could have echoes and animals hear them, the cat's head popped out of the square opening in the lid of the creel. It regarded Stranahan with unconcealed hostility, its mouth opening to show the long canines, its breath a hiss. Then it withdrew its head back into the creel's interior.

"I followed your snowshoe tracks. I didn't see hers," Sean said.

"Tatie's so light she doesn't leave paw prints. Besides, she makes most of the trip in the creel, which I lash to the back of my pack. I don't bring her here except in winter, when the eagles hunt at lower elevations. She'd make a meal, I'm afraid. But then, maybe not. She is a survivor, what Ernest would call a man of the world. That was his last short story—'A Man of the World.' Are you familiar with it?"

Sean said he wasn't.

"He set it in a town called Jessup, which is really Cooke City. Most readers, even Hemingway scholars, dismiss it as being simplistic, just a sketch about an old man called Blindy who bums drinks at the bars. Someone to pity, to hand a coin to when you're feeling generous. What they don't see is that under his stinking clothes, Blindy is one of Hemingway's unvanquished heroes. His eyes were gouged out in a drunken brawl with another man whose face was also disfigured in the fight. But where the other man is a recluse, unwilling to show the scars where Blindy had torn at his face with his teeth, Blindy himself remains undaunted. He's proud of his name. He's earned it. He is a man of the world, not someone who shrinks from it."

Sean had expected a confrontation, not a lecture. But it was an opening and he stepped into it.

"Is this one of Hemingway's stories?" He pointed at the typewriter.

"You tell me," Jackson said. "You can turn up the lamp if you want a closer look."

Sean turned the metal key, exposing more of the wick to the flame. It was the same sheet of typewriting he'd seen at the cabin. No, not exactly. The same characters, the man and the boy, but the narrative had taken them farther into the woods, where the river flowed, where the sky was a velvet slot crisscrossed by long snakes of mayflies, their wings pulsing against the walls of the forest.

*The trout rose as an intermittent rain,* he read, *and the hand on the rod forgot that it was old.*

The scene reminded him of the hatch he'd fished with Margarethe Harris on the Au Sable River, where the current parted around the island where she and a boy had shared their first kiss.

"Do you have the rest of the story?" he asked.

"Do I have the rest of the story?" Jackson seemed to look beyond the igloo walls. His cheeks glowed cherry in the lamplight. His beard shone like the pelt of a polar bear.

"That, Mr. Stranahan, is a question I've been asking myself for the last thirty years."

# CHAPTER THIRTY-ONE

# Changing Fortunes

"I suppose it's time," Jackson began. And slowly he nodded, as if he had arrived at a long-delayed decision. "I am only a man, with a man's desire to unburden his heart. I knew this day would come."

The cat's head again emerged from the opening in the creel, and the livered hand patted the flat head. "You stay here, Tatie," he said. And to Stranahan: "You'll want to get into your coat. The coldest hour is upon us, or will be when the sun breaks over the horizon."

Jackson ducked back outside the igloo, where he drew a stout, curved-blade instrument from where it had been stuck into the snow.

"This is what the Inuit called a *pana*," Jackson said. "It's used to cut snow blocks. This one's carved from a walrus tusk. I use it for its original purpose, but I also tap the ice with it to see where it's safe enough to walk."

He pointed toward the bay of the lake, only a couple hundred feet away. "You see that pressure ridge that begins near the shore and runs in a line toward the peninsula? It formed after a cold snap last month, when the ice began to warm and expand. When I shoed up here to build my spring igloo, I saw a mountain goat break through and drown. Who knows what other bones it joined on the bottom?"

It was gray light now, and Jackson followed what Sean could see was a well-trod path that contoured along the bay, into the half-eye of the sun. He turned where the peninsula extended into the middle of the lake. But for a solitary subalpine fir that had found roothold in the cracks of the rock, it was a barren landscape, making Sean think of images of the moon. At the terminus of the peninsula, the shallow water was rimmed with a pane of thin ice. Jackson tapped at it with the point of the walrus tusk and they saw the water underneath lap up against it. Jackson reached out farther, where the ice was thicker.

"What you want is a solid thump," he said, "not a hollow thunk." He jabbed the blunt end of the saw onto the ice. "Like that. This is solid. It's only melting at the edges. We can walk on it."

Where the snow cover was wind-scoured the ice was indigo blue. It was shot with bubbles, and with long ladderlike cracks that were colored the silvery black of the backs of mirrors. The cracks showed the depth of the ice as they walked into the hourglass of the lake.

"A guide at the ranch where I bought my cabin said that Ernest Hemingway rode a horse up here sometime in the middle 1930s," Jackson said. "This is where he tossed the Civil War pistol that his father used to kill himself. He fictionalized the incident in *For Whom the Bell Tolls,* writing that he saw himself holding the gun in the reflection of the lake. He wrote that it made bubbles going down and that when he last saw its glimmer, it was no bigger than a watch charm. Another version has him throwing it into the lake and being haunted by seeing the barrel point at him as it turned end over end. It gave him a premonition of his own death."

"And you think this could be the spot?" Sean had heard Bill Shaunnessey's version of the story, but asked the question to keep Jackson talking.

"A horse trail drops down to the lake at the base of the peninsula. He would naturally walk out to the point to lob the gun. This is as far as I could throw a three-pound rock, which is about what the Smith & Wesson would have weighed."

"How deep is it under our feet?"

"The maps show a sonar reading of sixty feet. Now, if Hemingway didn't throw the gun, but leaned out over a ledge and dropped it into the water, then that ledge just around the point is my guess. It's eighty feet deep right off the rocks."

"It's like you're a dot on an ocean," Sean said.

Jackson nodded. "There's nothing makes a man feel so small or philosophical about it as walking onto the ice of a big lake."

"Why do you come up here, Peter?" Sean asked. "I understand the connection with history, but it seems like a bleak place to write. Why not the cabin?"

"I do work in the cabin. But when I become stuck or get stir crazy, I find my solace and inspiration here. I minored in cultural anthropology and had the opportunity to live with Inuit seal hunters for a month off the coast of Greenland. That's where I learned to build an igloo. There's something about making your house to write in. It makes the experience more insular and gives you a personal connection. And the work you do with your hands stirs the creative juices.

"This basin"—he swept an arm—"this is where I feel closest to the man who has become a brother in my life in everything but blood. It's where I've come the closest to assimilating his spirit. Here he made a promise to himself. By throwing away the gun, he announced that he was a stronger man than his father, that he would not fall victim to the same urge that fought for purchase in his own being, and that he would live long enough to complete his work. Some would say he didn't succeed, but he succeeded for the next twenty-five years. He gave the world *A Moveable Feast* and *The Old Man and the Sea*. It is my mission, indeed my fervent prayer, that I will be able to channel his spirit to complete his unfinished work, which is my promise to him, as well as to myself."

"How could you possibly hope to finish it as he would have?"

"I have finished it many times, although never to my satisfaction. But to answer your question, I'll know I have succeeded when I have written one true sentence following another until the story is finished."

"One true sentence or one sentence true to Hemingway?"

"Both. Anything less would be failure, would in fact be fraudulent. I would not put our names on it."

"Our names?"

"The legal name I have adopted is a pseudonym Hemingway wrote under when he worked for the *Toronto Star.*"

For some time the men had stood facing each other, Sean, as he looked past Jackson's shoulder, able to make out the far shoreline, where a dark interruption in the rim of snow marked the pool of open water at the outlet stream. Now he saw a human figure emerge from the shadows, apparently following the trail he had taken before dawn.

*Sam,* he thought. At this early hour the snow would be hard enough to hold his weight. It was just like him, too, to change the plan, and the timing could not have been worse. For though Sean had not lost sight of the probability that he was in the company of a murderer, he was fascinated by Jackson's revelations and suspected he was closer to uncovering the secrets of the lost Hemingway trunk than he had yet been.

Acting as if he'd seen nothing, Sean shifted his eyes back to Jackson, who had begun to speak, picking up the thread of Sean's thoughts.

"Many years ago," he was saying, "I was offered the chance to examine a steamer trunk. It was early-twentieth-century vintage, a mono-grammed canvas Louis Vuitton with leather corners that had very little cracking, which is plenty rare, but it had a replacement handle and the cedar interior had been relined, which compromised its value. What caught my eye were the hotel stickers. That trunk had seen a lot of world, from Paris to the Port of Havana to Kenya in Africa—just the kind of places a romantic young man like myself dreamed of ad-venturing in. I had been drinking and the gentleman who owned the trunk had been drinking, and the hour was late, but let me tell you, when he opened the hinges and lifted the lid, I sobered up at once. There must have been a dozen bamboo fly rods in that trunk, most of them House of Hardy, several of American make, three-piece models so that they would fit. Good English fly reels, that wicker creel Tatie sleeps in, it was there—lines, fly wallets, miscellaneous fly fisherman's accoutrements. Nothing extraordinary from a collector's standpoint, mind you, but all first quality."

Sean took another glance past the man's shoulder. The figure had contoured the back bay and it was Sam all right; Sean could make out the red of his checked wool coat.

Jackson continued his narrative. "The fellow who had it said he'd found the trunk at a garage sale in Fond du Lac, up in Wisconsin. A woman was ridding the garage of her old man's stuff that he'd been storing for umpteen years, before he folded his tent and died on her. She wanted three hundred dollars, contents included. That was a lot of money in those days."

Jackson nodded, pulled back by his memories.

"My friend knew his bamboo and didn't dicker, but he didn't know what he had, either. Not at first. 'EMH,' the monogram on the side of the trunk, meant nothing to him. The gear itself possessed no obvious marks of provenance, except for 'EH' engraved onto a sheepskin fly wallet and a couple of old Hardy Perfect reels—that one I gave you for elk antler velvet was one of them. But of course thousands of people have those initials. It was only after he found a rolled-up piece of paper that had been stuck down one of the rod tubes that he realized he'd come into a windfall. It was a letter from the rod maker to Ernest Hemingway. My friend knew it could be fake, but his gut instinct told him that his three hundred had been money very well spent."

"Who was this man?" Sean asked. And immediately regretted the question, for it interrupted the flow and for a long moment Jackson fell silent. When he spoke again, it was in a different voice, a thoughtful, reflective voice.

"Does it really matter?" he said. "Just say he was part of an informal club I belonged to. We saw each other every so often, and I'd always ask to see the trunk. He was gracious enough to let me spend time with it. He even permitted me to fish one morning with a Hardy Fairy. This went on for five or six years, during which I moved up in the world. When my mother died, I came into some inheritance and moved up a little further. By this time I was a full professor at a small college, and I had developed a crush on Hemingway that was becoming a love affair. It wasn't what he chose to write about—beyond the obvious themes I have my own opinions, but I'll let the literati and the armchair psychiatrists nitpick his motives. No, it was the way he wrote. That spare eloquence that fundamentally changed the direction of American literature, that's what left its mark on me. The trunk provided a unique connection to him. Let me tell you, I fell victim to at least three of the seven sins each time I opened that lid. In time I came to believe that it should be mine, because only I could fully appreciate it. That's what a person does if he wants something badly enough. He justifies the means by the end."

Sean glanced over Jackson's shoulder. Sam was still a couple hundred yards away, but almost abreast of the igloo now. From where they stood he knew that Sam would be able to see him as well, and Sean could only hope that he wouldn't call out his name.

"Am I boring you? You seem distracted."

"No, not at all. I'm fascinated."

Sean shifted to his left so that Jackson would have to turn in order to continue facing him, and so would be looking in the opposite direction from Sam. It assured him of at least another few minutes of undisturbed company.

"Fortunes change," Jackson went on, "my friend's as much as my own, but his were in the opposite direction. He was trying to float a business that was failing badly, and one night he approached me about the trunk. He knew I had connections in the antiquities world and would I consider reaching out to them. He thought the trunk might be worth ten or twenty thousand dollars to the right collector, and apologized that he couldn't offer it to me, knowing my interest. It didn't occur to him that I might actually have the money. I was being honest when I told him that value and selling price weren't the same thing, and that the literati had turned their backs on Hemingway, and his reputation had suffered. Also, it would be difficult to establish provenance for most of the tackle, for anything but the one rod, really. Monograms and initials are not that difficult to forge, and collectors tend to regard them with understandable skepticism.

"I had five thousand dollars in savings and told my friend he could have all of it when the banks opened the next morning. He hemmed and hawed, but after another drink he agreed to the offer and I got a cashier's check to him before he could change his mind. I told myself I didn't cheat him out of it, but I did not act entirely honorably, either. I downplayed the value of what he had, and I emphasized Hemingway's loss of stature without explaining that literary criticism was a fashion industry, and that what was out in one decade might be back on top in another. In short, I took advantage of a friend. For a long time that bothered me. To be perfectly frank, I was never to face him or his family again. I really didn't come to terms with what I'd done until I found the manuscript, the story that Hemingway had started but never finished. Then I realized I had made the right decision in acquiring the trunk by any means necessary. You understand, it was my destiny to finish the story. It was no one else's. No, that's not right. I felt it was Ernest's destiny to finish it by guiding my hand. I am not Ernest Hemingway, but he is, in a sense, me. I can open myself so that his spirit speaks through me. I have done so."

Sean resisted the urge to check on Sam's progress. He held Jackson's eyes.

"Was the story in the trunk? Is that where you found it?"

Jackson conceded a small nod. "I told you the interior had been replaced. Where two boards joined, the tacks holding the cedar strips were loose and one had backed out so that I noticed. I drew the rest out with pliers and pried the board back. That's where it was. Not the page you saw in the typewriter. That isn't original. The original— three pages in all—was typed on the backs of stationery sheets. When I unfolded them—and my hands were shaking, as you can imagine— a lock of hair fell out. It was long, so I felt I was on safe ground saying it was a woman's hair. That puzzled me, but then I thought it must be Martha Gellhorn's, that she had given Ernest a lock of her hair when their courtship was being conducted in secret. Gellhorn was a blonde, and so was the hair. Perhaps he was hiding the story in the steamer trunk to keep it from the eyes of his wife, Pauline."

"How was it stolen in the first place?"

"I have a theory about that. The woman my friend had bought the trunk from said her husband worked for the Railway Express in Chicago. She thought the trunk must have been unclaimed baggage, and that her husband had helped himself to it. She said that the practice wasn't condoned, but was commonplace. Personally, I think it is much more likely that he saw who it was addressed to and recognized the name. Years after I came into possession of it, I found a letter that Ernest's son Jack had written about his father's tackle being lost in transit to Ketchum, Idaho, and that to the best of Jack's recollection, it was in 1940. That makes sense. Hemingway was staying as a guest of the Sun Valley Lodge that year. He probably had a lot of stuff shipped up from his house in Key West."

Sean felt like he'd been forcing a lock, picking at it and picking at it, and that finally the tumblers had fallen into place and the window to the past had opened. He remembered the unpublished profile Margarethe Harris had written about Jack Hemingway. She hadn't made up the story. The trunk truly had existed, and if Sean was to believe Peter Jackson—and he did believe him—it contained not only fishing tackle that belonged to Ernest Hemingway, but an unfinished manuscript with a value that could not be calculated.

"Peter," Sean said. "Where's the trunk now?"

# CHAPTER THIRTY-TWO

# Russian Roulette

"It's in the room where I sleep," Jackson said. "Down at the cabin."

"I was there yesterday morning, Peter. Nothing's in that room. Just an old trunk that's a replica, and all that's inside are blankets."

"I mean it was there. I had to hide it away."

His eyes found the ice underneath his boots. "I . . . She said she had velvet, that if I gave her something out of the trunk . . ." His voice caught. It was the first time Sean had seen him unsure of himself. He was only a man now, not the incarnation of his hero.

"Who are you talking about? Are you saying Freida took something from the trunk?"

A glance up, then the eyes sliding past. "No, Freida was a friend."

"Then who, Peter?" *Just say the name.*

"She calls herself a therapist. She made us friendship bracelets from threads. See, I'm still wearing mine." He removed his right mitten and tugged up the left sleeve of his coat, revealing a bracelet of colored threads. "But all she does is want stuff from you."

"What does she want, Peter?"

"Anything you have. Everything you have."

*He's talking as if she's still alive,* Stranahan thought. "Who are you talking about, Peter?"

"Jolene."

*There. It's out.*

"Jolene who?"

"Bailie is her last name. At least that's what she told me. She likes to say that it's on the house."

"What's on the house?"

"She is, but only if I give her what she wants. When she has her claws in you, she's like Tatie with a rabbit. I thought the experience would bring me closer to Ernest, a shared knowledge of the flesh. He'd had relationships with prostitutes in Havana. And I'm old, but I'm . . . a man. I live alone. I have a man's needs. Especially when my work isn't going well and I think God has sent me on a fool's errand. There are days when I think I should just let history be history."

"How did you know her, Peter?"

"Freida knew her. They came to install the chandelier. Jolene told me she was an actress. She picked up money helping Freida with the larger installations. Sometimes you needed a second set of hands, and she was used to working with her hands backstage, helping the grips build sets. She said I sounded lonely. She handed me a card that said she was a personal relationships facilitator. It's just another term for whore. I never told Freida that she came back afterward, or that I gave stuff to her I told myself I'd die before selling."

"Did you give her a creel that belonged to Ernest Hemingway?"

"No. I gave her one I found at a garage sale in Silver Gate. It's a typical midcentury Lawrence, sound condition but not desirable."

"But you told her it was Hemingway's."

"I was trying to pass it off. How do you know this?"

"I was at the house where she lived in Virginia City. Were you there?"

"No. She came here. I told myself I was the only one, but I suspect she had others. It . . . it became intolerable. I lost respect for myself. My work suffered. Freida had told her about the Hemingway tackle, at least I think so. Jolene knew, so she must have. I gave her the creel. It wasn't enough. I gave her a Hardy Princess fly reel with Ernest's initials on the case. Finally I gave her one of the Hardy Fairy rods. I was weak.

There's no other word for it. The flesh was weak. It had become an intolerable situation. I only have myself to blame."

The figure on the lakeshore was drawing closer. Sean drew a breath and took his chance.

"Is that why you killed her, Peter? Because it had become intolerable?"

"Killed her?" The question seemed to take him aback. "Kill Jolene May? I didn't . . . I mean, yes, I wanted to. Tatie, she hated her. She could smell the hound on her, smell the greed in her. But I'm a pacifist. Ernest was, too, that's something misunderstood about him. He loved war for the subject matter. But he abhorred it for what it did to human beings."

He was straying off track.

"So you marched her into the woods?" Sean prompted. "Because it had become intolerable."

"I would never—"

Abruptly, Jackson stopped. He'd heard something. So had Sean. Sean looked past Jackson's shoulder. Sam was coming around the point of the peninsula, Jackson's shotgun in the crook of his elbow. It *was* Sam. He stared at the figure. Wasn't it? Sam's coat, no doubts. But too big, draped loosely, the figure leaning back from the hips. Not Sam's forward lean, his bear's lumbering gait.

"Is that you, Sam? *Saa-mmm.*" Sean's voice echoed off the escarpment walls.

"There's no Sam here. Sam, he's got other things to worry about without climbing up here."

". . . *without climbing up hee-rre.*"

Echoes taunting each other, the figure drawing closer. Speaking again. "Worries. Concerns. Call them what you want. The pain is the same."

". . . *the pain is the saa-aame.*"

The man's hips looked wider than his shoulders, extending like ears. That's when Sean knew. The ears were the single-action Colts, cocked forward in the double holsters, pushing at the drape of the coat.

Jackson spoke. "What are you doing here, Leland?"

"We're on a first-name basis, are we? But I guess that's appropriate. Out here in this nowhere, all this country for a body to disappear in. Like an echo. Nothing but silence when it's gone. You need first-name friends this high. More important than money."

He was on the ice now, sliding his boots forward like skates.

Jackson drew to his height. "You don't scare me, Stokes. What are you going to do? Shoot me with your candle-wax bullets?"

To Sean: "He did that once. I was drinking in that establishment of his and told him something I shouldn't have. And he's a man who likes to exploit another's weakness. But I never said a word, not after he searched my house with a bogus warrant. Not even after he shot me. I never said a word then. I never told him where it was. I sure as hell won't tell him what he wants to hear now. You hear that, Stokes? In Africa we would classify you as a jackal. You scavenge the leavings of others. You're too much of a coward to do the killing yourself."

"You don't see me running away, do you? And that fella down the mountain, I don't think he'd call me timid."

"Sam would wipe the floor with you," Sean said. And felt his rage build inside him, the same rage he'd felt lying on the cold ground at the campground in Yellowstone Park.

"If you hurt my friend, I'll kill you," he said.

"From where I stand that seems unlikely. But not to worry, there's nothing wrong with him that a few grams of morphine won't cure. Of course, he could freeze to death. This kind of weather, a man needs his coat."

Sean gauged the distance. Ten yards, a little closer. Stokes had transferred the shotgun to his left hand. His right hand hovered over the bulge in the coat. Sean knew Stokes would have four shots in him from the right-hand revolver, the one with the full-power loads, before he took the second step.

"How did you find me?" Jackson's voice sounded genuinely curious.

"I have the GPS, old man," Stokes said. "The one you gave the woman for hauling your ashes."

"I don't own a GPS."

"You don't? Then it's hers and you must have told her where you hid the goodies and she entered the coordinates. Either way, she knew where to find you. And now we have the evidence that you killed her—your shotgun, your footprints over hers. Your gloves at the scene."

Jackson turned to Sean. "The only thing I ever do with those gloves is chop wood. I never killed anyone."

"Not the way it looks, old man. So tell me where it is. Show me, and maybe I'll put in a good word. You can go on living with your precious cat, borrow one of its lives until you finish your great American novel."

And Sean thought, *It was him all along.* Stokes was the killer, not Jackson. He had murdered Jolene Bailie over the coordinates in her GPS, the coordinates that she thought marked where Jackson had hidden his trunk. He'd slipped Jackson's big moccasins over his own boots to frame him, then had shot her with Jackson's shotgun. He set it up, probably figured it would be days until somebody found the body. That's why he took the gloves from the porch and placed them at the scene. They weren't like footprints; they wouldn't melt and disappear. They would implicate Jackson, and Stokes could use that to leverage the whereabouts of the trunk out of him. Stokes must have been surprised as hell when Sean stumbled across the body so soon.

Sean looked toward the igloo. Before entering it, he'd taken off his pack, and it leaned against the wall. He was too far away to make out the sag in the side pocket where he'd put Martha's gun, but as Stokes didn't have it, it had to still be there.

"What are you going to do?" Jackson said. "Kill both of us?"

"First things first, but that isn't a bad suggestion. Use the weapon used to kill the woman. Stranahan up here tracking down a murder suspect, trying to be the hero, letting the suspect get the jump on him. Then the man committing suicide. Shades of the great writer he idolized. That would be a twist of irony, wouldn't it?"

"You're forgetting about Sam," Sean said. "Explain away two murders? Maybe. But three?" His voice sounded hollow.

"God will take the rap for your buddy. Beat him with a big stick for a while and he'll be all bruised up. A slide'll do that to a man. They'll find his body—if they find it—'Poor Sam.' Spring avalanches are the worst, aren't they? Hard to believe the power of nature. He drove his buddy up here and look what happened to him. Buried in the snow and left to die. Where's the justice in the—?"

"Wait. I'll tell you," Jackson said. There was resignation in the voice.

Stokes smiled. "That's better, old man. Now you're making sense. You know, I'm genuinely curious. Ernest Hemingway's lost treasure chest. And here we've been sitting on it all these years, right here at the Top of the World."

"The trunk's gone. I haven't had it in forever." The defeat in Jackson's voice was amplified by the echoing walls. "I traded it all away. Everything. All the rods, all the gear. Nothing's left but a few pieces of paper. You wouldn't know what to do with them."

"I'll be the judge of that."

"They're in the igloo, but I'm warning you—"

"Shut up and lead the way. You, too, Stranahan. Keep your hands where I can see them."

They went in a line, Jackson probing ahead with the walrus-tusk saw, then Sean, counting the steps to his pack and wondering what to do when he got there, trying to come up with any reason that Stokes would let him even get close. *Think of something.*

"What are you muttering?" Stokes said.

Where the ice was thin at the point, almost to shore, Sean deliberately put the weight of his right leg on it, breaking through. He went down, punching his arm through the ice to stop his fall, then struggled to his knees, the front of his jacket dripping water.

"Jesus, that's cold," he said.

"You idiot," Stokes said. "No, don't even think of reaching under your jacket. Get up. Keep going. And you, old man, you don't need that fancy stick anymore. Just drop it before you get any ideas." Jackson dropped the pana onto the snow.

Sean limped forward, favoring his right foot. The genesis of a plan was kicking around in his head. It could work. It had to, for once Stokes realized that all that remained of the rainbow he was chasing was a few sheets of typing, probably nothing more than the manifestations of an old man's madness, he might well take up Jackson's challenge and shoot both of them.

Forty yards to the igloo. Thirty.

Sean began to shiver violently, his teeth clacking together. He remembered Freida Toliver, in the throes of her hypothermia, biting her tongue and breaking a tooth. He bit down now, once, once again, three times, the blood filling his mouth. He leaned over to spit it out, splashing crimson onto the snow.

Now his whole body was shaking. "I . . ." His voice jittered. "I-I-I . . . must have . . . broken a rib." He began to waver and caught himself from falling down. "Bring me . . . my pack." His voice coming in shudders. "I have to get dry . . . clothes."

As he staggered toward the igloo he felt, rather than heard, the footsteps coming up behind him. Judging the sound, he waited. And then swung round as hard as he could, his fist cutting through the brittle air, only to see Stokes's face draw back, then grin behind the blue-black mouth of the revolver.

"Didn't you get enough already? Do you really want me to shoot you? Well, if you insist."

At the crack of the revolver, Sean went down, clasping his hand to his throat. He felt the hot dizzying burn of the wax bullet and tried to draw breath. He struggled up to his knees, swallowing what felt like a golf ball in his throat.

"That's a good look on you," Stokes said. "All that's left is to see you beg." He holstered the handgun and drew the barrels of the shotgun over Sean's chest, then Jackson's.

"The only reason I didn't kill him," he said to Jackson, "is because I haven't decided what to do with him. Or you, old man. You say you have some papers. What are they?"

"An unfinished manuscript. Ernest Hemingway's unfinished manuscript."

"Really?" Greed was speaking, unveiled avarice.

"Well now, that's more like it." He nodded. "This is how it's going to work. You, Stranahan, stay right where you are. You try to stand, you try to *crawl*, the next bullet's lead. And you, old man, now listen closely to me, you go into your igloo and bring me out those papers. You don't bring out anything else. I see anything else in your hands, I don't have to tell you what happens."

"The papers are in a fishing creel. Do you want me to take them out of it?"

A moment of hesitation before Jackson spoke. And Sean, for just a second, forgot his pain, seeing the ploy taking shape.

"Then bring out the creel, by all means. I'll tell you what to do with it. But before you do, take off your jacket. We don't want any surprises."

Jackson reached for the zipper.

"The shirt, too. Drop it in the snow."

Jackson stripped to his waist. His skin was pale as death, the pectorals sagging, his arms ropy with old man's muscle. The hair on his chest was long and wavy, like a yeti's.

"Shoo now, shoo." Stokes flicked his fingers. "Go get it. I'll give you a count of ten. You aren't back out, I'll shoot you right through the wall. We'll find out if those XTP slugs penetrate as well as advertised."

Jackson pushed aside the blanket and disappeared into the igloo.

"Ten," Stokes said. "Nine . . . eight . . . seven . . . six . . . five . . . four—"

"I'm coming out."

Sean saw the blanket move and Jackson's head emerge from the entrance. He came out stooped over, his hands outstretched, holding the wicker creel.

"Put it over there in the snow," Stokes said. "No, farther away from the igloo. Right there."

Jackson put the creel down.

"Unbuckle the clasp."

Jackson unbuckled it.

"No, don't lift the lid. You reach inside, you'll lose the hand, first bullet. You'll lose your life, second bullet. Now go over and kneel by Stranahan."

Jackson did as he was told, avoiding Stranahan's eyes.

Stokes crab-walked around the creel until he was directly behind it, where he could keep his gun on the two men.

"If these papers aren't what you say they are . . ."

He bent and lifted the lid.

The movement was so fast that all Sean registered was a blur, then a frozen moment when the cat was plastered over Stokes's face, before its rear legs began kicking like a jackrabbit's. The claws ripped at Stokes's eyes and cheeks.

Its yowling started low, then rose in pitch like tomcats fighting at midnight. Every few seconds, inhuman screams punctuated the howling and echoed across the basin. Frantically, Stokes struck with his hands at the cat, but the claws were dug in. His face was a bloody mask as he reeled around and around, staggering toward the bay like a drunken man. Tripping at the edge of the lake, he fell sprawling on the slick ice. The cat hanging from him, he got to his feet and began to run, his legs pushing awkwardly across the frozen water.

Sean lunged for his pack. He ripped at the zipper to claim his revolver. As he drew it, there was a loud hissing as if the lake was exhaling a breath, then a rolling thunder as the ice cracked. The split, triggered by Stokes's weight, raced along the pressure ridge toward the peninsula. For several long seconds, Stokes straddled the split in the ice. His legs widened into an inverted V. Then he plunged through.

"Help!" he shouted, his head bobbing up. His right hand was still flailing at the cat. He scraped it off, flinging it into open water.

Sean saw Jackson, bare-chested, running past him out onto the ice. The ice groaned under his weight and cracks radiated with each step. He flung himself onto the ice and began to crawl toward the sloshing water the pressure ridge had cracked open.

"Tatie!" he called.

Sean looked around for a stick to extend toward the drowning man. Nothing. His eye caught the single tree on the peninsula. He ran toward it, pausing only to bend down and grab the snow saw where Jackson had dropped it. The diameter of the trunk was at best three inches, but it was green wood, fibrous and tough. Sean hacked at it with the saw, again and again, until the handle cracked off the walrus-tusk blade. He cast the pieces aside and bent the sapling over with his weight, one way, then the other, and again, the wood splintering until he could twist the trunk and finally wrench it free from the stump. He glanced behind him, saw two heads in the open rift in the ice. Jackson had fallen through, too.

Sean ran onto the ice. He dropped down and began to elbow across it to spread out his weight, pushing the sapling in front of him. He extended it toward Jackson.

"Grab hold," he said.

"Where's Tatie? I can't find Tatie."

"Grab hold," Sean said.

Jackson grasped at the needle branches and Sean began to worm backward, pulling himself with his toes. One foot. Another. He wasn't getting enough traction. He turned around and dug his heels into a thin drift of snow that clung to the ice. Kicked and pulled, kicked and pulled, like he was in a game of tug-of-war. Finally he was onto solid ice. He risked standing up and hauled with all his strength. Jackson's arms came out of the water, then his torso. A pause as he caught his breath, and then he was up and out, wriggling onto the ice like a seal.

"Where's Tatie?"

As soon as Sean judged Jackson to be free of the danger zone, he crawled toward Stokes, pushing out the branch.

"Stokes, over here."

"I can't see." The head bobbing, going under to resurface, the blood washing away and then filming over his face as he came back up.

"Unbuckle your gun belt. It's dragging you down."

"Can't. Going to drown. I—my God, it's cold."

"Forget the guns. The branch is right in front of you."

With suddenness, Stokes lunged forward, his hands grasping at the thin branches.

"That's it." Sean pulled at the branch. "Hold on."

"Can't . . . hold . . . on."

"You can."

But even as Sean said the words, Stokes let go of the branch. His head turned around once, then again as he kicked with his submerged legs. Sean saw the terror in his eyes as they cast frantically back and forth. Then he slipped under, out of sight. Sean waited, his heart beating against the ice. An arm came up, one of the Colt revolvers in a fist. Then the arm went down and the last of him Sean saw was the barrel of the Colt, going down like a periscope. Then he was gone.

"T . . . Tatie."

Jackson was staggering along the line of the break, his bare chest flushed and heaving, calling for the cat. He stuttered to get out its name.

"She . . . she's gone," he said as Sean came up. "My T . . . Tatie's gone. She . . . saved my life."

*She saved mine, too,* Stranahan thought. He ran his eyes up and down the zigzag split in the ice, where the water was as gray as gunmetal. He couldn't see the cat. But she was so tiny, he could have missed her.

"Maybe she got out. And thought, *Even if she did, she's soaking wet and she's only three pounds. How long would she last?*

"I can't . . . see her. Tatie. . . Ta . . . Tatie!"

———

Each time Sean called Sam's name, the canyon walls caught his voice and tossed it back and forth. It was as if the gods were making a game of catch out of his futility, mocking him, and when he finally stumbled down into the camp where he'd left Sam by the fire, he feared the worst. He could see the shape of the body, but there was no response when he called to him. The big man was curled beside the ashes of the fire with his wool watch cap pulled down, so that Sean couldn't see his face. Even after he'd approached to within a few feet, he couldn't see Sam's chest moving. Sean bent forward over the body's bulk, and in that instant, Sam whirled. The movement caught Sean off guard, and he was on his back on the snow without knowing how he got there. Sam loomed over him, pressing a sharp stick into Sean's chest, bearing down with his weight.

"It's me, Sam. It's Sean."

Sam's eyes blazed.

"It's me."

The eyes continued to blaze, then, slowly, the fire died and the eyes swam out of focus. Sean felt the pressure on his chest ease as Sam sat back in the snow.

"I thought you was him." His chest heaved from the exertion. He said he'd been holding his breath for at least a minute so there would be no steam from his exhalation.

"Didn't you hear me?"

"I heard. It sounded like you, but I thought he might have his gun on you. All I had was surprise. Fuck, man, how was I to know?"

Sean sat down, feeling the relief course through his body.

"Good spear, huh?" Sam said. "I fire-hardened the fucker before the ashes got cold."

"Yeah, Sam, good spear. Thanks for not skewering me."

"I wanted to put on some more wood, but I thought a fire would be a giveaway. My only chance was him thinking I froze to death. I damn near did. The sumbitch took my coat."

"He wanted me to mistake him for you. Are you okay?"

"Fuck no. The cocksucker shot me in the foot."

Sean saw a dark red stain where the heat of the blood had lanced a hole through the snow.

"Not with a fucking wax bullet, either," Sam said. "I think it took off my little toe. He was trying to make sure I didn't go anywhere."

"Well, you're lucky it wasn't the head."

"He shot me in the head, too." Sam pulled his hat up so that Sean could see the welts, one above his left eye, the other at the hairline on his right temple. "My mother called me a hardheaded child, said I inherited the Norwegian genes and I'd grow up with bolts sticking out of my head. Why wasn't I purty like my brother, who got his looks from the other side of the aisle? Good thing, though, I guess."

"What happened?"

"I don't want to talk about it. He took my pride, man."

"Tell me."

"The fucking bastard thought I knew more than I was letting on, so he played Russian roulette to get it out of me. He'd put two bullets in and spin the cylinder. 'Hmm. Wax bullet or copper-jacketed? Let me see.' Then he'd pull the trigger. *Click.* Spin the cylinder. *Click.* Spin it again. *Bang.* Like being hit by golf-ball hail. Then he'd put in another round and spin the cylinder, say, 'Hmm,' laugh when I winced. I thought I was going to die because, you know, why would he keep me alive? I could talk. People might not believe what I said, but I don't think he wanted to take that chance. He's just a fucking lunatic."

"What did he want?"

"He saw your tracks on top of the old man's and wanted to know who else was up here. I . . . I told him it was my buddy, that we just got a wild hair to go ice fishing. 'Course he saw right through that. I didn't have any ice fishing gear. That's when he pulled the gun. I gave up your name, man. I'm sorry as shit." His shaggy head shook, remembering. "Fuck, man, I thought he was going to kill me."

"I'd have done the same thing in your place. And he *was* going to kill you. He was going to kill all of us. But I think he wanted to see how it played out at the lake and keep his options open, how to make it look afterward."

"Well, what the fuck did happen?"

"What happened is he's dead. He's the one who shot Jolene."

"No shit?"

"No shit."

"What about the old dude?"

"I'll tell you on the way back. Can you hobble on that foot if I make you a crutch?"

"I still got nine toes."

# CHAPTER THIRTY-THREE

# Clash of Colors

Molly's eyes flashed from Sam to Sean, then to Sam again. She'd heard the truck pull up and was standing in her nightgown as Sam's key scraped at the lock and he hobbled in. She'd listened to his explanation while shaking her head, her upper teeth denting her lower lip.

"You leave without telling me where you're going. You come back at three in the morning and I'm scared to death, and you say you shot yourself in the foot but it's okay?"

"It was an accident," Sam said.

"Yes, you said that. You drip blood on the floor and say it's an accident. But you won't say where it happened, you won't say how."

She reached for the phone behind the display case.

"What are you doing?"

"Calling off search and rescue." She punched in 911, tapped her fingers on the glass top of the display case.

"Yeah, Cindy, it's Molly. The bastard came home." She set down the phone.

Sam gave Sean a pleading look. Sean knew the truth would come out. He had no intention of hiding what had really gone on up on the frozen lake. But Sam was more reluctant, knowing the consequences.

"Don't look at him. You tell me. The truth, this time."

"We were going to hike to some lake in the Beartooths where Sean was doing some work. But I shot myself as were packing up the packs. We took a gun because it's griz country."

"Then I guess I don't rate. Because when you take me hiking, all we have for protection is bear spray."

"It was my fault," Sean said.

"Did I tell you you could talk? I'm speaking to my husband, not to you."

Sean shut his mouth.

"Hey, shit happens," Sam said.

"You're going to go with the 'shit happens' defense, huh?"

"I'm in goddamn pain. I thought I might get a little fucking sympathy."

"Don't you dare raise your voice. You'll wake up Sarah." She looked at Sean. "That's what you're going to tell the doc in the box? That he shot himself and it was an accident?"

"I don't need no doctor," Sam said. "There ain't no toe left to attach."

Molly's eyes stayed on Sean. If they could shoot bullets, he'd be dead.

"He's going to the clinic and you're going to drive him," she said evenly. "I'd go myself if it wasn't for Sarah. So you better get your story straight on the way over. And while you're at it, you can say good-bye to him for a good long while, because you're not going to be seeing him."

"Why the fuck not?" Sam said.

"Because you're grounded."

"You can't ground me. I'm a grown man."

"I just did."

Her eyes flashed from one to the other. "Go. Out the door with both of you."

Sam leaned against Sean as he limped to the truck. The truck was still making clicking noises as the metals of the exhaust expanded to grate against each other. They hadn't been inside for more than five minutes.

Sean helped Sam climb into the shotgun seat.

"Isn't she magnificent?" Sam said.

Magnificent, Sean agreed, and scary. She was also true to her word. May wasn't halfway gone, but June would almost be over before Sean Stranahan laid eyes on Sam Meslik again.

————

When he heard the knock at the door of his art studio, Sean put the brush between his teeth. He'd known it was Martha for at least ten seconds, recognizing the cadence of her footsteps on the travertine floor. She was carrying a cardboard box sealed with yellow evidence tape and he made room on his fly-tying desk.

Martha ran her eyes along the walls. "You're a better artist than you are a detective," she said. "Maybe if you stuck to your watercolors, I wouldn't have to keep bailing you out of trouble."

"Does that mean I'm clear?"

Nearly two weeks had passed since Sean had called her from the clinic while Sam had his toe doctored up.

"It means you've been interrogated," Martha said. "It means you've passed a voluntary polygraph and two counties no longer consider you a suspect in the murder of Jolene Bailie, or in the probable drowning of Leland Stokes. It helped that Leland had a history. Since he's gone under the ice, half a dozen victims of his wax bullets have crawled out of the piney woods. Some still have scars."

"That's a relief, I guess."

"From your perspective, it should be. But I want you to understand something. That little treasure hunt you went on with your pal, Sam, and the time that elapsed before you reported back to the county, means I can't trust you. If I can't trust you, we can't have a relationship."

She looked at him until he nodded.

"It also gave Peter Jackson time to disappear before he could be questioned. You're lucky that your actions, or I should say lack thereof, haven't been interpreted as obstruction of justice."

"Let's hope Leland's part of a dying breed," Sean said, seeking to deflect the subject to anyone but himself.

Martha's "humpff" made him raise his eyes.

"Oh, I don't know. There's a few people in Hyalite I wouldn't mind shooting with wax bullets. You might be one of them."

"That's my Martha," Sean said.

She didn't smile.

"So, what's in the box?"

"What Jolene Bailie had on her person at the time of her death. It found its way to the crime lab and then got lost in the shuffle after Gigi had her baby. Just like I thought, the place is in chaos."

"Good for Gigi. A girl or a boy?"

"A boy. I offered my condolences."

"Just open the box."

"We will, but first I want to see if we're on the same page about something."

"What's that?"

"It's not what, it's who. Wilhelm Winkler. You're smiling. I don't see what's so funny."

"His name makes me smile."

"Not me. The only reason he's not a suspicious death is because the autopsy results fall within an acceptable realm of medical interpretation. For the death to be classified as accidental, that is. But he died under suspicious circumstances. Legally speaking, that's not the same thing. That means my investigation is still open."

Sean's "okay" was guarded.

"So I'm going to lay a sequence out for you and you tell me if you agree."

Sean nodded.

"We know that Wilhelm Winkler is Freida's stepbrother. That's how he knows about the missing trunk. That's how he comes into posses-sion of the rod that you and your buddies were oohing and ahhing over. Plus, he's originally from an area in Austria that Hemingway used to visit, so he's better acquainted with Hemingway than most people would be. Are you with me on that?"

"Vorarlberg."

"Who taught you that word?"

"You did, but I think the connection is speculative."

"Okay, strike Austria from the equation and you still have Winkler's involvement coming through Freida. Jolene Bailie worked for Freida, so its logical that Winkler meets her through that association. I'm guessing they knew each other in a biblical sense, sex being her stock-in-trade. But maybe not. Either way, they're in cahoots and went to the Bear Trap together."

"I'm with you."

"Except I don't see her as a sharing kind of person. I see her as a taker."

Sean shrugged. "She went with Winkler for the same reason I tagged along after Patrick—security in numbers. She's small. Winkler's larger. Plus he's a businessman. To me, Jolene doesn't seem like the type who could negotiate with Patrick Willoughby and come out on top. Her talents lay elsewhere. She needed Winkler to negotiate the deal."

Martha chewed on her lip, then slowly nodded.

"You know what I think happened that day? I think what started out as one thing became something else. They may have left the trailhead in cahoots, but then he tripped and fell. She smelled blood. She liked the smell. She figured she could do the deal herself. So she watched him die. But then you come along and she doesn't have time to retrieve the fly rod case from wherever they'd hidden it. That's why you and Sam saw her there the next day with her dog. She was coming back to look, but somebody else had found it first."

"You're painting a pretty coldhearted picture of someone you barely met."

"You're right. But I've seen her kind before. What did her mother say about her, that she thought she had glitter in her veins? I think what she had in her heart was cold black ice."

"Are you trying to convince yourself or get me to nod along?"

"Both. I just hate loose ends."

"Maybe the answers are in the box." Sean reached into his pocket for his folding knife, opened it one-handed, and stuck it point first into the table. "Quit keeping me in suspense."

Martha slit the tape and took out the list to check against the contents, which also contained notations on where the items had been found. Martha brought out the clothes first. Jeans, belt, the same flannel shirt Sean had seen her wearing when he'd met her in the Bear Trap. All brown with bloodstains. Panties, also bloodstained. Wool socks, poly liners. Also light hikers, moderate wear on the treads.

Martha held up one of the hiking boots. "By the way, Harold got back about the photo. He said it looked like the big tracks were made by someone who would have been a good bit lighter than Jackson, by the depth of the impressions. That fits in with it being Stokes. He could have pulled the moccasins over his own shoes to make it look like it was Jackson. Putting Jackson's gloves at the scene was a nice touch."

"That's a lot to infer from a photo."

"Maybe. Harold doesn't make many mistakes, though."

She dug deeper into the box, drawing out a plastic reclosable bag. She shook the contents onto the desk. A Celtic-design ring. The elk-tooth earrings Sean had seen Jolene wearing. The friendship bracelet Sean had seen on her wrist, all the colored strings broken but one.

"I guess even murderers have at least one friend, huh?" Martha said. "Didn't you say that Jackson was wearing one, too?"

"Yes, they exchanged them."

"Strange bedfellows."

"Where's her phone and the GPS, Martha? I put them back into her pockets."

"The phone was processed at the lab and is still there, as far as I know. There was no GPS at the scene, at least not that was recovered."

"Then Stokes took it before anyone else arrived. There's no other explanation."

"Why would he do that?"

"Because it had the coordinates to the bay on the lake. That's how he knew to climb up there."

Martha shook her head. "If he was going to take it, why didn't he take it before you found her body? Why wait until after?"

"People who commit murder can panic. Maybe he didn't think of it when he shot her. Maybe me finding her body was the trigger."

"If he coerced the location out of Jolene, he wouldn't need her GPS in the first place. Have you thought of that?"

Now it was Sean's turn to shake his head. "Even if Stokes didn't need the coordinates, it was still in his best interest to take the GPS from the scene. If it was taken into evidence, the waypoints could have been investigated. Stokes had wanted that trunk for a long time, ever since Jackson got drunk in his bar and told him about it. Any information of its whereabouts he wanted to keep to himself."

"Maybe, but I still don't like it."

"Anything else in the box?" Sean asked.

"Only this." Martha pulled out a second reclosable bag. It contained only one item, a silk scarf. The scarf was torn and two opposing ends were tightly furled, as if they'd been knotted together.

"It wasn't actually found on her body," Martha said. She studied the packing list. "Says it was caught on a thorn bush and found closer to the bridge. No hairs that could be useful for identification, but a set of tracks were found in the mud that matched the size and tread pattern of Jolene's shoes."

She raised her eyes to Sean's. "So it was either in her pocket and got caught on the thorns, or it was around her neck and the knot came undone and it got caught on the thorns. Or maybe she just got rid of it because it clashed with her shirt. That's humor, by the way."

Sean reached out to take it from her fingers. The scarf was a tangerine color, like the gill plates of a cutthroat trout.

Martha started speaking again, but Sean was no longer hearing her. He was looking in her direction, but what he was seeing was a splash of color through a rain-streaked window in a room overlooking a bend of the Au Sable River.

# CHAPTER THIRTY-FOUR

# A Good Month to Die

The crate she'd sat on while dipping her hands in hot water stood upside down on the porch. He'd passed the cottage up the road, her truck there, and had almost turned in. But he wanted to choose the ground on which he'd meet her and had decided to pick a place that was familiar. She would come when she heard the car drive by, had in fact already started, for he heard the motor as he reached for the iron door latch under the moose skull. The Great Room was shuttered, tiger stripes of light swarming with dust motes.

Sean chose the same heavy upholstered chair facing the fireplace that he'd sat in the night she'd told him her life story. He wondered how much of that was true now, as he heard the throaty idle of the pickup, and then the motor shutting off and the car door closing, and the door to the lodge opening and then closing, and the steps coming up behind him, the solid rap of the jodhpur boots.

"It's you," she said. "You . . . you should have called ahead."

"And ruined the surprise, Margarethe?"

"Well, it is a surprise. A good one, I mean. You can have the same room if you'd like. We were almost full up last weekend, but you caught me in a lull. Mondays and Tuesdays, that's when—"

Sean turned to face her. She was tall and square-shouldered and didn't lose her poise even when she saw the scarf in Sean's hand. Her own hand went to her throat. The scarf she wore today was a mint color, a shade or two lighter than the gray-green of her eyes.

"I . . . I've been looking for that. Was it on the porch? I thought I'd dropped it into the river during a float last week. I thought—"

"No," Sean said. "This was stuck on a thorn bush near a creek called Froze-to-Death."

"I mean, it looks . . . but no, I, on second look it's not mine, it can't be. I've never been to Wyoming. I always wanted to fish the Wind River. When I was in Montana I thought I might stop there on the drive back, but—"

"Who said it was in Wyoming?"

The room fell silent.

"You can drop the act, Margarethe. There's no one here to convince but me, and I know exactly where you were last month. I even know who you killed. In fact, I'm the one who found her body. What I don't understand is how you found out where Peter Jackson lived and how you knew Jolene Bailie. I'm not flashing a badge. Nobody knows I'm here. I just want to know why an old steamer trunk was worth people dying for. I assume you have it now. Maybe it's behind that door to your father's old study. Underneath the photos of all your heroes."

"You sit there and you judge me and think you know me, but you don't know the first thing about me."

So she would be defiant. That was okay, Sean thought. The defiant are not afraid to tell the truth.

"I know you marched a woman into a hollow in the woods and shot her with a shotgun. I know that."

"She was despicable." The word was spat out. "You don't know."

"Then tell me, Margarethe."

"I need a drink," she said.

"Get one. Make one of your martinis. I could use one, too. It was a long flight."

She walked to the bar at the end of the room. Sean didn't move from the chair. It was taking a chance, but if he'd said no, he was inviting her hostility. He wanted her talking, and was betting on the alcohol influencing the equation. She came back and handed him the glass. She sat in the chair next to him and let out a deep breath, her chest falling, and then her shoulders falling. She looked at the fireplace, or looked at nothing. If there was an expression on her face to be read, Sean couldn't read it.

"Would you mind starting the fire? It's ready to go. Just light the paper with one of those long matches."

He busied himself with the task.

"Are you still cold, Margarethe? Even now in the warmer weather?"

He sat back down and she reached across the arm of her chair and placed her hand on his wrist. He felt the icy press of her fingers.

"My ex-husband told me I was so cold I froze men's hearts. What a cruel thing to say. Of course he didn't know the truth. When you were here before, I asked you to make the cold go away. You comforted me, but you didn't take advantage. Even when I all but asked you to go to bed with me. You had a girl, and you were staying true to her. I admire a gentleman. My father loved me, but he was not so . . . conscientious."

Sean barely breathed. He could feel the artery in his wrist throb under the pressure of her fingers.

"Reynaud's is partly hereditary," she said. "They just haven't identified the genes. My father had it, and after my mother died, he would sit with me in the evenings, right here in front of this fireplace. There was a couch here then. He would say, 'Margee, I'm so cold I just want to jump into the flames. I can't go on like this.'"

She sipped the martini and looked critically at the reflection of the fire through the glass. She seemed to be somewhere else for a moment, and then she took another swallow and picked up the thread.

"It always started the same way. We'd be sitting shoulder to shoulder and he'd put his arm around me. Then he'd stroke my hair. It felt so good, so right. If he'd stopped there, how different my life would be. But he didn't stop. He'd massage my shoulder, and after awhile, his hand would work around until he was touching the side of my breast. He'd just barely press with his fingers. I'd breathe and tell myself it was okay, because he really was cold and he needed my warmth, and he'd been the sun and the stars to me since I was a little girl. I'd have this argument with myself, telling myself it was okay, and all the while he'd be going farther. I knew what he was doing, but I didn't have the courage to stop him. I was fifteen and my mother was dead and he was all I had. I couldn't stand the thought of losing his approval. Can you be raped by somebody if the only person you say no to is yourself? If you go along and then, finally, your head quits arguing with your body? Is that rape, no matter how old you are?"

"Margarethe—"

"No. You want me to talk. I'm talking. You want to know about Wyoming. What happened there, it started here. Right here in front of the fire."

She paused, and pressed down harder.

"When something like *that* happens, you look for a window to escape through." She flitted the fingers of her free hand. "You build a fantasy world you can fly away to. For me, that was fishing and writing stories. Remember what I said about everybody needing something, whether it was a martini at six o'clock or a good man at ten? What I should have said was a trout at six and a true sentence at ten. That's what I needed. Hemingway taught me that you can write about someone, or about something that's happening to you, and that it can be a cathartic act without spelling it out. I'm doing that now. I'm telling you that I wrote about my father without saying the words.

"Almost every night, after he'd fallen asleep, I'd tiptoe downstairs and open the steamer trunk and take out the rods and joint them and wave them like they were fairy wands. I'd fish them all up and down the river without taking them from that room. Then I'd roll a sheet of stationery into the typewriter and write until I'd lost myself in a world where my father was the man he was before my mother died, when I was only his daughter and didn't have to be his wife, too."

She turned her head and looked steadily at Sean.

"I can remember the exact moment I decided to kill him. I was eighteen, just a few weeks from graduation, and I was going with that boy who kissed me on the island. He picked me up one night and we drove into Grayling to go to a movie, and afterward, we went out to some property my mother's family had on Lake Margrethe. It's where we always went to go necking. That's what they called it in my time. It was odd about my father that way. He didn't mind if I had boyfriends. That was okay just as long as I didn't have sex with them. In his heart he hated himself for making me lose my innocence. He truly did want happiness for me, and that included having my own family. Just not yet, though. But that night, my boyfriend wanted to go all the way and I wanted us to, I just wanted to lose myself to him, but I came up against a wall and I . . . well, I couldn't. I couldn't be unfaithful to my father. How sick is that?"

"I'm sorry, Margarethe." Sean didn't know what else to say.

She'd finally let go of his wrist. Sean turned a log in the fireplace.

He heard her say, "And you came here thinking you knew me. How much do you know me now?" She laughed to herself, a sad, sad laugh, and when he turned to face her, her eyes were shining.

"But maybe you do know me," she said. "You know me better than anyone else. I've only been living with what I'm telling you for thirty-eight years. I suppose it's time, finally. And I've been thinking of you ever since you were here. Have you been thinking of me?"

"Yes."

"Just not the same way I was thinking of you."

Sean didn't say anything, and again he heard the sad laugh. "Story of my life."

"What happened with your father, Margarethe?"

"That's a good way of putting it—*with* my father. Because it was as much his decision as mine. When my boyfriend dropped me off that night I could see the light shining in the upstairs bedroom. I opened the drawer of his desk where he kept his .22 pistol. I picked it up, and I was looking at it when he came down the stairs in his socks. I hadn't heard him. He asked me how my date went. I said fine, and he said, 'Good. He's a nice boy.' He acted like he didn't see the gun. Then he almost said something, and all the rest of my life I've wondered what that could be. But he didn't, and he turned away. I heard him starting up the stairs—you couldn't see them from the study—and I counted 'one, two, three, four, five.' There were ten stairs and he stopped at five. Then there was just this awful silence. I felt like I couldn't breathe. I remember that almost better than anything. Finally, I heard him ask if I remembered how to load and shoot the gun the way he'd taught me.

"I didn't say a word. And then he started back up the stairs and I counted, 'six, seven, eight, nine, ten.'

"So after he climbed up there I followed him. I put the pistol on the nightstand and got into bed with him. Afterward, I was lying there crying and he said, 'It's okay, Margee darling. It's gone on long enough. I never wanted to hurt you. Please find it in your heart to forgive me.' I reached over and got the gun, but then I couldn't go through with it. And so I thought, 'I'll just end me,' and I was bringing it to my head, here"—she pointed to her temple—"and he put his hand over mine and said, 'No, you have your life ahead of you.' He said that he'd left a note for me to give to the sheriff when he came and that it was inside the steamer trunk. Everything in there was mine now. Then he told me to go outside and listen to the river.

"Dad used to say that after dark a river talked to you, that it was important that you listened, for that was the voice of its soul. We had an old porch swing at the upstream end of the property under a weeping willow tree. It was the place I'd gone to be alone since I was a little girl. I sat there and watched the lightning bugs and listened to the water like he told me. It seemed a long time before I heard the shot. He'd come outside the house and was lying in the riverboat by the dock. There wasn't much blood, just a little under his head. It was like he was asleep. I thought, 'I can't call anyone. And I can't give the note to anybody,' because it would get out that Dad had killed himself and

that would diminish how he was thought of. You see, I was still thinking of him, not me.

"So I tried to pull the boat up onto the grass, but it was too heavy,
so I went and got the truck and used the winch on the boat trailer.

"The rest is like I told you before. I set the boat on fire with him in
it. People burn slash piles all the time and we're remote enough here
that it was a long time before anyone reported the smoke. Finally Old
Kuck, who was the deputy sheriff, showed up, but by then I'd burned
the suicide note and scraped the bones and ashes into the river and
buried the skull back in the jack pines. I said he'd been swept off the
boat by the cedar sweeper and when I found him, he wasn't breathing.
I said I'd put his body in the boat and hauled it back up to the dock. I
could see he was thinking about it. I wasn't that big a girl, but I said
God gave me the strength. Some people came out the next day dressed
like they do in hospitals. But there wasn't any blood in the house or
any evidence that he'd died any way except how I told them. They didn't
like it that they hadn't found his skull, but what could they do? So that
was the end of it. Except for me. There's never been any end of it for
me. There never will be.

"There," she said. She held Sean's eyes. "Now you know more than
you wanted to."

*More,* Sean thought. But still less. She had yet to tell him about
either Jolene Bailie or the contents of the trunk.

"I'll tell you what," she said. "If you make us a couple more drinks
I'll show you what you came all the way from the Madison River to
see. You know how to make a martini, don't you?"

"I know there's an olive involved."

"All the fishermen in the Au Sable Club knew how to make a proper
martini. I was considering making you an honorary member until you
said that."

A change had come over her that started with a smile and moved
to her eyes, which were no longer overcast with impenetrable sorrow.

It was as if she'd been breathing carbon dioxide for years and had suddenly got a lungful of oxygen, all with the unburdening of her heart. Still, it seemed absurd to be following her instructions—a finger of vermouth, fifty swirls with the spoon to melt the right amount of ice to tamp down the bite of the gin—when only a few yards away, the door to the study stood ajar. When Sean handed her the glass, she led him wordlessly into the small room and switched on the lamp.

"It's under the desk. The leather on the side handles is pretty shot, so just sort of corner it out a little at a time. It's pretty heavy."

Sean moved the chair away from the desk and inched out the steamer trunk. The first thing that struck him were the baggage stickers from the hotels, several obliterated from chafing but others still legible— the Hotel Florida in Madrid, the Paris Ritz, the Ambos Mundos in Havana, the Stanley Hotel in Nairobi.

"My father used to say that Hemingway was a gypsy, that he didn't like to sleep under the same roof twice."

"These are some pretty exotic roofs," Sean said. "Peter Jackson told me that he bought it from a man who was part of a club. Am I right that he bought it from your father?"

"It was my father's, yes. But Mason, I mean Peter, didn't buy it from him."

"You called him Mason."

"That was his name back when I knew him. Mason Bradley. I still have a hard time calling him Peter."

"If he didn't buy the trunk from your father, then who did he buy it from?"

"From me. I went straight from high school to keeping this old ship from sinking. I had to pay the taxes and the trunk was the only thing I possessed that was a liquid asset. I held on to it for as long as I could, until the money from Dad's life insurance policy gave out— and then I had to let it go. I guess it doesn't sound so bad if he says he bought it from a grown-up."

"Where did you find the trunk, Margarethe? Was it at the cabin?"

"What do you mean? I didn't *find* it. I made a deal with Peter. Did you think I drove all the way to Wyoming to hunt him down? He contacted *me.* He'd run out of money and his supply of medicine had dried up. He said the woman who was his source had died inside a bear's den. I didn't believe him until I read about it on the Internet. He said he wanted to turn the trunk back over to me. I guess he'd grown a conscience about swindling it out of me all those decades ago."

"And he was just going to give it to you?"

"No, he had a condition. He was getting older and said he didn't know how much longer he could stay on at his cabin. He was worried about his eyesight failing and surviving another winter. If I would put him up in a room here at Wa-Wa-Te-Si, he said he'd work off the rent. He'd been a carpenter before he went into teaching and could do a little of this and a little of that. I was opening up the place and I could use a little of this and that around here. I wasn't sure he was telling the truth, though."

"He was," Sean said. "The rancher he bought the cabin from said he was a handyman."

"Then maybe it would have worked out. He'd always been a perfect gentleman. Maybe I could have forgiven him for taking advantage of me."

"When did this happen?"

"He called me in March. That's when he told me how sorry he was. He didn't tell me that he'd traded away almost everything in the trunk, but maybe I read something into his voice. Anyway, I had a feeling that if I didn't drive out there, but waited for him to come to me instead, there wouldn't be anything left to drive out there for. Then you showed up with your story about the Gillum rod, which had been in the trunk when I sold it, and I figured that I'd better hurry. So you see, it was you as much as Peter who set this in motion. If you hadn't walked through my door . . . But then you did, didn't you?"

She was silent. They stood in the room, the trunk at their feet forgotten.

When she spoke again, the venom in her voice was something you could taste.

"She called herself an actress. I guess that's one way to describe it. She'd been shacking up with him, and he was promising to pay her for her services, pay her with what belonged to me. She'd have robbed him blind, I'm sure, but he told her the trunk was up at some lake, that it was marked by a cairn and buried under rocks. It wasn't true, but she wasn't smart. I could tell that as soon as I walked in the door. Oh, she was pretty enough, but everything about her was hard. Her face was hard. Her body was hard. Her heart was hard. You could strike a match on her and it would go up in flame.

"I asked Peter what the hell was going on. He tried to assure me that he hadn't given her anything that was valuable and was just putting her off, that the trunk was nowhere near that lake. We ate dinner, the three of us. Can you imagine what that was like? We all just stared at each other. No, she and I stared. Peter tried to look anywhere else. She could sense that she was going to be the odd woman out and gave up all pretense of civility. She swore like a sailor at both of us, right there in the kitchen. 'I'm going to stand up for my rights,' that kind of thing.

"Peter, he couldn't stand confrontation. He said I could work out a split with her. Meanwhile he was going to take his shotgun and his cat and go for a walk. He'd no sooner left than she reached inside her backpack and pulled a gun on me. Told me to go outside, that we were going to take a little stroll. Said if I shouted for Peter or put just one foot wrong, she'd shoot me then and there. I believed her, but I couldn't believe it was happening. I mean, it was happening, but it was like it was happening to someone else. I thought, 'I'll go along and then I'll get the drop on her somehow.' She took me up in the woods and told me to lie down on the ground. I was going to act like I was dropping to my knees and turn and make a lunge for her, but I never got that far. As soon as I bent down, I heard the shot. I could actually hear the pellets rip through her. She came down on top of me and her whole body was like in spasm. She was gagging, had her neck stretched out and her mouth open. Then this long groan, like an animal sound, when the air went out of her. I could feel her blood soaking into my shirt, but I wasn't hurt at all, not a single pellet hit me.

"When I looked up, Peter was there. He'd thought something like this could happen, and he'd been following us. He said she'd raised the gun just before he shot. He fired the left barrel because it had a full choke and the pattern would be tighter and less likely to hit me. 'Thank God for a full-choke barrel,' I told him. It's strange the things you say when something like that happens. It's like you become giddy afterward.

"I'd harbored such resentment for him for so many years, but now we were bound together in this woman's death, and he'd saved my life. He was an old man with no one to call a friend, and the two of us shared a history. I wanted him to follow me back to Michigan. He could drive her car and drop it someplace like Bismarck, where it would never come back to him. I said I'd take him up on the offer of helping me with the lodge. But he wouldn't come. Do you know why? Because the shot had made the cat run away and he wouldn't leave without her. I said we'd wait for the damned cat. No, he didn't want to risk anyone seeing me with him. He was being protective. It sounds strange, but he treated me like I was a long-lost daughter. He said he'd follow me when it was safe, and not to worry about Jolene's car. He'd just drop it off somewhere and hitch back to the cabin. He was going to bury her and figured the body wouldn't be found until at least the next hunting season, and that was only if a bear dug her up. By then, he'd be long gone. Jolene was a loner. She didn't have any acting jobs coming up until the summer. Nobody was going to go looking for her."

"So you left him?"

"I expected him to show up here. But then I guess you found her body and he became a fugitive, and he had to run for it."

While she was talking, she'd been looking at the photos on the walls, all the gentleman anglers who'd inspired her schoolgirl fantasies of what a man should be. Sean saw her eyes stop on the photo of Jack Hemingway.

"Why did you write the story about him?" Sean said. "You already knew about the lost trunk, more about it than he did."

"That was a coincidence, not meeting Jack but that he knew about the trunk. I had no idea. But then when he told me about it, I thought if I wrote the story, maybe Peter would see it or someone would tell him, or somebody out of the blue would call and say they knew who had the trunk. Maybe Peter would even get in touch with me himself. At that time, I placed a great value on getting it back, but I had no money to hire an investigator and all my effort was in keeping this place from falling apart. I didn't know that he'd changed his name. It wasn't like today, when anybody can find anybody."

"So where was it?" Sean nudged the trunk with the toe of his shoe.

"Under his porch. He just had to pry out a few boards. He put it in a wheelbarrow and helped me get it down to the car. That's the last time I ever saw him, heading back up the hill to bury the body and look for his cat. Now you know as much as I'm going to tell you. I'm tired of talking. Aren't you going to open it and find out what you've come all this way for? I'll tell you right now you'll be disappointed."

Sean thought about those who'd opened the trunk or coveted its contents, starting with the Railway Express employee who had stolen it in the first place, and wondered if he really wanted to join that club. Freida Toliver, Wilhelm Winkler, Jolene Bailie, Margarethe's father— they had all died violent deaths. And Peter Jackson and the woman standing before him were damaged people who had not been made stronger in the broken places. Sean didn't believe in the Hemingway curse and he wasn't superstitious, but why tempt fate? And he found, to his surprise, that he wasn't that interested. Not now, not when he knew that the only real items of value were no longer under the lid.

"Why don't you just tell me what's inside, Margarethe?"

"Nothing compared to what I remember. There's one Hardy St. John and a Hardy Fairy rod, but one of the tips is broken. There's a pewter fly box like a Wheatley, but the springs are rusted out. The flies are so dry they're like mummified moth wings. You just breathe on them and they crumble into dust. There's a trout net, but the bow is cracked and all the netting's rotted out. Some gut leaders and old silk fly lines. That's about all. Peter must have bartered away the rest, because I remember at least a dozen rods and all kinds of gear. But the trunk has Hemingway's initials on it. And it's still in pretty good condition. If you could prove it belonged to him, then I suppose that's worth something."

"Peter said he found three pages of typewriting in the trunk. It was hidden behind the cedar lining. He thinks it was the start of a story or a novel that Hemingway was writing. He's spent the last I don't know how many years trying to finish it. It's his life's work. That's what the elk antler medicine was for, to prolong his eyesight and give him enough vitality to finish the story. I'm surprised he didn't tell you about it."

She was regarding him with an odd expression. "What was the story about?"

"There was a man and a boy walking through the woods. They were talking about a good month to die."

An involuntary muscle tugged at her face. For a moment, she seemed to pull into herself, into some dusty drawer of her mind, before her eyes went to the manual typewriter on the desk.

"It was typed on this old Royal," she said. "But Ernest Hemingway didn't write it. I can assure you of that."

"You said he visited here in 1939 or 1940. That's just before the trunk went missing. Why couldn't he have written it here? The time frame fits."

"Because I know who did."

"But . . ." Sean paused before he could complete the thought. He felt a flush like hot ice move up his body.

"Don't act so surprised," she said. "I had a good ear. I could write like all my heroes before I found a voice of my own. Out in the woods there was an old toolbox I'd taken from the boat shop to put my stories in when I finished them. But when I was writing late at night, I'd hide the pages behind one of the boards in the trunk until the next day. I'd fold them around a lock of my hair for luck. It's a Chippewa custom that old Shoppenagon, that Indian in the tintype on the wall, passed along to my grandfather. That story you're talking about, it must have still been in the trunk when I sold it."

"So the boy in the story, that's you?"

"I always made the character a boy. That way, if anyone found it, they wouldn't think I was writing about myself."

"Did you finish it? Peter only had a few pages."

"It's a long time ago. I think I only had the start."

"Do you remember what was going to happen?"

"They were going to fish the Hendrickson hatch and the man was going to drown in the river for his sins. Does that sound familiar to you? I had a title for it. 'April.'"

"Being the good month to die?"

"Yes." For a moment she looked stricken.

"What?"

"I must have had a premonition. My father shot himself on the twenty-ninth of April."

# CHAPTER THIRTY-FIVE

# Rio de Corazón Frío

At the José Martí Airport, the immigration official asked Sean if he'd prefer to have his passport stamped or unstamped. Not understanding Spanish, he said "Sí" and the stamp came down. Small and unobtrusive, just thin red lines, like broken blood vessels.

"You dumb fuck," Sam said when he greeted him outside security. "The goon posted stateside is gonna fry your ass when he sees that stamp. You're in violation of the Trading with the Enemy Act."

"Really?"

"Nah. Nobody checks anymore. It's just a matter of time now before Cuba's as wide open as a ten-peso whore. You're going to love this country. Nicest people you'll ever meet, and the women, oh my goodness gracious, it's like God was smoking crack when he put the pieces together. All colors, and every one just fucking beautiful. Come on. I'll buy you an octopus-head appetizer at Paladar Guarida. Then we'll order you up a leg of lamb big enough to feed a pack of wolves. Once you got your strength built up, we'll hop into a '52 Chevy Bel Air a buddy of mine owns and go dancing. This whole place is hanging together with pastel paint and piano wire; it's like those Kuwaiti villages we went through after Saddam got done pissing on them."

"I'm monogamous now, Sam."

"Hey, I'm a married man myself, but no harm looking. Actually there is, though. You so much as turn your head in the direction of a *jinetera* and it's like peeling chrome off a bumper hitch to get her head out of your lap.

"Hey, hey," Sam raised his hands. "You want to put a lock on your zipper, Sam can hide the key. I'll get you down to Playa Larga an innocent man, or close enough, anyway. Smoking Cohibas and drinking rum doesn't count."

"He's there? You're sure?"

"How many gringos sit around typing all night long with a cat on their shoulder? In Playa Larga? Ain't that big a place, Kemosabe. He's there."

———

The house was one of a half dozen beachfront rentals connected by a strip of sand. They were near mirrors of each other, with seaside patios for the guests. Two boys were swimming with an old swayback horse in the light surf as Sean walked down the beach. They rode the horse out onto the sand, its ribs showing like stripes, the boys laughing and dripping seawater and offering shy smiles as Sean passed by.

Casa Vinola y Zuleyda had an island bar and palm trees that made starfish silhouettes against the sky. Sean walked under the aqua-painted columns of the archway onto the outdoor patio and he wasn't there. At least he wasn't in any of the chairs before the array of plastic tables.

"Buenas tardes, señor."

The bartender's mustache lifted with his smile as he built Sean a mojito. Sean sat in one of the chairs facing the sea. He sipped the drink while the water, which was the washed-out-penny color of the sand, began to shade into a darker copper.

Hearing the tapping of a cane on the outdoor tiles, he turned to see Peter Jackson pulling out a chair at a table a few yards away. Jackson looked younger and fitter than he had when Sean left him at the frozen lake, after he'd covered him with the elkskin robe in the igloo and lit the hurricane lamp for warmth. Sean had been in a hurry to hike back to Sam and had heard Jackson utter "Tatie," still more concerned about the cat's welfare than his own.

Jackson turned his head in Sean's direction and then to the sea and back again. His hair was cropped short now, hugging his skull, and his beard had turned as white as snow. Sean saw that the pupils were drawn and his eyes were a beat or two behind as they followed the turning of his head. They never quite settled into focus.

"I'll have a mojito as well," he said as the bartender approached. Then to Sean, he said, "When one of your senses dies, the others become enhanced. I can smell the sweetness of your drink and isolate it from the conflicting scents of the evening. I find that this colors my work so that I write less about the sights than about the scents and the sounds of the country."

"How far are you along in the story?" Sean said.

Jackson's eyes made an attempt to focus. He leaned forward.

"You have come a long distance, Mr. Stranahan. Did it take all this time to find me?"

"A friend is helping some local people set up a guide business at Las Salinas. I would have come here sooner or later."

"Is he a big gringo? A beard like mine but red like the flames of a fire? I heard he was inquiring. He thinks his Spanish is better than it is, though I'm told he swears with some proficiency."

"That's him."

"Does this mean that I will never be able to return to the States? Not that it matters. My brother-in-law owns this house. I am happy here in one of the small rooms. My needs are simple, and as Cuba has no extradition policy with the U.S., I am quite safe."

"If you mean have I told anyone where you are? No. Only Margarethe Harris. She said to tell you that the offer stands."

Jackson fell silent. Sean looked past the white-taped trunks of the shade palms, out toward the darkening sea and into the past. He was thinking back to when he had taken leave of her less than a week earlier, at the Wa-Wa-Te-Si Lodge. He'd carried the bucket of hot water to the porch and she was sitting with her hands dropped into the water when he drove away. The last words she'd said were, "You'll read about me someday. I'll be the woman who froze to death on a hot summer night."

"I did her a grave injustice," Jackson said in a measured voice. "I'm truly sorry for it." His beard dropped onto his chest, then he shook his head. "God bless her."

He lifted a hand and the bartender began making two more mojitos.

"Have a drink with this old dreamer," he said to Sean.

Sean pulled out the chair opposite Jackson and saw that under the table, by one of Jackson's splayed-out bare feet, was a small dead lizard. It was growing dark and the bats had begun to flit around the electric lights hanging from the archway.

The bartender brought the drinks.

"Gracias, Marquez," Jackson said.

"Should I bring the typewriter, Señor Jackson?"

"Sí, gracias. Please set it at the regular table."

Jackson smiled for Sean. "I have two regular tables. This one for its greater sense of the sea, another back under the awning for my work."

"How is the work coming?"

"It comes. Ernest said that all he ever tried to do was write as well as he could and that sometimes, if he was lucky, he could write better than he could. That, I've found, is as good a description of the process as any. Now that I have to write by the feel of the keys, I find I focus better and losing my eyesight wasn't the blow that I anticipated. I will have this next drink with you and then I will have to say good night. If you will be here long, please come by with your *babosa* of a friend so I can add to his vocabulary of maledictions. Spanish is a far more colorful language to curse in than English."

Sean sat back as the drinks arrived and saw that there were now two dead lizards by Jackson's feet. The next time he looked there were three, and he still had not seen the perpetrator of the minor murders.

Jackson smiled when Sean mentioned it.

"Tatie thinks I'm too old to hunt, so she provides me with her kills. She would be sleeping on my shoulder by now, if you weren't here."

"When did you find her?"

"She returned to the igloo after you left. She hopped onto my chest and we warmed each other."

"How did you smuggle her into Cuba?"

"I folded fifty convertible pesos into the hand of an immigration official at the harbor. Now, I really must get to work." He paused. "I have finally found a title. If I show you, will you promise to keep it our secret?"

Sean promised.

Jackson drew invisible circles on his left palm with his forefinger and the bartender brought over a pen. Jackson scrawled on a napkin and handed it over. "Please wait to read it until you leave. It makes me uncomfortable to have my work examined in my presence, even something so short as a title."

A few minutes later, Sean walked out onto the sand with four Spanish words buttoned in his shirt pocket. He could hear the clacking start up behind him, pause, and then start again. He had never found a way of telling Jackson that the story he was attempting to complete had been started by an eighteen-year-old girl, or that she already had a title for it. But perhaps that was for the best. As a woman with lake storm eyes had pointed out, everybody needs something to live for, whether it's a martini at six o'clock or one true sentence at ten. That, Sean thought, and the luck of a black-footed cat.

# Epilogue

The bean-hole beans, when the pot came out of the ground, were overcooked, crusted, and practically inedible. The brats were good, but there weren't enough to feed the swelling number of well-wishers who'd arrived by early evening. But then Sam drove up with a barrel grill strapped down in the back of his pickup, with smoke coming out of its twin smokestacks. Two suckling pigs had been taking turns on a spit since three in the morning. The aroma was incredible.

"Kemosabe," Sam said, coming around the truck and crushing Sean's ribs in a bear hug. Escaping the massive arms, Sean could see the white welts on his forehead where the wax bullets had made impact.

"So Molly's finally relented?"

"I wouldn't go that far. But you can ask her. She's waiting for the babysitter and then she'll be driving up in the Forester. I think the best you can expect is probation."

The wall raising had come off without a hitch. Or rather three of the walls had. The south-facing would have, too, if the stakes holding the retaining brace hadn't pulled out of the ground. It had fallen back with a thunderous crash and everyone stared and no one spoke, and the only sounds were all the dogs barking, for this being a Montana wall raising, there were almost as many as there were people. "Somebody blow a trumpet and see if the rest come down," Walter Hess said, breaking the silence. None fell, and the wall went back up.

By seven o'clock, Patrick Willoughby and Kenneth Winston had driven the eighty-odd miles from the Liars and Fly Tiers' clubhouse and the only person missing from the party was Martha Ettinger. It was, Sean decided, too much for her to forgive him—too much more than too soon, for nearly a month had passed since she'd visited his studio. Not only had he gone behind her back tracking down Peter Jackson at the lake, he'd compounded the betrayal by flying to Michigan and then Cuba while keeping her out of the loop.

Sean was looking up the road toward her house when Willoughby walked up behind him.

"She'll come or have a good reason why she can't," he said.

"I'm afraid I'm the good reason, Pat."

"Don't talk like that. Come have a drink with us. Ken's uncorked some hard cider that's been jugged for almost two years."

They found themselves talking about the drama at the igloo, as they had the day after Sean and Sam had limped off the mountain. Sean realized that he'd never told them about the walrus-tusk pana that he had broken trying to cut down the sapling.

Willoughby smiled, then nodded.

"Someone will find it and wonder what a walrus was doing by a lake in the Beartooth Mountains," he said. "It's like the mummified leopard carcass in 'The Snows of Kilimanjaro,' one of Hemingway's most famous stories. What was it searching for at twenty thousand feet?"

"What was it searching for?"

Sean waited for Willoughby to sip his cider.

"The western summit of Kilimanjaro is called Ngaje Ngai—'House of God.' The leopard is frozen in time. It's a symbol of immortality. Peter Jackson also seeks immortality. He believes it will be his reward for completing the story."

He peered at Sean over his glasses.

"Not to change the subject, but I do wish you'd lifted the lid of that trunk when you had the chance. You have only her word for what was in it."

"I'm sorry, Pat. I was traveling on your dime. I should have looked. It's just . . ."

He stopped, trying to find the words.

Willoughby waved a hand. "The money is unimportant."

Sean shook his head. "There was death in that house. It started when Margarethe's father brought the trunk home from Wisconsin. His wife became diagnosed with cancer only a few weeks later, and after she died, he took to drink and ending up molesting his daughter and committing suicide. I don't believe in the Hemingway curse, but no one who had anything to do with the contents of that trunk was ever the same again."

"I suppose we'll just have to be happy with the Gillum rod," Winston said. "You said that the department is going to return it to us."

"I already picked it up. It's in the Land Cruiser. Are you still planning to donate it to the Hemingway Trust?"

Winston looked at Willoughby. Willoughby smiled his enigmatic smile. "It will find a home where it may be admired by others in the fullness of time. For now, the rod will reside at the clubhouse, where it will serve as a symbol of our misadventure and of the consequences of uncontrolled avarice. It is a fishing tool foremost, and any member who wishes to fish it shall have the opportunity. Now, if you'll excuse us, Ken and I are next up in the team horseshoe toss."

By nine o'clock all that was left of the pigs were eight hooves, Sam having eaten the apples roasted in their mouths. Molly arrived, and Sean girded himself as she walked up to him. She put her hands around the back of his neck and kissed him on the mouth.

"Sam says you're family, so I'm going to give you a second chance," she said. "He's still a boy, that's part of what I love about him. He adores you and he'll follow you anywhere, and I don't want to lose my husband. So we're friends again. But here's my promise. If you ever put him in danger again, ever, I'm going to tell him that you tried to kiss me and put your hand under my shirt. Then we'll see where his true allegiances lie. Won't we?" And with that she kissed Sean again, bit his lower lip lightly, and walked away.

They were the last to leave, Sam and Molly, and as their taillights glimmered and jerked their way down the canyon, Sean saw the figure of Martha walking down the road. She was with Goldie, the dog leading the way with a flashlight clamped in its mouth. Sean felt the way he always did when he saw her, an awareness of the intake of his breath, and a slight sensation of lightheadedness. He would temper the tendency to make a fool of himself by a show of confidence, and his nervousness would be masked with a display of nonchalance. And just as the walls of his house had gone up a few hours earlier, so would the walls he erected as a barrier to keep the two of them apart.

"Have you forgiven me, Martha?" he said, keeping his voice light. "Molly has, finally. Sort of."

"Sort of," she said, musing over the words. She knelt down and took the flashlight from Goldie's mouth and shone it over the walls of the house.

"That's a good way of putting it. But I wasn't avoiding you. There was an emergency at the office and I couldn't get free until now."

"What was the emergency?"

"What wasn't? Just the usual circus. Are you going to give me a tour?"

Sean walked her around the house, pointing out the staircase to the loft, which stopped at a point in space, the loft yet to be timbered in, and two roughly framed rooms. Martha made appreciative sounds at appropriate intervals.

"Another few weeks," Sean said, "and 'Your place or mine?' won't be a joke."

"Why wait? We can bring some blankets over from the tipi. We'll be able to see the stars."

"Really?"

"Just for tonight," she said.

"In that case . . ."

He bent down and put an arm under her knees and lifted her up.

"This isn't *Gone with the Wind*," she said. "Put me down."

He carried her up the unfinished steps and through the unframed door, to the place inside the walls.

# Acknowledgments

Ernest Hemingway was a gypsy, a traveling man who spoke or mangled at least five languages and might write one sentence on one continent and the next on another. As this novel is based upon a true incident in his life, it became apparent early on that for Sean Stranahan to follow the trail of the lost steamer trunk, he would have to update his passport.

Much of my story takes place in northwestern Wyoming and Cooke City, Montana, and for help in bringing this corner of Hemingway's world to life, I thank my wife, Gail Schontzler, who reported on Hemingway's time here for the *Bozeman Daily Chronicle* and suggested the title—*Cold Hearted River*. Also, my thanks to Chris Warren, who leads Hemingway tours out of Silver Gate, Montana, and set up an exhibit of Hemingway memorabilia in the Range Rider Lodge, where Ernest is known to have bent an elbow. If my novel has inspired you to learn more about the writer's life here, contact Chris through his Web site (hemingwaysyellowstone.com). Thanks also to Bill Bilverstone, Michael Keating, and Sue Hart, creators of the Montana public television documentary *Paradise and Purgatory: Hemingway at the L Bar T and St. V's*, which chronicles Hemingway's first visit to the L Bar T Guest Ranch in 1930 and his recovery from auto accident injuries at St. Vincent Hospital in Billings, Montana.

For help in the Cuba portion of the book, I owe a deep debt of gratitude to Valerie Hemingway, who was Ernest's traveling companion, close friend, and personal secretary in the late 1950s, and who, after his death, married his son Gregory. Valerie lived and worked in the Finca Vigia, Hemingway's home in Havana. Along with Ernest's widow,

Mary, Valerie retrieved many valuable papers and belongings from the Finca after the revolution. With her help, I was granted full access to the Hemingway home, the interior of which is no longer open to the public. Valerie proofread this novel with an eye to all things Hemingway, and many of the details that give the book its verisimilitude I owe to her encyclopedic memory. *Muchas gracias* also to Señora Ada Rosa Alfonso Rosales, Valerie's friend and the curator of the Hemingway home and museum. Ada Rosa not only opened the doors of the Finca but graciously gave me an extensive tour of the grounds and museum.

For help on the Bay of Pigs chapter, I thank Lazero Vinola Sr. and his son for their hospitality, and Felipe Alonso Rodriguez, the best bonefish guide in Cuba.

Key scenes in *Cold Hearted River* are set in upstate Michigan, where Hemingway spent many summers and where the waters of my own history run deep. Wil Cwikiel took an afternoon from his day to guide me to Hemingway haunts in Petoskey, Horton Bay, and Walloon Lake. Thanks, Wil. And for help with the Au Sable River scenes, I thank Bill Buc, who hired me to work on the trout habitat restoration project he spearheaded for the state in the 1970s. Thanks, too, to Bill's friend Steve Sendek. Bill and Steve floated me down the river in a classic Au Sable River boat past the island Bill calls the Masterpiece, and which in the novel is called Margarethe's Island. I built that island more than forty years ago. Little changed, it acts as a lodestone to pull me home, where last fall I was able to say hello to old friends, present if only in memory, including fellow river crew workers Big Dave Myer, John Hirvela, Bruce Milnes, Joe "Slick" Kuck, Doug Wonder, Johnny Hale, Mike Orzokowski, and Dean McNeal. Those who take me further back still include Ray McVicker, Jerry Derring, Kay Wallace, and Mason Bradley. And thanks to Vicki Ankney, the girl who loved Johnny Mathis, whose songs bring back fond memory.

Last, I must thank the late Jack Hemingway, my fellow field editor at *Field & Stream*, for telling me the story of his father's missing steamer trunk, and Patrick Hemingway, for filling in details of the lost tackle.